STRAIGHT BOY

Jay Bell Books
www.jaybellbooks.com

-=Books by Jay Bell=-

The Something Like... series
#1 Something Like Summer
#2 Something Like Autumn
#3 Something Like Winter
#4 Something Like Spring
#5 Something Like Lightning
#6 Something Like Thunder
#7 Something Like Stories - Volume One
#8 Something Like Hail
#9 Something Like Rain
#10 Something Like Stories - Volume Two
#11 Something Like Forever
#12 Something Like Stories - Volume Three

The Pride series
#1 Pride High: Book 1 - Red
#2 Pride High: Book 2 - Orange
#3 Pride High: Book 3 - Yellow
#4 Pride High: Book 4 - Green

The Loka Legends series
#1 The Cat in the Cradle
#2 From Darkness to Darkness

Other Novels
When Ben Loved Tim
Kamikaze Boys
Hell's Pawn
Straight Boy
Out of Time, Into You
Switch!

Aknowledgements

Before we begin another tale filled with racing hearts and wistful sighs, I would like to acknowledge a select group of people for helping make this story possible. I'm grateful to all of my readers for their faithful patronage, but those listed below have gone above and beyond in supporting the artistic dreams of a very silly human being. As soon as I get my cloning device working, I intend to thank each and every one of you in person.

Jacob Allman ♥ Mark Andrews ♥ »annismckenzie« ♥ Daniel Attaway ♥ BhamGhostwriter ♥ John Bloomer ♥ Kevin Bowling ♥ Jos Bowmaster ♥ Ivan Brisbane ♥ Chris & Kai Burton ♥ The By George Farm Boys ♥ Ricky Castaneda ♥ Josh Chernos ♥ Matthew Christian ♥ Edward Cleofe ♥ Andrew Corvin ♥ Dee Damiano ♥ Jeff Davault ♥ Chantal de Pessemier ♥ Todd Doty ♥ Mark Edwards ♥ Shaun T. Erickson (AKA Marcello) ♥ Travis Falla ♥ Tallian Fisher ♥ Zac Ford ♥ Jeremy Friend ♥ Jim Frier ♥ Damian Lavaun Gaskins ♥ George and Paul ♥ Alex Mario Gonzales ♥ Tomas Gradin ♥ Tiffany C. Graham ♥ Sal Guenette ♥ Jeff Hall ♥ Stephen Hurwitz ♥ Daniel Hutchinson ♥ Jarter ♥ Jason Jermyn ♥ Laura Jones ♥ Leigh Juhlke ♥ Ingrid Birgitta Karlsson ♥ Eric King ♥ Shaun King ♥ Jonothon Laycock ♥ Eric LaMonte ♥ Brennan Lennox ♥ Brittany Rose Lewis ♥ Lisa Lieurance ♥ Edward Lopez ♥ Robert Lucas ♥ King Maples ♥ Susen McBeth ♥ Jini McClelland ♥ Lindsay Moffat ♥ Carol Molinari ♥ Simon Monroe ♥ Sam & Julia Morris ♥ John Neumann ♥ Michael Oaks ♥ Olivier Ochin ♥ Zara Park ♥ Scott Pearson ♥ Anthony Reeves ♥ Matthew Richards ♥ Dayanne Roa ♥ Jason Robertson ♥ Kent Victor Schuelke ♥ Ethan Scroggs ♥ John Smeallie ♥ Jamie Snow ♥ Anna Solomonov ♥ Heather Somma ♥ Jo Sowerby ♥ Sebastian Stidham ♥ Rose Stovicek ♥ Stephanie Sullivan ♥ Michael Swearingen ♥ Gary Taylor ♥ Ian Thomson ♥ Guillermo Tirimacco ♥ Bob Turnure ♥ Cindy Ullmann ♥ David W. Van Zyl ♥ Brian Verwiel ♥ Anthony Vo ♥ Michael Wallace ♥ Henrik Wehle ♥ Jason Weigel ♥ Michael D. Williams Jr ♥ Bernard Randall Wilson ♥ Paige Yodanis ♥ Francesco Zambotti ♥ Srulik Zand

In Memory of V.I.P.
(Very Important Puppy)

Straight Boy

by Jay Bell

Chapter One

This is a new beginning. I can be anything I want. A jock with impressive biceps, the round curves glistening with sweat as I cock my arm back to throw a ball. Or a theater-obsessed drama student who says everything in a vaguely foreign accent. I can paint myself in mascara and drape myself in black leather, and everyone at school will assume I've always been that way. A snob, a nerd, a burnout… I can be absolutely anything, which makes it ironic that all I am is bored out of my mind.

And homesick. I pull out my phone, which has become like a pacifier that a toddler refuses to part with. I know I don't need it anymore. I just can't let go yet, even though the life that used to course through my phone has slowed to a trickle. Calls and video conferencing were the first to go. Now I'm hardly getting any texts, and when I do…

Brace yourself, Andrew! You'll never believe it. Piper broke up with Seth!

My response is a pathetic, *Who?*

The guy who works at the car dealership. I guess you moved before meeting him.

Oh. Is she upset?

Not after Dixon dumped Gina the next day. They're totally going to hook up.

I don't let on that I'm clueless as to who either of those people are. A lot can change over a single summer. That's what I had been counting on. I just thought the change would be in my favor—that I would be the one toning down my adventures so my friends back home wouldn't feel too envious and start to resent me. Instead, I'm worried they're starting to forget me. I'm so far away from everything I once knew. Before the move, that had sounded so appealing. A fresh start. In Chicago! A city of endless potential. A sprawling metropolis where all my dreams would come true. Or where I could sit in my parents' backyard while mourning everything I've left behind. Yay.

I lower the phone in an attempt to remind myself just how awesome it is here. For starters, I'm sitting outside without feeling as if my eyeballs are going to fry like eggs, or that my skin will dry out and crack open. Summers in Albuquerque can be brutal.

I find them much more tolerable here. Especially now, at night. The cool air moving through the leafy trees is soothing instead of dusty and biting. We never got much green in New Mexico. I'm surprised there's so much here. When my parents first started talking about this move, I pictured us crammed into a small condo downtown. The reality is that we live a fair distance from the city in a village called Oak Park, which feels more like one of Chicago's many neighborhoods. Maybe it had once stood on its own before the endless sprawl from the city overtook it. Oak Park is now indistinguishable from the miles of tightly grouped buildings and crowded streets that lead east, where it's possible to see the skyline on a clear day. My brother and I once climbed up on the roof of our house to do so. That had made for an awesome selfie and resulted in an outpouring of "You're so lucky!" from my friends.

Yeah. Super lucky. I raise my phone again, needing one more suckle on that technological rubber nipple, despite the lack of notifications. I go to Instagram this time, and when seeing my friends only makes the pit in my stomach open wider, I look at my own profile instead, hoping to remind myself that I'm still having an awesome adventure. I can get a little morose at times. These moods never last long, but they're pretty potent when they happen. After browsing my photos, I have to admit that my life does indeed look happy. Plenty of images show me with sun reflecting off my blond hair. White teeth, free from braces at last, flash at the camera as I try catch the attention of my future—and so far nonexistent—boyfriend. Behind me are all the impressive sights: Lake Michigan, the view from the Willis Tower, the shiny surface of the Cloud Gate, and many more. I detect a theme as I scroll back up. My older brother, Reed, is in most of these photos, looking like a total heartthrob, even though it nauseates me to acknowledge that. His appearances taper off around the time Reed met his girlfriend. A series of photos with my parents comes next; my expression not quite as certain. The most recent photos are of me on my own. I'm no longer smiling in them. I do appear kind of thoughtful, so bonus points there. I probably look like I've gotten really mature from this move, when in truth, I feel like I haven't grown at all. I'm still the same person. It's only my body that's been displaced.

"No, *you're* not listening!"

I don't know who shouts this, but the voice is male and raw with emotion. Drama in the neighborhood! At this point, I'll take whatever action I can get, even if that means snooping. At least I'll have a story to tell my friends back home. To be honest, I *love* snooping. I'm nosey by nature, and a diversion is just what I need to return my thoughts to the present. So long as this little domestic dispute doesn't turn violent. If that happens, I'll call the police or knock something over to distract them. A trashcan probably, since the voices are coming from across the alley.

I snort, recognizing how inner-city that sounds, when really Oak Park is full of charming brick houses, wooden front porches, and droopy old trees. It's kind of gorgeous, but our neighborhood does have its ugly side. Much like a facelift, all the unappealing stuff is yanked toward the back, to where I'm walking now. Beyond our miniscule backyard, past the stand-alone garage and through the gate, *that's* where it truly looks like we live in the shadow of Chicago. Large plastic trashcans bake in the summer heat, the fragrance gag-worthy when they're full. Utility poles are covered in posters warning of vermin and poison traps, the occasional scurrying rat not impressed with the efforts to get rid of them. Sometimes we'll even get someone pushing a cart down the alley, rummaging for metal to sell. I'm tempted to stop and take a selfie to make it look like my new life is rough and I've been forced to develop street smarts. That's when I hear the voice again.

"You don't know what it's like for people like me!"

This gets my attention. I've said that phrase myself, in my more emotional moments. Usually during a holiday, when I'm forced to be around relatives who aren't quite as understanding as my parents. I walk faster, a number of fantasies playing through my mind. I had given up on most of them as the summer went on, but I'd settle for a late romance rather than none at all.

"As soon as they find out, everyone treats you differently."

Yes, they most certainly do! I practically run down the alley until the voice is to my right instead of in front of me. I have to be stealthy, even in the dark. This house's fence is chain-link instead of the wooden planks that shroud our yard in privacy. That's both good and bad, because I'm able to see a teenage guy around my own age and an older couple who are likely his parents. The unobstructed view means I can be seen too. I keep walking until hidden behind their garage. Then I press my back to it and listen.

"It's not in my head!" the guy shouts. "To your face, they act like they understand. Like they're sympathetic, but as soon as your back is turned, they start making jokes."

Yeah. I've been there too. My mind races, trying to find any other interpretation of these words other than what I want them to mean. I can't really hear the other half of the conversation. The parents have kept their cool so far, but I don't care about them. I just want confirmation that—

"What am I supposed to do? I was born this way!"

All my willpower is needed to keep me from marching into that backyard while waving an invisible rainbow flag. I've never been into Lady Gaga. She's great! It's just not my style of music, but I'm glad she popularized that phrase. I was born this way too. I peer around the corner of the garage, trying to get a better look at this guy. The street lights aren't helping. Only a small porch light is on at the back of their house, whereas I'm lit up for everyone to see. I risk a glimpse. The guy's back is to me, and he's shaking his head at whatever his parents are saying. One of them moves away, so I duck behind the garage again. I wait there, but the argument must have run its course, because I can't hear more. When a car turns down the alley, I keep walking, like I have a destination in mind. When I reach the next street, I turn around and head back, my pulse picking up as I pass by his house again. I don't stop this time, but I do look over.

And I see him. He's alone in the yard now and facing my way. The shadows make it hard to tell, but I'm pretty sure he's handsome. He sees me and gives an upward nod. I don't know if I do the same. I'm too busy trying to get my knees to bend as I totter forward like a complete virgin who has never caught the attention of another boy before.

I'm *not* a virgin, for what that's worth, but I might be out of practice. My face is burning when I reach the back gate of our yard. I slip through it, hoping he hasn't wandered out into the alley to investigate. Once I'm safely shut away, I stand still and listen. I don't hear footsteps or anyone calling out, "Hey gorgeous! Get your ass back here so we can kiss!"

Wouldn't that be something? I return to the deckchair where I was sitting earlier and resume warming the seat. I mentally play back the fragmented argument, trying to make sure I'm not deluding myself, but I keep reaching the same conclusion.

I have a neighbor who, like me, is gay.

I make it through an entire day without thinking of him. I don't mean the guy across the alley. *He* fills my thoughts with fantasies, each of them welcome like a much-needed cure, but it doesn't last. I'm sitting in my room when it happens. Spotify recommends the wrong song. Just a cover version, but it's still enough to send my mind racing back to Albuquerque. To a different bedroom. The furniture is still the same. Only the shape of the room is different. And I'm not alone. A guy with poofy red hair and glasses is smiling down at me, his palms on the mattress to either side of my head. His naked body is pressed against mine, and with a doofy grin he says, "Remind me again where I'm supposed to put it?"

Scott always joked around like that. My sides often hurt from laughter when we hung out. Just an ache, compared to the pain that came later, when Scott found someone that made him laugh too. I tried to be grown up about it. I did research online and found articles that assured me attraction is mostly out of our hands. We want who we want, simple as that. Choice isn't involved. At times this made me feel better. Scott didn't cheat. He just explained things one Sunday afternoon, and for once, he hadn't cracked any jokes or used funny voices. Instead he sat on the edge of my bed and fidgeted, every other sentence an apology.

I wasn't completely surprised. I knew that he was more into the idea of having a boyfriend rather than me in particular. That's how it started for both of us. We wanted to be gay in practice, instead of just theory. That required another person, and neither of us was picky about who. Then I fell in love. He didn't. The last semester of my junior year was pure hell until my mom mentioned the job transfer. I couldn't believe my luck! I was certain physical distance would help.

It didn't. Maybe I need physical closeness instead. Not for the first time, I browse a cruising app on my phone. Normally I try to ignore the photos of toned torsos, since those guys are looking for one thing only. This time I go straight for the meat, but I soon feel repulsed. There's nothing wrong with casual sex. I just know that it would be a struggle for me. I'd have too many questions, want to talk and get to know the guy first. Ideally I would have dinner with him a few times to make sure he wasn't a total creep. Once I was comfortable around him, *then* we could get freaky. In other words, I wanted a relationship, not a hookup. With that in mind I switch to a different app, but after some swiping left and right, I give up. I can't stop thinking about a freckled back and pale skin, or lips that press against my neck and blow, resulting in a fart noise.

The memory alone is enough to make me laugh. And close both apps. I'm still not ready. Am I? I think of my mystery man again, who is perfect by virtue of anonymity. I wouldn't be able to point him out in a police lineup. I don't know anything about him except his rough age and where he lives. Oh, and that he feels misunderstood and ill-treated, which isn't a rarity. Most of my friends could make the same claim. Only the specific reason why might make him special, and that's still a giant assumption. I want more than just a fantasy. I'm willing to explore the reality. I just don't see how we'll ever get to know each other or even meet. I rack my brain trying to find a way, mostly because it's better than dwelling on the past.

The next day, my brother comes up with the perfect excuse. Inadvertently.

My bedroom is in a finished basement, next to the family room. If my brother ever moves out, I'll have the bottom floor all to myself. My parents tend to watch TV and socialize on the upper floors. They don't like the temperature in the basement, and yeah, when they're running the air conditioner it can feel like a refrigerator, despite the carpeted floors and insulated walls. Needing an extra blanket is a small price to pay for getting to feel like I live by myself. I already come and go through the rear entrance of the house to further enhance this illusion. For now, I have a roommate. My brother often sprawls out on the couch while channel-surfing. He never settles on anything for long, although when he does, it's usually to the sound of a roaring stadium.

I hear a referee's whistle when I leave my room, and sure enough, Reed is taking up most of the couch while watching a game. He looks a little like me if I did pushups every day and dyed my hair brown. I suppose I'd need to start chugging protein shakes too, because I'm nowhere near as beefy as he is.

"Hey," he says, raising the remote to mute the television. "Mom's cat is still missing."

The cat has a name, Hufflepuff, and she belongs to all of us technically, but Mom takes care of her. As far as the cat is concerned, no one else exists.

"What's it been?" I ask. "Three days?"

"Yeah," Reed replies.

"Is that a long time?"

"Long enough to be worried." My brother sits upright. "You know how I feel about that cat. Still…"

"We don't want Mom to be sad," I say.

"Exactly."

"Flyers?"

"Already did them." My brother tosses the remote on the table. "The online equivalent, anyway. I guess we could put some up. Maybe go door-to-door."

"Door-to-door?" I ask.

My brother looks at me like I'm stupid, which is fine. He's been doing that since I was born. Sometimes I wish I had a younger sibling, just so I could act superior and do the same. Right now, all I can think about is one door in particular. "Worth a shot."

"Good." Reed picks up his phone. He doesn't explain what he's doing. I have to stand there and wait, like I'm his servant. "I just emailed you the flyer. Go upstairs and print it out."

"Yes, sir!"

When he reaches for the remote, I grab it and throw it across the room, just to mess with him. I have to run afterwards, because Reed loves nothing more than putting me in a headlock and making me beg for mercy.

Once I'm in the office and the printer is churning out page after page, I'm tempted to create another flyer. One with a silhouette of a male figure on it instead of a cat photo. The flyer would read, "Missing! My soulmate. Intelligent, handsome, funny, and kind. Last seen walking through my dreams. Reward: One barely used heart. No questions asked."

After thinking about it, I decide that last line would have to go. Eventually, when I find the right guy, I will ask a question. A very big one. For now, I'd settle for getting to meet him.

— — —

I haven't lived in Chicago for long, but I've already picked up on patterns in the weather. Clouds that cover the sky from horizon to horizon are a lot more common here, for instance. Such days are usually warmer than normal. When the sky is open and blue, it tends to be windy instead. I'm not sure why. My grandparents are too weather-obsessed for me to look up the reason. I'd feel old if I embraced that interest. All I know is that the wind makes taping up flyers a real pain in the ass.

I only printed twenty, figuring that a cat couldn't go that far. It's already taking longer than I expected for Reed and me to get them all posted, our progress slowed by our need to keep an eye out for Hufflepuff. That, and we're both constantly distracted by the smallest details because so much is different from New Mexico. Like the street signs that say *Speed Hump*. This makes more sense than *Speed Bump*, since the raised concrete stretches across the entire street. Definitely more than just a bump, but surely we aren't the only ones to find the word choice amusing.

"I'm totally going to steal one of those," Reed says. "Maybe a few so I can send some back home."

"Speaking of home," I say, tilting my head in the direction we'd come from. "Maybe we should double back."

"Then again," Reed says, still eyeing one of the signs. "Do I really want that hanging above my bed? Could be misconstrued."

I laugh. "Probably best not to advertise that you finish too early."

"Hey!" Reed says, swiping at me, but I'm too quick and dodge away.

"Even if you're not ashamed of the truth," I continue, "stolen street signs aren't the classiest way to decorate. You're not in high school anymore."

"Then I know what I'm getting you for your birthday," Reed says. "You're right. Let's go home. We'll take a different street and put up the rest of these."

We only have five flyers left, which we tape to poles at the end of every block. Once they're gone, my palms start to sweat, because we haven't knocked on any doors yet. My mystery man lives another block away, but I figure I'd better start now so it isn't completely obvious what I'm up to.

I feel guilty after the first door. The woman who lives there seems genuinely upset over our missing cat, which makes me think of all the bad things that could have happened to Hufflepuff. I may not be overly attached to the animal, but I want her to be okay. I start to take the job more seriously, not letting Reed skip houses that he feels look shifty. By the time we reach the next block, I'm not thinking about my mystery man anymore. Not until we reach his house. I already walked by it the other day, just in case he decided to have another argument with his parents, maybe in the front yard for a change of scenery. And yeah, I was hoping to see a car with a rainbow sticker or anything that confirmed my theory. No luck on either front. Now I have a real chance of finding out the truth. And it intimidates me.

I'm not sure why. Maybe because if I'm wrong, I won't have anything left. The fantasy has been nice. I've spent a lot of time escaping into it, imagining how we could meet and how our story would play out from there. I've blown through three or four different versions. In the most recent, we ended up divorced and fighting over the foster kids, but we still got our happy ending because the passionate arguments made us realize that we were still into each other. We renewed our vows and ended our lives old and married.

"You go ahead," I say, pulling out my phone like I have something important to do.

Reed shrugs and walks up to the front door. I hang back, closer to the sidewalk where I can still see. A parent will probably answer the door anyway. Then again, it's summer and a workday so—

The door swings open… and it's him! I'm able to confirm one thing right away. He's handsome! His hair is chestnut brown and just the right length to stand up on its own, peaking in the middle. His eyebrows are dark, as are the eyes beneath them. His skin is tan and there's plenty of it on display, since he's only wearing sweat shorts, which look way hotter on him than they have any right to. I don't see a six-pack, but his chest is wider than his narrow waist.

I already regret not approaching the door with my brother. Would it be too obvious if I went up to it now? Reed is talking and jerks a thumb over his shoulder at me. The guy's eyes start to move in my direction, but I'm quicker, looking down at my phone and seeing my embarrassed expression reflected in the screen. I'm not usually shy. Until I am. Why now?

My thumb taps of a bunch of things, but my brain takes in none of it. Only when I hear the door shut do I look up to see my brother walking back to me. He's grinning, which is confusing.

"Good news?" I ask.

"Nah. He hasn't seen her either." Reed nudges me as we resume walking down the sidewalk. "Still... Could be a nice friend for you. Same age. And everything."

"What's the everything?" I ask, hoping he found out something.

"You know," Reed says, nudging me again. "He was good-looking. You don't have to be gay to tell that."

"He's probably straight," I say, trying to feign disinterest, but I can't help myself from asking, "Unless you were getting a vibe?"

Reed is already shaking his head. "I don't have gay sonar. Sorry."

"It's gaydar, you dumbass!" I tease. "As in gay radar."

"Oh. Either way, maybe you should get to know him. It would be good to have a friend when school starts. Are you nervous?"

"Yeah." I exhale. "Terrified, actually."

"It's rough," Reed says, nodding in sympathy. "You were around the same group of kids your entire life, and now, when you're about to start your senior year... This is when you're supposed to be celebrating with those people, not stressing about being a total stranger."

"You're not making me feel better," I complain.

"Sorry. I get it, man. That's all I'm trying to say. I miss my friends too."

"Then why did you move up here? You already had a place of your own."

Reed shrugs. It takes him a while to answer. We're walking past houses, but I'm not so interested in knocking anymore. "Because it sounds cooler to be a bartender who works in Chicago. That's more impressive than Albuquerque, right? I'm hoping something more will happen here. Bigger city, bigger dreams. Does that make sense?"

"Totally."

"It's normal to be nervous," Reed says. "I bet Mom and Dad are too. New workplaces, new bosses. Hey, let's try this house."

I follow him. He knocks. Then we wait.

"Things will work out for us both," Reed says. "You'll be the new kid in school. That makes you interesting by default. Everyone else is old news. You'll make a bunch of friends, start dating again, and go to lots of parties. I'll find a better place to work than that dive, and things will really pick up when I move in with Dakota."

My head whips around, and I see that he's serious. "What? Is that happening soon?"

"Yeah. At least I think so. Her roommate is moving out in two months, and Dakota and me... I know we haven't been dating for very long, but I think she's the one."

"Wow," I say, turning back to the door, which still hasn't opened. "Have you asked her yet?"

"No," Reed says. "Keep your fingers crossed. This will make us both happy."

"How so?"

"When I'm gone."

I picture an empty couch. Since he's always hogging the entire thing, I usually have to beg before he'll let me sit. That's annoying, but without him there, the basement will be a lot colder. I don't mean the temperature. I'm going to miss him. Reed might be a pain in the ass, but he's also been my best friend since we moved here. "It'll suck when you're gone," I reply.

Reed looks over at me in surprise. Then he starts laughing. "Honest Andrew."

My family has always called me that, ever since I was a kid. I have a filter. I just don't see the point in pretending I feel one way when I actually feel another.

Reed wraps an arm around my neck, but only so he can put me in a headlock. "You're really going to miss me, huh?"

"Not really," I manage to gasp. "Let go!"

He releases me, and we both turn and step off the porch, deciding that nobody is home.

"I'll still be around," Reed says. "Whether you like it or not."

I'm glad. I don't tell him that, though. Being honest doesn't mean I have to be transparent. Besides, I'm pretty sure he knows how much I love him. Reed has always looked out for me and been on my side. When it comes to the important things, at least. That's how I know he loves me too.

He grabs my arm, his grip so powerful that it hurts. "Look!" he hisses.

I follow his pointing finger to a house across the street. A gray and white cat is hunched in front of the door, staring up at it and meowing. Hufflepuff!

"The stupid thing is at the wrong door," Reed says. "Come on!"

We hurry across the street, and as soon as Hufflepuff sees us coming, her eyes get big. Does she run to us in relief? Of course not. Instead she darts into the nearest bush. Reed and I position ourselves at opposite ends of it, and it's me who has to crawl on my stomach to reach her. She runs before I can grab her, but Reed snatches her up. I wiggle free from the bush, cussing to myself along the way, until I see what a mess she is. No blood or anything, but she's dirty, freaked out, and probably hungry.

"Let's get her home," Reed says, cradling her to his chest. "We'll make sure she's cleaned up and fed so Mom doesn't have to see her like this."

"She's going to be so relieved," I say.

Reed and I exchange a look, the emotion in our eyes attesting to the same truth. We're relieved too. Me especially. Now I can go back to dreaming about the life I want here in my new hometown. I'm not sure of the details yet. Just that it'll involve a guy with chestnut brown hair.

Chapter Two

New clothes have a lot in common with a new school. One begins with a timid courtship of sifting through the racks of a department store, the other by driving up to the educational institution. Once the outfit is put together, or the school is enrolled in, confidence rises and so do dreams of a future filled with potential. That doesn't last for long. Not for me, anyway. The new clothes feel weird now. The way the fabric and denim grip my body is just as unfamiliar as the hallways I'm walking through. I want to check a mirror and consult a floorplan, because in both cases, I'm worried I look like an idiot.

If there's one thing New Mexico has, it's space. No amount of housing developments and strip malls will ever fill the massive desert. The schools I'm used to are single-story and sprawling. In Chicago, everything is crowded. The high school I'm in now is three stories tall. Four, if you count the basement level. The hallways are stuffed with students, which doesn't make it easier to figure out where I'm supposed to be. Everyone is paired up or in groups, socializing while walking on autopilot. Only the tiny freshmen appear confused and lost. I try hard not to be one of them.

I feel naked and vulnerable without my friends by my side. I'm trying my best to make new ones though. During third period, I strike up a conversation with the guy next to me. This goes well until he realizes that I'm new and imparts the following wisdom:

"Just stay away from the black kids."

Great! You're a racist asshole. Fuck off.

I don't say these things, but I already have plans to switch to a different seat tomorrow. I'll claim I can't see or hear well enough, if need be. Lunch is predictably awkward, since I don't have anyone to sit with, but I'm prepared for that. I spend most of it texting old friends. I try not to let it bother me that their responses are slow or don't come at all. They're probably having a blast being the new ruling class of the school.

By the time I'm walking to sixth period, World Literature, my spirits are low. I had a lot of fantasies about someone noticing me in the crowds, maybe due to some lingering aura from my life in

New Mexico. My new friend would bound over to me, introduce themselves, and then show me off to their crew. Instant social circle! I'm not vain. I don't actually think I'm any more interesting than the next person. I'm just an optimist who likes to daydream, a combination I'm beginning to consider a major personality flaw.

Too often I'm disappointed by my own inflated expectations. This runs in the family, judging from the way Reed thought that moving to Chicago would somehow make everything better. He probably expected to be flipping drinks in the air and performing bartender stunts at some rooftop club downtown. Instead he's struggling to learn Spanish at the little corner bar where he works so he can communicate better with the customers. Reed doesn't complain much. He treats it like an opportunity to expand his mind and add skills to his resume. Optimism. It's relentless in our family.

I try to get myself back to this mentality, but I'm still not there when I find the right classroom and walk inside. I keep my head down and sit, pulling out my phone and using the camera to check my hair. I wish I hadn't gotten it trimmed. It still has length, the natural waves touching my ears, but like my clothes, the new cut isn't comfortable yet. I feel like squirming in my own skin as I wait for the final period to begin so it can end. I just want to go home. Back to the house a few blocks away. Back to New Mexico miles away. Anywhere but here.

The teacher walks in just before the bell rings. After the shrill sound ceases, he introduces himself as Mr. Thorp. His argyle sweater vest is tight against his slender torso, his beige pants as pressed and fastidious as the rest of his appearance, including his short and tidy hair. The only casual touch is the dress shirt sleeves, which are neatly rolled up to reveal black skin.

"I know you were expecting Ms. Funk," he explains. He holds up a hand when some of the students laugh. "Just be happy you didn't have to go through high school with that particular surname. I can only imagine how much character it helped her build. Anyway, Ms. Funk will be back soon. For now, you're stuck with me. Let's start with a riddle. I want you to imagine a prison cell without windows. The walls are solid cement twenty feet thick and there are no doors."

"How can the prisoner breathe?" asks a kid who has class clown written all over him.

"There are hundreds of needle-thin holes in the ceiling," Mr. Thorp says unabashed. "They let in air and natural light. Now then, what's the one thing you can give the prisoner so they can escape? Just one object. Anyone?"

"A jackhammer!" someone shouts.

Mr. Thorp shakes his head. "There's nothing to plug a jackhammer into."

"A metal file," someone else tries.

"Nice idea," Mr. Thorp says, "but a file would be worn down and useless before the prisoner could create a tunnel big enough to escape through. The same with a hammer and chisel."

"A teleporter pad," the class clown says again. "Or a magic wand."

Mr. Thorp smiles. "Now those are some creative ideas! But this is the real world. Any more guesses? No? How about this?" He holds up a book. "No matter how dire your situation, you can go anywhere and be anything when reading. Even impossible places that have teleporter pads and magic wands."

Most of the class groans, but I like it. I've always enjoyed reading, which is good because I'll be spending a lot of time escaping into fictional worlds if things don't improve soon.

"If there aren't any doors or windows," the class clown says, "how does the prisoner eat?"

"They shove pudding through the airholes," Mr. Thorp says without missing a beat. "Let's take roll call and then get started."

As he says each name, I look at any person I can comfortably see and wonder if any of them will be my new friend. Or more.

"Mia Cardenas?"

"Present."

Mr. Thorp's eyebrows rise above his glasses. "Are you new here?"

"Yes," the girl answers.

"Come on up then." Mr. Thorp smiles. "Don't be shy. Front of the class, please."

The girl hesitates. Then she stands and walks up front to wait. He's going to make her talk about herself. Crap! I thought they only did that on television. None of my other teachers singled me out. I'm hopeful I won't be noticed, but as Mr. Thorp continues his way down the list...

"Andrew Evans?"

"Here," I reply.

His eyes dart to me and away again, and just when I think I'm safe, he does a double take. "I don't recognize you either. Are you new?"

"Nope." Honest Andrew fights against this answer, but I push back, because this is survival!

Mr. Thorp blinks. "Really? Who did you have for American Literature last year?"

"Mrs.—" I blank. All I need is a last name, but I realize that I don't know any of the right ones, so I say the only thing that comes to mind. "—Pants."

The entire class laughs. Mr. Thorp doesn't look too upset though. "Mrs. Pants, huh?" he says with a smirk. "How fortunate. She's one of our better teachers. Very in charge, because she wears… Ahem. Get on up here! I know it's embarrassing, but this is a great way to meet everyone."

Mia and I are the only two new students. I size her up, wondering if she'll become my new bestie, but she looks awfully straight-laced. So does Mr. Thorp, but he's been cool so far, so I reserve judgement. When she's asked to say something about herself, Mia quickly starts talking about church and her participation in the Business Professionals of America club. I'm not sensing a lot of common ground here. Then I panic, because I realize that I should have been focusing on what I planned to say.

"Thank you, Mia," Mr. Thorp says, extending an arm to direct her back to her seat. "Andrew Evans… Tell us a little about yourself."

I decide then to go for it. When I came out of the closet, I did so because I had finally accepted myself for who I am. I still want to learn and grow, but ultimately, I took that leap so I could be me. I wouldn't have met Scott if I had kept pretending to like girls. Coming out now might help in that same regard. Scanning the class, I see a few guys I wouldn't mind getting to know better.

"Hey," I say, starting out easy. I want them to realize that I'm just like anyone else. "My name is Andrew. My family just moved here from Albuquerque. I prefer PlayStation over Xbox, and I think the *Game of Thrones* TV show is better than the books, although the opposite is true of *The Shannara Chronicles*." Was I losing them? How about music instead? "I prefer Childish Gambino over Bruno Mars, and Beyoncè over Rihanna." When did this become about choosing sides? I could just say I prefer turkey without hating on chicken. I was probably losing more of my audience with every line I drew in the sand. Time to get to the point. "And when it comes to my personal life, I'm into guys and single so… You know. Call me."

Dead silence. That's bad enough. Then the snickering starts.

"That's enough," Mr. Thorp says. He turns to me and nods. "Very interesting, both of you. I can tell we're going to have a variety of different viewpoints this year, which is great. That'll result in some lively discussions, I hope. Thank you both. I'd like to get started by—"

I rush back to my desk, hating how my cheeks are burning for everyone to see. I don't want anyone to think I'm ashamed. I'm proud of who I am. It's only the situation I find embarrassing. I'm about to sit down at my desk when the guy seated behind me snorts. He has floppy black hair brushed to one side, his bangs partially shading cruel green eyes. He's shaking his head like I'm an idiot. I glare to show what I think of his opinion and then I sit. Or I try to. I hit the ground instead. Hard! I land on my tailbone. A cry of anguish escapes my lips. It sounds whiny and nasal, which only adds to my embarrassment. There's no way I missed my chair. I know I didn't pull it out that much. As I twist around to see what happened, I notice the chair is as far back as it can go. The guy behind me is leering. The expression only lasts for a second before he hops to his feet to help me, with a very convincing, "Oh my gosh! Are you okay?"

If my face was burning before, it's molten lava now. I'm still grimacing in pain, so I must look like a real beauty. The next thing I know this jerk is pulling me to my feet. He's grabbing my arm so hard that it hurts, and in a barely audible grunt, he says, "Fag."

"Get away from me!" I shout, jerking away.

The guy lets go just as suddenly, my feet scrabbling on the tiles before I sort of lean-fall against my desk. At least he's backed off. When I look over, he's wearing a mask of false concern.

"I was only trying to help!" he says, green eyes trained on the teacher.

Right. This isn't the first time I've been picked on. Not by far. I don't look as tough as Reed, but I've learned a lot from my older brother. Being gay will always make me a target. That doesn't mean I have to be an easy one. Standing up to a bully can get your ass kicked, but as long as you land a few punches, they'll usually think twice before messing with you again. Not that it was a good idea to come out swinging. A demonstration was often enough. They just need to see that you've got some fight in you.

And I do.

As soon as I'm on my feet and stable, I get up in his personal space. "If you want to mess with me, bring it!"

I focus on anger instead of my growing fear, because I'm just now noticing how much weight this guy has on me. I'm skinny. If I physically push him, I'll probably end up stumbling backwards, so I compensate with attitude instead. I'm confused though, because I'm not getting the same attitude back. His face is slack, the green eyes big as they turn to the teacher for help.

"I was only trying to pick him up!" he says.

"Pick this up!" I snarl, sweeping my arm across his desk and sending everything there to the floor.

It's a mistake. I can see that now because his only reaction is a barely perceptible smirk. There are bullies, which are common as can be. And then there are psychopaths, which are rarer, and much *much* more dangerous.

"Mr. Tucker!" the teacher says at last. "Please take your seat."

The other guy complies instantly, adding an all-too-convincing, "Sorry, sir."

"Mr. Evans. If you could please pick up his things and apologize, then we can—"

"Fuck you!" I snap. Sometimes anger stays with me for days, giving me strength. Other times it flees just as quickly as it comes, leaving me empty, weak, and on the verge of tears. I know I've made another mistake. The teacher seems like a nice guy, but the day hasn't been anything like I'd hoped, and I'm tired of feeling lost, awkward, and alone. I refuse to add victimized or afraid to that list. "Sorry," I mumble.

"I'm sure you are," Mr. Thorp says, his tone clipped. "Now pick up those books and take a trip to the school counselor. Talking to her will help you calm down. All right?"

I pick up the fallen items as quickly as possible, not being neat or gentle when I set them down on the desk again. The guy, whoever-he-is Tucker, isn't fazed. He just whispers, "See you tomorrow." Before I turn away, he takes something out of his pocket and sets it on the desk next to the mess I made. He doesn't move his hand off it completely. It stays obscured, but I see enough. A wooden handle. A gleam of silver metal. It's a knife, the kind that has to be folded open before it can be used to gut a fish.

Yeah. I've made a big mistake.

Fear has often been my nemesis. An intimately familiar enemy. I used to grapple with fear on a daily basis. This stopped me from being my true self, from being happy, from finding love. It's one of the reasons I now strive to be honest. People only lie when they're frightened of the consequences that truth will bring. Fear is the puppet master of dishonesty. Other despicable behaviors too. I often imagine a hierarchy of miserable emotions with fear at the top, like a mob boss who rules over them all.

I thought I had conquered fear, vanquished it completely, when I came out. Now fear has caught up to me, snapping at my heels as I walk down the hall. I want to run. I'm not worried about getting in trouble. My parents are reasonable, even though they drive me crazy. I know they'll see my side of things. They might not agree with what I did, but I'll freely admit to them that I regret my actions. I don't fear what the school counselor will say, or how Mr. Thorp will view me from now on. My concerns all center around one particular person.

Tucker. I don't know his first name and don't need to because he is fear personified. Just not in the monstrous form I had always imagined. The incident had gone by in a blur, but I remember floppy black hair and a face that could be whatever it needed to be: innocent, concerned, cruel. If fear had crippled me emotionally before, now it was capable of stabbing me in the gut with a pocket knife while staring straight into my eyes with calm emerald irises. I'm not going back to that class. Not for anything or anyone.

I wander down the halls trying to find where to go. When I finally locate the right door and open it, I'm surprised. The school counselor must be in high demand, because she has her own waiting room. The usual utilitarian school furniture is absent here, replaced with a love seat and a table surrounded by comfortable chairs. A window on the far wall reveals a private office. The counselor sees me enter and holds up a finger, indicating that I should wait. Then she continues addressing someone across from her, but I can't see who because a curtain hides them from view.

I sit on the loveseat and start working on potential defenses, eventually settling on the truth. If fear and I are going to do battle again, I'll try what killed it last time.

When I hear the office door open, I look up and the breath catches in my throat. It's him! I'm pretty sure it is anyway. I've only seen him twice. Once at night and again from afar, but I'm certain it's my dream guy. *Mystery man*, I mean. He's wearing torn jean shorts and a maroon hoodie, and despite his outfit looking a lot more comfortable than my own, he doesn't appear to be having a good day either. The school counselor isn't far behind him. Her hair is red and curly, her glasses small and round.

"Just have a seat in here," she says to him, "and read through the pamphlet. Take your time! There's no pressure. Go at your own pace. We can talk about it afterwards, and I'll be happy to answer any questions you have. Okay?"

My mystery man nods. His eyes meet mine briefly, but they don't light up in recognition. He chooses the table instead of the loveseat. I stand and follow the counselor into her office. On the way, I try to scope out the pamphlet he's been given in case it reveals more about him. All I can see is that the front is sky blue.

"Right in here," the counselor says at the door to her office.

She lets me go in first. The room isn't very big. Just enough space for a desk, chairs, a bookshelf, and a potted plant. The nameplate on the desk identifies her as Ms. Beaulieu. Way too many vowels, so I'm relieved when she introduces herself as Jill instead.

"And what's your name?" she asks.

"Andrew Evans," I answer. I offer my hand and add, "It's a pleasure to meet you, ma'am." Tucker isn't the only one who can be excessively polite to authority figures!

Jill smiles. I can tell she sees right through my act, because while typing my name into her desktop she ruefully says, "What could bring such a nice young man to see me?" Maybe it's already there on the computer screen. I don't know how things work in this school. She's still smiling though, which makes me like her because at least she's giving me the benefit of the doubt.

"I messed up," I admit. "It was a bad situation. And not completely my fault."

"In my experience, the blame rarely rests on one person's shoulders." Jill doesn't sound judgmental when she says this. Instead she hits the arrow key a few times in quick succession, like she's scrolling through a file. Then she leans back, seeming satisfied. "Tell me all about it."

I do so by setting the stage. *I'm new, the day was stressful*, etc. While going over the basics, I can't help but look to the waiting room window. I can see the table where the guy is sitting. He's facing away from us, but some infuriating part of me decides that even the back of his head is worth staring at.

"Just a second," Jill says. She stands and closes the curtain the rest of the way. "These office walls are thick. Nobody can hear anything you say, don't worry. You have complete privacy."

I continue my story, relieved that she mistook my infatuation for concern. I'm at the part where I'm baring my soul in front of the class when I find something else to distract me. I notice more of the sky-blue pamphlets off to one side of her desk, displayed upright with a variety of others. Now I can see that the background is a literal blue sky, and that the font on the front is stylized to resemble fluffy white clouds. The text reads, *No More Classrooms*.

"So you identify as…"

"Gay," I clarify.

Jill nods, as if to reassure me that she's okay with that, and I believe her.

"Everyone at my old school knew," I continue. "Some people had a problem with it, but most were fine. I thought the same would be true here, but when I returned to my seat, the guy sitting behind me pulled my chair out and I hit the floor. He denies it but I *know* what happened."

"What's the name of this student?" she asks.

"I'm not sure." That's true enough. A last name isn't much. I don't want to implicate Tucker and give him even more reason to hate me. It's the same reason I don't mention the knife. I tell her the rest though, including how I lost my temper with the teacher. By the end of my story she's shaking her head.

"Andrew!" she scolds.

"I know. It was one of those moments you regret right after it happens."

"Well, Gerald is a very understanding teacher. I'm sure he would appreciate an apology —"

My stomach sinks. I look back to the pamphlet and its promise of no more classrooms. If only.

"—and I'm sure the rest can be worked out if you and this other young man are given a chance to talk it through."

That's the last thing I want!

Jill notices my panic. "I would be happy to mediate. This will take place in a safe environment."

"Sorry," I say, pointing at the pamphlet. "What exactly is that? In New Mexico, they have these home study courses. I think it's called virtual education."

"Virtual education?" Jill repeats this like she's sounding the words out.

"Yeah. You do it all from home on your computer. Or how about old-fashioned homeschooling? Or getting my GED? Will I still be accepted by colleges if I get that instead? My SAT scores are high!"

Jill stares at me. Then she blinks. "My goodness, you're really shaken by what happened today, aren't you?"

"It's not just that," I say before she can march down the hall, pull Tucker out of class, and force us to bond. "It's *everything*. I thought it would be fun to move to a new state, but it's too much. I don't know anyone here, and I'm confused by how this school works. I didn't think everything would be so different, but it is. I'm losing touch with my friends back home, I've already screwed myself socially here, and I'm… I'm freaking out."

This isn't an act. I wish it was, because now my throat feels tight from holding back emotion. Jill looks me over. Then she turns her attention to her computer again, which seems like a cold move. At first.

"We have your transfers from your old school," she says. "Your grades are excellent and you didn't get in much trouble."

"Just a little," I say.

Jill reaches over and pulls the pamphlet free. "This is a new program. It still takes place at this school, but in the library instead of classrooms." She opens it so I can see, but it's her words I'm hanging on. "People have a wide variety of needs in life. That includes education. Designing a universal system that works for everyone is impossible. In this program, students are given more personal responsibility. You'll be shown what academic goals you are expected to meet, and it's up to you how you get there."

"Like a magnet school?"

"Yes! Very similar."

"I would love that!" I've gotten in trouble for reading in class way too often. Books have even been taken away from me. Not because of the content, but because they weren't assigned by the school. That always infuriated me. If I'm reading, shouldn't that be encouraged? Or if a school insists on sticking to the tried and true classics, couldn't they let students choose which of those books appeal to them? Reed had been assigned *To Kill a Mockingbird* freshman year. I read it over two separate nights and was excited to read it again when I reached that grade, but instead I got stuck with an English teacher who was obsessed with wars and only assigned books that centered around them. So an alternative to traditional education sounds good to me. The excuse to avoid Tucker makes it all the sweeter. "Sign me up! Please!"

Jill looks amused by my enthusiasm. Then she bites her lower lip and asks, "Can I introduce you to someone? He's a new student here too. I think you could both benefit from spending time together."

No! She couldn't be referring to *him*. Could she?

I shrug casually. "Sure."

"Just a moment. He's the student I was talking to a moment ago."

As she gets up and leaves the office, my excitement turns to dread, makes a U-turn toward anticipation, and then does a sharp right toward anxiety. This is good, this is terrible, and it's too late. He walks into the room and sits right next to me, and I pray we're not expected to shake hands, because my palms are covered in sweat.

"Carter, I'd like to introduce you to Andrew. Andrew, this is Carter."

I even love his name! This is it. He has to be the one!

"Hey," I manage.

"Hey," he responds.

We have so much in common already.

"Andrew is from New Mexico," Jill explains as she takes a seat behind her desk. "And Carter, you're from…"

"Phoenix," he says.

"Then we used to be neighbors," I joke. I refrain from pointing out that we're currently neighbors too.

Carter flashes me a smile, then looks at Jill with unease. I stare a second longer before doing the same because he's even better than my fantasies. Not hotter. I have a very vivid imagination fueled by all sorts of unrealistic and unattainable visuals. I blame the photoshopped fashion industry. And certain porn websites. Carter is *real*, though. A normal guy leaning toward handsome who I've just decided is exactly my type. I love the thickness of his lips and the way the back of his neck is a little hairy past the buzzed line, like he's got a touch of werewolf in him. And are those dimples in his cheeks? I'm dying! I force my eyes away to focus on what Jill is saying.

"—and so I thought you might be interested in getting to know each other, since you're both new here. It never hurts to have more friends. Am I right?"

Carter looks over at me and smiles. I'm pretty sure I melt into the chair, which is pathetic, because it's only a mere glance in my direction. His head is already turning toward Jill again.

"We can hang," he says. "Sure."

"We'll totally hang!" I say, eager to back him up. Worried this could be interpreted as sarcasm, I add, "We're bros now." Yeah. Much better. Maybe I should try a fist-bump and high-five combo next. Ugh.

"Andrew was expressing interest in the Open Classroom Project," Jill continues. "Did you have time to read through the pamphlet yet, Carter?"

"Yeah," he answers. "It all sounds good."

"Wonderful! Well, let me get everything set up, and I'll print out permission slips for your parents to sign." She starts typing on her computer again before our mutual stares pull her attention away. "Why don't you two relax in the front room? I don't see any point in sending either of you back to class."

The idea of being stuck in a glorified waiting room with Carter… I'm not sure how I feel about that, but I already know it's preferable to getting knifed by a psychopath. I hang back as we walk into the waiting area, unsure of the logistics. I'd love for us both to sit on the loveseat, but naturally he returns to the table, the same chair as before, and pulls out his phone. I don't. I sit across from him, taking the opportunity to stare until he looks up.

"So," I say. "What are you in for?"

He catches on quickly, a smile tugging at his cheek and causing a dimple to appear. "Killed a man."

His voice is artificially gruff when he says this. It reminds me of the night I heard him yelling at his parents.

"You?" Carter asks.

"Robbed a bank," I say. "I needed a place to hide the money until the heat dies down, so I brought it here. Jill works for me. She's kind of my gal."

Carter laughs, the sound coming from deep in his chest. It's loud enough that I see Jill check on us through the window, but she seems pleased.

"Seriously," I say. "How'd you end up here?"

His smile fades, and I find myself wanting to do everything possible to make it return.

"I got into a fight," Carter says, looking away.

I wonder if he had his own brush with a homophobic bully. Maybe our entire lives have been running parallel to each other, leading to this magical point where they finally intersect. "So did I."

The brown eyes return to consider me. "Ha. For real though."

"I did!" I protest. "It wasn't exactly a fist fight but—"

"That's what I thought."

My mouth drops open. "What's that supposed to mean?"

Carter shrugs, his eyes glimmering playfully. "You don't look like you'd do so well in a fight."

"Because I'm skinny?"

He shrugs again. "Something like that."

"You leave me no choice." Puffing up my chest, I put my elbow on the table with a thud and splay my fingers wide. "Arm wrestling time. You and me. Winner takes all. Including the stolen bank money."

Carter grins and puts his elbow on the table too. I was just being silly. I didn't think this through, and I'm glad because we're about to touch. We don't even know each other's last names and now… Now we're holding hands. His feel strong in a way mine never have. My fingers are thin and my palms are soft. His feel rough. I wonder how they got that way.

"On three," he says. "One…"

"Wait, do we start right when you say three?"

"Two…"

"Or do you count to three, and *then* we go?"

"Three!"

Carter's hand tenses around mine as he pushes. I push back. I know I can't beat him. His bicep bulge is way bigger than my own, but I'd still like to impress him as much as possible. I last about five seconds before my arm begins to shake. When it gives in, he doesn't slam it on the table mercilessly. He eases up right before that happens, and for one glorious moment, the skin of our forearms press together, his hand gripping mine. I'm more than happy to submit to him permanently if it means we can remain this way, but he barks laughter and releases me.

"You're not here because you got in a fight," he says, like he can read my mind. "You're here because you *lost* a fight and you needed Jill to soothe your shattered ego."

"Busted," I say, relieved that I'm not so transparent. Then again, part of me *wants* him to know my thoughts, if only so I can see how he reacts.

"Oops!" Jill says this from the other room. Maybe she dropped a pen or clicked the wrong icon. All I know is that it seems to break the spell.

Carter's face becomes troubled again. "Do you think your parents will be upset about the open classroom thing?" he asks.

"Why would they be? It says a lot that we're being accepted into the program. I don't think everyone gets in. Jill checked my grades and my—" I snort and say the next two words sarcastically to prove I'm cool. "—*permanent record* before she made the offer."

Carter looks confused. "Really?"

"Yeah. She didn't do the same for you?"

He only shrugs. Carter seems to do that a lot. Maybe I should too, so my shoulders become nice and rounded like his. We could make it a trend. The apathy workout!

"Either way," I say, "just sell it to your parents like it's a big honor. They'll be proud."

Carter laughs. "Right. Maybe they'll even take me out for ice cream."

"Make them take me too," I say. "You heard Jill. We're best friends now."

Carter grimaces. "So embarrassing. Don't worry, I've got friends already. I'm sure you do too."

"Tons," I say. "The only problem is, they're all over a thousand miles away." I feel myself starting to blush again, but I don't care. It's the truth.

"Oh," Carter says. "When did you move here?"

"At the beginning of the summer."

"Huh."

"What?"

"Nothing," he says quickly. He messes with his phone for a second, maybe to escape the awkwardness. I'm wondering if that's the end of our story when he looks up again. "Sounds like we're going to be classmates."

"Yeah."

"So we might as well be friends. I don't know anyone else in this open classroom thing."

"Open Classroom Project," I say, turning my attention to the pamphlet to draw attention away from what just happened. "You down with OCP?" It's the first thing that comes to mind.

Carter looks confused. "Huh?"

I try again, making myself sound more like a rapper. "You down with OCP?"

This time it clicks. "Yeah, you know me!" Carter's voice is booming when he sings this. Then he shakes his head and grins. "Great song, man."

"Yeah. Super cool. My dad listens to it all the time."

"It's my grandma's personal favorite," Carter shoots back.

"I'm not surprised," I say. "You know what OPP stands for, right?"

"What?"

I lean to the right to make sure we're not being watched. Then I whisper, "Old people penises."

"No way!"

"For real." I manage to keep a straight face. "Look it up."

To my delight, Carter actually starts to, but I can't hold it in. I splutter laughter.

He rolls those beautiful brown eyes at me. "What's it really stand for?"

"I honestly don't know. Here." As a peace offering, I look it up, and it turns out I'm not far off. We're busy snickering over the real meaning when Jill walks back into the room and places a piece of paper in front of each of us. "have your parents sign these tonight, and bring them back to me first thing in the morning. If for any reason they don't sign… Well, I suppose it's still good for you both to report back here so we can find a different resolution to your situations."

That piqued my interest. What exactly is Carter's situation?

Jill checks her watch. "School is out in ten minutes. You can leave early, if you like."

We both stand a split second later. An offer to leave school early is *never* debated or questioned. We try to squeeze through the door at the same time, Carter playfully shoving me behind him. I look back before I go and see that Jill's cheeks are rosy as she watches.

That's when I promise myself to invite her to the wedding.

Chapter Three

Once Carter and I are outside the school, I keep walking, wanting to get away from there before other students flood out of the building. I see parents already waiting to pick up their kids—an especially embarrassing end to a stressful day for many freshmen. I instinctively walk toward home, knowing that Carter will also have to go in that direction.

"What should we do?" he asks.

Shirtless back massages would be a good start, but of course I don't suggest this. "I don't know. We could go to the mall." It's a lame idea, and I can tell from his muted response that he's not impressed, even though he agrees. I don't want him to regret being friends with me. I can do better. "Do you have a car?"

"No need. It's walkable."

That's not what I meant. If he had wheels, I would have suggested going somewhere cooler, but if we're stuck in our area, I can't think of anything better. Carter seems to know where to go, since he turns at the next corner.

We take only a few steps before I stop us. "Our backpacks! We left them in Jill's office."

"Oh, right." Carter looks back toward the school. "We'll see her tomorrow morning anyway. I've got my wallet."

"I do too," I say, patting myself down.

"Then if our packs get stolen, it's no big loss."

Fair enough. We walk in silence as I struggle to find a topic of conversation.

"What do you think of Chicago?" I say, purely out of desperation. It's a question I'm sick of. He probably is too, so I decide to play off of that. "I bet you haven't been asked that recently!"

Carter chuckles. "Nobody has told me about winter yet either and how terrible it's going to be."

"Oh my god! *Every single person* I meet keeps warning me about it. Especially when they find out that I'm from somewhere warm."

"Just do what I do: Tell them you own only shorts and ask if you'll need something warmer. They practically have a heart attack."

I laugh. "I'll guess we'll find out how bad it really is. You can be honest with me though. No need to worry about hurting the feelings of the locals. Do you like it here?"

Carter frowns. "It's okay. Different from what I thought it would be. I was picturing—I don't know—Gotham City or something."

"Yes!" I say. "Chicago is supposed to be skyscrapers and mob bosses and hot dogs. Not an endless suburb."

"It's weird, right? In Arizona, when you leave a city, you're surrounded by desert. Here it just goes on and on."

"And on. My brother and I got sick of going downtown all the time, so one day we decided to drive in the opposite direction."

Carter looks over at me as if interested. "What did you find?"

"The traffic thins out a little, and it's more like the suburbs I used to know. Just a lot greener. All the good tanning beds and nail salons are out there too. It's glorious."

Carter laughs again. I'm loving that he gets my sense of humor. "And past that?" he asks.

"Farms and then the next town."

He nods like he expected as much. Then he sighs. "It's definitely different from back home."

"Why did your family move?"

He traps his bottom lip between his teeth. I watch as it slowly slips free again and wonder what his mouth would feel like pressed against mine. "My parents came up with the idea," he says. "They said it would broaden our horizons, which is ironic because that's the one thing you can't see here. You?"

"My mom got a promotion."

"Must have been a big one to move you guys across the country."

"We're basically billionaires now, yeah." I'm sneaking as many glances at him as I dare. His demeanor isn't as carefree now. Maybe it's the topic. I think I understand. Even when I'm having a good time here, a stray memory from my old life can bring me down again. "Do you ever get homesick?"

"I miss..." Carter trails off. Minutes seem to drift by. I'm tempted to fill the silence, but I'm also dying to know what he's going to say. Is he thinking of an ex? Someone (please let it be a guy!) he was forced to part with who he still longs to see? "I miss the nature," he says at last.

"The desert," I say incredulously, not hiding my disappointment. "What you really want to get back to is all that dry, cracked dirt."

"And the mountains," he says defensively. "Arizona has some beautiful rocks."

"You're such a Boy Scout," I say jokingly, hoping to lighten the mood.

Carter winces. "I was… Until they kicked me out."

"What? I need the full story. Now!"

My mind fills with images of a Scoutmaster unzipping a tent and catching Carter and another boy in a compromising situation. In my own defense, I'm imagining him at his current age, and the other boy just happens to look exactly like me.

"You know that line in *Toy Story*," Carter says, "where Woody talks about having a snake in his boot? It's one of the things he says when someone yanks his pull-string." He puts on an exaggerated country accent. "'There's a snake in my boot!' I was a lot younger at the time, and I thought it was the funniest thing in the world. We were out camping when I decided that would make a good prank, so um… The Scoutmaster wasn't happy. Mostly because it was *his* boot I chose."

I laugh, even though I still like my version better. "Did he get bit? Or did the poor snake get squished?"

"Neither. The Scoutmaster kept his boots in his tent because he wasn't an idiot. Kind of an asshole, but not an idiot. I figured if I unzipped the tent enough to slip in the snake, it would naturally find its way to one of his boots. I was young," he stresses when I make a face. "And I thought the snake I caught was harmless."

"Thought?"

"Young," he reminds me. "Anyway, the Scoutmaster must have heard me, because he woke up and turned on his flashlight at about the same time I was setting the snake loose. I got lucky. He shined the light on it instead of me. When he started hollering, I started running, not that it mattered. I was the prime suspect because of course I'd been walking around quoting Woody for most of the trip. When the Scoutmaster went around checking tents, he must have heard me laughing."

"So in summary," I say with a devilish grin. "A cowboy named Woody convinced you to put your snake in another man's tent."

"Dude!" Carter says with a belly chuckle. "That's seriously messed up!"

Why? Because he was young and the situation wasn't remotely sexual? Or because he thinks anything gay is messed up? I decide to give him the benefit of the doubt. It *was* a trashy joke.

"I get why your Scoutmaster wouldn't be happy," I say, "But I'm surprised they kicked you out for a harmless prank. Kids do dumb things."

Carter's face turns a little red. It's adorable. "The snake was the final straw. I had a history."

"You're trouble," I say warmly. "Aren't you?"

He shoots me a wink that just about knocks me over. "Stick around long enough and you'll find out."

Just try to get rid of me, I'm tempted to retort. I don't. In fact, I struggle to find words. I've gotten in trouble before too, but only for normal things like talking in class or passing notes. I haven't had too many brushes with authority. I don't have any cool stories to share. Even worse, I'm taking the guy who likes nature and cowboys to an air-conditioned mall. I don't see myself winning any points that way, but it's too late to turn back. I can hear the rush of cars and see the main road ahead. Our destination is across the street and a little further down.

"Have you been to this mall already?" I ask.

"Yeah. It's small."

"It's not the size of it…" I say, but even I don't laugh at my joke, too focused on the impending disaster. I imagine us sitting quietly on a bench, listening to the piped-in music while moms push strollers past us. "We can go to Starbucks instead."

"They have one there," Carter says. "Sort of. It's just a booth. They could use a real one. A bookstore too."

"You like to read?" I ask.

"Yeah." We reach the street corner. Carter hits the pedestrian signal with the butt of his fist, striking it a few times as if already frustrated by the wait. "Why do you sound so surprised?"

"I'm not. Okay, maybe a little, but only because you seem more like the sporty type."

"Now you're saying that athletic people are too stupid to read." Carter shakes his head. "That's hateful, Andrew."

I laugh, he smiles, and I'm happy that I get his sense of humor too. "I pictured you playing baseball. Or maybe football. How many sports are you enrolled in? Help me out here. I'm still trying to label you." Boy, isn't that the truth!

The pedestrian light turns from orange to white. He leads the way. "I was in gymnastics when I was younger."

"Why'd you quit?"

"I found a different sport I liked better."

"Which one?" He probably feels like he's being interviewed at this point, but I can't help it. I want to know everything about him.

"Hiking."

Carter pauses before saying this. Not as long as before, but I'm convinced he's not being honest. The answer is too weird. Hiking is athletic, but it's not exactly a sport. People don't compete and get medals or trophies for walking around in the wilderness. Do they? Maybe he was a male cheerleader, or into ballet. Anything that he would feel the need to hide, lest people make assumptions about his sexuality. Right now, I'm all about making those assumptions, so I try a different angle.

"What sort of books do you read?"

"The kind that're filled with photos of sports equipment."

"Seriously," I say, pushing him playfully. "Who's your favorite author?"

"Rowling." He says this in a deep voice, like he's desperate to make it sound cool.

"J.K.?" I ask.

"No, I'm not just kidding."

It takes me a second to get his joke, and I'm impressed, because it's not only witty banter, but she's one of my favorites too. "I am *obsessed* with the Harry Potter books," I say. "I've read each one three times."

"Same here," he replies, matching my happy expression. "I'm not sure of the exact count, but it's high. When I was little, I even dressed up as Hagrid for Halloween. It didn't work out so well. Most people thought I was supposed to be a bum or a caveman."

I laugh at the mental image, and refrain from sharing that I wanted to dress up as Hermione. My parents wouldn't allow it. This was years ago. These days my mom would probably do my make-up and hair. I opt instead for less embarrassing evidence of my dedication. "We have a cat called Hufflepuff. My parents let me name her."

His head whips around, and I realize what I've just given away.

"Were you knocking on doors the other day? She went missing, right?"

"That's right!" I say, and in the hopes of steering the conversation away, I add, "We found her the same day. She's fine now."

"Good. I remember you!"

Now I look over at him. For once my face doesn't betray me. I'm not blushing, but I am curious. Maybe I made an impression on him too. "Really? My brother did most of the knocking."

"Bigger guy, yeah. You didn't come up to the door. You were texting or something."

"Sounds like me," I say. "That sounds familiar. I think your house is just a couple down from mine. We live on the other side of the alley but—"

"No way!" He sounds excited.

That makes two of us. "I'll show you where I live later. Just in case you ever want to stop by."

"Man..."

He says this while wearing a dopey grin. I'm not sure how to interpret that. He either likes me, or he *really* likes me. Either one works for me. We spend the next few minutes talking about our favorite series. Both of us have taken the quizzes on Pottermore and were sorted into Ravenclaw, to our mutual delight. We're talking about which wizarding classes we'd most like to take when I notice Toys R Us. I can see the mall now too, but it's not the right place.

"Let's go in there," I say, nodding at the massive toy store. "If we hurry, we'll beat the afterschool rush."

He laughs and agrees. Once we're inside, I come up with a plan. All I want is to spend time with him, and in order to get the maximum amount, I say, "We have to go up and down every aisle. That's the only way to do it."

"Okay," he says. "Except for the baby stuff. We can skip that, right?"

"Nope! All of it. Starting with the far corner."

He groans. The aisles we are heading toward are predominantly pink. This is an intentional choice on my part. I still can't figure him out. I really am struggling to put any sort of label on him. A jock who doesn't play sports? A geek who just happens to be cool? As for his sexuality, I keep second-guessing myself, but I figure his reaction to all these dolls might help me figure it out. Gay guys aren't necessarily into girly things, but we do tend to be less intimidated about crossing gender lines.

We make fun of what we see in the girls' section. I'm sure we'll do the same when we get to the boys' stuff, but I make sure to pause in front of the Barbie display, especially the Fashionista dolls that include a variety of cute teenage guys. It's not just blond-and-boring Ken anymore. And yes, I've stood in this very spot a few times over the summer, wondering if a tiny plastic boyfriend was better than none at all.

"Dude!" Carter says, sounding excited. He grabs one of the boy dolls off the shelf and practically presses his nose against the package to take in all the details. "Ginger would love this!"

"Who?"

"My youngest sister. She always likes the nerdy guy in any show she watches." Then he holds up the doll and squints at me, as if doing a comparison. I can only see the back of the package, which shows a picture of a doll wearing glasses and a plaid shirt.

"That's how you see me?" I say in mock offense.

"You like to read, so that makes you a nerd," he teases. "Taste of your own medicine!"

"You like to read too. And I don't even wear glasses. Oh hey, they have one that looks like you." I grab a female doll with black skin and an afro. She's one of my favorites, and yeah, I've been tempted to buy myself some fake friends too.

"That *does* look like me," he says. "Spitting image!"

I put it back on the shelf but he holds on to his.

"I'm buying this for her," he explains.

"How many siblings do you have?" I ask as we keep walking.

"Two. Both younger than me. You?"

"Just the older brother you met. That's Reed. We get along okay."

"My sisters are brats," Carter says dismissively. "I can't stand them."

I don't buy it. He must love them or he wouldn't be proudly carrying a doll around the store. I can't decide what this says about him. He's either cool or gay or some mixture of both. No matter what, I like being around him. We have fun as we explore more of the store. In the action figure aisle, we swap memories about the shows we liked best. I find myself wishing the next *Fantastic Beasts* movie was due out sooner so there would be more Harry Potter related merchandise on the shelves. We could have bought matching wands or something cute like that.

"Hey!" Carter says when we reach the next section. "Bikes! I miss mine."

"You didn't bring it with you when you moved?"

He shakes his head. "It was a mountain bike. I figured it would be useless here, and I needed the money, so I sold it."

"I used to have a dirt bike," I say. "After I got too old for it, I inherited Reed's ten-speed, which I don't really like."

"You're never too old for a dirt bike," Carter says, setting aside the doll and lifting a bike from the display rack. He gets on it and grins, even though his knees are practically up to his shoulders.

I whip out my phone to take a photo. Carter is a good sport and poses. Then he gets up and takes a bigger bike off the rack. He looks around at the empty aisles and smiles. "Hey. Grab one for yourself."

"Why?"

"Come on! Just do it!"

I choose a bike that's similar to his, and as soon as my butt hits the saddle, memories of slow summer days come rushing back to me. We don't need to discuss what happens next. We both start pedaling. Slowly at first. I've never ridden a bike indoors. The cramped aisles make me nervous, the handlebars wobbling until we pick up speed. Carter whips around a corner, and I give chase.

"Excuse me!" The employee is a blue-shirted blur that we blow past. A few customers have to dodge out of the way, but Carter and I don't slow down. Nor do we stop laughing.

"Hey!" A different employee this time, who runs after us.

Carter seems to have a plan. He leads us to the far corner of the store. There he skids to a stop. I do the same. Carter holds up a finger, eyebrows raised like he's listening. We both grin at each other when we hear footsteps. As soon as they near, Carter takes off in the opposite direction. I'm right behind him. He leads us back to the bike section, where he quickly hops off the saddle and returns his to the rack. He helps me do the same.

"Act casual," he says, grabbing the doll and walking down the aisle. I follow his lead, even though I'm not nearly as good at keeping a straight face.

"You two!" the employee pants, catching up with us at last. "What… are you… doing?"

"Buying my little sister a present," Carter says, holding up the doll as evidence. He appears legitimately confused. I try to stand behind him as much as possible, because I'm on the verge of losing it. The employee is bent over, hands resting just above his knees, as he tries to catch his breath.

"Where are the bikes?" he manages to wheeze.

"I think that section is next to the strollers," Carter says, pointing away from us.

"Maybe you should ask someone who works here," I manage to squeak out.

The employee glares, then seems to decide that we aren't worth the trouble. He musters a "don't do that again" before hobbling away.

We wait until he's out of sight. Then we bust out laughing.

"This one's mine."

We're standing outside my house. I already know that I want to invite him in. After our trip to the toy store, we went to the mall, but only for a cookie. Carter was restless while we snacked, so I suggested we head back home, mostly so we could be alone. I'm hoping that, once we're hanging out in my basement, conversation will become even more personal.

"It's awesome that we're neighbors," Carter says, beaming at the place.

"I think so too," I say. "Wanna come inside?"

"Nah." Carter turns away from the front of the house, looking instead toward where he lives, even though he can't see it from here. "My mom will want to hear how today went. She keeps texting."

"Really?"

"Yeah," Carter says sheepishly. "You know how it is. New school and everything. Besides, I need to sell them on the open classroom thing."

"Just ask them if they're down with OCP," I say.

This earns me a grin, but it doesn't last long. Carter seems worried.

"Us getting into this project is a good thing," I say. "Remember that. Tell them it's a major achievement. An honor! You have to get them to sign, no matter what. I won't do this without you! We're in this together or not at all." I'm laying it on thick, I know, but the more I keep talking, the bigger his smile becomes. "You're a champ! The other seniors won't know what hit them. None of the others will either. Soon you'll be the king of the school!"

"All right, all right," he says with a laugh. "Shut up already. And I *am* the king."

"That's the spirit!"

"No, I mean it. That's my last name."

"Carter King," I say. With a sigh. Oops! I quickly thrust out my hand. "Andrew Evans. Pleased to meet you."

He shakes my hand and his head. "You're so weird." He says this like it's a good thing, so that's how I take it. "See you tomorrow."

I want to ask if we'll walk to school together, but that sounds cheesy, so I let him go. I practically swoon once I'm inside my house. If only we had a fainting couch. I'll talk to my parents about getting one. They're still at work, but I can hear the television downstairs. Reed hasn't begun his shift yet. I follow the sound of studio applause and find him sprawled out on the couch. As usual.

"Hey!" he says when he notices me, sitting up like he'd been waiting. He even reaches for the remote and turns off the TV. "How'd it go?"

"Fine," I say, but he can see from my expression that it was better than that.

"You're one of the popular kids now, aren't you? I bet they're already setting you up to be homecoming king."

"No, but I wouldn't mind being the queen." That sounded cooler in my head. Carter is a King, I want to be his queen, and maybe I should take a vow of silence, because now my brother is shaking his head.

"You're such a dork," Reed chastises. "I take it back. There's no way you're popular."

"I'm not, but I did make a new friend. Do you remember that one door we knocked on? The guy my age?"

I tell him everything. Almost. I don't mention Tucker and how the school day had gone from bad to worse. I skip over all of that, because it won't matter tomorrow. Instead I go into embarrassing detail about what Carter and I got up to. Our antics at the toy store don't sound nearly as entertaining when I try to describe them. That happens again when I'm in my room and texting my old friends. My enthusiasm gives away too much. Eventually, they all ask the same question that Reed did. "Think you'll be more than just friends?"

The answer is that I don't know. While we were at the mall, I came close to asking Carter if he has a girlfriend, but I worried that—by assuming he's straight—he might feel pressured to go along with that. Just like I used to when still closeted. Making the question a neutral "Are you seeing anyone?" sounds too much like a proposition, and I wasn't about to ask if he has a boyfriend. I regret that now. I should have found some way to bring it up.

The easiest would be letting it slip that I'm gay and seeing how he reacts, but sixth period had shown me that upfront and direct wasn't always the best approach. I'll let people get to know me first, like the way it happened in New Mexico.

I should have at least exchanged phone numbers with Carter. Steering a conversation was much simpler with texts, since I could strategize before each reply. Coming out to him that way would be a lot easier too, but I'd rather see his face when I do. That way I'll know how he really feels. That, and I just really like his face.

I flop onto my bed, phone in hand, and pull up the photo of him: Carter on a ridiculously small bike, revving the handlebars like it's a motorcycle. I zoom in, checking out different details. Some naughty, others nice. All of them have me dreaming. I've never said this before in my life but…

I can't wait to go to school tomorrow.

Chapter Four

When I reach for my phone the next morning, it's because I'm hoping to see a text message from Carter. Then I remember we haven't exchanged numbers yet, and I panic, like we had made it all the way to the altar only for me to realize I don't know my groom's last name. How could I have skipped over something so basic? If anything, phone numbers are *more* important than last names, since they are used on a daily basis. Last names are only useful when you have something to mail, or if you're listening for your name to be called in a waiting room. Even then they seem fairly disposable. I'd rather give up my surname than my cell phone.

I rush through my morning rituals while trying to figure out how I can meet Carter before school. Each idea is more desperate than the last. I mentally go from knocking on his door to leaving early and sprinting circles around his house, just so I won't miss him when he exits. I don't know if he'll leave through the front or back door, which is why I would have to keep rushing between the two.

In the end I decide I'm being foolish. I know he'll be in Jill's office. Unless his parents didn't sign. If that's the case, then surely he would have texted last night… except he doesn't have my number. Ugh!

I'm a nervous wreck when I leave home. I use the side entrance. We don't have a back door exactly. The houses in Chicago are arranged like books on a shelf. The narrowest part faces the front. I'm guessing this allows for more homes to be built on less land. The weird side effect is that the view from most of our windows is of our neighbors' brick walls. The houses on either side of us are separated by a mere six—maybe eight—foot gap. I haven't tried it yet, but I'm pretty sure I could lie down with my feet pressed flat against our house and still reach out and touch the neighbor's place.

We do have a door toward the rear of the house, but it leads out to a paved walkway smooshed between buildings. That's where I am when I hear someone call my name. I'm trying to lock the door behind me, and when I look over, the keys slip out of my hand. In the misty light of morning, I see Carter striding toward me. His grin is confident, the basketball shorts and hoodie he wears confusing my imagination because the material of one is light and slick, the other soft and thick, which would make for one weird hug if our bodies were to rub together. That doesn't happen. Instead he holds out his hand at a weird angle, and just before I attempt to shake it, I realize that I'm supposed to slap it instead. I let him slap mine in return.

"Hey!" he says. "I was hoping to catch you. I wasn't sure which door you use."

"I was wondering the same thing about you," I admit. "I'm a backdoor kind of guy."

He guffaws, which is the best possible start to my day. Maybe not the best start *imaginable*, but then my noggin is capable of conjuring up some pretty wild scenarios. Such as a squirrel running up one of Carter's legs and down the other with his shorts trapped between its teeth. "Did your parents sign?"

"Yeah!" he says, all traces of worry gone. "Yours?"

"Yup!"

"Cool."

"Cool," I parrot. Would it be too much to offer my arm before we begin our walk? I manage to restrain myself.

"I'm still not sure what I signed up for," Carter says as we head out.

"Me neither. I flipped through the pamphlet last night, but it was boring. For all we know, we might have agreed to be slaves in a salt mine."

"Salt mine? Is that a bad thing?"

"Yeah. Just imagine how much worse our wounds will hurt after we get whipped. The salt gets everywhere." I nudge him. "But the good news is that everything we eat will taste better, because our lips will be encrusted with the stuff."

Carter shakes his head. "I think it'll be more like animal testing. The school will inject us with experimental drugs. If we're lucky, we'll both end up with super powers."

"And if we're not lucky?"

"We'll have eyes and noses growing out of random parts of our bodies."

"Gross!"

We walk a few paces in silence. "But if you *had* to have an extra set of eyes," Carter says, "where would you want them to be? I'd put them on the back of my head. That way I could see behind me, and I could also grow out my hair to hide them."

"Or you could wear a turban like Professor Quirrell did to hide his extra face." The Harry Potter reference earns me a fist bump. "I'd want my extra eyes to be on the palms of my hands. One each. That way I could spy around corners or point them in any direction I want to see."

"That's a good idea," Carter says. "Except it would make jacking off awkward."

"That would only be a problem once a day. Sometimes twice."

Carter snorts. "More like five times a day."

Is he serious? Because that's hot. And maybe of concern. I make a note to buy him some lotion before he chafes himself so bad that it falls off. "I'd just wear gloves," I reply.

"Smart." Carter nods musingly. "And it makes it feel more like someone else's hand."

"You speak from experience?" I say. "I meant that I'd wear gloves all the time Not just while I'm beating off. I don't want to shake someone's hand and have them feel my secret eye squirming against their palm."

"Back of the head is better," Carter insists. "Hands are needed for too many other things."

This debate continues until we switch to suggesting the most ludicrous place an extra pair of eyes could go and a justifiable reason for each. "Eyes on the bottom of my feet," I say. "That way I can see if there's a snake in my boot."

His laugh falters as we reach the doors to the school. He seems nervous again. I'm not. We squeeze past other students to get inside. I look over at him, trying to copy his confident grin from earlier. "We'll make it fun. No matter what it turns out to be."

I hope I can make that true. It'll suck if we're shown to separate tables in the library and expected to study on our own. I've mostly forgotten about Tucker. The new reason I'm doing this is to spend time with Carter.

Jill seems happy to see us when we enter her office. We collect our backpacks and mess with the contents while she types more information into her computer. The bell for first period comes and goes, and I start to hope that we'll stay in her office for most of the day, signing papers and being prepped for whatever comes next.

"Okay," Jill says at last. She rises and walks to the hallway door. "Time to meet your new classmates."

We're standing in the school library, a place that usually fills me with the same warm coziness that I get while reading. Libraries, much like books, are some of the best places to escape into. Usually. Jill forgot to mention one crucial detail about the Open Classroom Project.

"—he'll be your teacher for every subject," Jill is saying. She turns to the man in question. "You've already met Andrew. His friend here is Carter King."

Not even that name can take me back to my happy place, because my head is filled with storm clouds, and in their center stands Mr. Thorp.

He smiles at us both, and while his tone is as kind as his expression, I tense each time he speaks. I'm worried he'll out me to Carter. Technically I outed myself when I stood in front of his class and spoke my truth. That was then, when I didn't have anything to lose. Now is different. I know I'll have to open up to Carter about who I am, but I want to do so on my own terms. I've always had this fantasy about having a best friend I fall for, and when I finally reveal that I'm gay and madly in love with him, he does the same. What better way could there be to begin a relationship? Best friends, right from the get go!

"You're both welcome here," Mr. Thorp says. "We'll get you settled in right away." He looks at Jill. "Unless there's anything we still need to go over?"

"No!" she says, seeming eager to hand us off. Or not, because she lingers, her attention divided between Carter and me. "If you need anything, including a sympathetic ear, you know where my office is."

I thank Jill and watch her go. Then I get nervous, because I know what's coming next. I've been in one of Mr. Thorp's classes before. We'll soon be standing in front of the class and be forced to tell our life stories. A number of tables, chairs, and sofas are set up in one corner of the library, most of them filled with students who are already sizing us up.

"Let's introduce you to everyone," Mr. Thorp says, walking us to the center of this assembly. "Yesterday we each took turns saying a little about ourselves." He glances over at me. "Although we can make it a quick introduction if you prefer."

"Quick sounds good," I say.

Carter backs me up with a simple. "Yeah."

"Your attention please," Mr. Thorp says loud enough for everyone to hear. "I know we've already done roll call today, but we have two new people joining us so… If you don't mind."

He gestures to a girl with blue hair that spills over one shoulder in a gentle wave, the roots just as black as her eyebrows and long eyelashes. Her right nostril is pierced with a simple silver hoop. When she speaks, she has a faint Spanish accent, which is nothing unusual for this area. "Hey," she says. "My name is Olivia Torres."

"Patricia Seiler," the girl next to her says.

"Eddie Bergman," says a guy at a nearby table.

And so it goes. There are only about twenty of us, and it strikes me halfway through that everyone is allowed to say their own name, instead of the teacher calling it out. The order is random instead of alphabetical. It's a small detail, but I like it.

"Yo. Carter King. I just moved here from Phoenix."

"Yo yo yo," I say after him, barely managing to keep a straight face. Who says "yo" anymore? Besides him. And now me. "I'm Andrew Evans, and I'm fresh outta Albuquerque."

I'm hamming it up, but I get the result I want. Carter laughs and shakes his head.

"And I'm Gerald," Mr. Thorp says. "Okay! As you were, everyone. I'll get our newcomers acclimated." He's quieter when he continues speaking. "There aren't any seat assignments, but for the sake of convenience, let's start at that table over there so there's enough room for us all to sit. Why don't you go ahead, Carter?"

He shrugs and walks that way. I turn to Mr. Thorp… Or Gerald as he apparently calls himself here.

His voice is especially low now. "The Open Classroom Project isn't for students who *are* trouble," he says. "It's for students who are *having* trouble. I'd like to know which category you fall into."

He manages to make the question sound less accusatory than we both know it is. I don't blame him, considering the scene I made yesterday. My goofy introduction a second ago probably didn't help my reputation either.

"I'm overwhelmed," I tell him.

"By?" he asks.

I consider my answer carefully before I speak. "All of it."

He nods, as if finding this acceptable. "I've seen your transfers. You seem to have thrived academically at your old school. I assume that was in a normal classroom environment?"

"Yes," I respond. No sense in denying it.

"I know that doesn't necessarily mean that *you* were doing okay." Gerald takes a deep breath. He looks to where Carter is now sitting and then back at me. "Still, I expect a lot from you. Your work here will need to be impeccable. That doesn't mean leaving others behind. I'd rather you help them keep up, if necessary."

"Okay." I'm not sure what I'm agreeing to. I just want to join Carter again.

Gerald seems satisfied. We walk the rest of the way to the table and sit, and from then on, he treats me no differently than he does Carter as he explains exactly what we've gotten ourselves into.

"You have a cake," Gerald says, "that you have to eat before the end of the school year. It's up to you how you eat this cake. If you prefer little slices, that's fine. If you'd rather shove your face right in and munch hands-free, that's fine too. In many regards, you get to choose the flavor of the cake, the shape of the pan it's baked in, the color of the frosting, and so on. The school's only concern is that you finish the cake with a reasonable understanding of what you've eaten." He looks at a clock on the wall. "And now I'm wishing lunch wasn't so far away, because cake sounds delicious."

Carter chuckles, and I try not to feel jealous that another guy has made him laugh.

"These are the key ingredients that will bake your cake," Gerald says.

He presents us with a list, and at first I feel like we've been conned because it's the usual combination of science, math, English, and other basics.

"Math isn't the most flexible, I'm afraid, but when it comes to science, you may choose which topics interest you most and focus on those. Likewise with your World Literature course. As long as the books you choose meet a few basic qualifications..."

I perk up at this. "So we could read *Harry Potter*?"

"Yes," Gerald says, "although I'd rather you challenge yourself with *The Casual Vacancy* or one of the mystery books that Rowling wrote under a pseudonym. Her *Cormoran* series is a stronger effort, in my opinion."

"You like Rowling?" Carter asks, clearly impressed. "Want to join our secret fan club?"

Gerald smiles but stays on track. "Ultimately it's up to you what books you read. Keep in mind that you'll need to produce a compelling essay for each, which will be more difficult the simpler the source material."

The other subjects are handled in a similar fashion. The school sets a minimum we have to achieve, and it's up to us how we get there. This is soon put to the test.

"And with that, gentlemen," Gerald says, "you're free to do as you see fit."

Carter turns to me. "Are you any good at math?"

"I do okay."

"Let's blow through all of that first and get it out of the way."

We look at Gerald, who is observing but doesn't offer any objections.

"Is it okay if we work together?" I ask.

"You can stand up and teach the class if that's what you all agree on," he replies. "I don't want to see anyone copying answers, but if you reach the same conclusion together…"

He soon rises to check on other students. Gerald seems to be there to offer advice, or to tutor and teach when need be, but he's not the constant presence that most teachers are. I'm really liking this concept. Carter does too, so we put a dent in our math assignments with the minimum of goofing around. We want to make this work, and we're not alone. Even when Gerald leaves to fill in for Mrs. Pants or whatever her name is, the class stays on track.

When it's time for lunch, I feel more satisfied than tired. Most of the kids from the OCP sit at the same table, including Carter and me. We're at the very end with an empty seat next to each of us. That means privacy, which I'm eager to take advantage of. Carter is more interested in his phone. I poke at the tray of warm and gloppy food in front of me. Then I give up on being polite.

"You can text your former friends all you want," I say. "Just be aware that, as I become your new best friend, you'll eventually cease to find them interesting."

Carter looks up, his brow crinkled. "Huh? Oh. Sorry. It's not my old friends. It's Bobby."

"Who?"

"A guy I hung out with during the summer. He's giving me crap about the OCP. I think he's jealous."

"Who could blame him?" I say, feeling a little envious myself. "Does he go to this school?"

"Yup." Carter finally sets down his phone. "We had a couple classes together, but that was yesterday. He's not happy about the switch."

Sounds like I have competition. I mentally declare war on this Bobby person. "Hey, can I get your phone number?"

"Yeah! Duh. I keep meaning to do that."

He rattles off the number to me, my fingers practically trembling with excitement as I type it into my phone. Then I send him our first text.

Hey! It's Andrew, your new best friend. Bobby called to let me know that he's giving up the title, and that he wants me to have it.

Carter reads this, his lips moving a little. I'm worrying he won't get the joke and think I'm crazy, when he finally laughs. "Bobby isn't my best friend."

"No?"

"No. He's cool, but…" Carter shrugs.

I'm not deluded enough to think that I'm his best friend either. Not after a single day of knowing each other. "Is your BFF still in Phoenix?"

Carter seems to think about it. Then he nods. "Yeah. You?"

I can understand the delayed response, because I have to think about it too. "Kind of. She started dating this guy, and he's got a sister that she really connects with. It's like she's become a part of their family. We promised to stay in touch, but we don't have as much to talk about now. I don't hear from her so much anymore."

"Bound to happen. Things change."

Good. That means he won't stubbornly cling to his former best friend, giving me a chance. I don't know Carter well enough to judge how close we'll be, or if we have true romantic potential, but in my experience, connections with people don't need much time. You either click or you don't. We decide to finish our meal in the same way we're tackling our OCP course load—by cramming it down our throats as fast as possible—a contest Carter wins by a fraction of a second. At the end of lunch period, I'm more certain than ever that we click.

"Gotta use the gents," I say on the way to class.

"Just don't let them use you," Carter shoots back.

"Ha!" My response is automatic. It's only when I'm standing at the urinal that I wonder what he meant. That it would be bad to let the other guys in the restroom use me as a toilet? Or did he mean sexually? Was the comment homophobic? Or meant to be funny, which it's not, because being gay doesn't mean having bathroom sex. To each their own, but I can't think of an environment that's a bigger turn off. Except maybe my aunt's house, which always reeks of vegetable soup. No idea why. I've never seen her eat a drop of soup in my life.

I'm still pondering this when I return to the library. I cut through one of the aisles of books. Then I stop and stare, because Carter is sitting atop the table we'd been using. So is the girl with blue hair. Olivia. Her eyes are shining as she titters at whatever Carter is saying. She looks like she's covered from head to toe in the happiness that had, until now, belonged to me.

I hang back until the bell rings. Olivia gets up and returns to her seat. Carter stays where he is, still wearing the same dumb expression, even though she's gone.

"Hey," he says in a conspiring whisper. "Did you see that?"

"Sure did," I say, sitting in one of the chairs and pulling my math workbook close. "Ready to keep going?"

Real smooth. Nothing wins a guy's heart like reminding him that there's arithmetic to be done. I want to pout. I really do, but that ceaseless optimism of mine kicks in. Maybe I was telling myself the wrong story just now. I love women. I find it easier to talk to them, and that includes joking around or sharing intimate details. This seems like a fairly typical preference for most gay guys. Carter could be the same way. Or maybe he really was flirting. So what? He could still be bisexual or any of the other flavors out there. Not straight though. Please don't let him be that!

"What did she say?" I ask, shoving away the workbook.

Carter finally sits next to me. "She has family in Arizona. Says she goes there once a year."

"Oh." I don't care about her history. I just want to know one thing. "Was she hitting on you?"

"I don't know." Carter's voice is a whisper. "I think so."

His grin says he doesn't mind. Or maybe he finds it amusing like I do when women mistake me for something that I'm not. Either way, we need to have the talk. That's right, *the* talk. Just not in school. After, at his house or mine.

Gerald comes over to ask how we're doing, and that's our cue to get back to work. So we do. Eventually we tire of math and use the last hour to plan when and how we'll tackle the other subjects. I want to decide on what we'll be reading, but Carter seems reluctant. Or maybe he's just distracted. More than once I catch him glancing in Olivia's direction. When the bell rings, I can't wait to get out of there. I'm worried that Olivia will approach us and ruin everything, but she's one of the first to leave. I'm about to suggest we go to my place when Carter waves his phone at me. "Bobby and the others are hanging out at Scoville. Wanna go?"

"Sure." I'd rather be alone with him. I just can't find a way of saying so that doesn't sound needy or pathetic.

Scoville Park isn't far from the school. Nor is it very large. It's the size of a city block and surrounded by artsy little shops that I've already browsed multiple times. I've noticed the park before, but this is my first time walking through it. The park is fenced in by trees, which helps create a natural barrier against the surrounding traffic. The center of the park is mostly a mowed grass field. That might not sound exciting, but the open space is a welcome break from the constant congestion. I turn my face up to a blue sky, letting the sun warm my cheeks, and feel relieved to have made it through another day of school. I'm curious about the situation I'm walking into, and a little apprehensive. A person's friends say a lot about who they are, so I reshuffle my perspective until I'm looking forward to meeting Bobby. If I'm lucky he'll spill lots of details about Carter that I don't know yet.

"We always hang out at the war memorial," Carter says.

He nods to the far end of the park, where circular steps lead up to a large white statue that stands over three smaller figures made of bronze. Each member of the trio wears a different military uniform. Above them, the flag of the United States waves in the air. I give all of this only a cursory glance, scanning the sidewalks and benches until I spot a group of students our age. The dais of the war memorial is made up of steps, and that's where five of them sit.

My stomach sinks. One of the people we're walking toward

gives an upward nod of his head, his black floppy hair needing to be pushed back into place. Then he locks eyes with me and I'm certain it's him, because that stare is so cold it gives me chills.

"Tucker," I say.

"You know Bobby?"

Carter's words hit me like a sucker punch, and for one mad moment, I wonder if this is some sort of elaborate trap. "I— I don't know," I stammer. "Is that Bobby's last name? Tucker?"

"Yeah."

I don't have time to respond or to scramble for an excuse to leave, because we're within earshot now. Even worse, Bobby Tucker has risen to join us.

"Who's this?" he says, still focused on me.

If I'm lucky… If I'm really *really* fortunate, he won't remember me.

"Andrew," Carter says. "I texted you that he was coming with."

"Right." Bobby's smile is slow and deliberate. "I just didn't realize that—" He laughs and shakes his head. "Are you fucking serious? *Him*?"

"What's your deal?" Carter says. "Don't be a dick."

"I'm just screwing with you, man." Bobby laughs again, eyes wild as he looks at me. "Come on."

He throws an arm around my shoulder as he turns around. I glance over to see that he's done the same to Carter. He's leading us toward the rest of his friends. Every instinct tells me to run, but the arm on my shoulders has moved higher. Now it's around my neck, and it feels a little tight.

"How did you two become so close?" Bobby asks. "Don't tell me. You're dating."

"Ha ha," Carter deadpans. "We're in that new program together."

"The one for retards?"

"Fuck this," Carter growls. "We're leaving."

Hope explodes inside of me until I look over to see them both grinning. It's only banter. Offensive, annoying banter.

"You're missing out," Carter says. "We get to do whatever we want. The teacher isn't even there most of the time."

"Maybe I'll join," Bobby says. Hard green eyes lock onto mine. "You'd like that, wouldn't you, pretty boy?"

Pretty boy? If one of them is gay, please don't let it be Bobby! "I thought I heard that the program is full now."

"You'll put in a good word for me, though. Won't you? See if they can squeeze me in?"

"First thing in the morning," I say, relieved when he finally releases me.

Now we're standing in front of the war memorial's steps and staring down at four other people. Bobby runs through a list of names, and I size up each as a potential threat. Mick must weigh a ton, his straight blond hair shoved under a John Deere cap. Pedro barely looks up at me, too busy rolling a joint. Felipe is scrawny with a pitiful goatee, his blue-collar clothes out of season and out of style. And then there's Jackson, a black guy who is giving me the eye. He's about my size. Not quite as skinny, but I find him a lot more intimidating when Bobby introduces him as "my right-hand man." Bobby even makes Mick scoot over so he can sit next to Jackson. Carter and I remain standing.

"So how did you two lovebirds meet?" Bobby asks.

Carter answers, but I don't hear what he says. I'm too unsettled by the way Bobby smirks each time he looks at me. I start listening again when his head tilts in my direction and he says, "You know about him, right?"

"Know what?" Carter asks, expression puzzled.

Bobby grins, like this is the best news possible.

"Know what?" Carter asks again, sounding less patient.

"This guy is trouble," Bobby says, leaning back and stretching out a leg. "He flipped out in sixth period and started throwing stuff around the room. Didn't you, Andrew?"

I go along with him, hoping it will buy me time or earn me respect. Maybe if I'm funny, the rest will be overlooked. "I just have these moments," I say, clenching my hands while pulling the craziest face I can, "where the tension builds and builds until I… I… *hulk out!* Nrrrraaaaaagh!"

Bobby stares. Then he laughs. The rest of them do too, but it doesn't sound mocking. "You're crazy, man," he says. "Hey, Pedro, hurry up with that joint. The rest of you, move over. I want to get to know this fool."

Is that how it works? Is acting crazy all it takes to earn the respect of a legitimately crazy person? Maybe I can make a career of this and be an ambassador to the insane. I'm not thrilled to be sitting next to Bobby, but Carter is to my left, which provides some comfort. I try to focus on him. Before long, a smoldering joint is being offered to me.

"Your turn," Bobby says, choking on the words as he tries to hold his breath—and the smoke—in his lungs.

Drugs aren't a regular thing for me, but I've indulged enough to know that getting stoned is best done in an environment where I feel secure. Weed magnifies emotions, good or bad. I'm already jumpy enough. I know that will only get worse if I partake, and yet, I also can't refuse. I'm being watched, like this is a test, which it probably is. I take the joint and inhale, but I make sure not to draw very hard on it. Once I blow out smoke, Bobby slaps me on the back.

"There ya go!" he says. "Now you're one of us!"

"It's not my first time," I shoot back. When I notice him tense, I add, "My grandma let me take a drag of her cigarette when I was nine. This is the same thing, right?"

Everyone laughs, and once again I'm safe because I'm silly. A lot of gay people learn this defense. If you're amusing enough, people forget to hate you. I bet that's why Oscar Wilde was so witty all the time. The clever things he said and wrote helped distract from his preference for hot young lords.

I pass the joint to Carter, who sucks on it and blows out again immediately. I don't think he knows how to inhale, but his secret is safe with me.

"So how did you and Carter meet?" I ask Bobby.

The story isn't very interesting. At the start of the summer, Carter was doing lawn work for extra cash, and one of those yards belonged to Bobby's neighbor. They talked a few times over the weeks until Carter asked him what people do for fun in Chicago.

"So I told him about drifting down on Lower Wacker Drive and took him there the next weekend," Bobby says with a wicked grin.

"You should have seen his face," Jackson chimes in. "You had fun, though, didn't you?"

"Yup!" Carter says. "We gotta show Andrew that too."

I don't know what they're talking about and I don't care. I'm just happy that Bobby is too distracted to notice I'm not really smoking the next two times the joint is passed to me. There are seven of us, and that's enough to burn it down to a roach. My head feels light, but I'm not fried by any means. My heart *is* pounding though. Something about Bobby's energy — the way his every word is an affront to kindness and sensibility — makes me nervous. Go figure.

Conversation goes on without me for a while. The topic moves from the most fun that can be had in Chicago to some guy named Dirk who moved away last year, but who, by all accounts, made everything fun. I can't keep up with all these names. Maybe it's the weed. I can't even remember who the scrawny dude is, or the name of the big guy who looks like a farmer.

"Holy motherfucking Mary," Bobby says suddenly. He gives an appreciative whistle. "Who invited the mermaid?"

Three girls are approaching us. I recognize only one. The blue hair is hard to forget. Olivia is here. Great. Just when I thought it couldn't get worse.

"Dibs on Blue," Bobby says.

Then again, if he's interested and it works, that would remove her from being a threat. Him too, depending on how wrapped up in the relationship he gets.

"She's mine," Jackson says.

"Don't be greedy," says one of the other guys. "You've already got Harper."

One of the girls, a redhead, raises her hand and waves.

Jackson waves back. "Maybe it's time for me to upgrade."

Classy. I can see why he's Bobby's right-hand man.

"Shut up," Carter says. "Both of you. The mermaid is mine."

"She doesn't belong to anyone," I spit. "Especially you losers."

Bobby chuckles as if I'm being cute. "Which one do you like, Andrew? Becca? Harper? Or the new one? Come on. Who would you like to finger? Or eat out."

I grit my teeth. "You know the answer to that."

"Barking up the wrong tree, am I? How about Jackson here? I bet you're dying to shove your tongue in his butthole. Or is it me? I saw you checking out my package earlier. No wait… I think I get it now. You want—"

I shoot to my feet. To my dismay, a hand grabs my arm and yanks me back down.

"If you leave now," Bobby whispers, leaning in close, "I'm

going to follow you home and beat the fuck out of you on your own lawn, right where your mother can see."

I yank myself free and stand. "Let's go then. Come on home with me. Let's tangle!"

Bobby grins. "I guess he likes me after all."

Everyone laughs. Except Carter. He looks confused.

"I'm leaving," I say to him. "Are you coming?"

Carter glances at the girls. That's all the answer I need. I turn and stomp toward the nearest street. I'm about to cross it when I feel someone grab my arm. I ball up my hands into fists, ready to swing, but the fight goes out of me when I spin around and see Carter's worried face.

"Hey! What's wrong? Why'd you run off like that?"

"I'm gay!" I snarl. "That's what's wrong!"

Carter looks like I slapped him. "You're gay?"

I take a deep shuddering breath. "Yeah."

"I'm not!"

I get it. Even though it feels like a line drawn in the sand, I understand that in a split second, he must have seen the previous forty-eight hours in an entirely new light. Every compliment, every brush of physical contact—no matter how small—must now seem like I was desperately hoping for more. He would, of course, be exactly right.

My face is burning. I'm embarrassed by my own actions, or at least my thoughts, which I had believed were private and invisible, but I guess not. "Okay," I say. Then I turn and cross the street.

I'm halfway down the next block and pushing through an incomprehensible jumble of emotions when I hear his voice just behind me.

"I don't get why you're mad. What did I do wrong?"

He sounds hurt and confused. I would have preferred hateful and cruel. That would be easier to deal with. Instead I'll have to explain what I'm feeling. I don't want to. Not at all, so I deflect.

"I'm mad at him," I say, pointing in the direction of the park. "Tucker. Bobby! Whatever his name is. Remember when we met?"

"It was yesterday, so yeah." Carter tries a goofy smile, and it almost works. It ends up hurting me instead, because I still find him so damn cute.

"I told you I got into a fight. Remember? Well, it was more like an argument. Gerald was substituting during sixth period—"

"Our teacher from the OCP?"

"Yeah. He was subbing for the usual teacher. Gerald wanted me and another girl to say something about ourselves and…" I tell him what happened, feeling pathetic instead of vindicated. I should be able to fight my own battles; I don't need him to. I just want him to know what an asshole his friend is.

"Fucking Bobby," Carter says, shaking his head. "I know he can be a dick but—"

"He flashed a knife at me!"

Carter rolls his eyes. He doesn't sound surprised. "That stupid knife. Listen, man, Bobby is all bark. He likes to rile people up. That's just his way. He did the same thing to me. Don't feed into it and he'll stop. Think of it as a sort of initiation. Once you get past it—"

"I don't want to be his friend! He threatened to follow me home and beat me up once I got there. Isn't that messed up? It's like he wants me to know that I'm not safe, even at the place where I should feel the safest. He's crazy!"

"He's full of it."

I shake my head in disbelief. "Now I know that you aren't gay, because if you were, you would get it. People like me get beat up. We get *killed*. Ever heard of Matthew Shepard?"

"No."

I laugh, but there's no humor in my voice. "Seriously? They tied him to a fence, beat him, and left him there to die. And he did. Would you tell Matthew the same thing? That he shouldn't have fed into it?"

"I… I don't know." Carter says. "I'm confused."

"Great. You be confused. I'm freaking scared. Of him. Tell Bobby that and see how he reacts. Before you do, imagine if you found out that someone was frightened of you. Ask yourself how you would react, and then ask him, because I bet his response won't be the same."

Carter's mouth opens and closes.

I'm done. He'll never understand what it's like to constantly be on guard, just because of who I am. "Never mind. I'll see you around."

I walk away. Carter follows, even when I go faster, so I stop again.

"What are you doing?" I demand.

"Walking you home," Carter mumbles. "I don't want you to be scared."

That gets me right in the heart, which sucks, because it's tender enough already. "I don't need your pity, Carter. I don't need you at all! Leave me alone."

He looks hurt as I storm off. The expression remains on his face, even when I look back over my shoulder, but he isn't following me anymore. I got my wish. I'm alone. That's the problem with filling yourself with pride. There's such a thing as too much of it. Even now, because I can barely admit that I was wrong. I am scared, and I do want him with me.

Chapter Five

I've ruined everything. I pace my bedroom, the light growing dim outside. My stomach grumbles with hunger. I couldn't eat dinner. My mom made lasagna, which I normally love, but the pit inside of me can't be filled so easily. I've lost my only friend in Chicago.

Even worse, we share every single class now. The OCP was supposed to be my escape. Now it will be a prison where I'm forced to share a cell with my victim. Or am I the victim? It's so confusing. All I know is that Carter didn't do anything wrong, short of not understanding what it's like to be gay. How could he? And yet I still made him feel horrible. I can't face that guilt every day. Maybe I could transfer back to my normal classes. That would mean I'm forced to be around Bobby Tucker again. I could switch that class too, but he'll probably find me eventually. In the halls or after school, and this time I'll be alone. I want to go home. To Albuquerque.

"What the fuck?!"

Reed sounds terrified as he shouts this from the next room. Probably just a spider. He's a total wimp about bugs. The door to my bedroom is thrown open, my brother ignoring my complaints as he rushes to my window.

"Someone's out there," he says.

My blood runs cold. "What did he look like?"

"Dark hair, your age."

Bobby! It has to be. They are probably done hanging out at the park. Carter has surely told him everything. Bobby knows I'm vulnerable, and now he's come to fulfill his promise. "Grab a weapon," I say, creeping toward the window.

"Huh?"

"A baseball bat! Hurry!"

Reed's face twists up. "Why would I have a bat?"

"Because you like sports!"

"I don't play baseball. I've never played baseball."

I shoot my brother a glare. "Get anything! He's got a knife!"

"A *knife*?"

"Yes!"

"GAH!"

A face appears in the window, but it's not the nightmare I've been dreading. The hand I expect to be brandishing a knife is empty and waving at me.

"Wait a minute," Reed says. "I've seen him before."

"It's Carter," I say with a chuckle.

"Why didn't he ring the doorbell? Or text?"

My phone is powered off. I do that when I'm upset and want to cut myself off from the world. As for the doorbell, I don't know. Maybe he wanted to avoid my family so we could talk alone.

Reed isn't done fretting yet. "Why's he sneaking around with a knife?"

"He's not," I say, already rushing out of the room. "I was thinking of someone else."

"You need to find better friends!" Reed calls after me.

A few seconds ago, I was certain I didn't have any friends at all. I'm still not sure I do. Carter is standing there when I open the back door. I can tell he's feeling just as self-conscious as I am, because he's kicking at the walkway and not making eye contact.

"Hey," he says. "Can we… Um… Can we talk?"

"Yeah." I step outside and am about to close the door behind me, before I realize this sends the wrong signal. I don't want to shut him out of my life. "Do you want to come in?"

"Sure," Carter says.

I lead him through the finished basement. Reed is standing there with his arms crossed. I just know he's going to embarrass me.

"Do I need to pat you down?" he says to Carter. "Hands against the wall. Spread your legs. And your cheeks!"

Yup. I was right. "No need," I say. "He made it through the metal detector." The only explanation I offer Carter is an apologetic shrug.

Now I wish I had put more effort into my bedroom. It's not the largest space. I have a bed of sorts. The mattress and box spring rest directly on the carpet. No frame. I like it that way. I have a few low shelves loaded with books and a dresser with Bluetooth speakers on top. A canvas chair is in one corner, and that's about it. There's not really a place for two people to sit.

Carter looks around and notices a photo collage on the wall. My old life in New Mexico. He peers at the pictures, the faces meaning nothing to him since they're all strangers. Maybe that's why he stares longest at a photo of me and Scott at White Sands. We have our arms around each other, but I'm guessing it's the pristine desert in the background that interests him most.

"Do you miss it?" he asks, looking over his shoulder.

"Yeah," I answer.

"Me too. Is this your boyfriend?"

"He was. We broke up before I moved here." I chew my bottom lip before asking, "Did you have a girlfriend in Phoenix?"

"Not when we moved. I wasn't talking to anyone at that point."

"How come?"

Carter turns to face me. "I'm really sorry about the way I acted earlier. I was kind of high."

I fight down a smile. "No you weren't. You don't know how to inhale."

"True," he says, "but I thought I felt a little funny."

"Sometimes it's the thought that counts."

He smiles, and as always, he's fucking beautiful when he does. Then the smile convulses and becomes a grimace. "I read about Matthew Shepard. I looked him up."

"Oh."

Carter walks toward me, and before I know what's happening, he grabs me in a hug. "I won't let anyone hurt you," he says over my shoulder. I hear a wet sniff. "I swear to God. I won't!"

This isn't pity. It's love, of a sort, and even my pride can't resist it. My arms are at my side, and I want to hug him back, but I'm also petrified he'll misinterpret that as me wanting more. Which I do. More than ever.

He releases me and spins around so he can wipe his nose. "Sorry."

"It's okay," I say. "And thanks." While his back is to me, I speak my own confession. "I wasn't mad at you earlier. Not really. I was angry at Bobby. You just got caught in the crossfire."

"I've been there, man," Carter says, his shoulders shaking with the sort of laughter that is verging on tears. "Ugh. What a shit day."

It wasn't, though. Just the end of it. "I liked the OCP. I'm still down with it. Are you?"

"Yeah, you know me," Carter says, turning around again. He looks me over, and I can tell that he's trying to put all the pieces together.

"I'm still the same person," I say.

"I know. It's just… You should have told me."

"Yeah. I should have." I get down on the floor. The box spring and mattress are just tall enough to use as a backrest, so I sit and pull my knees up to my chest. Carter does the same, except he's facing sideways towards me, with an elbow on the bed and his legs stretched out. "I really like you and want to be your friend," I continue. "I just never know how people are going to react."

"You *are* my friend," he says. "And I would have been fine with it. I am fine with it. If Bobby isn't, then he's not my friend anymore."

"Thanks," I say. "Hey, how did things go with Olivia? You like her, right?"

"She's really pretty," Carter says, the dreamy expression interrupted by concern. "Is that okay? Are you—"

"I'm good!" I hurry to say. "Although if you were gay, I'd be putting some serious moves on you right now, because you're hot."

He grins. "Yeah?"

"And charming and all kinds of things that I'm sure she'll love, the lucky hag."

Carter snorts. "Hag?"

"First thing that came to mind. For what it's worth, I also think she's pretty. But I'm not interested. Obviously. Did you two talk much tonight? Did you get her number?"

"Oh." Carter looks away, his cheeks red. "I didn't go back to the park."

"Why not?"

"Because I was trailing you."

It takes me a second to understand what he means. "You followed me home?"

"I was worried about you. What you said really got to me."

God he's sweet! "I had no idea! Maybe you should be a detective."

"I'd rather be a ninja," Carter says, sitting upright and pantomiming throwing razor-sharp stars. He even makes little whooshing sounds.

Predictably, I find this adorable. "I don't suppose you have a gay brother?"

"Just the little sisters," Carter says. "The oldest is only a year younger than me, so if you ever change your mind…"

"If you ever change yours!" I shoot back.

He laughs. "Fair enough. Is it offensive if I ask how you know?"

"That I'm gay?" I shrug. "I've always known. Even all the way back to the third grade. There was a guy in my class who—well, he looked like a younger version of you, to be honest. I wasn't a shy kid, but for some reason, I couldn't bring myself to talk to him, but I did have dreams. Nothing sexual. He just kept showing up in them, and I kept feeling this *excitement*. Like I was really happy that he wanted to hang out with me. Years later, when all my guy friends stopped acting like girls were gross and became obsessed with them, I felt left out. Simple as that. Around the time you started noticing girls, I started noticing guys in a whole new way."

"Was it hard to come out?"

"Not to my parents. My mom figured it out before I did and kept telling me that if I was straight or gay or anything in between, that she and my dad would be fine with it. My brother was tougher, because he kept giving me advice about women. I could tell he felt proud that he could guide me or whatever, and I didn't want to hurt his feelings by telling him he was wasting his time." I laugh. "My friends were the hardest. That seems like a joke now because they aren't even around."

Carter furrows his brow. "It sucks how things change. You don't get a choice. Life just takes people from you."

I'm not sure I understand. The phrasing sounds weird to me, but I don't want to ruin the moment by telling him I don't get it. Then again, he's working hard to understand me. The least I could do is the same. "You make it sound like someone died. Did they?"

He shakes his head. "I just mean that it's hard to lose a friend." He looks at me sharply, and the intensity of his stare makes me feel like I'm the most important person in the world to him. "I'm not going to let that happen again."

"Me neither," I say. "Let's take an oath. We'll cut open our palms, spit in them, and shake while swearing to be friends until our dying day."

Carter winces. "I *really* want to do that. Just without the blood. And the spit. What's that supposed to do?"

"I think that makes it binding somehow. We can take the easy way out and sacrifice a virgin instead. We'll use Bobby. All we need is a giant rock to tie him to and a hungry dragon."

Carter laughs. Then he grows somber. "I want to take an oath. For real."

He holds out his hand, elbow on the bed—the classic arm wrestling pose again. I shift to my side so I can do the same. I'm worried that he won't want our hands to actually touch, but I see nothing in his gaze except determination. Our palms make contact, neither one of us trying to overpower the other. Instead we're in perfect harmony.

The words come to me like I've always known them. "I swear to always be your friend. From now until the last breath escapes from my lips."

"And I swear to be your friend, even beyond that. Oh. And to protect you until my dying day."

He grips my hand tighter. I do the same. Then he effortlessly pins my arm to the mattress and laughs.

I don't care that I've only known him for two days. I love him. For better or worse, one way or the other, I love Carter King.

"It's Friday."

Carter doesn't sound enthusiastic. It's the end of our first week of school, which should be cause for celebration. Instead he's fidgeting his way through lunch. He keeps looking at his phone, or down the table to where Olivia is sitting. They talk sometimes during class. Usually in the morning before things get started, or occasionally he'll finish eating early and follow her back to the library. I'm not sure why he doesn't invite her to join us at either location, but I'm glad. I like having him all to myself.

"What do you want to do?" he asks.

"Tonight?" I gnaw on a carrot stick while thinking about it.

Carter shakes his head at this. "Why don't you eat chips like a normal person?"

"I'm trying to watch my figure."

"You're so skinny! You can eat whatever you want!"

I roll my eyes. I've heard this a hundred times before. "That's not how it works. I'm skinny *because* I watch what I eat. My dad looks like he's nine months pregnant. I'm not going to let that happen to me and then start dieting. Prevention is key. Think of this as my version of a dietary abortion."

Carter stares. Then he groans. "You're so messed up."

"Thanks! But if you want, just this once, we can order a greasy pizza tonight. We'll binge on that and Netflix. Sound good?"

"Yeah," Carter says, but he still doesn't seem excited. "Or, uh…" His fingers touch his phone subconsciously. "Bobby mentioned a party."

He's still friends with Bobby. They hung out together the other night. I know because Carter keeps saying—

"I talked to him."

Right on cue. Carter sounds like he's pleading with me as he continues.

"Bobby's sorry about the way he acted. You're both my friends. It would be cool if you got along. And this way you wouldn't have to be scared of him anymore."

"I'm not scared," I say. "It's like tigers. I'm not scared of those either, but I'm also not stupid enough to go anywhere near one."

"I just thought it would be fun." He looks at Olivia again. "Eh, maybe not. Did I tell you that they're together?"

My mouth drops open, pulped carrot nearly falling out before I hurry to close it and swallow. "Bobby and Olivia are *dating*?"

"Yeah," Carter says, sounding miserable.

I look over at her, searching for signs of a recent head trauma. My interactions with her have been limited, but she never seemed stupid.

"Bobby Tucker," I say in disbelief. "Olivia is willingly dating him. No way! Blackmail must be involved. Or maybe he took her family hostage."

"I keep telling you, he's not always an asshole. I've seen Bobby crank up the charm with girls. He's got some serious moves."

"Wow." I can't imagine anyone wanting to touch Bobby without him forking over a wheelbarrow full of cash. I guess he's not the worst-looking guy. He might even be considered handsome if he wasn't such a jerk. "It won't last."

Carter perks up at this. "No?"

I shake my head. "She's too smart. She'll see through him eventually. Even if he does have a good side, it's not enough to keep a girl like her."

Carter takes another bite of his cafeteria burger, this time with more enthusiasm, and I have to admit it looks better than what I brought from home. I want him to be happy. Pizza and TV won't cut it, but I really don't want to go to that party. I need to offer him something better.

"Do you like beer?" I ask.

"Uh, yeah! My uncle brought us kegs of German beer a couple years ago. He's in the air force and was stationed there. He kept telling my parents that, in Germany, I was old enough to drink legally. They didn't buy it. At first. Eventually they were drunk enough to agree, and I got plastered. First time, but not the last. Why? Do you have a fake ID?"

"Better," I say.

Reed is going to kill me. I'll be a chalk outline on the sidewalk by sundown, but I don't care. I want to make Carter happy.

The bar where my brother works is a dump. I'd call it a dive, but those are trendy right now, and often intentional. They're also usually surrounded by other thriving businesses. The place where Reed bartends is in a residential neighborhood, on the bottom floor of an apartment building. It has enough regulars to stay in business, but I'm guessing most of them are still at work when our school day ends. At least I hope so. I'm running on what Reed has told me. We're also literally running in spurts, because the earlier we get there, the more likely my plan is to work.

"Where are we going?" Carter asks when we are forced to stop at a busy intersection. He uses an arm to wipe away the sweat on his forehead. "How is this fun?"

"You'll see," I say. The pedestrian light turns white and we're off again.

Please don't let there be a bouncer! That's the one detail I can't remember. I keep picturing a roped-off area on the street and a guy with arms the size of pudgy children. I'm relieved when, glancing down at the GPS on my phone and the empty sidewalk ahead, I see nothing but a street-corner business with neon signs behind dirty windows.

"Get your beer face on!" I declare. I'm not sure what that means. It just feels right. Carter is too distracted to notice, his expression puzzled as I press my back against the door and start to push it open.

"They'll kick us out," he whispers.

"Will they?"

I honestly don't know the answer to that question. Our chances get a lot better when I see all the stools are empty. There's only one person there, standing behind the bar and looking increasingly panicked.

"Drew?" Reed says. I hate it when he calls me that. I haven't gone by that name since I was a little boy. "What's going on? Why didn't you call? Are Mom and Dad—"

"Everything's fine!" I say.

Reed notices Carter and gets suspicious. "You guys can't be in here."

"We're thirsty!" I say. "It's super-hot outside and we're dehydrated. It's your civic duty to help us before we croak."

He grits his teeth and starts to shake his head.

"Please," I whine. I try to show it all with my face, how there's a guy I want to impress, even if he's not gay. I'm new in school, I finally have a friend in Chicago, and this is my one chance to win him over.

Reed jerks his head toward the very end of the bar. "Get in the corner where it's dark. If you see a police officer—no, *anyone* who looks even remotely responsible—you hightail it out the back. Understand?"

"Yes!" I exchange a victorious grin with Carter, who is definitely into this. He's looking around the place like it's a wonderland. I do the same on the way to our seats. This is my first time in a bar too.

"What can I get you?" Reed asks once we both hop up on a stool. He's regained some of his sense of humor.

"Two beers," I say.

"Nope! We've got water, cola, orange juice…"

"Aw, come on!" I give him my best baby-brother eyes. "Just this once."

Reed glances over at Carter again. I hope he's imagining a pretty girl there instead. I almost ask him to, knowing it's the perfect translation. Reed checks the door again, then turns to consult a clock on the wall.

"I can do a rum and Coke," he says. "That way if someone walks in, I'm just babysitting you until our parents get here. You got lost because everything is new and confusing, and like you said, you were getting dehydrated." He looks at Carter, no doubt seeing a great big hole in his story.

"I'm new to the area too," Carter says quickly. "I'm from Phoenix."

"He really is!" I say. "Show him your old school ID."

"Don't bother," Reed grumbles. "If I get fired over this, you're both supporting me financially for the rest of your lives."

"I mow lawns," Carter says helpfully.

"Great." Reed sighs and walks toward some bottles on the wall.

"Make it a double!" I call after him. I think that's like ordering a large Coke instead of a small one.

While we're waiting for our drinks to arrive, Carter and I slump over the bar and pretend to be exhausted from our jobs. We take turns trying to out-complain each other ("The only thing that hurts more than my bones is writing my ex-wife another alimony check.") and when the rum and Cokes are set on the bar, we take a million selfies with them, turning to capture as much of the background as possible.

"Post those tomorrow, not today," Reed says, "and don't you dare tag the location."

He leaves us alone after that. Or he's standing at the other end of the bar to watch for anyone coming inside. Carter and I clink glasses. Then we drink. Reed didn't hold back on the rum. He poured them strong, which makes him a good brother because if we don't get a buzz from this little stunt, it will be lame.

"This is cool," Carter says, his head bobbing as he surveys the bar.

"Enjoy it while it lasts," I say. "I don't think he'll let us do this again."

"Your brother is awesome."

"He is. Do you get along with your sisters?"

I'm intentionally inching us closer to the subject of his family because they're still a big mystery to me. I want to know about that argument I overheard before we officially met. To me it sounded like the lamentations of a gay man, but if Carter was closeted, surely he would have come out to me already. Right? I need more information, but every day that we've hung out after school has been at my place. I don't feel right inviting myself over, and he hasn't offered. Coincidence, or does he not want me to meet his family?

"They're okay," Carter says. "When we were younger, my sisters were closer to each other. Girls versus boys. That sort of thing. When we got older, Vicky and I were going to the same school, so we connected more. Back in Arizona, anyway."

"And now?"

He shrugs. "We each do our own thing."

"What made that change?"

Carter toys with the weird skinny straw that came with our drinks. He's staring down at it, and for the moment he looks like a patron who has been coming here for years. He doesn't answer my question.

"What about your parents?" I ask, wanting to get him talking again.

"They're cool," he says, "aside from worrying too much. I guess that's their job, but I wish they would have a little faith."

He takes a swig. I copy him and wish I knew how to make him trust me completely. I know he has secrets. He's said too many weird things and had too many odd reactions to not be hiding something. I don't think he's been abused, physically or emotionally. He seems too happy most of the time. He can't even inhale so it's probably not a drug problem, and he's not drinking like his life depends on it, although I wouldn't mind getting him drunk just to see if that helps the truth slip out.

I could ask him about the argument directly, and I might, but not yet. Our friendship is still new, and he's had to put up with a lot, considering that I don't get along with his other friends and told him off while coming out. What a mess! I don't want to admit that I was snooping around his backyard before we met, and then ask about something potentially embarrassing. He might decide I'm more trouble than I'm worth. Instead I go back to acting goofy with him until our drinks are drained. I'm definitely feeling buzzed.

"Another round, my good man!" I say, holding up my empty glass.

My brother looks at the entrance again, as if expecting a SWAT team to bust down the door. Then he marches over.

"You guys are done here," he says. When I open my mouth to protest he adds, "There's a bottle of vodka in my nightstand. You're welcome to it. Just don't let Mom and Dad find out."

"In your nightstand?" I tease. "Do we need to stage an intervention?"

"I have a kid brother I've been hiding it from," Reed shoots back. "Go easy. Don't leave the house once you've been drinking. Have a sleepover or something."

I look over at Carter, who nods like this won't be a problem.

"Now get going before I throw you out," Reed says.

We stand up. Carter fishes a ten dollar bill out of his wallet and slides it across the bar surface. A tip, I guess. I think it's cute. Then we finally leave. I let Carter go ahead of me, so I can turn to Reed and say, "Thank you."

He smiles in return, like he totally gets it. Best brother ever.

Chapter Six

My parents usually work late, but my mom takes off early on Fridays. She's home when we get there. I always have gum on me. We're chewing like mad so she doesn't smell the alcohol on our breath. She's thrilled to see that I have a friend. My mom is beaming at Carter so intensely that I'm scared she'll start pinching his cheeks. It's not like I've never brought friends home before. Then again, I had a very active social life in New Mexico, which probably made the long summer without friends worry her. She gives us the green light for Carter to stay the night and we're free to go to my room. We hang out in the adjoining family area instead, since we have the entire basement to ourselves. Carter texts his parents for permission to stay, and we're about to raid my brother's room when my mom shows up, asking what sort of pizza we'd like delivered. Only after she returns upstairs do we sneak into Reed's bedroom.

Unlike me, he's messy. His room is stuffed full of things. To all appearances, it looks like he's lived there for years, not months. I go straight for the nightstand. Carter is more interested in browsing the clutter.

"Holy shit," he says. "Are these porn mags?"

He clamps a hand over his mouth, but I'm not worried. My parents are liberal about such things, and I doubt we can be overheard.

"My brother collects them," I explain as I shift through the nightstand contents. "Just the vintage kind. He won't buy anything that's not nineties or earlier."

"I have *got* to get an older brother!"

I laugh. "Those magazines are tame compared to what's on the internet. Most of them only have photos of girls." My fingers bump into something hard and cool. I grab it, my hand wrapping around the neck of a bottle. "Found it!"

I stand and turn around to find Carter enraptured by my brother's magazines. I can't help looking him over, just in case his jeans are tighter than usual. Is it always going to be this way? Me longing for what I can't have? It's not a deal breaker. I just hope my attraction to him doesn't remain this intense. I've had straight guy friends before, and I've certainly had naughty thoughts about a few of them, although this time feels different somehow.

"These *are* really tame," Carter says. "This one barely has any photos."

I tilt my head so I can see the cover. "*Penthouse Letters*! Those are hilarious. It's supposed to be filled with 'true' stories that people send in. Bring it with. We'll read some of them."

He looks a little apprehensive at the suggestion.

I roll my eyes. "I'm not trying to seduce you. Respect works both ways. You're cool with me being gay. I'm cool with you being straight. Neither one of us should try to change the other."

This only seems to increase his discomfort. I'm totally lost. We go into my room and hide the booze, having agreed that we should wait until after the pizza gets here. That way we're less likely to get caught by my mom. Still worried that he's uncomfortable, I add, "You can crash on the couch tonight, if that makes you feel better. Or I'll sleep there and you can have my bed."

"No!" Carter says. "I mean… I never do that with my other guy friends. Why should I with you, right?"

His smile is reassuring. I'm still confused, but I try to let it go. I'm his first gay friend. That's bound to take some getting used to.

We return to the family room and play video games until the pizza arrives. My father brings it down, ogling my new friend in a way he usually doesn't. Then it clicks. My mom is probably trying to figure out if this is a boyfriend and she wants my dad to get a read on him. Not that it would matter either way. Scott was allowed to sleep over, despite us being a couple. Liberal parents are awesome. Especially when they make themselves scarce.

"I thought he'd never leave," I say while my dad is still within earshot.

He flips me off as he walks down the hall. He and Reed have a lot in common. The same build, interests, and attitude. I'm a lot more like my mom in most regards.

"Think it's better to drink before we eat or after?" Carter whispers when we're truly alone.

"Both," I say.

We go into the bedroom and pass the bottle back and forth. It's like drinking gasoline. I hate it. I can tell that Carter does too, because his eyes are watering.

"I keep hoping it'll get easier," I say after another swig. "Like I'll get used to the burn."

"Same here." Carter is wearing a permanent grimace now. "Hey, if rum and Coke go together…"

"It can't be worse than this."

As it turns out, it's a big improvement. Pizza also helps chase away the aftertaste of rubbing alcohol. We're both buzzed at the end of the meal, and when we pour our next drinks, we go easy on the vodka. That helps keep the fumes down. I'd like my food to remain down too. We watch TV until that becomes boring. Then we go into my room and put on music. I notice the magazine on my bed, so I grab it and flop onto the mattress. Carter joins me on the bed. Our backs are against the wall, our shoes are off, and I have this urge to nudge his foot with mine. I resist. I also promise myself, while I'm still sober enough to think, that I won't make a move on him. Having a new boyfriend would've been awesome, but a new best friend is almost as cool. Maybe even better, since we won't get into the type of arguments that accompany romantic relationships.

"Are you going to read me a bedtime story?" Carter asks.

"Absolutely." I open the magazine to a random page. "Here's one from Belinda in Boca Raton, Florida. She says 'I was having an ornate four-poster bed frame delivered. The frame was imported from Italy and very heavy, but thankfully, free installation was part of the deal. Boy did my imagination run wild when I opened the door to discover two tall Haitians standing there. I invited the delivery men in, making sure to watch everything they did so I could check out their big biceps and tight buns.'" The guys, as it turns out, don't speak great English, so when the bed is finally set up, Belinda tries asking how much weight it can bear. When words fail, she lays on the bed and starts bouncing to try and show them, which they take as an invitation. She doesn't mind, and the rest is kind of hot—especially some of the descriptions. It's all contrived and clearly written by a man, but we laugh and snort our way through it anyway.

We're having too much fun to stop. I breeze through a bunch more letters until we get to one about a guy who works at a shoe store. A woman keeps trying on pair after pair of shoes until she's the last customer and the store closes. Then it really gets freaky. "'She shoves her dainty little toes into my nostrils, my ears, my mouth—'"

"Ew!" Carter says. "In that order?"

"I guess so." After scanning the rest of the letter, I shake my head. "It's all foot stuff. They don't even have sex! Or does that count? I mean, they're both turned on by it. Either way, I'm buying my shoes online from now on."

Carter guffaws. "Same here."

"Your turn," I say, passing him the magazine. "The next one is called Sexy Circus. I'm hoping for clowns. Or a bearded woman. Or both!"

"Oh." Carter squints at the text. "I don't think I can read right now. I'm way too drunk."

"So am I! You heard how many mistakes I made. Don't be shy."

"Which one is it?"

"Sexy Circus. Right here." I tap the correct column of text. "Bonus points if you read it like a ringmaster making an announcement."

"Dear Penthouse Letters," Carter says. They all begin that way. Then he looks away from the page. "Hey, can I get another drink?"

"When you're already too drunk to read? First I get my erotic circus fix. Then I'll pour you another."

He lets the magazine flop onto his lap. "To be honest, I'm kind of sick of this."

"Getting too turned on? Do you have a thing for feet? Because if you're really nice to me, I'll shove my toes in your nose. But first you've gotta read me a letter. Just one. Then we'll stop."

"I have to pee."

Carter gets up and leaves the room. He doesn't look back, but on the way out the door, I swear his face is bright red. Once again, I feel like I'm missing the obvious. He wasn't getting turned on by the letters, was he? Is he in the bathroom jacking off, right now? I'd be surprised. After the first letter was hotter than expected, I had made sure to choose only those with ridiculous titles. I even scanned ahead to make sure we weren't getting into uncomfortable territory, like one involving a threesome where the two guys got a little hands-on with each other. Still, I had been awfully insistent. We're drinking while on my bed, so yeah, maybe I'm coming across as creepy.

"I know how to keep my hands to myself," I say the second he's back in the room. "I'm not trying to get you to jack off with me or anything like that. The letters are funny. I thought you'd think so too. And hey, you're the one who asked me to read them to you."

I'm getting defensive. It's probably the booze, but it's hard not to feel insulted. Being gay doesn't mean I'm some man-crazed nympho with no self-control.

"You're fine," Carter says, voice strained.

"Then why are you acting so weird? Just read the damn letter!"

"I can't!"

The words stun me. Then I almost laugh, because I know he can read. We've talked enough about books for me to be certain. He's not faking it by watching movies. He knows too many details. We've even had a lengthy discussion about scenes that were better in the Harry Potter novels versus the movies. And at school...

What are we doing again?

It's a phrase I've often heard Carter utter when we sit down to tackle our work. We've mostly been focusing on math, but we've also discussed *The Cuckoo's Calling* during the week. I know a TV show exists, but we've kept pace with each other chapter by chapter. Still, in retrospect, I do spend a lot of time explaining assignments to him.

"What do you mean?" I ask.

Carter goes to the bottle of vodka and takes a direct swig. Deliciously dramatic, but the gasp followed by a "blegh!" undercuts this severely. He's still not talking.

"Best friends don't keep secrets from each other," I say. "We took an oath, remember? If it helps, I think I've got it narrowed down to two possibilities."

He nods, giving me permission to proceed.

"I either make you uncomfortable because of my sexuality—"

"You don't! I'm totally cool with you being gay. Why else would I—"

"—*or*," I interrupt, refusing to be sidetracked. "You can't read."

Carter glowers at me. I'm worried he's going to tell me to shove the oath and our friendship up my ass, but then he sits on the mattress with his back to me. "I *can* read," he grumbles.

"Then what is it?"

"I'm dyslexic."

"Okay." I try to remember what I know of that disease. Or is it a condition? A disorder? "So you swap letters around sometimes."

Carter's laugh is hollow. "I wish. It's more like… Have you ever tried to read while walking? You know how it all bounces around and you can't keep your place? Imagine that, except you're running instead."

"Oh. You must do okay though. You read a lot of books."

Carter turns to glare at me. I'm not sure where his anger is directed, but he grabs the magazine, which is still open to the same page. "Dear Penthouse Letters," he says smoothly. He glances up long enough to say, "I've learned to fake it wherever I can." Then he resumes reading. "I even tog— *thought* when the circle make to own, that I would half my own big aben… abent?" He looks back at me again. "How am I doing so far? If you're getting turned on, I swear I'm not trying to seduce you."

I don't laugh. Instead I scoot across the mattress until I'm sitting next to him. Then I gently take away the magazine because I can already imagine Reed's expression if I have to explain that part of his collection was ripped to shreds in a drunken rage. I look down at the first sentence of the letter. *I never thought, when the circus came to town, that I would have my own big top adventure.* Okay, so he was pretty off.

"I'm not the best at reading aloud either," I say diplomatically.

Carter rolls his eyes. "It's nearly that bad when I read silently, which I never do. Not if I can help it. Being dyslexic doesn't mean I'm stupid. Albert freaking Einstein was dyslexic, but I shot myself in the foot a long time ago, because I managed to hide this until high school. If I had fessed up sooner, they probably could have taught me to work around most of it by now. Instead I made it to the middle of ninth grade."

I'm unable to contain my surprise. Maybe if I was sober, I would have done better. I know he sees it on my face, so I ask the most obvious question. "How? Does someone read to you or—"

"Audiobooks. If you're wondering if I'm really into all those stories we talk about, I am. I love books. I always have, even when I was little. I just need someone to read them to me."

"That makes sense, but school work—"

"Voice recognition. That's how I write most of my papers. I

just talk into my phone or laptop and it writes it all down for me. Spellcheck catches most of the mistakes. I guess. I almost never get an A, but I do all right. If I need to read something, there's an app for that too. Ever heard of OCR?"

I shake my head.

"Optical character recognition. I can take a photo of almost anything, have it convert to text, and then make my phone read it to me."

"And you've managed to pass every grade so far by doing this."

Carter shrugs. "I don't have as much trouble with numbers. Dyslexia is different for everyone. I got lucky when it came to math. The rest has been hard. I always fail tests since I can't use my phone for those. Teachers assume it's nerves tripping me up. A few thought I was cheating somehow, like somebody was doing my homework for me, but it's always in my handwriting. If I get a worksheet with blanks to be filled in, I can't print out my answers like I would an essay, so I copy it all down by hand after I get it figured out on the computer. I've also done a ton of extra-credit assignments to scrape by with a passing grade. That's saved my ass more times than I can count."

I stare at him, still baffled, but for another reason. "You're a genius!"

Carter narrows his eyes. "Did you not hear what I just said?"

"That you were clever enough to make it to high school despite having a huge disadvantage? One that you managed to keep hidden? Yeah, I heard all of that." I'm laughing now, because I really do find it amazing. "That's a huge accomplishment. Seriously. Give yourself credit!"

Carter looks puzzled before he grins a little. "When you put it like that…"

"For real. It's nothing to be ashamed of. You were born this way, right?" That's when it clicks. The argument I overheard between him and his parents must have been about this. *As soon as they find out, everyone treats you differently.* He would have been concerned about being labeled before starting at a new school. I'd had similar fears, but coming out had braced me for such things.

"You've just got to own it," I say. "Everything you achieve is that much more impressive because of this. Take pride! You should be bragging to people about this, not hiding it!"

Carter laughs and shakes his head. "Only you could turn this into a positive."

"For real! It's not like this is going to trip you up much. If you can make it through high school, you're ready for the real world."

His smile falters. "I'm not getting into any colleges. I flunked my SATs."

"Oh. Lots of people don't go. Reed didn't." I wish I could say I wasn't either, just to make him feel better. "College isn't for everyone. You might not need it, depending on what you want to do."

"I want to be an author." Carter clenches his jaw, his eyes searching mine. "This is the part where you're supposed to laugh."

"Why? You can do the voice recognition thing, can't you? I'm sure other authors write by… what's it called? Dictation."

He's already shaking his head. "A high school essay is one thing. To be a writer, you need to have style. I have tons of ideas, but they all come out flat."

"Then you just need a good editor."

His eyes continue to bore into mine, but now the feeling is different. There isn't as much anger behind them. "Are you always like this?"

"It's annoying, isn't it?"

"Yeah." He shoves me playfully. "Let's have another drink."

"I told you, only after you read this letter." He starts to get upset, until I nod at his phone. "Show me how you do it. I'm curious."

"For real?"

"Yeah!"

Before long, we're listening to a robotic voice describe an orgy involving a lion tamer, a couple of trapeze artists, and the strong man. It's even better this way. Best of all, there's no more tension between us. We're too busy laughing and drinking for the real world to bring us down.

Carter is the first to fall asleep. I lay there watching him while replaying every conversation we've had that my intoxicated mind can recall. Most of it makes sense now. But certain things still don't add up. *It sucks how things change. You don't get a choice. Life just takes people from you.* What the hell does that mean? And didn't Carter say he stopped talking to everyone before he moved? Why? Because of his dyslexia? Did all of his friends make fun of him? Disown him?

Carter rolls over in his sleep, his eyes opening briefly to meet mine, and I swear they smile. He's drunk too, or maybe he's in the middle of a dream and doesn't actually see me. All I know for sure is that my heart skips a beat. If I can fall in love with him so quickly, plenty of others must have too. I bet most people, after learning about his dyslexia, just want to help him. I can't imagine anyone turning their back on him. Even I don't. When I finally close my eyes and succumb to sleep, I'm still facing Carter.

"There's nothing wrong with his brain."

A requirement of the Open Classroom Project is accepting one-on-one tutoring. This happens daily, although some of my sessions are so short that they basically consist of Gerald asking if I'm doing all right, and me reassuring him that I'm fine. Carter's sessions with him tend to take longer. Much longer. Now I know why, although I still have many questions.

"Isn't that the cause of dyslexia?" I ask. "Carter's brain is somehow…" I glance over to be sure he's still at our table and that we can't be overheard. "Malformed?" I finish at last.

Gerald's smile is patient. "I'm sure his brain is very shapely. It simply utilizes a different set of neural pathways. Think of it like speaking a different language, or a computer using a different operating system. If you suddenly found yourself in Greece, you too would struggle with some of the most basic tasks. Or if you prefer Windows and have to use iOS for the first time—"

"But those things can be learned," I say. "Carter already knows how to read. He just can't… See right?" I shake my head. "I don't get it."

Gerald sighs. "The truth is, much about dyslexia remains a mystery. What we *do* know is that plenty of people have learned to work around their difficulties and are still able to thrive."

"I want to help him," I say. "If there's something I can do when we're working on assignments together, I will. Although it would be even better if he doesn't need to rely on me or anyone else."

"We all need to rely on each other eventually," Gerald says, "but I share your sentiment. I'll need to discuss it with Carter first, but if he's open to the idea, you can sit in on some of our sessions and get a feel for the skills that I'm trying to teach him."

"Yes! Sign me up!"

"I'll let you know." Gerald clears his throat and pushes his glasses higher up on his nose. "Speaking of which, I'd like to help you increase your skillset too."

"What do you mean?"

"The reason you joined the Open Classroom Project."

"Because I was overwhelmed? I'm not anymore. I love this program."

"I'm glad to hear that," Gerald says. "I was referring more to your altercation with Mr. Tucker. Have you heard of anger management?"

"Yeah, but *he* was the one who pulled my chair out from under *me*!"

"True, but you were the one who became angry."

"Of course I did. He physically hurt me! What am I supposed to do, laugh it off? Maybe I shouldn't have shoved the books off his desk, but he's a jerk. He had it coming!"

Gerald raises his eyebrows. That's it. He doesn't say a damn thing in reply. That's when I realize that he's made his point.

"I get emotional sometimes," I say, trying my best to sound calm. "And you have to admit that there were mitigating circumstances."

"I agree," Gerald says, "which is why, as you may have noticed, you weren't punished."

I hadn't really thought about it. If anything, getting to join this program felt more like a reward.

"Was he?" I ask.

Gerald cocks his head. "Do you remember how he reacted after you hit the floor? When you stood up and told me what had happened."

"He lied and said—"

"Yes, but *how*. What was his demeanor?"

Just thinking about it makes me grit my teeth. "He stayed calm."

"Which is a tremendous advantage. I have bad news for you. People like him exist outside of high school. In your adult life, you'll find yourself in a number of unpleasant situations where you might have justified cause to be angry. The problem is, the other person usually feels justified too. When both parties react with anger, matters can escalate until it leads to injury or even the loss of life. The next time you yell at someone, attack them, or touch their property, you might find yourself on the receiving end of violence. I'm sure you're aware of the gun problem in this city."

I swallow. "Yeah."

"Learning to stay calm will allow you to think on your feet. It's a crazy world out there, Andrew. As you've already experienced, you might not be doing anything wrong when you're unfairly targeted. That's why I'd like to go over some basic skills with you in a future session. Consider the idea and let me know. Okay?"

I nod, but I don't need to think about it. Gerald is right. When it comes to people like Bobby Tucker, I need any advantage I can get.

Chapter Seven

"There's another party this weekend," Carter says.

We're at school, in the library, and I'm reading through the instructions for our next assignment. The timing is good, since I can pretend my scowl is one of concentration. It's been two weeks since we got drunk together. I knew it was just a matter of time before this issue came up again. I just didn't think it would be so soon.

"Where?" I ask.

"Bobby's place."

"Say no more!"

Carter sounds excited when he replies. "You'll go?"

"No, I mean that literally. Say no more. I don't need the details, because there's no way in hell I'm going."

Carter sighs, and I give up pretending that I'm concentrating.

"Everyone deserves a second chance," he says. "Besides, I'm going, and I want you there too."

"Why?"

"Because you're my best friend."

Bastard! I don't know if he does it on purpose, but nothing melts my icy heart faster than him speaking those words. In truth, I don't want to be apart from him either, especially on the weekend. I can accept that Carter has friends I don't like, but it does suck being bored at home when we could be having fun together. I'll be on my own again after school today while he's hanging out with the others. Maybe it's time to give Carter's friends a second chance. Straight into the viper's pit though? I don't like the idea of being around Bobby in public. His home sounds even worse.

Carter is studying me, hope reflected in those syrupy brown eyes that I find so hard to resist.

"I need you to start wearing sunglasses," I tell him.

"Huh?"

"Never mind. Think I can tag along tonight?" If I'm going to do this, I want to get a feel for the situation, preferably somewhere safe.

Carter looks over at Gerald, who is tutoring another student.

Once certain he can get away with it, Carter pulls out his phone and types a text. He shows it to me before hitting send.

Andrew wants to get petsa to. Cool?

"Pizza," I say, scribbling the word in the margins of my text book. "Two z's. Don't ask me why. Two o's on the second 'to.'"

"I knew that."

I believe him. Carter's brain tends to write things the way they sound. If anything, this reflects poorly on the English language more than on him. I refrain from pointing out that the vowels in "pizzazz" sound completely different from those in "pizza", despite the similar spelling, and that's just one example of many. It's a miracle that anyone can master written English.

It doesn't take long for the response to come. Carter's smile tells me what the answer is, even before he relays it. I'm having pizza with Bobby tonight.

After school, Carter and I return to our homes. I still haven't been to his place. I'm not sure why. I figure he'll invite me when he's ready. We meet again an hour later, and I notice that Carter has freshened up. He's restyled his hair and, judging from his minty-fresh breath, brushed his teeth. We walk toward the mall again, but this time we don't go as far.

"Ever been to Blaze?" he asks.

I shake my head.

"I'm not sure we had them back home," he continues. We might come from two different states, but they border each other, and so we talk about them as if they're the same place. "It's like Subway, except instead of a sandwich, they make the pizza right in front of you. You get to choose the toppings and everything."

That sounds cool, although I'm nervous as hell when we enter. I scan the place and see, toward the very back, Bobby's entire crew. Even the girls. The only person I don't spot is his right-hand man. Whatever his name is.

"I need you to give me a refresher on their names," I say on the way to the table. Carter rattles off a few, and I instantly forget them again. Maybe I have a learning disability of my own. I focus on what he's saying and try to commit a few to memory.

"The big guy is Mick. The skinny one is Felipe. And you already know Olivia." Carter sounds disheartened when reaching her name. "Oh, and Jackson."

He gestures behind us, which is almost enough to make me jump, but when I look back, Bobby's favorite henchman is standing behind the counter. I guess he works here.

"Carter!" Bobby says, having noticed us. "Andrew! The happy couple!"

I still hate him. Especially for voicing my deepest desire.

"Hey!" Carter says. Then he tilts his head in my direction. "You guys remember Andrew?"

"Hi!" I say, managing to sound upbeat. I'm going to try my damnedest. For Carter. "How's it going?"

"That man—" Bobby says, pointing at me. "There's no one in this world I'm more jealous of. He stole Carter away from us!"

"I might be willing to share," I say, nodding at the two pizzas on the table. "If you are."

"No need," Bobby says. "Jackson gets an employee discount. It's free. You should order one of your own."

"Really?" Free food sounds good to me. I need to find a job. My parents don't give me an allowance, with the exception of a little cash to use at the school cafeteria. The only food I normally eat is what I get at home or from the school district.

"Really," Bobby replies. "Before you do that, come outside and smoke with me."

"I don't smoke," I say. Recognizing how square this sounds, I add, "Not cigarettes, anyway."

"I'm saving the good stuff for the party," Bobby says. He's all smiles. I see what Carter means. He can be charming when he wants, which helps explain why Olivia is still sitting at his side. "Come keep me company anyway."

Bobby wants to talk. This could be good or bad. I want to reassure Carter that I'll be all right, but he's already sitting, his attention on Olivia. Some bodyguard. But I'm not too worried. Bobby is crazy, but even he wouldn't knife me to death just outside a pizza place. Right?

As soon as we're standing on the sidewalk out front, I feel better because we're facing a busy road. The kind full of witnesses.

"He's not gay," Bobby mutters, the artificial cheer gone from his voice as he lights a cigarette. "Is he?"

"Carter? No. He's not."

Bobby grunts. "Neither am I. Or any of my friends."

"I'm not surprised." I press my back against the brick exterior. "I'm used to being the only one. It sucks."

He looks me over, his eyes slightly narrowed. "I bet it does. You seem all right, though. You're not a pussy."

I decide to take this as a compliment. "Thanks."

"Carter sure likes you. And I like him. So I guess any friend of mine… Wait. What's the stupid saying?"

"I get what you mean."

"Good." Bobby pulls long and hard on his cigarette. Probably just to show me he can. He sizes me up again, and when he exhales, I expect it to be in my face. Instead he blows it off to the side. "You keep your hands off me, and I'll keep my fists away from you. Make sense?"

"Yup."

"Excellent. Think you can get some beer for the party?"

Did he know about the trip to the bar? If he ever asks to go there, I'll refuse. No matter what it costs me. I would never do that to Reed. I will, however, beg my brother to buy a couple of twelve-packs. "I'll see what I can do."

"Nice. Do that, and we're good."

I'm not surprised by this request. I didn't expect unconditional love, friendship, or anything else remotely nice from Bobby.

"You screw around with a lot of guys?"

I also didn't expect a question like that. "No," I say. I'm tempted to keep my answers short, but maybe this is a chance to dispel a few myths. "Not all gay people are promiscuous. I'm more the relationship type."

Bobby laughs like I'm being funny. So much for spreading enlightenment. "It'll be interesting to have you around," he says. "Do me a favor. Stay close to Carter. You're good for him."

"Okay," I say, relieved that I don't pronounce this with the giant question mark that fills my mind, because I have no idea what he means. Some mysteries aren't worth solving. Bobby tosses the cigarette to the pavement and crushes it beneath his heel. Then we go back inside.

"Get yourself a pizza," he says on the way back to the table.

"Thanks," I say, and I hate it because I sound like one of his lackeys. I don't owe him anything, gratitude especially.

Now it's time for round two. I approach the counter. Jackson crosses his arms over his chest, like he's thrilled to see me.

"Hey," he says, his voice as deep as it is gruff. "What do you want?"

"Is that the standard greeting here?" I reply.

He loosens up enough to unfold his arms. "Only on bad days."

"Is this one of them?"

He shrugs.

I look above him at the menu, trying to figure out how it works. I understand the basic premise, but there are different crusts, sauces, cheeses...

"The spicy sauce is the best," he says helpfully. Or maybe so I'll go away sooner.

"What about the dough?"

"Don't do the gluten free. Or the vegan cheese. They both suck."

"Okay. Ummm..." I focus on the toppings as he gets the basic dough and sauce ready. Then I start rattling them off, one by one, and try to ignore how he's giving me the eye. I'm sure he's judging each selection and thinking, "Of course the gay guy wants broccoli." I should have just chosen the meat-heavy pizza. I'm sure that's what most guys get.

Once all of that is done, we move to the register. "It's really free?" I ask. "Bobby said you get an employee discount."

"Yeah," he says. "I'll call your name when it's ready."

"Thanks."

I'm on my way to the table when I realize I forgot my drink. I turn around and see Jackson closing the register. He notices me and quickly shoves his wallet in his back pocket. My first thought is that he's stealing money. When his expression shifts to embarrassment, I realize that he just paid for the pizza himself. And I feel terrible.

"I don't have any money on me—" I start to say.

"It's free," he says, handing me my cup. "Don't worry about it."

While I'm standing at the soda fountain, I wonder if this is how it works with Bobby. Maybe we're all expected to bring something to the table. Communes work that way too. So do cults. How good or bad this is usually depends on the leader, and I don't have much faith in ours. Yuck. As I put a plastic lid on my cup, I promise myself to never think of Bobby in those terms again.

— — —

I'm unsure what to expect when arriving at Bobby's place on Saturday. Chicago is an odd city. Walk a few blocks in one direction, and you could be in a bad neighborhood. A few blocks from there, you might find yourself surrounded by million-dollar homes. Chicago is a patchwork of income margins and cultures, and while these neighborhoods are all united under the same quilt, the city itself still feels tragically segregated.

What I imagined is easy: It's unfair, and I chastise myself for it, but I expected Bobby to come from one of the poorer areas. I figured that anyone who did such a bad job of raising their kid would also be bad at managing their own life, including finances. Says the guy who had to beg his brother not only to go into a store and pick up beer but to pay for it too. The truth is, I've had friends whose parents run a good home despite struggling financially. And I've known rich kids who were lazy and spoiled. I've seen the reverse too. I know I shouldn't go into new situations with any sort of preconceived notions. It's fairer to wait and judge accordingly.

Like tonight. As we pull up to Bobby's house, I see that he too lives surrounded by middle class vagueness. Anything could be behind the doors of this neighborhood: a rundown home that was paid off back when real estate was cheap, a glistening modern interior that was recently renovated, or anything in between.

"You all right?" Reed asks. Probably because I'm still sitting in the car and staring at Bobby's house. "Want me to walk you to the door and tell his parents what to do if you wet the bed?"

"Yes," I say.

Reed puts the car in park and gets out, but only so he can pop the trunk and help me unload the beer. "This is the last time," he says. Again. This song has been on repeat all day. "If one of your friends gets drunk and decides to go for a drive. It'll be bad enough if *they* die." He notices children playing down the street and takes inspiration. "What if they run over some poor kid?"

I can tell he's about to change his mind and close the trunk with the beer still inside, so I hurriedly say, "Last time, I promise. Really. I'll make sure no one drives."

Reed shakes his head, but at least he resumes unloading. "I always wanted to be the cool older brother. Totally not worth it. From now on, I'm going to be the kind who rats you out anytime you do something wrong."

"When are you moving out?" I tease.

We carry two twenty-four packs to the door. Reed stands there, like he's waiting for me to knock so he can meet the parents… who are out of town.

"Can you still be the cool older brother until tomorrow?" I say.

"Nope." He raps on the door, musses my perfectly styled hair, and laughs all the way back to the car.

He's already driving down the street when the door opens. I'm still trying to fix my hair. Luckily it's only the scrawny guy who answered. Felipe, I think his name is. He barely seems to recognize me, but his eyes light up when he sees the beer on the porch.

"Wanna help get this inside?"

I don't need to ask twice. I ogle everything on the way to the kitchen. The house feels lived in. Everything is somewhat cluttered, but typical for a normal family life. I'm eager to scope out the refrigerator, hoping it will be covered with photos of Bobby when he was little and, presumably, less frightening. Maybe that'll make it easier to be around him.

We never get to the kitchen though. Felipe leads me instead down a set of carpeted stairs to a finished basement. Things here look more dated. Much of the large area is taken up by a bar, the padded surface about eight feet long before it curves and touches the wall. Behind this are mostly empty shelves. No alcohol bottles, just a few knickknacks and some dusty glasses.

"He came through!" Bobby says from the other side of the room. I notice a couch, a couple of chairs, and an older widescreen TV that's boxy instead of flat. Beyond this is an open door where I can see a messy bedroom. That's also the source of the pumping music. Stale cannabis smoke hangs in the air, but from the way people reach for the beer, not everyone has partaken or feels that weed is enough.

"Nicely done, Andrew," Bobby says, clapping me on the shoulder.

I manage not to recoil from his touch, focusing instead on doing a head count. Everyone is here except Carter, the one person I feel comfortable around. I make small talk and open a beer for myself, being sure to say whenever people ask how I managed to buy booze: "Called in a favor. I won't be able to again." I use exaggerated frustration, just to drive home the point.

The room is split into two groups at the moment, one clustered around the bar, the rest with Bobby on the couch and chairs. I remain close to the bar, where I have nothing in common with anyone, and silently curse each minute that passes without Carter showing up.

"Andrew! Hey!"

I turn away from a conversation I'm only pretending to follow and see a girl with blue hair.

"Hey!" I say back, my enthusiasm very real because at least Olivia and I are from the same world. I don't know much about her, but we're classmates. I also find it easier to talk to girls, for some reason.

"Thanks for the beer," she says, holding up two cans and shaking one, which is clearly empty.

"Slow down!" I say, but to show I'm not judging, I shake my own empty can, which I drank one nervous sip after the other.

"I'm still working on mine." Olivia glances toward the couch, where Bobby is slapping his knee and laughing at his own story. "He sent me for a refill."

"Wow," I say with a smirk. "You found yourself a true gentleman. Better hold on to him. They're rare these days!" I'm taking a risk, but she doesn't seem to find this offensive.

"I know, right? I was about to tell him to get it himself when I realized that, if one of us is going to leave, I'd rather it be me."

Talk about a loaded statement! I walk around the bar to the fridge and grab two more cans. She follows, which is good because now we have more privacy.

"So…" I say. "You and Bobby."

Olivia does the cutest eyeroll I've ever seen. It's not vapid, but more like she's aware of her situation and has decided to have a sense of humor about it. "He's a handful!"

"Ew."

"Not what I meant," she says. "I take it he's not your type?"

"God no!" I say. Then I look to where he's sitting, and I can see that Bobby is a decent looking guy. It's just… everything else. Still, I don't want to offend her. "I have weird taste. You guys make a hot couple though!"

She scrunches up her nose. Then she finishes off her can, so I hand her a fresh one. "I've always liked the bad boys," she says, toying with the tab instead of opening the beer. "I know what I'm getting into each time. I'm not new at this, but Bobby is… pushy."

"In a bad way?"

She raises her eyebrows, her expression wry. "There is no good version of pushy."

"Oh. I'd offer to beat him up, but he scares the living hell out of me."

"I can take care of myself," Olivia says. "I'm sure you can too. Don't be scared of Bobby. He puts on a big show."

I believe her. I think everything Bobby does is exactly what he wants his audience to see, but I could be wrong. This is the second likeable person who has told me that he's not so bad, but they've also failed to explain what's so great about him.

"Carter sure is a sweetheart," Olivia says.

My favorite subject! I crack open my beer, she does too, and we bump cans. "He's awesome," I say. "Living here sucked before I met him. Funny how much difference a single person can make."

"So you like Chicago now?"

"Yeah!"

"And you know about—"

"The winters?" I laugh. "Yeah. I think someone might have mentioned those to me."

Olivia smiles. "At least you'll be able to keep each other warm. That should help you get through the first one."

"Exactly!" Wait… what? I feel my phone vibrate and pull it out, the timing perfect because now I can keep my confused expression without needing to explain it. I'm pretty sure she thinks Carter and I are dating. That's who the text is from, as it turns out.

I'm outside. Nobodies answering.

Voice recognition? Or did he write this on his own? I've become obsessed with Carter's typos. I feel like, if I truly knew him, I should be able to tell which are his and which come from the software. "Speak of the devil," I say, holding up my phone.

Olivia smiles and says, "Don't keep your prince waiting. They're even rarer than gentlemen."

Oh my god. I don't let myself laugh until I'm safely upstairs. I manage to hold it in until the door is open. Then I see Carter, and it all comes out in snorts and chortles.

"What?" he says, looking even more confused when I step outside with him.

"Olivia," I say, trying to catch my breath. "She thinks we're dating."

"What?" Carter's face falls. "That blows!"

My expression becomes a lot more serious too. "Thanks a lot!"

"You know what I mean." He turns around and looks skyward. "Ugh! It doesn't matter anyway. She's still with Bobby. Right?"

"Right."

I don't tell him that she seems unhappy in that relationship. I know I should, but a selfish little goblin in my heart doesn't want to give him away so easily. Besides, Olivia prefers the bad boys. She said so herself. Carter is sweet. She probably wouldn't be interested even if she was single. I don't want Carter to feel sad though.

"Girls *love* gay guys," I tell him. "They feel like they can let down their defenses around us. That works both ways, which means you're probably getting closer to her than you would have otherwise."

"Yeah?" Carter says, looking more optimistic.

"Yeah. And if Olivia and Bobby ever break up… Who knows? She'll need a shoulder to cry on."

Carter squints at me while nodding slowly. "You're a stone-cold player, aren't you?"

"A born heartbreaker," I say cockily.

Carter makes a face. "Rewind a second. I'm not a girl. Are you saying you don't feel comfortable around me?"

"I didn't at first, but it's different now that you're my boyfriend." It feels good to say, even if it's not true. When his concerned expression doesn't fade, I roll my eyes. "Of course I feel comfortable around you. Why, you're practically one of the girls!"

Carter shakes his head in exasperation. I promise him a beer for his troubles and lead the way inside. I enjoy myself a lot more from then on. His presence makes it fun. The beer helps too. Everyone gets drunker or higher, and the party gets louder. Carter and I talk to Olivia, and I'm tempted to slide my hand around his waist as a joke, but I don't. The topic of us dating doesn't come up again, thank goodness. When I get bored of watching him lust after her, I mingle because I'm feeling buzzed enough to socialize with anyone. Except Bobby. Even my inebriated instincts tell me to keep my distance from him.

"Hey!" I say when I spot someone tall, dark, and slightly less scary. "Jackson!"

"Hey, man," he says with an upward nod. "Thanks for the beer."

"No problem. I feel like I owe you one anyway. Speaking of which…" I pull out my wallet, which contains a ten and a five. I take out both bills and force these into Jackson's hand. "For the pizza."

"You don't have to—"

"I want to," I say, closing his fingers around the money. He yanks his hand away, but I'm intoxicated enough that I'm not offended. *The gay guy has gay germs. Ewwww!* Whatever. I'll put up with anything from him right now because the pizza incident has bothered me ever since it happened. Enough for me to ask my parents for lunch money, and then to bring a sandwich to school instead. "I know it cost more like twenty, but I'm broke. I need to find a job."

Jackson shoves the money in his pocket. Then he looks me over again. I'm getting tired of feeling like I'm in a sideshow.

"We're hiring," he says.

"Really?" My cooking skills are limited to a few basic dishes, but I can definitely handle rolling out dough, spreading sauce, and sprinkling toppings.

"Yeah," Jackson says. "We've had a bunch of people apply already, but I can get you the job if you're interested. The manager has a thing for me."

I snort. "Is that why your girlfriend broke up with you? She caught you flirting with the boss?"

Jackson smiles. He's got teeth and everything! Obvious, I know. I've just never seen him do that before. "Almost. Harper walked into Blaze while I was sitting down with a fine-ass customer."

"Oooh," I say, wincing in sympathy. "That can't be good."

Jackson shrugs. "I had it coming. So you want it?"

"The job?" I shrug. "Sure!"

"You gotta come in and fill out an application. I'm on the grind tomorrow afternoon."

"It's a date!" The word choice is intentional, just to get back at him for pulling away from me.

Jackson takes it well. He barely recoils at all. "How'd you really get this beer?" he asks.

"Older brother," I admit. "Don't get excited. He's already cut me off."

Jackson laughs. "I used to hit up my cousin. She cut me off last year."

"What's up with that?" I ask. "Are we going to be as boring as them when we get older?"

"Probably."

I make more small talk after that. Enough to not be rude, when what I really want to do is check on Carter again. I'm glad Jackson and I have a chance to interact anyway. I don't know if he and I will ever be close, but I should be able to work with him. Everyone else I've spoken to at the party or at Blaze seems okay too. If only they didn't all have Bobby in common. I try to imagine how ideal life would be if he wasn't around, but that's not how the world works. *In everyone and everything, good and bad are inseparable.* My mom always tells me this, so with it in mind, I grab another beer and bring it to the host, all in the name of maintaining diplomatic relations.

"That was awesome," Carter says.

He's behind me as we climb the basement stairs. We're still at Bobby's house and have already said goodbye. Now all that's left is to stumble home, and hopefully, get inside without my parents scrutinizing us. We're just about to leave when something catches my eye.

"Whoa," I whisper. "Check it out!"

I lead the way through the living room to a framed photo on the wall. It reveals a happy family of three. On the right is a woman with black hair that might have been floppy if it wasn't so long. Next to her is a balding man with green eyes, although without the psychopath glint. Between them is a boy of six or seven years old. Bobby is missing teeth in the photo, but he still looks like trouble. One of his cheeks is kind of dirty, and he looks way too amused, like he just kicked the photographer in the shin before getting into position.

"Only child," I say. "Can't blame his parents for not wanting more."

"What are you doing?"

We spin around like thieves caught red-handed. Bobby—the current and much more intimidating version—is standing not far away. He looks past us at the photo and snorts, not seeming too concerned. Instead he focuses on Carter.

"You can crash here if you want," he says. "Olivia is taking off soon. So are the others. It'll just be us."

"Oh." Carter looks at me with discomfort, but it's his offer to accept or decline. When I don't come to his rescue, he jerks a thumb at me. "I'm supposed to be staying with him."

Bobby spares a brief glare in my direction, like I'm somehow to blame. "They won't know the difference."

Carter turns to me again, and I know I should keep quiet but I can't help myself. "His parents live next door," I explain. "If they come looking for him tomorrow and he's not there, it'll mean trouble. My parents won't be happy with me either."

"You're both fucking square," Bobby says, staring at Carter like it'll make him change his mind. Then he flashes a vicious smile. "Have a nice night, lovebirds."

Carter gets his back up. "We're not—"

Bobby laughs. I do too and shove Carter toward the door. I don't really think it's funny but, once again, my survival instinct kicks in. I want to keep Bobby happy so he doesn't do something crazy. More than ever, I need those anger management lessons that Gerald offered. Maybe he can teach me how to clamp down on my fear too. I suck in cool night air as soon as we're outside.

"So awkward!" I say.

"I wouldn't mind staying with him," Carter says. "I just like your place better."

"It was interesting to see where he lives," I say as we begin the walk home. "I always find that revealing. Like it tells a story about that person, whether they want it to or not."

Carter is quiet for a few paces. "What did Bobby's place tell you about him?"

"Not much, to be honest. I don't think his parents use that downstairs area at all, so they probably give him a lot of leeway. Same with mine."

"His dad isn't around anymore," Carter says.

"Oh." That's news to me. "I didn't get much of an impression really. He needs to clean his room."

"You should see mine."

"Is that an invite?" I know it's not. I'm just tired of waiting.

Carter shrugs. "I guess. I still like your place better."

"Than your own home? I can relate. It gets boring being in my bedroom day after day, night after night, week after week!"

"Okay, okay!" Carter says with a chuckle. "I get it! Shut up!"

"Month after month," I continue, "year after—"

"You haven't even lived there for a year!"

"It feels like I have. The monotony is killing me!"

"Fine. My place. Tomorrow night."

"I thought you'd never ask." In my mind, I rest my head on his shoulder, he puts an arm around me, and we walk home in contented silence. In reality, we take turns making stupid jokes, only being quiet when we reach my street. I'm not sure which version of events I prefer. Both would be nice. For now, I'll take what I can get.

Chapter Eight

Two more weeks pass by before I'm allowed to visit Carter's house. He keeps telling me he needs to clean his room first, which is ridiculous, because he's seen mine messy plenty of times. He's helped *make* it messy! I shouldn't have told him all that stuff about a home revealing a person's story. I have a feeling that, since then, he's been editing his own story before I can get to the rawest and juiciest parts. Carter still has a secretive side that I can't crack, but today I'll get another chance. Right now in fact!

"Ready?" I say, grabbing my already packed bookbag and standing as soon as the bell rings. "Let's go!"

"Calm down," Carter grumps. "We're not going to Disneyland."

"Your house might be even cooler, for all I know," I say, jiggling the back of his chair. "Come on! Hurry up!"

"No point in rushing," Carter says, getting to his feet with the speed of a turtle addicted to horse tranquilizers. "We have to get Vicky first. She's walking home with us."

"I get to meet one of your sisters?" I practically shout.

Carter shakes his head. "You're sad. Really. I pity you."

"Fine with me. Let's go."

I try to rein myself in as we walk and I scan the crowds. Even from a distance, the family resemblance makes Vicky easy to spot. Sure, I've seen photos, and yeah, she's the only one waiting in the designated place—beneath the flagpole—but even without these indicators, I would have known anyway. She looks too much like her brother. Vicky has the same earthen tones, the skin almost dusty, like she's been working on a farm with no showers but plenty of wind and erosion. Her hair is the same dark chestnut color as Carter's, a baseball cap yanked over it. Even with the ponytail running down her back, I bet she's often mistaken for a boy. She dresses like one, wearing a no-frills T-shirt, jeans, and sneakers. Her posture isn't very ladylike, either. I love her already. As we near, I'm surprised by how small she is. She's short and slender, resembling a freshman more than a junior.

For whatever reason, she lights up when she sees me.

"Hey!" Vicky says, thrusting out her hand. When I do the same, she doesn't shake it, but instead she curls her fingers against mine to link them before pulling away. Then she beams up at me. "This is so cool. You're really gay?"

"Yup!"

"Come on," Carter says. "You can walk home with us. That's the deal. We're not standing here the whole afternoon."

She makes a face at him, then falls in beside me as we begin the journey. "I think it's awesome that you're out and everything," she says. "I would be too."

Interesting. Is she trying to tell me something?

"I'm not gay," she continues, as if hearing my thoughts. "But if I was, I'd be *the* loudest and proudest. Too bad I love guys. Hey! Do you have any brothers?"

"Just an older one, sorry."

"I like them older."

Carter groans as if in pain.

"Yeah," I say, "but he's a *lot* older. Reed is twenty-three. And taken."

"Let me know if that changes," Vicky says with a cackle. "Do you have a boyfriend?"

I shake my head. "I wish."

Vicky looks past me to scowl at her brother. "Why can't you be gay? That would be so cute!"

Oh, I definitely like her! "Yeah, Carter," I say, "pushing him playfully. "Why can't you be gay?"

"I hate you guys," he grumbles.

Vicky returns her attention to me. "But you've kissed a guy before?"

"Yeah."

"Guys? Plural?"

I nod. "Yup."

"And other stuff?"

"Vicky!" Carter snarls.

I'm not offended by the question. Not at all. "I had a boyfriend in New Mexico," I explain, "and we did all the things that boyfriends do." I can feel Carter's glare without needing to look at him. It nearly burns a hole in my head, so I hasten to add, "Things that you should only consider if you're in love with someone."

"And married," Carter says.

I scrunch up my face. "Well…"

"I'm with him," Vicky says, jerking a thumb at me. "It's like that old saying: Never buy a cow without milking it first."

"I don't want to hear this," Carter says, picking up the pace. "Come on you two. We're almost there!"

Vicky rolls her eyes. "He thinks he's my dad, and that girls need protecting from all the naughty things that boys want to do. Like I'm some naïve damsel. The truth is, I practically assaulted the first guy I ever—"

"Text me," I say for the sake of my best friend's sanity. "We'll pick this up again later."

By the time we're done trading numbers, we've arrived. I've already seen Carter's house from the outside. Like mine, it's old, two stories tall, and wooden with a small front porch. We enter through the front door. The ground floor still has the original hardwood floors, which I envy, although the carpet we have means I don't hear footsteps as much when I'm in my bedroom. We pass way too quickly through the living room. I want to check out the family photos, but they are only blurs as he leads us to the kitchen.

"Thirsty?" he asks, opening the refrigerator. He hands out cans of Pepsi without waiting for an answer. Then he closes the fridge, turns to his sister and points, as if telling a dog to leave the room. I'd think that was cruel if Reed didn't do the same thing to me all the time. Younger siblings tend to get away with more, but we also have to put up with a lot.

Vicky rolls her eyes. Then she offers me a fist bump and says, "Text me," before leaving the room.

"I like her," I say, looking past Carter to the drawings on the refrigerator door. "And these. Is the pink horse one of yours?"

"It's a unicorn," Carter says. "And no."

I bite my lip in an effort to contain my smile. "So…"

Carter sighs. "I'll give you a tour."

He walks me through the public areas of the house, and I finally get to see photos of him when he was chubby-cheeked and gap-toothed, but most of the rooms don't interest me. When we go upstairs to his room, which I've built up to legendary proportions in my mind, I get excited again. The door is shut. As soon as we enter, I'm surrounded by his scent. There's a hint of air freshener too, but I do my best to try and filter it out. When it comes to the visuals…

"Do you like to decorate?"

"Why?" Carter asks, sounding defensive.

Because everything is so coordinated. Carter doesn't always put together the best outfits. I like to tease him that he's also fashion dyslexic. The room is perfection. The walls are painted navy blue, which complements the blue and white sheets. The rich wood of the headboard pairs nicely with the desk shoved up against one wall, complete with lamp and laptop. A striped rug in the middle of the floor helps add a playful splash of yellow, the wall-to-wall carpet beneath it a dark gray. I feel like I've walked into the pages of a decorating magazine.

"Geez," I say sarcastically. "What a dump." I turn to him in disbelief. "Why do you like hanging out in my room so much?"

Carter shrugs. "I don't know. I guess because it's so… you."

That makes my heart flutter. "Want to trade? Seriously. I'll live here from now on."

Carter laughs and seems to relax. "You really like it?"

"Yeah! I'm just surprised you have a knack for interior design."

"For what?"

"Making rooms pretty," I say patiently. He really is straight, isn't he?

"Oh. To be honest, I had my mom help me. That's why it took so long to have you over. I wanted my room to look nice for you."

Or maybe he's gay and is trying to seduce me, because that's one of the sweetest things I've ever heard. It's also a little frustrating. I want to get to know him better, not his mom. "She has good taste. I think. How much of this was her idea?"

"Most of it," Carter admits. "Some of it was you."

He gestures to a collage of photos on the wall. I rush over to inspect it, hoping it's not just photos from his life in Chicago. I'm in luck! Blue skies, beige dirt, and unfiltered sun dominate the backgrounds. Now this… *this* feels like a treasure trove. I'm finally able look into Carter's past. Some photos amuse me, especially those of a skinnier guy with braces who I would've mistaken for a younger brother if Carter had one. Age has only made him handsomer, which might be why a pretty girl with blonde hair began appearing in many of the more recent photos, including one where she's kissing his cheek. I feel victorious instead of jealous, because this means he likes blondes. Yes! She's not the only recurring character. In fact, she's just a guest star compared to the guy with bronze skin and buzzed black hair who is in nearly every photo. Whoever he is, he's as handsome as Carter. Maybe even more so, because as time passes from photo to photo, his muscles grow the biggest and become the most defined, his confident smile casting a shadow over Carter's own.

I touch the strong chest with the tip of my finger. "Who's this?" When I don't get an answer right away, I look over to see Carter staring at the photo, his features tight. Then he notices me and swallows, like he's holding back emotion.

"Renzo," he says. "He's my— Never mind."

"Your what?" I ask.

Carter winces. "Don't get mad. That oath we took, I meant it. I still do."

"He's your best friend," I say.

Carter nods.

I smile. "That's totally cool! To me, a best friend is more of a status. It's higher up than a normal friend. You can have more than one."

"Really?"

"Yeah! Why not? We make the rules. I'm your best friend here, and he's your best friend there. Right?"

Carter grins and nods. "Thanks."

I return my attention to the photo. "Do you guys stay in touch?"

"We try, yeah."

"And is he straight too? Because he's freaking hot."

Carter groans. "Girls were *always* noticing Renzo instead of me. It drove me crazy. He thought it was funny."

"I bet. You must have had some luck though." I point to the blonde girl.

"Melanie." Carter's voice is soft when he says her name. Almost reverent. "She was my first girlfriend. The only one, actually."

"No way! The only one? Really?"

Carter shrugs. "There were a few girls I dated before her, but nothing like a real relationship. Sophomore year, it was all about me, her, Renzo, and Tracy." He points out a photo I haven't noticed yet. A group shot of four.

"What about junior year?" I ask.

Carter is quiet again.

"Did you guys break up?" I press.

"Kind of."

"Kind of? How's that work?"

"We were still together," he says. "Until I moved."

Ugh! Could he be any more enigmatic? And would I still be into him if he wasn't? Because it draws me in and drives me crazy every time. In a good way. I think.

"Check this one out," Carter says, clearly attempting to distract me.

In the very center of the collage is my ugly mug. That's intentional. We were making the dumbest possible faces while taking selfies, and lucky me, my face just happens to be very expressive.

"Aw!" I say. "I made the wall!"

"Of course you did," Carter says, grinning at me. "You're my best friend."

I chuckle at the compliment. Still… "Couldn't you have chosen a better photo? One that makes me look cool? You and Renzo are so National Geographic together."

"Huh? Oh. You mean the rock climbing."

"Yeah. Look at you guys, hanging out—no, hanging *on* together." I scope out the photos again. Many are of taut flexing muscles as Carter and Renzo take turns dangling from ropes or clinging to stony surfaces. "You guys seem legit. Not like people who go to those silly indoor climbing places."

"That's where we started," Carter says, sounding proud. "And where we met."

"Yeah?"

"Yeah. I taught Renzo a lot." He grins. "I guess you could say that I showed him the ropes."

"You should show me too," I say. I'm not much for athletics, but I don't want to miss out of any part of his world.

Carter snorts. "Yeah, right."

"What's that supposed to mean?"

"Let me see your palms."

I hold them out for him to inspect.

He barely even looks before he starts shaking his head. Then he holds out his own. "See mine? I'm out of practice, and I still have way more calluses than you."

"Big deal," I say. "I'll get calluses too. You didn't start with them, did you?"

"I had more muscle when I was twelve than you do now. You'll need to start doing pushups."

"I'm tougher than I look."

He's clearly not convinced. "Do we need to arm wrestle again?"

Forget the arms. I can wrestle for real. For as long as I can remember, Reed has taken great pleasure in pinning me down, getting me into headlocks, or putting me into any hold that makes me beg for mercy. This became more fun once I was big enough to fight back. He always remained stronger and more experienced than me, but I learned a lot of useful skills along the way.

Such as the element of surprise.

I grab Carter's wrist and deftly step behind him to pin it behind his back. Then I place my other hand on his shoulder and push, causing him to stumble forward as I steer him around. "Where you goin'? Where you goin'? Huh?" Reed used to do this to me all the time, the bastard.

Carter is the perfect victim until he recovers from his shock and braces his legs. This allows me to bend him over, which is fun but not my usual preference.

"Let go!" Carter growls.

"Make me."

"Fine! You just picked a fight you can't win!" He changes tactics and falls first to one knee and then the other, bringing me down with him. We're on the rug, which will have to act as our mat, because I'm not done proving my point. I'm about to wrap an arm around his neck when Carter grunts and flops to his side, pulling me along as he goes. I get spooked and release him so I can brace myself for impact, allowing him to slip free.

Carter doesn't flee. He's too intent on revenge. When I see him coming, I try to roll away and get up, but I'm not quick enough. Before I know it, Carter has his legs wrapped around mine in a scissor hold, and one of his arms is constricted around my neck like a python.

"Now who's tough?" he says.

I gasp. When I suck in air, it sounds haggard. I do this twice in a row, the sound horrible, like I'll die at any second. "Can't—" I manage to gasp out. "—breathe. Please!"

He releases me, and I roll over onto my hands and knees, coughing and retching. In the corner of my eye, I see him reaching for me with concern, so I lunge and knock him flat on the ground. Then I sit on his hips, laughing victoriously. "I can't believe you fell for that!" I say, making the fake choking noise again. "If you had a brother, you'd know these things. Oh, and to answer your question, *I'm* the toughest."

Carter is raising his legs up, like he wants to loop one around my neck, but he's not that flexible. He flings his arms at me too, but I knock them away. I'm about to beat my chest and give a Tarzan yell when his hips rise up and down again, like he's doing the worm. It's enough to buck me off, and while I'm in the air, he grabs me and rolls to the side. Before I know it, he reverses the situation. Now I've got my back on the floor and he's sitting on me. Still not my preference.

I'm skinny, which means there's less of me to hold on to, so I start squirming. This might not set me free, but it makes me hard to hold down. Carter keeps trying anyway, telling me to submit. I won't. Not without a fight. He manages to pin my legs beneath the tops of his shoes and trap each of my wrists in one of his hands. I refuse to make it easy. I keep moving until Carter stretches out, pressing his full weight against me and…

Until this moment, there was nothing sexual about us touching. I had a few fleeting thoughts, but they were humorous rather than hot. I was too caught up in the struggle to even recognize how good his hands feel, and how the warmth from his body is radiating against mine. His chest heaves as he tries to catch his breath, a victorious smile mere inches from my face, and I start to react. I mentally clamp down on it because I don't want him to think I'm after cheap thrills. I'd rather be his friend than a fling. If anything more is going to happen between us, I want it to be emotional.

"Well?" he says, still grinning. "Who's the toughest?"

"You are," I say, hoping that if I submit, he'll get away from me. I don't really want him to. But I need him to, if that makes sense.

Carter rolls over onto his back, one of my arms trapped beneath his neck like a pillow. I find this easier to deal with. For my own comfort, I roll over onto my side. I'm facing him now and fighting the urge to place my palm on his chest. Not to feel him up or anything. My free hand simply needs to go somewhere, and I wish I could rest it on him.

This is getting rough. I've lusted after straight guys before, but with Carter I also feel affection. I want to tell him how much I like him, maybe even love him, and that it's okay if he can't feel the same way about me. I want him to know anyway, but only if it won't mess with what we have. For now, my hand becomes a fist, my emotions balled up inside it. I rest this on the carpet, knuckles touching where his ribcage meets the floor.

"Will you teach me anyway?" I say.

"Huh?"

"Mountain climbing."

"It's rock climbing," Carter says with a laugh.

"But will you?"

He's quiet.

I sigh.

"Sorry," he says. "Renzo and me, that's kind of our thing. I don't do it with anyone else."

"Not even Melanie?"

He scoffs. "Never."

"What about Olivia?" I say, my tone more playful. "Would you teach her?"

"Hm. I'd need to think about that."

"You suck."

Carter snorts. "You wish."

He's got that right. I know it's probably just guy banter, but it makes me wonder yet again if he's aware of my feelings. As it turns out, the topic is on his mind. Sort of.

"I feel weird about that whole situation with her," he says.

I raise my head to look at him. "What do you mean?"

"How she thinks we're a couple."

I laugh and let my head fall back down. "So tell her the truth."

"It's like you said. Olivia is more comfortable around me because she thinks I'm not interested in her. And now I've sort of been lying, or at least not correcting her when she assumes stuff."

"Like what?"

"Like outfits. She wants to know what you and I are wearing to homecoming. She thinks we should wear matching suits."

The thought makes me smile. "Are we going together?"

He looks over at me, his ear tickling my bicep. "If you want, but I'm not getting dressed up or buying you a corsage."

"I don't care as long as I get my slow dance. I want a free meal too. Take me somewhere nice."

"No problem," Carter says. "Burger King or Wendy's. Lady's choice."

I swat him with my hand, and yeah, maybe I let my fingertips brush against him as I pull away again. Then I remember another tactic that has won me many a battle, and I thrust those fingers into his armpit and start tickling.

"No fair!" Carter cries between howls. "Stop! Stooop!"

I take advantage of his writhing body to slip my arm free. Then I get up and tackle him again, and for the remainder of the match, we're not gay or straight. We're not lovelorn or oblivious. We're just two boys, trying to pin each other to the ground.

The only problem with my new job at Blaze Pizza is that every shift means time away from Carter. Over the past few weeks, I've tried to make sure my schedule interferes with my social life as little as possible. On weekends, that means working during the day when Carter is more likely to be out mowing lawns. On weekdays, I start during the dinner rush when Carter is expected to be home with his family. That at least gives us a couple of hours after school to hang out.

Aside from needing to maintain my addiction to him, I love the job, or to be precise, the money I earn. It allows Carter and me to do fun things, like when we borrowed the car and drove to Barnes & Noble where we finally were able to buy magic wands—thanks to the next *Fantastic Beasts* movie coming out. So at least one of my dreams for us came true, even if we didn't get matching ones. We don't get matching suits either. He never formally invites me to homecoming, and I don't really expect him to. Probably for the best. A guy like him would be mobbed by dateless girls, which I can't handle. Even the idea of watching him slow dance with someone else is upsetting. Better not to risk it. Instead we do our usual thing and hang out at each other's houses, watch TV, play video games, wrestle, or edit his stories.

Carter has allowed me see some of them, and he's right, the prose itself is terrible. The structure is workable though, and the ideas are good. We're often shoulder to shoulder, me reading aloud from his laptop and making suggestions, which he then reacts to. We've already polished off two short stories and showed them to Gerald, who seems genuinely impressed. Carter keeps referring to "the big project" that he wants my help with. Eventually. He won't say anything more about it than that. No surprise there. He likes to keep me in suspense.

The best part of spending so much time at home with him is that it allows us to save our money. We want a car. We're both in the same situation, having to beg and borrow the family vehicles if we want to go anywhere. My parents are also fed up with this, which is why they made me a lucrative offer when I took this job. They'll match whatever I manage to save. So if I can raise five thousand dollars, I can get a ten thousand dollar car. Carter is willing to pitch in too, or as he puts it, "You get the car, I'll take care of the rest." He means gas, oil, insurance, repairs... the rest. I love this, since it's like we're married and pooling our finances.

This becomes my motivation for smiling at every customer, since part of every dollar they spend is going toward my new car and endless adventures on the road with Carter. Although with some customers, I don't have to fake that smile at all.

"Welcome to Blaze Pizza," I say, grinning from ear to ear. "Have you been here before?"

"Once or twice," Carter says, grinning back at me.

He seems especially excited, and I don't understand why until the door opens and a girl with blue hair walks in. Olivia is biting her bottom lip, attention still on her phone. She's scowling in concentration, her face pretty even while doing so. Then, with one final tap of her thumb, she looks up, sees us, and smiles.

"Olivia!" I manage to say without it sounding too strained. "Hey! Where are the others?"

"It's just us," Carter says, breath a little short.

He fixes wide eyes on me, his head bobbing as if urging me to reach a conclusion I really *really* don't want to reach. Last I heard, Olivia was still dating Bobby. I wait until she's peering at the menu before I shoot him a quizzical expression. He shakes his head, just once, and I nearly sigh in relief. Nothing has changed. He's just excited to be alone with her, which sucks, because alone is what he and I do best. That's supposed to be our thing.

"What'll it be?" I ask.

Olivia opens her mouth, but before she can say anything, Jackson comes bounding over from the pizza ovens. "Hey!" he says. "Where's Bobby?"

A very good question, I want to say. *Let's call him and correct this oversight.*

"At the police station with his mom," Olivia says. "You know that guy who keeps calling me Smurfette? He fell down the stairs today and broke his arm. Bobby just happened to be behind him at the time, so he got the blame."

"Taking care of his girl," I say in approving tones. "Nice!"

I try my best to ignore Carter's incredulous expression.

"If Bobby has to do time because of that guy," Jackson grumbles, "I'll break his other arm."

"Do you think he will?" Carter says, looking a lot more chipper. "Do time, I mean."

I wouldn't mind that either, especially if Olivia remains faithful to him while he's behind bars.

"He just sent me a text." Olivia holds up her phone. "Bobby says that the guy's family is pushing for him to pay the medical expenses, and that he convinced them it was an accident."

"Damn straight it was," Jackson says. Then he returns to his station before any pizzas burn.

More customers are coming in, so I need to get back to work too. "What'll it be?" I press.

Olivia looks at Carter. "What sounds good to you? We're sharing, right?"

Carter stares back at her. "Yeah! Whatever you want is fine."

"Are you sure?"

"Uh-huh!"

I'm on the verge of vomiting. Depending on where I aim, they might not have as many toppings to choose from. Olivia gives me her order, and when one of her choices is artichokes, which Carter *hates*, I look at him to see that he's still smiling. And it hurts. What a stupid thing to get emotional over. My face is burning when I make sure to put artichokes on only one half of the pizza so he won't have to eat them. Carter doesn't ask for this. He doesn't need to. If Olivia cared about him half as much as I do, she would know better.

I try to calm down when they go to find a table. They aren't dating. She's still with Bobby who is, by all accounts, being badder than ever. That should keep her interested, although it's not the real issue. What bothers me is Carter's obsession with her. He's straight and has told me as much on more than one occasion, but I keep hoping that I'll awaken something in him. Or, like some of those books I read and never talk about, that he could be gay-for-me. Does that happen in real life? Ever? Because if not, it seems like a really fucked-up thing to write. Don't those authors realize that they're selling false hope to people like me? Do they not care?

"You all right, man?" Jackson asks.

"Why wouldn't I be?" I snap.

"Uh, because you're pacing back and forth like a caged wolf. You're supposed to be over there."

He's right. I'm standing by the ovens now, partially because I can see Carter and Olivia better from here. And because when the pizza is ready, Carter will come for it, and I want to be there to… I don't know. Say something to him. I'm just not sure what.

"Can we switch?" I ask Jackson. "Just for a little bit. Please?"

"Oh-kay," he says before slinking away.

"Thanks," I murmur, my attention still on their table. I watch them so intently that I nearly forget to check the oven. The pizza's crust is dark brown when I take it out, but it's still presentable. "Carter!" I yell, wanting to get him away from her. Now it's just a matter of finding the right words to make the entire world change to suit my needs.

Carter doesn't share my struggle. He has plenty to say. "I told her that I'm not gay!" he whispers. "I thought she would hate me when she found out, but she doesn't! She was surprised, that's all. I think she's okay with the real me."

I stare at him. I'm so stunned by what he said that, for a moment, I forget my own pain. "You know what this means?" I ask.

He shakes his head.

I laugh. "Carter… You just came out!"

He thinks about it. Then he guffaws. "I guess I did!"

"This is major!" I walk around the counter to give him a hug.

As I cling to him, the sorrow returns, because it's just a matter of time. Who wouldn't want Carter King? He doesn't need to be a bad boy or anything else. He's perfect the way he is. Olivia is too smart not to recognize that. I hope she's watching us now. I hope she sees my face and realizes what she would be stealing from me. Carter might not be gay, but right now, he's all I've got. Please don't take that away from me. Please.

"Dude," Carter says, humor in his voice. "I'm happy too but…"

"Sorry," I say, releasing him at last.

"I better deliver this pizza," he says ruefully.

I consider my options. Knock the pizza to the floor to buy myself time, or maybe tackle him so he can't get away. In the end, I impart some wisdom that Reed used to give me before I came out. "Never keep a woman waiting."

"Good advice. Have anymore? I'm nervous as hell!"

He doesn't know how I feel about him. He can't. Carter has too good of a heart to ever put me in this position. I give him my best answer anyway, telling myself that it's a way to silently prove my love, and that maybe someday he'll recognize the sacrifice I made. "Make sure she knows this wasn't a joke at her expense. Tell her the truth—that you liked how open you could be with each other, that her thinking you were gay took the pressure off and made it fun. And that you want it to stay that way."

"Should I tell her how I feel?"

I look him right in the eye. "What's the point of telling the other person when you know you can't be together?"

He nods. "Okay. Thanks, Andrew."

"That's what I'm here for." As I watch him carry the pizza over to Olivia—who claps like he worked some sort of magic—I wonder if that's all I'll ever be: The guy who helps others get what they want while always going without.

My mood steadily plummets during the rest of my shift. I'm no longer smiling at customers or bothering to distribute toppings evenly. I don't ask if they'd like anything else when ringing up their orders. I just want them out of my way. I keep looking at Carter and Olivia's table, even once they're gone, like the ghost of their memory might help me make sense of it all. I have a pocketful of text messages I'm ignoring because I'm convinced they're all about her, but this small abstinence doesn't help either.

I want him. I keep telling myself that he's straight. Over and over again, but somehow I can't get it to sink in. I want Carter so badly that it feels like I should be able to make the impossible happen. Why can't we be together? Besides the obvious, but that seems like such a small detail in the face of such a huge emotion. Isn't love supposed to conquer all?

I take my frustration out on the dishes after the restaurant is closed and the doors are locked. I'm slamming trays around and jet-blasting plastic containers clean like they've done me personal harm. I guess I'm making a lot of noise, because Jackson comes to investigate, mop in hand.

"What the fuck?" he says.

"That pretty much sums up my life," I reply. "What the fuck."

He stands there and watches me, but with an audience present, my actions feel less like venting and more like being ridiculous, so I shut off the water.

"You all right?" he asks, leaning the mop against the wall. He's not a touchy-feely guy, so this takes me aback. I can't remember Jackson ever wanting to talk about feelings. So far, everything we've ever discussed has been strictly external and completely superficial.

"No," I admit. "I'm not okay."

He crosses his arms over his chest. I don't think he's comfortable being around me, even though we've worked together for nearly a month. "Anything I can do?"

"Hire a hitman?" I grimace and shake my head. I can't even joke about it. I *like* Olivia. I just wish that Carter didn't.

"If someone's messing with you—" Jackson begins to say.

"It's nothing like that. I'm fine. I'm just pathetic and alone, but whatever. Could be worse."

Jackson studies me, like I'm a confusing puzzle. I don't expect him to solve it, but I should have known better, because today the world is determined to prove me wrong at every opportunity. "Are you in love with Carter?" he asks.

This pisses me off. Maybe because it's just a matter of time before he tells everyone else and it becomes a big joke. "Are you in love with Bobby?" I shoot back.

Jackson looks hurt. I've never seen him wear that expression before. He rages against it, as I so often have, trying to drown the sorrow in anger. He balls his hands into fists, works his jaw, and pulls back his lips like he's tasted something sour. I'm convinced he's going to beat the living hell out of me. Instead he walks over to one of the plastic trash cans and kicks it once, twice, and then a third time. My heart is pounding in my chest, and I'm genuinely scared. When he turns around to face me...

The anger is gone. He just looks sad, like nothing ever goes his way. Jackson walks over to the sink and grabs a towel. "Come on," he says, attention on the dishes. "I'll help you dry."

"Thanks," I manage.

We work together in silence. It's not until we've finished closing up and step outside into a humid night that he speaks to me again.

"Want a ride?"

"Okay."

He leads me to an old beat-up Camaro. I've seen it before. I used to think it was Bobby's. That's how often Jackson lets him drive it, which makes me wonder if I hit on the truth by accident. Maybe I'm not the only person to know the sting of unrequited love. We don't talk on the way home. Jackson's music is too loud. I just point and he drives. He turns down the stereo after pulling over, and I say the only words that come to mind.

"I'm sorry."

"Yeah." He reaches across me and yanks the handle so the door opens. Then he leans back. "So am I."

I'm tempted to shut the door again and ask how he feels, or maybe explain what I've been going through. Instead I get out of the car. As I watch him drive away, I realize that—despite knowing exactly where I am—I've never felt so lost.

Chapter Nine

Nothing has changed. All my fears have, so far, amounted to nothing. Olivia and Bobby haven't broken up. Carter is still transparently infatuated with her, and I'm still crazy about him, although I don't think he realizes that. Jackson hasn't told anyone yet, as far as I can tell. He's probably as uncertain of my situation as I am of his. Despite how friendly we've become at work, neither one of us seems eager to talk about our feelings again.

I'm pretty happy about that, actually. The status quo is better than what I thought would happen. I try to put my worries behind me, which isn't hard because there's a great big event coming up to distract me. Halloween! I used to love the holiday as a kid. I still do, but somewhere around junior high, I started feeling like it no longer belonged to me. Probably because a few people slammed the door in my face and told me that I was too old to go trick-or-treating. That, combined with the universal desperation to be considered cool at school, meant childish things had to be set aside.

Screw that! I'm about to begin my life as an adult. Before I graduate from high school, I intend to go out with the most childish bang possible. Carter shares my outlook, and together we convince the others that we should all dress up. Best of all? Our costumes will have a unified theme.

"I always wondered what it would be like to have a little sister," Reed says.

He's staring at me aghast, which I try not to take personally. And fail.

"You don't think I'm pretty?" I ask in a deeper voice than normal, facing the couch with two fists on my hips.

"I thought…" He reconsiders whatever he was going to say and tries again. "When you came out, I asked if you were into drag or anything like that, and you said you weren't."

"I'm not. It's Halloween! This is a costume, stupid."

"In that case, you're very pretty. You're supposed to be one of the Harry Potter kids, right? The girl. Hairy Midget?"

"Hermione, and no, I'm way cooler than her. I'm Luna Lovegood!" I wave my wand with a flourish as I say this. He's not impressed.

"Bring me back some candy," he says, turning off the TV. "I gotta get to work."

I can't believe he's not blown away. We went all out on these costumes! That meant taking a serious chunk out of the car fund, but the end results were worth it. Carter and I decided to go the school uniforms route, which made it a lot easier. I hurry to the bathroom to check my appearance. I look freaking fabulous, thanks to the blond wig I found at a thrift store that isn't the cheap and frizzy kind sold at costume shops. It's pretty convincing, actually. My mom helped me style it. The uniform is perfect. I'm wearing a dress shirt and tie mostly hidden beneath a black sweater with the Hogwarts crest on the chest. The matching skirt makes me laugh, but it looks fine. I opted for black thermal underwear instead of tights because Chicago is already getting cold. I even found a cork to put on a string to replicate Luna's necklace. I wish we were going to a costume contest, because I would win hands down. I'm sure of it.

My phone chimes at me, and when I check it, I see a text message from Carter.

On my wae. The guys are to.

Hand typed. He's trying. I hurry back to my room to grab a pillowcase. He's not there when I step outside, so I walk to the alley to wait for him. The breath catches in my throat when I see him coming. Carter looks stunning in all black. Like me, he's wearing a Hogwarts school uniform, but he's still all man. One in particular. I had the hugest crush on Cedric Diggory when I first saw the *Goblet of Fire* movie. Less so when a friend made me watch the *Twilight* movies, but Cedric will always have a special place in my heart as my first infatuations. I even had a photo of him that I tore out of a magazine and taped to my bedroom wall. Carter couldn't have chosen a better character to be. He is, quite possibly, even hotter than Cedric was.

"You look amazing!" I say when he's near enough to hear me.

Carter just stares. He doesn't laugh. He just shakes his head and says, "Wow."

"Good wow, or bad wow?" I ask.

"Good," he says. "Hey, you even have the Butterbeer cork necklace!"

"Hell yeah I do!"

We bump fists. Then we start waving our wands around

and casting spells. Probably good to get that out of our systems before the others show up. We go to the front of my house to meet them. When they arrive, I'm seriously creeped out, despite already knowing who everyone planned to dress as. Bobby is Voldemort. Of course he is. He bought a costume complete with a mask, gloves, and a black robe. Next to him is Olivia, or should I say Bellatrix Lestrange. She looks sexy in the dark lacy dress. She even curled her hair and sprayed it black. When I catch Carter panting in her direction, I wish she had taken my advice and dressed as Professor McGonagall instead, although I have to admit this does make more sense.

Pedro and Felipe both chose to dress up as Dementors. They bought generic grim reaper costumes, but it works. I'm disappointed in Mick's costume since he only has a fake beard, a brown coat, and an umbrella that isn't the correct color. Not much of a Hagrid. At least he has the right build. That just leaves Jackson, who hasn't shown up yet.

"Are you fucking serious?" Bobby says, cackling while pointing a pale-white finger at me. "You look ridiculous!"

"No he doesn't," Olivia says. "He looks beautiful!"

She takes my hands, which is maybe something that girls do. I don't know.

"Did you do your own makeup?" she asks.

"Yes," I lie, because I know Bobby will only keep laughing if I tell him my mom did it for me.

"You're a natural," Olivia says. "You should do mine sometime."

"Or not," Bobby mutters. "Where the hell is Jackson?"

We spot him coming down the street in a hurry, purple robes flowing behind him, a matching cap on his head. He looks cool, but Dumbledore just isn't the same without one crucial detail.

"You forgot the beard!" I complain. "And the wig."

"Uh-uh," Jackson says, trying to catch his breath. "I realized that when I leave those off, I look more like—"

"Kingsley Shacklebolt!" Carter and I say in perfect unison.

This leads to a round of high-fives.

"I had to spray-paint the cap," Jackson explains. "That's why I'm late. It's hard to find purple paint. This works better with the robes too, since I couldn't find them in lavender."

"You look awesome!" I enthuse.

Bobby isn't as impressed. "And here I was looking forward to killing Dumbledore, like in the movie."

That's not what happened in the movie or the books. I don't tell him that he did, however, kill Cedric. That's kind of creepy, come to think of it.

"What did you do for his wand?" I ask Jackson.

"Still the Elder Wand," he says. "I'm pretending that Dumbledore gave it to Kingsley for safekeeping and—"

"Enough of your gay-ass book club," Bobby says. "Let's get this show on the road."

That means trick-or-treating, and we do visit a number of houses, but along the way, Bobby takes great delight in tormenting kids who are little enough to be scared by his costume. One even drops her bag of candy before she runs off, but Carter picks it up and chases after her to give it back. I freaking hate Bobby sometimes. Most of the time. Olivia doesn't seem happy either, since they get into an argument shortly after.

"I didn't know you were into Harry Potter," I say to Jackson as we walk between houses. "Just the movies or...."

"All of it," he says. "My mom is obsessed and made me read the books. She literally paid me to. Or withheld my allowance until I did. Depends how you look at it."

This makes me laugh. I'm about to ask what his favorites are—book, character, house, movie—when we hear someone yelling at us from behind.

"Carter!"

I recognize that voice. I turn around to see Vicky running toward us. Her costume doesn't match the source material as well, and the bright red fright wig isn't exactly ginger, but if I'm not mistaken, she's supposed to be dressed as Ginny Weasley.

"Who the hell is that?" Bobby asks with a snort. "Your girlfriend?"

"My sister," Carter says through gritted teeth. "What are you doing here, Vicky? I thought you were out with your friends."

"They are *so boring*," she says. "I ditched them. What are you guys doing? Let's get wasted. Or high!"

"If you've got booze or weed," Bobby says, "you're welcome to hang with us."

"You're the seniors," she retorts. "You're supposed to hook me up. The first one is always free. That sort of thing."

"How did you find us?" Carter asks, not sounding pleased.

Vicky holds up her phone. A GPS map is on the screen, a pulsing blue dot showing our current location. "I just followed my heart," she says.

"Good," Carter replies. "You can follow it back to your friends. Now!"

"She can hang with us," Bobby says. "Why not?"

They glare at each other, which I've never seen before.

"I'll keep an eye on her," I say, hoping to dispel the tension. "We girls have to stick together, right?"

This gets a few laughs, but not from the two guys who are still staring each other down.

"Let's try this house," Olivia says, pulling on Bobby's arm.

That does the trick. For one of them, at least. Carter watches them walk away, his face twisting up even more. Then he turns to his sister. "Don't leave my side," he growls.

"Okay," she says. "I promise. Sorry. Your friends are more fun than mine. I don't mean to be the bratty little sister."

"It's fine," he says, seeming appeased. "Just stay away from Voldemort."

Interesting. Carter is always so nonchalant about Bobby's shortcomings, but he isn't stupid. I'm sure he's aware that Bobby is disturbed. This is just the closest I've heard him come to admitting it.

We hit about ten more houses. One of them sends us away, so Bobby kicks in the faces of their jack-o-lanterns once the door is closed. That's practically good behavior for him. For a while we just wander the streets, eating candy and talking, which I like. That changes when we pass a house where the bass is really thumping.

"They left the candy bowl on the porch," Mick points out. "Should we help them out with that?"

"Forget the candy," Bobby says. "That looks like one crowded party."

He's right. Through the bay windows we can see that the front room is stuffed with adults.

"I don't think they're riding a sugar high," Bobby says, turning to face us. "Here's what we'll do. A few of us will go inside and see what kind of booze they've got. The rest of you go to the back door and wait. We'll pass the goods to you there.

Mick, you're coming in. You look like you're thirty."

"I'm in too," Carter says, puffing up his chest.

"You sure you can handle it, queer bait?"

"Oh, I can handle it! Can you?"

Ugh. Straight male posturing. If they're so determined to prove who has the biggest dick, why don't they whip them out and grab a ruler? It would be a lot more entertaining for the rest of us.

"I'm in too," Vicky says.

"Fine with me," Bobby says.

"She's *my* sister," Carter shoots back. "You don't get to decide that!"

"She looks too young," I say before they start swinging. "I'll go. Jackson, you too. The rest of you wait, okay?"

The grumbles I get in response are as close to an agreement as we're likely to reach. In truth, I don't want to go at all, but I'm getting worried about the tension that's building between them. At least if I'm there, I can talk Carter down if necessary. I'm hoping Jackson will help keep Bobby calm too, but I can't exactly ask him for help right now.

I'm nervous as hell when we approach the front door. Five people is too conspicuous. Or maybe not, because when I imagine someone sneaking into one of my nonexistent parties, I picture one person, not an entire group. Bobby doesn't knock. He just opens the door and strolls right in. I guess that makes sense too. Other people are coming and going. A few push past us as we follow him.

The air inside is humid and stale from so many bodies being crammed together. I'm worried I stand out the most. I look like a teenage girl. At least Carter and Jackson can pass for college age. Mick and Bobby are fairly hidden behind their costumes. I feel vulnerable in mine, so I try to hide behind Mick's bulk.

We don't go unnoticed. I hear a few people call out our character names or compliment us on our costumes. Nearly everyone here is dressed up, which helps us blend in. When we reach the kitchen, I swear under my breath because it's just as packed as the other rooms.

"Hey! What are you guys doing here?"

I swear again, because now we've been caught.

"Hey! I'm talking to you guys!"

We turn as one to face Harry Potter, of all people. Sort of. He's in his forties, a pot belly stretching the Hogwarts sweater he wears. His glasses are taped in the middle, and after pushing them up, he slaps the drawn-on lightning bolt scar in the middle of his forehead.

"You better get out of here!" he says to Carter. "My scar is burning. He-Who-Must-Not-Be-Named must be nearby! Ha ha!"

"What's your deal?" Bobby says helpfully.

"It's me, Harry Potter," the guy says. "You know, from the epilogue."

"Oh yeah!" I say.

"Nice!" Carter says, offering the guy a high five.

"Hey," grown up Harry Potter says. "You gotta come meet my wife. She's dressed up like Ginny."

Good thing Vicky didn't come in with us. The guy we're talking to seems a little smashed. Who knows what he might have done.

"Actually," I say, "we just got here and we're hoping for uh… a Butterbeer."

"I've had about twelve of those," our new friend says with a snort. I should have kept my mouth shut, because now he's peering at me. "Hey… How old are you?" Now he's squinting his eyes at the others too. "You guys are teenagers!"

"All part of the costume," I say hurriedly. "Convincing, huh?"

The man stares at me. Then he responds with a very drawn out "Pffffffft! I know exactly what you're doing!"

"So?" Bobby challenges. "What are you going to do about it?"

The man gives a theatrical wink and beckons for us to follow him. He shoves his way through the crowd with drunken disregard, leading us straight to a keg. He grabs one of the plastic cups and turns around with a wobble.

"Are you sticking around?"

"We were hoping to get it to-go," Carter says.

The man taps a finger to his nose. Then he yells. "The keg is kicked! We need a new one. Hey! The keg is kicked!"

I feel like running because a lot of attention is now directed our way. This soon shifts along with the crowd as a new keg is brought in.

"Better take the old one while you still can," the man slurs.

Bobby and Mick leap into action. Nobody seems to care about the old keg as the new one is tapped.

"Thanks," I say to the man.

He puts a hand on my shoulder, one of his eyelids lower than the other as he wobbles in place. "I used to be young once," he says with a sigh. "Happy Halloween."

"Come on," Carter whispers to me.

My friends are already shoving their way to the back door. When we finally get outside, we see the others checking a bunch of silver barrels. Other empty kegs.

"Leave those," Bobby hisses. "Hamhead or whatever your stupid movie name is, open that umbrella. We don't want anybody seeing this."

Soon we're like an entourage of bodyguards, the keg safely in our center, as we hustle down the sidewalk.

"Where are we going?" I hiss.

"My place," Bobby says.

It's about ten blocks away, and I swear with every step that we're about to hear a police siren and see flashing lights, but we make it.

"This thing is freaking heavy!" Bobby says. "It must be nearly full!"

I don't know about that, but once we've smuggled it inside and Bobby has returned from assuring his mom that we'll keep it down, we quickly discover that there's enough for not just one round but two. Maybe even more!

"That's enough," Carter says to Vicky. "Two drinks is your limit, or I swear to god, I'll call Mom and Dad and rat us all out."

She complains, but in the end she agrees. I let her take sips from my third cup anyway. I can't help it. The tension is gone, spirits are high, and this is guaranteed to be one Halloween that I'll never forget.

We drop Vicky off at her house before walking to my own. Even though Carter hadn't liked her showing up, she got along great with everyone and was often the life of the party. Probably because she was still sober enough to be witty. The rest of us were too trashed. I still am. Carter must be too because I follow him to my place and we spend a few minutes trying to unlock the door before realizing that we're at my neighbors' house. We run away while spewing laughter, and when we finally reach the safety of my room, we lock the door as if everyone we wronged that night is hot on our trail.

"That was epic," Carter says, collapsing onto my bed.

"It was," I agree, "but I can't wait to get out of these."

I don't mean my shoes. I kick those off, but it's the stupid thermal underwear that's driving me crazy. It had kept me warm when outside, but now I feel unbearably hot. I'm about to hoist up my skirt to take the underwear off when I notice Carter staring at me. He's propped up on his elbows, his butt on the mattress, his legs stretched out over the floor.

"What?" I say.

"Nothing. It's just…" He grins and shakes his head. "Nothing."

"I hate it when you do that. Just say it!"

He rolls his eyes, but he's smiling, like he has a secret to share. "You make a very pretty girl."

"Thanks," I say. "Between you and me, I'm glad I'm a boy. Being a girl is way harder than I thought it would be."

"How so?"

"Ever shaved your legs?" I ask.

"No. You?"

"This morning."

Carter scoffs. "You did not!"

"I did! I was originally going to wear tights until I read online that the hair would poke through." I pull the thermal underwear down and off. So much for being ladylike. Then I walk closer so he can see. "Feel it," I say. "I cut myself about ninety times, but I'm silky smooth."

Carter sits upright. I expect him to swipe an index finger along my leg in the same way a person might check for dust. Instead he puts an entire palm on my leg and slowly moves it up until the tips of his fingers touch the hem of my skirt. His eyes move up to meet mine and they're filled with lust.

"This is so confusing," he says.

"Hold that thought." I move to my shelves and switch on a small lamp. Then I turn off the overheard light. Now the room is dimmer. Cozier. I return to the bed where I was before, the breath short in my lungs. My head is woozy from alcohol and I know… I know this is a bad idea, but I don't care. I want him too much. "Keep going," I say.

"What?"

"Let's pretend. Who cares? Tonight, I'm a girl."

Carter licks his lips. He looks anything but certain, but then he touches my leg again, moving his hand up and down and sending tingles along my skin. I know if he reaches all the way up my skirt… Well, even the power of imagination has its limits. "Scoot back," I say, keeping my voice soft.

Carter shimmies further onto the bed, but he's still on his back, which is ideal. "Like this?"

"Yeah." I lay beside him, but I'm not quite as close to the headboard. I need to hide my face from him. I don't want to break the illusion. Not when I'm so close. I grab his sweater and shirt and pull up, exposing his stomach. When I place my hand there, I expect him to wince and pull away, but he doesn't, so I slide my hand up and down, and I nearly cry, because it feels good to touch him so intimately. I swear he's getting hard. The black jeans he's wearing look fuller than I've ever seen them. I'm terrified to reach for his belt, but I do so anyway. I'm starting to undo it when I look up. I can't help myself. I need to see his face.

Carter is still propped up on his elbows. He's watching me. I don't see any conflict there. He wants this too. We're finally walking alongside each other instead of me having to give chase. Sex is no longer important. I still plan on going there, but I need him to know first. I need to say how I feel, so I move upwards and bring my face close to his, our lips about to touch.

"Carter—"

That's as far as I get. He flinches and the spell is broken. Maybe my voice is too deep or too familiar. Maybe I should have just gone down on him and left the rest for another day. All I know is that he's rolling away and getting to his feet. He can't even face me as he inches toward the door.

"Wait!" I plead. "We'll start over. I messed it up. Please!"

I shout this last word. I'm not proud of how pathetic I sound, but I'm so freaking desperate for him that I'll beg if need be.

I almost start to when he turns on the overhead light. Then he glances at me and away again. "Take off the wig. Please."

I don't want to. I feel like it'll rob me of my power and that I won't be able to cast the same spell again. I guess that's the point. I reach up and pull it off. "Okay."

He looks over his shoulder at me. "I can't… I can't do that with you. I'm not like that."

"I don't care," I say. "It doesn't have to mean anything."

"It would to me," he says.

And I know I've lost, because it would mean everything to me. Absolutely everything. "I shouldn't have said that," I mumble. "I just… Do you know what it's like to want somebody so bad that it hurts?"

"Yeah," he says, voice hoarse. "I do."

For a second I think he means me. Then my brain sobers up enough to remember that he and I aren't the only people in the world. I like to pretend that we are, but no. She's out there. Maybe I should have bought a blue wig instead. "I'm sorry," I say. "I'm really drunk."

"So am I," he says, turning around at last. "Drunk and sorry."

"Okay. Will you please stay? I won't… It'll be just like how it always is."

"Yeah. Okay."

Silence fills the room. That's never happened before. Not with me and him. We're always talking. We get in trouble for it at school, my parents have had to ask us to keep it down, and even our friends complain when we get lost in private conversations. And now it's like we've run out of words.

"We should probably crash," Carter says at last.

I can only nod. He turns off the overhead light again and then the lamp. I take off the rest of my costume. We always strip down to our underwear before going to bed. Not him. Not this time. I hear his shoes hit the floor but nothing more before he crawls into bed. When my eyes adjust to the darkness, I notice his back is to me. That's how it remains for the next hour as I lay there and stare at the massive gulf between us.

"Andrew! Carter! Time to wake up!"

I groan loud enough to assure my mother that we're awake. Halloween should never be followed by a school day. Ever. I lay there for a second, puzzled by the remnants of a dream in which I was shopping in Diagon Alley for the perfect wig. When I found it, it was already being worn by Voldemort, who looked rather demure with long silky hair flowing over his shoulders.

Then the events of the previous night come rushing back to me and I sit upright. Carter is already up, his back to me.

"You okay?" I ask.

"Yeah," he says. "A little hungover, but it's not too bad."

"That's not what I meant."

"I know."

I wait for him to say more. When he doesn't, I decide to get to the point. "I don't want to lose you."

He looks over at me in surprise. "Are you kidding? I took an oath! So did you!"

That he takes the promise so seriously fills my heart with warmth. "Right. I'm just worried that last night freaked you out."

"Kind of," he admits. His brow furrows up before he looks away again. "How do I tell if I'm bisexual?"

I exhale, because it's a big question. If last night was a spark, then the smartest thing I can do is fan it into a flame. I should insist that he is bisexual, and that he needs to explore that, but the truth is... "I don't know."

"How did you figure it out?"

"That I'm gay?" I think about it. Hormones have led me down some very odd paths. I've looked at all kinds of porn and entertained all sorts of fantasies. Some of those worked; the rest didn't. That was all part of discovering who I am and what I like, but the gay stuff, seeing two guys together, that got in deep, no matter how hard I resisted. "Let me ask you this. Have you ever had thoughts about other guys that you can't get out of your head? Because when I figured out that I was gay, I went into denial, but part of me knew anyway. I fought against it, but I still knew."

"I've wondered if other guys are bigger than me," Carter says.

I refrain from asking him for measurements. "Right, but were you thinking about them naked and getting turned on?"

"No."

"Oh. Have you ever thought about kissing another guy?"

"Yeah," he says. Then he glances over his shoulder again. At me.

"Before last night."

"No. Never. I guess I might have seen two dudes kissing on TV and wondered how it would feel. Like if it would be different than kissing a girl."

"It is," I say. "The only real difference is the scruff."

Now he turns his body to face me. "But you're—"

"It took me a while to figure things out. I kissed girls before I ever kissed a guy, and it was fine. It felt weird the first time, but kind of nice after that. When I finally kissed a guy, it was electric, and I knew for sure.

An unspoken suggestion hangs in the air. He should kiss me. If he really is straight, then at least I'll have this moment to treasure.

-knock knock knock-

"Andrew! Are you awake? You have school!"

"Yes, Mom!" I shout. "We're getting ready. Stop worrying!"

I sigh and smell stale beer. Morning breath and parents. Double mood-killer. "Maybe we should talk about this later."

"Okay."

I throw off the sheets. He's seen me in my underwear before, and I've seen glimpses of him, although we're both usually quick to get dressed. Not this time. I pick up my clothes and walk around the bed to stand by the door. He glances at me and away again, but I don't get dressed.

"Hey. Look at me. Seriously. Really look at me. Does this do anything for you?"

His eyes move up and down my body. They even linger on my underwear. Then his expression becomes apologetic. "I want it to," he says.

That's sweet. But it's not the answer I was hoping for.

Chapter Ten

The morning got off to a rough start, and the rest of the day follows suit. School is awkward. Carter is quiet for most of it, aside from a few breaks in the clouds when things feel normal between us again. The clock is running slower than usual today, I swear. The final school bell doesn't help much either because I have to rush to work right after.

I manage to muscle through to the end of my shift, but now I'm exhausted, and when I step outside, it's pouring rain. I can't walk home in this weather. Reed is working too, which means I need to call my parents for a ride. Yay. I'm reaching for my phone when headlights turn on in the parking lot and catch my attention. The engine of an old Camaro sputters to life before driving over to the curb. The passenger side door opens and I see Jackson inside.

"Want a ride?" he says.

"Yes!" I run for his car and dive inside just before the rain gets even worse. "My hero," I say, grinning at him as I shut the door. "What are you doing here?"

"I stopped by to pick up my check."

I make a face at him. "You don't do direct deposit? I didn't see you inside."

"Fine," he says. "I was looking at the schedule and noticed that you're working tonight. The weather sucks, so…"

"Thanks!" I say. "You didn't have to, but I'm glad you did."

"I was on my way home anyway." He puts the car in drive and we're off. His music stays off this time. The patter of rain on top of the car accompanies us as we slowly cruise through the adjoining neighborhood. "Last night was wild," he says.

"You aren't kidding," I breathe. "I'm still recovering."

He shoots me a sly smile. "That just means you need to practice more."

"No thanks," I say with a chuckle.

"You left at a good time."

"Why's that?"

His grip on the steering wheel tightens. "Bobby and Olivia got into a bad argument. It was loud."

"Oh. That sucks."

"I don't think they make a good couple."

"Me neither," I admit, "but I have a hard time imagining Bobby being with anyone."

He's quiet. I regret my words for a couple of reasons. I'm bad-mouthing his best friend, and if Jackson does have romantic feelings for him, that makes it twice as rude. "Sorry," I say. "I only meant the other girls we hang out with. None of them seem like a good match either. Definitely not Becca. Or the other one. Whatever her name is. I really need to write these things down."

Jackson laughs. "I think they've had it with us anyway. Ever since Harper and I split, she and Becca haven't been coming around as much."

"You're such a player," I say, wanting to build him up. "Breaking hearts and ruining friendships."

"Yeah." For whatever reason, Jackson gets quiet. He remains that way until we pull over in front of my house. "Carter sure got trashed last night."

"Yeah. I did too."

"He stayed the night with you, right?"

"Right." I feel like he's asking a different question. In fact, I'm so confident that I choose to give him the answer he really wants. "Nothing happened between us. I'm starting to think it never will."

Jackson looks over at me. I can't tell his intent. I find him incredibly difficult to read. "Are you okay with that?" he asks.

"Not really. Are you asking because you want to know? Or did Bobby send you to find out? Because I'm worried about him and Carter. Things got tense last night."

"Bobby is all right," Jackson says.

"Is he? I don't mean to hate on him, but Bobby seems a little crazy. Like, the dangerous sort of crazy. I'm sorry if that seems judgmental, but the first few times I met him involved personal threats and injuries."

Jackson chews his bottom lip and doesn't reply.

There's something he's not telling me, so I press the issue. "You don't think he's slightly unhinged?"

Jackson puts the car in park and kills the headlights. "Bobby has been my best friend since the third grade."

"Oh. I didn't know that."

"Yeah. Before I met him, I used to live in North Lawndale. You know that neighborhood?"

"No."

"It's not far from here. Bad place to live. My dad was shot there when I was little."

"Jesus! I had no idea! I'm sorry."

Jackson nods. "He was a smart man. Had a life insurance policy. It wasn't much, but my mom used it for a down payment on a house here. She had to try seven different banks before she found one willing to take a risk. My aunt and grandmother pooled their money too. They did it all for me and my cousin. They didn't want us growing up in a neighborhood where that sort of thing can happen. I guess it can happen anywhere in Chi-Town, but it's a lot less likely in Oak Park. When we first got here, I wasn't the only black kid, but I wasn't used to the neighborhood being so mixed. I felt like I stood out, and that made me shy." He narrows his eyes, like he's waiting for me to make fun of him.

"I'm not surprised," I say. "You had just lost your father. That must have made you feel vulnerable too."

"Yeah," Jackson says. "It was a rough time. School especially. I was scared I would lose my mom and wanted to be with her. Things got better when I met Bobby. He came right up to me one day and acted like we'd always known each other. We've been best friends ever since. When his dad ran off, that only made us closer. It's not just me though. Everyone in our clique, we're outcasts. Bobby sees that. He notices the lonely people and gives them something to belong to, no matter how fucked up we are or how screwed up he is. So, yeah, he can be an asshole, but at least he brought us all together."

"I didn't mean to badmouth him," I say.

"I get it," Jackson replies. "His methods are questionable. Pedro barely spoke English when we met him, and Bobby kept giving him shit about it. Called him a stupid spic and things like that. Pedro even broke down and cried once, but Bobby kept making him talk, and when *someone else* called him a spic, Bobby punched that guy in the mouth."

I don't hide my shock. "There's got to be a better way. I'm sorry, but couldn't he have encouraged Pedro or tutored him?" I snort and shake my head. "I know how cheesy that sounds, but seriously."

"I'm with you, man," Jackson says. "I've tried to keep Bobby in check, but it's not easy. He's good practice, actually."

"For what?"

Jackson licks his lips and glances over at me. "I'm going into the academy after I graduate. I might get my bachelor's first. I need to figure that out soon, but I'm going into law enforcement."

"You're going to be a police officer?" I say in disbelief. "The guy who helped us steal a keg last night?"

"I was a passive observer," Jackson says, a hint of humor in his voice. "I didn't lift a finger to help."

"You weren't so passive when it came time to drink the beer!"

"Ha! I guess not."

"What's your last name?"

"Pearson. Why?"

"That means you'll be Officer Pearson. I just wanted to check how it sounds. I think it works."

"I won't be a mere police officer. I'm going to make detective. You'll see."

"Detective Pearson," I amend. "I know you'll get there because you have a huge advantage."

"What's that?"

"Years of direct access to a criminal mind. What if the day comes that you have to arrest Bobby?"

Jackson grimaces. "I won't even go there. I'll get him on the straight and narrow before then. For now, we're still in high school. We're supposed to do stupid shit."

"I'm with you on that," I say. "That's what Halloween was about for me."

The rain finally lets up. Now's my chance to get inside the house without getting wet, but I don't have to go alone. "Do you want to come in? Hang out for a while?"

Jackson chews his bottom lip again. Then he shakes his head. "Better not."

"Okay. Well… Thanks for the ride."

Jackson leans over, just like he did last time, and pulls the handle to open the door. "It sticks," he explains. I catch a whiff of his cologne before he leans back. My first impression couldn't have been more wrong. I'm not entirely sure what to make of him, but I stare long enough that he tilts his head toward the house and says, "Better go. The sky isn't clear yet."

"Yeah. Okay. Thanks!"

I make a run for it, and he's right. Just after I reach the

covered porch, the rain comes hammering down again, which makes it hard to see his car as it drives away.

Does your brother seem okay to you?

I'm sitting in the downstairs family room. The TV is off because the shows failed to suck me in, and picking up a video game controller feels like too much effort. I'm exhausted from one very long day, but I can't seem to concentrate or get my eyes to close long enough to sleep. All I can think about is lifting up Carter's shirt the night before and how good his skin felt. I keep picturing the arc of his belt when I started to loosen it. I wish I could go back and do it all over again. I would keep going instead of worrying about consequences. Or I wouldn't do anything at all, because he's not texting. We usually send a few messages back and forth before bed to make plans for the next day. Not tonight. So instead I have my legs balled up beneath me in one corner of the couch as I text his sister.

I guess, she writes back. *Why?*

He's been really quiet today.

Quiet how?

Wasn't that obvious? *Quiet as in not talking very much.*

Her response is almost instantaneous. *But he's talking? He says things back to you?*

I make a face at the phone, even though she can't see it. *Yeah. Of course. How come?*

Because the quieter Carter gets, the more upset he is.

Shit. So he is unhappy with me. Or us.

Did something happen? she texts.

We just drank too much. That was the cause, not the effect, but it's technically not a lie.

Okay. If he ever stops talking, tell me right away.

This is getting weirder and weirder. *Has that ever happened before?*

Why do you think we moved here?

My stomach sinks. I remember Carter saying something about how he stopped talking to everyone before coming to Chicago. That had seemed odd at the time, but I figured he meant he had distanced himself from everyone.

You tell me, I send back.

Then I wait. And wait. I'm about to point out that *she's*

stopped talking when a response finally comes.

I just checked on him. He's fine.

Good. I still want to know why you guys moved here.

Leave it, she sends back. *If you care about him, just leave it alone. Please.*

If there's one thing I'm certain of in my increasingly confusing life, it's that I care about Carter. So I let the subject drop. This doesn't help me find sleep though. Resigned to my fate, I turn on the television again and stare unseeing at the screen.

"You're in high spirits today," Gerald says. His glasses are off and he's polishing them while smiling at me.

I match his expression. Another week has gone by, and like an elastic band that was stretched to its limit and carefully relaxed again, things have returned to their normal shape. Mostly. I still feel like Carter is abnormally cautious around me, and the resentment between him and Bobby remains, but it's not growing. The situation seems stable. The elastic band isn't going to break or go shooting off into space. We're all okay.

"I'm glad," Gerald continues, returning his glasses to his nose, "because today's exercise is going to be challenging. And a little strange."

"Sounds fun." I'm really enjoying the anger management stuff. Schools teach us a lot of different things, but they never offer much guidance on who we are or how our minds work. This baffles me, since learning how to control our emotions and understand our thoughts should take priority over memorizing who signed the Declaration of Independence or knowing the capital of Libya. If schools taught us more about ourselves, maybe people like Bobby wouldn't be so crazy.

To my surprise, he's the subject of the day.

"I want you to go back to your first day of school here," Gerald says. "Except this time I'll give you a super power."

"Shape-shifting!" I say instantly.

"I'm afraid you don't get a choice. You have the power to stop time."

"Nice!"

"With a catch," Gerald says. "Time freezes for everyone except those who are looking directly at you in that moment. Now then, put yourself in the following scenario: It's sixth period, and a well-meaning teacher has asked you to introduce yourself. You do so, and just as it happened in real life, when you go to sit down…"

"I stop time."

"Not yet, because you don't expect there to be a problem. You can't predict the future. Only once your butt hits the ground do you use your power. Everyone in the classroom is now frozen except for you and Bobby. What happens next?"

"I punch him," I say. I know it's not the right answer, but they don't call me Honest Andrew for nothing.

"Okay," Gerald says, seeming open to the idea. "How do you think he would react? Be realistic."

That's easy. Bobby would get angry and pull out his knife, and I would end up bleeding to death. I don't want to tell Gerald about the knife, so I keep it simple. "I'd get my ass kicked."

"In other words, the situation would escalate and end poorly. Let's rewind and try again. What else could you do?"

"I could run."

"That's often a wise choice. Many people feel the need to cling to their pride, but what use is pride if you're lying in a hospital bed, or worse, a coffin? It's better to remove yourself from any potential harm. Good job! For the sake of this exercise, let's assume that Bobby had only intended to pull a prank and nothing more. You don't feel like your life or safety is threatened. What else could you do?"

"I guess I could try to reason with him."

"Okay. What would you say?"

I think about it, and I'm surprised how emotional the answer makes me. My throat feels tight as I try to get the words out. "I'd say that he can hate me all he wants and be mean to me, but it won't change who I am. I didn't choose to be gay. I'd ask him to imagine himself in that situation—how total strangers would hate him for who he is. I'd point out that, no matter how bad it gets or how much abuse he takes, he still wouldn't be able to change. It's a hopeless situation. Or it can feel that way at times. So yeah… If all that doesn't get through to him—" I shrug. "I'd start time again and talk to you about being moved to a different seat or class."

"Excellent," Gerald says softly. "That's a very wise course of action."

"But," I say, "isn't it important to stand up for yourself? Isn't anger useful in that way?"

"In my mind, that *is* standing up for yourself, but by using reason instead of rage. You could have told Bobby that he was being—ahem—a small-minded asshole, which to be honest, was my personal assessment. As we've discussed, this would only have made him angrier no matter how good he is at masking it. By taking the higher road, you aren't feeding into his anger or increasing it. You have a chance, no matter how slim, of getting through to him."

"He could also decide that I'm an easy target."

"I don't think so. It takes tremendous courage to stay calm in the face of adversity and to express the truth of who you are. That having been said, there are legitimately disturbed people out there. If an attempt at reason fails, as you said before, it makes the most sense to remove yourself from the situation."

I rub my forehead and try to imagine staying calm in that scenario. It's not easy. "Don't you ever get angry?"

"Oh yes," Gerald says. "I was extremely angry that day, but I didn't act on it. Instead I thought quickly and sent you to someone I trust. Jill is very good at assessing a student's needs and guiding them in the right direction. I also filed a complaint with the principal. Bobby's actions didn't go unnoticed. In fact—and I probably shouldn't be telling you this—but he was in another altercation recently and played innocent then too. The incident involving you was taken into consideration by the principal when deciding his punishment. Bobby was suspended for a week, and if anything similar should happen again, he will be expelled."

Wow. I knew that Bobby had been suspended, but I didn't realize that him messing with me was partially responsible. I was the first strike out of a potential three, it would seem.

"This isn't an easy lesson to learn," Gerald says. "Like any skill, anger management takes practice. I'll teach you some techniques that might help, but the most crucial of them is using your mind. If you can think quickly and imagine different outcomes, just like we did today, then you'll soon learn to rely on logic rather than impulse."

"You want me to become a robot," I say teasingly.

Gerald smiles. "Not at all. Emotions are a wonderful

asset. Some more so than others. We wouldn't be human if we abandoned them completely."

I look to where Carter is sitting, and I agree. There are some emotions I would never willingly part with. No matter how bad they sometimes hurt.

"There's something I've been meaning to talk to you about," I say, pulling my eyes away from him.

Gerald nods. "Go ahead."

"You've worked with Carter long enough now to know how smart he is. The way he faked his way through school all those years, in the most honest way possible. It's not like he cheated. He didn't have people slip him the answers to tests or anything like that."

"He's a very clever young man," Gerald says, sounding amiable.

This makes me feel confident enough to propose my idea. "I think he should be allowed to use his phone when taking a test. You or another teacher could sit there and make sure he's not looking up answers. He only needs his phone to help him read. And to help with how he writes. That's not an unfair advantage. Everyone is walking around with a phone in their pocket these days. It's like when we're allowed to use a calculator in math class, since—"

Gerald holds up a hand to stop me. "I agree with you."

"You do?"

"Yes. I've had similar thoughts myself. I plan on discussing this with the principal before the end of semester exams."

"Cool, but I'm dreaming bigger than that."

Gerald humors me with a smile. "Oh?"

I glance over at Carter again to make sure he isn't listening. Maybe I should have talked to him about this first. "He failed his SATs," I whisper. "So I figured, if he can retake those and use his phone, he'll do a lot better."

Gerald exhales like it's a tall order. "That won't be as easy to arrange."

"He deserves another chance. You've seen his writing. It'll only get better if he goes to college, but first he needs to be accepted. He gets really down on himself about the dyslexia, so just imagine what a boost to his confidence it would be for him to pass his SATs and have options after we graduate."

"I'll have to discuss the idea with a few people. I can't make any promises, but I'll try." Gerald studies me for a moment. "You really want the best for him, don't you?"

I nod because it's true. Even if I can't have him, I want to give Carter all the good things he deserves.

Carter and I are on the couch in the downstairs family room. His laptop is half on his leg, half on mine, which I love because it means we're sitting so close that our shoulders are touching. When we're at his house, we sit at his desk in separate chairs. I much prefer our current situation. Reed hasn't moved in with his girlfriend yet, but lately he spends most nights at her place, so we often have the finished basement all to ourselves.

"What do you think?" Carter says, looking at me with a vulnerable expression.

He's always like that when revealing a new story idea. I still don't know what his big mysterious project is, but we're at the point where he's trusting me with his outlines before he begins to write a story. That's new. I have to admit that I'm struggling with the most recent one.

"So let me get this straight," I say. "A flying saucer lands on Earth—"

"Near Roswell."

"Naturally. And when the door or whatever opens, an elf steps out."

"Yeah!" Carter says. "Because it turns out all those fantasy worlds we read about are actually their own planets. That makes sense, right?"

"Yes," I say, thinking of the typical maps in front of fantasy novels that show vastly different land masses. "But elves who have advanced so far technologically that they have space travel wouldn't be elves anymore. They'd be, I dunno, Vulcans instead."

Carter's eyes go wide. Then he blinks. "They *are* similar, but Vulcans don't use magic. Elves do."

"Sure," I say, "but it's sort of like nerds. Some are really into math, some are into science, and some are into books."

"Like us?"

"Yup. Vulcans are just elves who are into logic instead of magic. Neither are known for their sense of humor, right?"

"Whoa! You're right! Vulcans are just space elves. Hey! Do

you think that Martians are actually space goblins?"

"Both are small and green," I say. "Dragons are just fire-breathing dinosaurs."

We entertain ourselves for a while by finding more parallels. Before long, Carter starts to despair.

"So my whole idea doesn't work," he says, shoulders slumping.

"It could!" I reassure him. "How about instead of a flying saucer, the elves land in some other kind of craft. A boat made of willow tree branches. Maybe it was grown for that purpose and is still a living plant. Imagine if their magic progressed like our technology did until elves have space travel."

"We could set this in the past," Carter says excitedly. "What if space elves came to earth a long time ago and took some of us back to their planet for a visit? That would explain how fantasy concepts became a part of our culture."

"I like it!"

Together we rewrite his outline until my fingers get so cold that I start making typos. It's late November in Chicago, and that winter the natives have so often warned us about is creeping in.

"Do you have any coffee?" Carter asks.

"Why? You hate coffee."

"True, but at least it's warm. I'm freezing my balls off!"

"It is chilly down here, isn't it?"

"Uh, yeah. Why do you think I'm wearing my coat indoors?"

Because it looks so adorable on him? I helped him pick it out when we were shopping at the mall. It's beige suede with a fluffy fleece lining. I feel like shoving my popsicle fingers inside it to warm them. And as an excuse to touch him.

"Do you think your parents would mind cranking up the heat?" Carter asks.

"I wish. It's nice and toasty upstairs. It's only the basement that's so cold. We could go up there, but you know… my parents." There's nothing wrong with my mom and dad per se. It's just hard to have as much fun when we can't talk openly.

"That's okay," Carter says, no doubt having similar thoughts. "How do you sleep down here though? It's like an icebox."

"It's not so bad," I say. "My mom bought me a really heavy comforter. A couple minutes under that thing and I'm warm again."

We look at each other. Then, without needing to speak a word, we set the laptop aside and race to my bedroom. Carter dives beneath the down comforter first. I'm not far behind. We pull it up to our necks like our lives depend on it.

"Isn't there a bedroom you can move into upstairs?" Carter asks.

"I *love* the basement," I say. "Usually. I like to pretend I live on my own." With him. I don't have to say everything that comes to mind, right?

"So you're going to spend the entire winter under this blanket?"

"Correct."

"Man…" Carter says, sounding relieved. "This *is* way better. I'm getting warm already."

"Lucky you," I say, my teeth nearly chattering. "I'm still freezing."

"That's what you get for being so skinny. You need to eat more."

"For real? I'm on the verge of getting hypothermia, and you're lecturing me about how I eat? If someone was dying of a heart attack, would you tell them they need to get more exercise?" I roll over and press my back to him. "Warm me up before I croak."

I want the body contact. That's no accident. But I didn't expect him to roll over and put an arm around me. His strong chest presses against my back, and his knees nestle into the crook of my legs. We're spooning!

"Better?" he asks.

"Getting there," I say, willing myself to stay cold so that this will last as long as possible. Over the past couple of weeks, there hasn't been a hint that Carter is interested in me or is still questioning his sexuality. I haven't brought up the subject, not wanting to scare him off, but I think about it every single day. I wonder if he does too. If so, he's done a remarkable job of hiding it. I want to reach down and take his hand. I resist this urge as the minutes tick by, but eventually the temptation is unbearable. I compromise by placing my arm against his and hugging it to my body.

"This is helping," I say. "Thanks."

Carter is quiet. Which, according to Vicky, means he's upset. I want to get him talking again, so I grasp for a topic.

"Maybe I can move upstairs for the winter," I try. "Like how rich people flock to Florida or wherever. The basement will be my summer home."

Silence. Almost. I feel Carter's chest shudder against my back right before I hear him sniff. It sounds wet, like he's crying. When I roll away to check, I catch him wiping at his eyes to hide the tears.

"What's going on?" I say.

"Nothing." Carter clenches his jaw. He's looking everywhere but at me.

That's obviously not true. "Would you just tell me? Please?"

Carter's breathing is heavy as he tries to get himself under control. "I miss Renzo," he says. These words are nearly enough to make him start crying again. I watch as he struggles to get himself under control. "I miss home."

"Then when we get the car, that'll be the first road trip we take." I'm willing to do anything to make him feel better, even though I'm starting to feel as envious of Renzo as I am of Olivia.

He keeps me waiting, but thank goodness I get a response. He even sounds tentatively hopeful. "Do you have enough saved up?"

I nod. "With my next paycheck, I'll have three thousand." I've been ridiculously stingy lately, but it's paid off. "Think I can get a decent car for six thousand?"

"If you want a car with two-hundred-thousand miles."

"I've seen a couple of options on eBay with fairly low mileage," I say, "but you're right. They all cost closer to seven."

Carter's eyes light up with an idea. "I can give you five hundred. That way, when your parents match what you've saved, you'll have seven grand to go shopping with."

"Would you still be able to help out with gas and insurance?"

"Yeah. Easily."

I prop myself up on an elbow in my excitement. "Then let's do it! We need a car anyway. I don't care how close the school is. I refuse to walk in the snow."

"And we'll take a trip down to Arizona?"

"Yup! We have five days off next week for Thanksgiving. How long will it take to drive down there?"

Carter reaches beneath the comforter and pulls out his phone. Soon we're shoulder to shoulder again—this time sitting up in bed—and making plans. I find myself increasingly distracted. I could understand if Carter needed to cry over missing a friend. Straight guys are under a lot of pressure to hide their emotions, but they still have them. What puzzles me is *when* he was moved to tears… While holding me. Why? Did that remind him of something that happened with Renzo? Were they that close? Because straight guys might have feelings, but I don't think they ever cuddle with each other. Do they? It's more than the winter I want to escape by driving south. I can't stand the suspense anymore. I want to finally solve the mystery of Carter. Getting to see where he came from is my best chance.

Chapter Eleven

"I get that you and Bobby are best friends," I say diplomatically.

Jackson is driving me home from work, which has become a regular thing. Normally only when we share a shift, but if the weather is particularly bad, he often makes an excuse to come get me.

"And that you probably tell him everything," I continue, "because that's how it works. But can you keep a secret? For me?"

Jackson's right hand is on the top of the steering wheel, his seat slightly reclined. Music is playing in the background, but it's soft and soulful. He doesn't look over at me. His dark eyes stay fixed on the road as he says, "This is about Carter, isn't it? As in, you and Carter."

I swallow and hope that I'm not making a mistake by confiding in him. Just the suggestion that something is going on between us is enough to stir up rumors and put a strain on my relationship with Carter. "Yeah."

"Bobby and I don't talk about that kind of thing," Jackson says. "Ever."

"Oh."

Just once, could the people in my life please say something that doesn't confuse me? I hesitate long enough that Jackson finally looks over.

"You can trust me," he says.

And I believe him. "Carter and I cuddled yesterday."

I expect him to laugh or make a joke because now that I've said it out loud, it sounds silly.

"Cuddled how exactly?" Jackson says. "What were the circumstances?"

I tell him. All of it. Even the part about Carter crying, which feels like a betrayal. He didn't swear me to secrecy, but I know Carter wouldn't want anyone to know. As the car pulls over in front of my house, I eagerly await Jackson's assessment. All he does is puff up his cheeks and blow out.

"Let me ask you this," I say. "Do straight guys have moments like these with each other? Do they get emotional and let themselves be vulnerable?"

"I'm not the right guy to ask about that sort of thing."

I feel like he's alluding to more, and it's not the first time, so I decide to be direct. "Why not?"

Jackson scowls. He puts the car in park. Then he turns his head toward the window on his side of the car. I wonder if he's looking at my house and hinting that I should go.

When he speaks, his voice is so quiet that I barely hear him. "Can you keep a secret?"

I reach to turn down the stereo. "You already know one of mine," I say.

"Yeah, but mine's a lot bigger."

I could easily make that into a joke, but his voice is raw, so I don't. "I swear I won't tell anyone."

"Even Carter? Even if you end up together? Because I've never told anyone this."

"I swear on my grandmother's grave," I say. For me, it's the most sacred oath I can take.

Jackson finally looks at me, and he almost seems angry. Or I guess he's just defensive. I have an idea of what's coming. I think Jackson might be gay. Or at least bi. If so, it won't be a shock to me. In fact, I'd feel a lot less lonely.

"Bobby and I, we used to mess around."

My mouth drops open. "You mean sexually?"

Jackson is rapping his knuckles against the steering wheel, one of his legs bouncing up and down. He's jittery and nervous, but his body goes perfectly still just before he nods. Once. If I had blinked, I would have missed it.

"Okay," I say, trying to come to grips with this new information. "When? Recently?"

"No," Jackson says. "Junior high. Mostly. And it was always him asking me to do things. He didn't reciprocate."

"Oh." They say that guys experiment with each other. That's normal. I was too closeted to ever risk it, but from what I understand, it's usually when they're just figuring things out. Or sometimes in college, but I don't think it means anything. Unless… "If you don't mind me asking, did you like it?" I shake my head. "That's not the right question. Did you… *Do you* like him? Bobby. Do you love him?"

Jackson swallows. "Yeah. At least I did."

"Then you're…"

Jackson shakes his head. His jaw is clenching and his expression becomes hard. "I can't afford to be anything but straight. I have to pass a psychological screening to become a police officer. Blacks statistically fail those more often than white people. Did you know that? They did a study in Philly. I wasn't surprised by the results. Let me ask you this: What color are most police officers you meet?"

"White," I answer, "but I really don't see what race has do to with—"

"The odds are already stacked against me. My family is depending on me too. Not financially, but they have all these dreams for me, and they're religious, so I can't. I can't be anything like that."

"I felt the same way." I turn in my seat to face him. "I don't know what it's like to be black or to worry about becoming a police officer, but I thought I would be letting everyone down. I was sure my parents would be disappointed in me, even if they didn't show it. I also have religious relatives, but in the end, all of them kept loving me. Some of them don't get it or approve, but I feel the same way about aspects of their lives. Especially who they vote for. Family is weird. We're like strangers who have agreed to stick it out together, no matter how little we have in common."

"That's not always how it works," Jackson says. "I've heard stories. Some people end up on the streets."

"If that happens, you'll come live with me. My brother is moving out anyway, and once we graduate, we'll get a place together."

Jackson raises an eyebrow. Then he starts laughing. "You're serious, aren't you?"

"Yeah! Why not? But I bet it won't come to that. So, um… Just between you and me, do you think you're gay?"

Jackson licks his lips, and it takes him a while, but he nods. "I'm pretty sure. Yeah."

"Then let me be the first person to congratulate you on coming out."

"Hey," Jackson says, holding up his hands and shaking his head. "I didn't say anything about wanting to come out."

"You did anyway. You came out to me. You don't have to tell anyone else until you're ready. It's usually a gradual process. You tell those who you think you can trust, and when that goes okay, you tell the people you're a little less certain of and so on. When and how is up to you. For now, I'll keep your secret."

"Thanks," Jackson says. "I've been dying to talk to you about it, ever since that first day at the park. I thought Bobby was just giving you shit until you stomped off. Afterwards, he told me what happened—how you admitted to the entire class that you're gay. And how he pulled out your chair when you were trying to sit. I was pissed. I couldn't show it, but I was."

"That makes me feel better," I say. "Wait a minute. Why is Bobby such a homophobic asshole if you guys used to mess around? Oh. Never mind. It's a sad fact of life that the most vehement homophobes are usually closeted. That's another reason to consider coming out. When denial isn't enough, some people turn to hate. It's bad enough when that's directed inward, but the worst of us turn it on our own kind."

Jackson nods musingly. "You're right, but I don't think Bobby is gay. He's never shown any kind of emotion toward me. What happened between you and Carter yesterday—I would have killed for Bobby to do that with me."

"Would have," I repeat. "What about now?"

Jackson shrugs. "Sometimes I want to hate him, but maybe it's like you said: Hate is what we use to cover up how we actually feel."

I exhale, hoping that it never gets that bad with Carter and me. "So what exactly happened between you and Bobby? If you don't mind me asking."

Jackson looks at me like he's still trying to decide if I'm trustworthy.

"You're in too deep," I say with a chuckle. "Both of us are. We might as well bare our souls to each other."

"Heh. I guess so. Okay." He takes a deep breath. "We used to look at porn together at my house. Bobby's mom had a parental lock on their internet. Believe it or not, she used to try to keep him in line. I guess he wore her down over the years. Anyway, we were young. Hormones and all that. That led to…"

His expression is pleading with me to fill in the pieces, so I give it my best guess. "You used to beat off together?"

"Yeah," Jackson says. "Just a few times. I was really into it because even back then, I knew I liked guys. When did you figure it out?"

"Really early on," I say. "Although I didn't put a label on it until I was twelve or so."

"Same here. Anyway, one day Bobby suggests we do more. He didn't have any luck with girls back then, and he wanted to experience... certain things. So he suggested we take turns."

"Oral?" I ask.

Jackson's skin is too dark for me to detect a blush, but he manages to look plenty embarrassed. "Yeah. He told me to go first, and that he would repay the favor. He never did, but I didn't care. The same thing happened again a few days later. After that, he stopped pretending he would do anything for me. It was always one-sided. When he finally found a girl he could have sex with, all that stopped, and I—" Jackson's face becomes a mask of pain. He hides this quickly, but I still ache for him. "I felt like my heart was breaking, and that's when I knew for sure. I'm gay, and I love him. Loved him. Whatever."

"That's rough. I'm sorry."

Jackson chews his lip and nods. "Bobby never called me names. Not like he does with you. He never accused me of being gay. Maybe because he worried it would implicate him too. That, and I always made sure to act more reluctant than I really was. I think, to him, it's just a power trip. But it's weird sometimes. Do you remember on Halloween, how he wanted Carter to stay the night?"

"Yeah," I say, my skin already starting to crawl.

"I swear he had that same look in his eye, like he wanted to see if he could get another guy to serve him in that way. I know Bobby doesn't have feelings for Carter. I'm sure of it. All he does is talk about how in love with Olivia he is."

"We should probably hate her," I say.

"I've tried," Jackson replies.

"Me too." I never go out my way to talk to her, but each time we interact, I always find myself liking her against my will. "So you think Bobby wanted to sleep with Carter?"

"I don't know. He didn't invite me to stay the night, I know that much. I did anyway."

"Oh." A question reaches my lips, but I stop it before it can escape. Jackson is staring out the windshield, but he keeps looking at me nervously out of the corner of his eye. I can't help it. I have to know. "Did anything happen?"

"Yes," Jackson says. His lip trembles. "Please don't tell her! I know it was wrong. Usually it's only when he's between girls, but Olivia wasn't putting out, and Bobby was frustrated, and fuck, I guess I am too and have been for years." He wipes at his eyes. "I don't want to love him anymore. It hurts too much."

I put my hand on his shoulder and squeeze. "Then you've got to stop. He won't. To Bobby it's just convenience, or like you said, some sort of twisted powerplay. You have to be the one to end it."

"That easy, huh?" Jackson growls. "Could you end it if it was you and Carter?"

I don't take offense at his anger. I know it's not directed at me. I'm just the first person he's been able to express it to. And he's right. Part of me envies him. I'm so desperate for Carter that I'll take anything I can get, but I know if he put me through the same thing, if he only gave to me—or took, I suppose—when he didn't have a girl in the picture, it would slowly eat me up inside. Maybe I would start to hate him too. That would hurt even more.

"I'd quit while I was still able to love him," I say. "I feel like that's worth hanging on to, even if it's never reciprocated."

Jackson shakes his head. He's looking out the window again when he finally says, "You're right. I know you are."

We talk a lot after that. Jackson has questions, and I try to give him answers. Most of it revolves around coming out, or how I've dealt with fear, homophobia, or the uncertain future, because gay people don't have a lot of guideposts. We don't bank on settling down with someone and having kids. Not all straight people do either, but at least they have a Plan A to accept, alter, or reject.

Jackson seems fixated on the negative aspects of being gay, so I talk about the good stuff. How amazing it is to finally find that first special person; how liberating it can be to let go of preconceived notions and embrace discovery. Learning not to care so much about what other people think is pretty great too. While we're still on the positive, I invite him inside, thinking it will be good for him to see how accepting my parents are.

"No way," Jackson says with a smirk. "I've heard your place is one big refrigerator."

"Just the basement," I say, "which is where I basically spend my every waking hour."

"Raincheck," Jackson says. "I need to head home. Thanks for letting me get all this off my chest."

"You too," I say. "I like that we can confide in each other now."

"Yeah."

I reach for the door handle and pull, but nothing happens.

Jackson reaches across me, like he always does, and I swear he doesn't do anything special, but this time the door opens. "Like I told you," he says, "it sticks."

He smiles, and so do I. This time, when I walk to my house, he doesn't drive away until I'm safely inside.

I'm on the couch, watching TV under three layers of blankets, when Reed enters the family room lugging a big box in his arms. Even beneath a thick sweater, I can see his biceps bulging, which annoys me to no end. When the genetic dice were rolled, I sure wouldn't have minded getting some of those muscles.

"What's that?" I ask him.

"You got a package," Reed says, setting it down with a thump on the coffee table. "Or somebody left this for you. I don't think they mailed it."

I peer at the graphics on the box and read the words aloud, trying to make sense of what I'm seeing. "Oil-filled radiant heater?"

"Probably so you don't freeze to death down here," Reed says. "And then there's this."

He peels a yellow sticky note off the box and hands it to me. I read it, my confusion turning to amusement.

Welcome to Chicago. -J

It's only been a day since Jackson and I had our big talk. Maybe this is his idea of a thank-you present. If it keeps me warm, I'm open to trying anything.

"Is this from your boyfriend?" Reed asks.

"No. I don't have one."

Not that the thought hadn't occurred to me. It's not often that I meet another gay guy, and whenever I do, I always consider the possibility. I imagine it's like being part of a nearly-extinct species. In the rare instances when you cross paths with another of your kind, the potential for pairing up is most definitely on your mind. I don't see it working in our case. Jackson and I are too wrapped up in other guys. I still haven't given up hope on Carter. Not completely.

Reed plops down on the couch next to me. "We need to talk."

I hate that phrase. It always fills my stomach with dread. "Okay."

"Dakota asked me to move in with her." Reed gets this dopey grin on his face. "For months now, I've been trying to work up the courage to mention the idea to her, and then in the middle of dinner last night, she asks like it's not a big deal. 'Maybe you should move in.' Can you believe that?"

I can. I had even convinced myself I was looking forward to this moment, but now that it's here, I just feel sad. "When?"

"Thanksgiving weekend. Hey! Can you help me move a few things?"

"If I'm in town." I tell him about my plans with Carter.

"Oh. That's cool. If things don't work out with the car…"

I sigh, but not because I'm irritated. This sucks. That's all. "Of course I'll help."

"Thanks." Reed slugs me in the arm, but not nearly as hard as he usually does. "Listen, I know how crazy senior year can be. It's way too easy to get into trouble."

"You mean that time you got arrested for skinny dipping?"

"Yeah," Reed says. He opens his mouth to continue, but I don't let him.

"It wasn't even a lake or a public pool. That would make sense. Instead you were swimming naked in some old lady's backyard."

"I remember," Reed says through gritted teeth. "And if you don't shut up and let me talk, I'm going to strip you down and throw you in *our* neighbor's backyard!"

I grin shamelessly. "Make it Carter's yard and you've got a deal."

"You are so twisted," Reed says, sounding exhausted. "What I wanted to say is that I haven't had any luck finding a new job yet. I'm still working at the same crappy bar, so I'll be around. I meant what I said about not being the cool older brother who buys you booze, *but*, if you do get into trouble and you need someone to help bail you out, you can always call me. Okay? I mean it. Just because I'm moving doesn't mean I won't be there for you."

I'm touched by this. I don't want to be, but I am. I put on an exaggerated frown. Then I slowly lean in his direction until I topple over. He catches me in one arm, and for a moment, we just sit there, my head resting against his chest.

"You suck," I say.

"I know. I love you too, baby brother." He gives me a noogie and shoves me away. "What are you watching?"

I tell him, and we stare at the television together while we still can. I guess this is going to be a lot less common from now on. When I finally get restless, I rise and open the box for the new heater and plug it in. If I'm destined to be alone, at least I won't be cold.

We don't get the car as soon as we hoped. What looked like a promising eBay listing turned out to be misleading. If my dad wasn't with me, I probably would have bought the car anyway, despite all of its unadvertised faults. Mostly to make Carter happy. All he talks about is how we're driving down to Arizona. I beg my dad to look at a few more cars with me, but he isn't satisfied with them either. Time is up. Thanksgiving break is here. I help Reed move out, which is bittersweet, and to keep with that theme, I finally do get my first car, but it's on the last day of the holiday when it's too late to go anywhere.

Carter is cool about this. We make new plans to drive down during our winter break, which is even longer and will give us more time to get down there and back.

It's business as usual until then. School is going well. Carter is really thriving. He was allowed to take his finals using his phone, and his grades have improved. Even better, Gerald fought tooth and nail for Carter to retake his SATs under special conditions. He was successful. Carter and I studied for them together and had some stressful nights, but all the effort paid off. Carter received a passing score. We've since sent applications to the same universities, and I'm praying that his recent academic improvement will be enough to get him into one. Preferably a college that wants me too.

My friendship with Jackson continues to flourish. He remains reluctant to come inside my home, and he hasn't invited me over either. I don't take this personally. I know he's struggling with coming out and accepting himself. Some days he refuses to acknowledge the subject. On others he's eager to discuss it again. We often cover the same ground, but I remember needing frequent reassurance. Aside from that, we have a lot of fun together at work, although I do sort of miss the rides home with him.

The new car is awesome. It's a cherry-red 2012 Fiat 500 hatchback. I never expected to get anything so cute. It has a few dings and the motor isn't powerful, but I only needed a car to get around in. It's a very small car though, and Chicago's streets are half asphalt, half potholes, so it's not the most comfortable ride. I've learned to swerve down the streets like a drunk to avoid the larger craters.

When I first got the car, it only had forty thousand miles on it. Now that the last week of December is here, we plan on adding over three thousand to that number. Our families pressure us into staying for Christmas, especially since this will likely be our last one at home. The day after the holiday, we hit the road, and I couldn't be happier. An entire week alone with Carter!

That's become rare as of late. Olivia now sits at our table in the library. She eats lunch with us too, and more often than not, after school we hang out with her, Bobby, and everyone else. I only really mind when I let myself dwell on it. She's still likeable and—thank goodness—tied up in a relationship. I just miss having so much one-on-one time with Carter. Without it, my progress in getting through his last remaining barriers seems to have stalled.

Not anymore. Now we're free to talk about the dumbest things again without worrying about losing anyone, or Bobby making fun of us.

"The Sorting Hat is the real villain of the series," Carter says, sounding supremely confident in his assertion.

Me? I'm all doubts. "That doesn't make sense."

"Think about it." Carter says from the passenger seat. "All the kids with evil potential get sorted into Slytherin. How is that a good idea? Take someone like Voldemort. When he was still Tom Riddle, the Sorting Hat should have put him in Gryffindor. Surround him with a bunch of heroic-types, so he grows up with good influences. Instead, the Sorting Hat keeps all the bad kids together where they only get worse. Doesn't that seem odd to you?"

"It's segregation!" I say, finally seeing his point.

"Exactly. And when you're raised in an environment where that's considered normal—"

"And acceptable!"

"—then of course you get racist turds like the Death Eaters."

"We should write a fanfic about a new generation of students who feel misplaced in their houses, and who team up to destroy the Sorting Hat."

"One student from each house," Carter says.

"Yeah!"

I have to ease off the accelerator in my excitement. This is too good. Carter and me. That's all I want from now on. I can forgive Reed for moving out if this is how it feels when he's with Dakota. I hope it is. We take turns driving, and on occasion, we crank up the music. But most of the time we're talking. This makes the trip go by in the blink of an eye. A very long blink. More like a nap, really, but we reach our halfway point without either of us feeling like the trip has lost its luster.

We're in Oklahoma when we check into a hotel, my Christmas gift to Carter. The original plan was to drive south until the weather became warm enough to sleep in the car. The Fiat is tiny, and neither one of us was really looking forward to overnighting in it, so my parents helped me book a place for the drive down and up again.

I feel ridiculously grown up, staying in a hotel without supervision. Especially so far from home. Carter and I examine every detail of the room, which is nothing special, but because it's ours—even for just one night—it all seems enchanted.

Enchanted enough for something to happen between us? Maybe. We go out for some fast food, and later we put on swimsuits and hit the indoor pool. All part of my plan. I've seen him in his underwear plenty of times, but a wet swimsuit clinging to his hips (and everything in between) is something special. Besides, going swimming while everyone back home is freezing their asses off makes it twice as enjoyable, even if we are still indoors. Once we're back in the room, we crack open the window to enjoy the fresh air.

It's been a long day and we're both tired, but the good kind that feels relaxing. We're sitting on the bed together—I booked a double instead of a twin, pretending not to know the difference—and flipping through channels when Carter grabs the remote and switches off the television.

"There's something I've got to tell you," he says.

I look over at him. His face is serious. He's not about to burp or fart or anything silly like that. I'm on the verge of learning one of his secrets. I can feel it in my gut and see it from the struggle he goes through before he finally speaks.

"I'm not from Phoenix."

I stare. This isn't what I expected. "What?"

"I'm from Tucson."

"*What?*" I repeat, this time with added disbelief.

"Tucson. It's a city in Arizona."

"I know what it is," I say. "I just don't get why you would lie about something so trivial."

"Because it sounds cooler to say I'm from Phoenix. It's like telling people we're from Chicago, when technically we live in Oak Park."

"It's nothing like that!" I shoot back. "We live in the greater Chicago area. Tucson isn't that close to Phoenix, is it? And what about the museum I wanted to—"

"We can still do that," Carter says hurriedly. "Tucson is only an hour and a half away."

"What about the address I gave my parents?"

"Oh." Carter grins at me sheepishly. "I looked it up online. I don't know who lives there."

"You're such a turd!" I say, thwacking him with one of the pillows. "I can't believe you lied to me."

"You never have?"

"My family calls me—"

"Honest Andrew, I know. But have you?"

We're sitting on a bed that I intentionally feigned ignorance over, so no, I'm not completely innocent. Still, it kind of stings. "Do you lie a lot?" I ask.

"Only when it helps me seem cooler than I really am." He nudges me with his elbow. "Don't be mad."

"I'm not," I say, and it's true. I don't think I could ever be mad at him, or at least stay that way. He's my secret weakness. "What else haven't you told me?"

He gets quiet. *Really* quiet. The silence is deafening. Whatever his true secret is, I haven't learned it yet.

"I want to know who you are," I say, sounding vulnerable.

He notices, his reaction a guilty wince. "Sorry. You will. It just takes time. There are things you haven't told me yet, right?"

"Yeah." He doesn't know about Jackson. I had promised to keep that secret, and so far, I have. "You don't have to try to be cool around me. I already think you're cool. Like... the coolest friend I've ever had."

"Really?

"Yes." I say this firmly, so he'll know it's true.

His eyes shine in response. "I think you're amazing too."

I want to say what else I feel for him. He's right though. There are things I haven't told him, some of them major, because I also want him to think I'm cool. Cool enough to handle having a straight friend who I don't pressure into being something that he's not. That's a self-made promise I've kept so far, but if it turns out that he's bi or even curious, then I'm done holding back. I only need a clear sign from him—a signal that leaves no room for doubt. Drunken fumbling or confusing tears during a cuddle don't count. I need him to say that he wants me, or for him to make the first move. That's obviously not going to happen right now, so it's back to having fun.

"Wanna hit the vending machines?" I ask.

"Hell yeah!" he says. "And the ice machine. Something about filling a bucket with ice makes me ridiculously happy."

"Simple pleasures," I say. Like the time we spend together. I push him until he falls out of bed. Laughing, Carter launches himself over the edge of the mattress and drags me to the floor with him. Then we rise and walk out into the hall, turning each minute into magic.

Chapter Twelve

The closer we get to Tucson, the more nervous I become. I didn't have concerns before this trip began. I was looking forward to meeting hunky Renzo. I've stared at his photos plenty of times, but only when Carter wasn't in the room, because no matter what the girls may think, Renzo simply can't compare. Now I'm worried about how *I'll* measure up. What if we get to Tucson and I'm on the sidelines as Renzo and Carter exchange inside jokes and go racing off to climb cliffs.

I wish I could afford a hotel for the entire time we're there. Instead we'll be staying with Renzo's family, which is practical but it also means I'll be the third wheel until we begin the drive home.

Carter is increasingly quiet as we near his home town. He peps up somewhat when pointing out familiar sights, or when we step outside the car to fuel up and bask in warm weather that we appreciate more now that we've experienced the infamous Chicago winter.

For the final ten minutes of the drive, the GPS is the only voice in the car. *Turn left. Turn right. The destination is on your left.* We pull into the driveway of a large ranch-style house. I put the car in park and look over at Carter, but he still has his seatbelt on. He's in no hurry to leave the car. Despite my nerves, I'm eager to stretch my legs, so this really confuses me. Carter doesn't seem excited. I would be, if I was about to reunite with one of my best friends.

"Ready?" I ask.

"Before we go inside," Carter says, "we need to talk. I've been meaning to tell you about this the entire drive down. It's just... hard."

My stomach sinks. "Okay. I'm listening."

Something catches his eye through the windshield. Then he swears under his breath. I look in the same direction and see a woman coming toward us. She has a total mom vibe as she smiles and waves. Someone is behind her.

"Don't you dare laugh," Carter mutters under his breath. He turns a glare on me that's totally unexpected. "Swear you won't!"

I don't know what he's talking about. We don't have time to

discuss it. All I manage is a nod before Carter undoes his seatbelt and opens the passenger-side door.

I get out too. I notice Renzo right away, mostly because he's making a lot of noise. My first impression is how much he's changed. His skin is paler than what I saw in the photos. Granted, it *is* winter. Sun is never in short supply down here, but people do tend to go outside less in cooler weather. His impressive physique, from what I can see from the light breeze blowing against his T-shirt, hasn't remained so toned. In fact, he's a little flabby. What really baffles me is the way he walks, like somebody took him apart but didn't know how to put him back together correctly. His every step is awkward and lurching, like a zombie in fast-forward. And the noise he's making…

"Kah-tuh! Buh-dee! How was duh drive?"

It takes me a moment to realize that he's speaking in a funny voice, and I feel repulsed because this is the sort of joke I would expect from someone like Bobby. Only he would be insensitive enough to make fun of someone with a mental disability. If this is the kind of humor Carter and Renzo share, I'm not going to enjoy this visit at all.

Carter shoots me a glare full of judgement, and it finally clicks. This isn't an act or a joke. Something happened to Renzo between those photos and now. Something life-changing.

I watch as Carter turns his full attention on his friend. They hug, and it's pretty touching because they obviously love each other. I don't know if it's platonic or not. I'm done making assumptions for the time being, but they clearly have a deep affection for each other. Renzo's face is serene as he rests it against Carter's neck. Then he raises his head and notices me for the first time, his facial expression moving in slow motion as realization dawns.

"And-ruh?" he says.

"Hey!" I hurry forward and offer my hand. I really *really* wish Carter had prepared me for this, because I'm uncertain how to act. Part of me knows that I should just be myself. That's the best way to treat anyone—with unbiased equality. That's difficult when I'm struggling to keep up with the plot. "It's nice to finally meet you," I say.

"You too!" Renzo takes my hand, but his grip is at a weird angle. It's not like shaking hands with most people, but we manage. His smile seems genuine enough. I hope mine does too.

"How was your trip?" Renzo's mother asks. "You must be exhausted. Come inside. Oh! Do you have luggage? We can lend a hand."

"It can wait," Carter says. "Except for one thing."

The present. It's been sitting in the back seat the entire trip, gift-wrapped and mysterious. I knew it wasn't for me. Carter already gave me a Christmas present—the car stereo we listened to on the ride down. It's the only thing the Fiat had been missing.

"Heeeey!" Renzo says. "Is dat for me?"

"Yeah," Carter says, grinning at him as he tucks the present under one arm. "I hope you don't have it already. I know you didn't when I bought it, but Christmas…"

"Wha' d'you get?" Renzo asks.

Soon I'm walking behind them and trying not to stare at the odd way in which Renzo's body moves, so I turn my attention to his mother.

"Thank you for letting us stay here."

"It's going to make Lorenzo so happy," she says. "How sweet of you to drive down with Carter. I'm Maria, by the way."

"Andrew," I say. I'm sure she knows that already, but it's just one of those formalities.

"Are you hungry?" she asks. Then, in a louder voice, she says, "We've already ordered pizza, just like you boys always used to. It should be here soon. You're right on time."

"Sounds good to me," I say. "We're both tired of burgers."

I tune in to the conversation Carter is having with Renzo, eager for any hint I can get.

"—so cool that you don't need a walker anymore," Carter is saying.

That implies a gradual recovery. Some sort of accident? I don't get to hear more because now we're inside where a beagle is jumping around our legs, and an older man—Renzo's father—introduces himself to me as Diego. We're ushered into the living room where Renzo wastes no time tearing the wrapping paper off his gift. A man after my own heart.

"The dine-ah!" Renzo exclaims.

He and Carter are on the carpet in front of the coffee table. I move closer to see the box better and notice that it's a really big LEGO set of a three-story tall building with an old-fashioned diner on the bottom floor. It seems like an odd gift for an eighteen-year-old to give another. Then again, not so long ago Carter and I were waving around toy wands.

"Those sets are expensive!" Maria says, placing a hand on her cheek. "You really shouldn't have."

"I wanted to buy the Assembly Square," Carter says to her, before returning his attention to his friend. "That one is *really* expensive!"

"I got it!" Renzo exclaims. "For Chriss-mus."

They keep talking about LEGO, and I feel increasingly uncomfortable. I don't know much about the topic, and I'm unsure what to say to the parents. I'm still trying to figure it all out. Does Renzo have the mind of a child now? If so, why?

The doorbell comes to my rescue. The pizzas have arrived, and we're asked to take a seat in the adjoining dining room. Carter has to help Renzo to his feet. While he does this, I catch a glimpse of something on my friend's face. At first I think it's sorrow or sympathy, but that's not right. Only when I take my seat do I remember seeing the same expression from the night before. It's guilt.

We're joined at the table by a guy in his early teens. Renzo's little brother, Alex. Maria makes the introductions, and Alex spares me a quick, "Hey." He's more interested in talking to Carter, who is sitting across from us, next to Renzo.

"How long did it take to drive down here? What sort of car? What's the fastest you went?"

Carter answers these questions, while I try to watch Renzo without being impolite. I notice his frustration when his mother tries to serve him a slice of pizza, and how he pulls away his plate so she can't. Then he reaches for the box in the center of the table and picks up a piece, but it's a jerky ride back to the plate. His first bite isn't the most graceful either, but he does okay.

Then he catches me staring, and my stupid cheeks start to burn.

His response is friendly. "You might not believe it," he says slowly. "But I'm a really good dancer."

After a split second of shock, I smile and blush harder. "You're probably better than me, but that's not saying much."

Renzo laughs, the sound gleeful. "Do you know much about me?" he asks.

"I know that you're Carter's best friend."

"Am I still?" Renzo says, looking playfully at Carter.

I'm getting used to the way he speaks. It's slower than most people and he has trouble pronouncing some letters, but my mind fills in the blanks for him.

"Always," Carter says, his eyes darting over to meet mine.

I nod my approval.

Renzo looks at me again. "Do you know about the accident?"

"Ugh!" Alex says. "You don't need to tell everyone your life story."

"You're just jealous," Renzo says. "Nothing interesting ever happens to you."

"And I'm glad!" Alex shoots back.

Renzo rolls his eyes. His head wobbles slightly as he reorients his gaze on me. "Carter and I were climbing. Five point eleven. Right?"

"More like a five point ten," Carter says. He looks miserable. "Maybe with a b."

I have no idea what any of this means, but I don't dare interrupt.

"I messed up and fell," Renzo says. "Flipped over and hit my head." He places a palm flat against his forehead. "I was so embarrassed that I went to sleep for two weeks so I wouldn't have to face anyone."

"He was in a coma," Diego says from the end of the table. "You'll have to excuse his sense of humor. He thinks he's funny."

Renzo laughs, like he's being naughty. "The best part was that I didn't have to go back to school again. Eight months..." He struggles to get the words out, changing them once he does. "Nine months of summer."

"That's how it should be for everyone," I say. "Just reverse the current system. Three months of school, nine months of summer."

"Yes!" Renzo says. "That was my intent. I did it all on purpose."

If my cheeks were burning, Carter's entire head is on fire. I've never seen him so red. I can guess why. He must blame himself, for some reason. Because he was the one who taught Renzo how to climb? Maybe he wishes he did a better job, or that he never taught him at all. I'm not sure, but I wish we were alone so I could reassure him that he shouldn't feel guilty.

"We need to watch videos!" Renzo says. He starts to get up until his mother tells him to sit.

"Eat first," she says. "There's time for that later."

Conversation is much lighter from that point on. Renzo's parents ask me polite questions about where I'm from and what the move was like, before the topic turns to Chicago and what Carter and I think about life there.

At the end of the meal, I'm feeling a lot more relaxed. Until another curveball is thrown my way. It's just a small one, but it reminds me that I've never been exposed to anything like this before.

"Time to go," Renzo says.

"I'll take care of it," Alex says, hopping up.

He hurries around the table and helps his brother stand. No one else rises. Carter's clenching jaw makes me realize they're on the way to the restroom. I'm not sure what kind of help Renzo needs. Maybe it's too hard to get his pants undone on his own or something like that. All I know is that the dynamic couldn't be more different from my relationship with Reed. He's always the one who takes care of me. I might have helped him with his recent move, but I've mostly been a burden on him, not the other way around.

"Lorenzo has been so excited about your visit," Maria says. "We're all happy to see you again. Really."

"Thanks," Carter murmurs. "He's doing so much better."

"He really is!" Maria says. "He's even been… Well, he'll never forgive me if I ruin the surprise. Why don't you boys go into the living room? We can watch those home movies when he's back."

We help clear the table first. Then we take a seat on the living room couch. We only have a split second of privacy before Renzo returns. Carter scoots over to make room so he can sit between us. I'm okay with that. I kind of figured that's how much of this week would work. The circumstances are different than I expected, but I'm adjusting.

Or so I think. When the videos start, it's like a gut punch. The first one is the cheesy sort that someone makes when they're first learning to edit videos. It's a bunch of clips set to a hip-hop song. Renzo looks strong and toned, like he did in those photos I saw in Carter's room. Most of the footage is at an indoor climbing gym. Renzo is amazing. He swings from grip to grip like Tarzan grabbing vines, never seeming to slow or miss his mark.

"Show off," I hear Carter say. "That's not climbing."

"It's better," Renzo replies.

Carter is in the videos too, and he does seem more intent on scaling up and down than swinging around. He looks a little younger, and happy in a way I've rarely seen him. We've had a lot of fun together, but in the video there's something especially carefree about his smile. He even stands a little taller. The next shock comes when the music ends and the two friends are shoulder to shoulder and addressing the camera.

Renzo's voice is completely different. It sounds deeper. He speaks smoothly and without effort. "Life goals?" he asks.

"Everest," Carter replies.

"Too easy," Renzo shoots back.

"Blindfolded," Carter says.

"Already done it," Renzo replies. "With my hands tied behind my back. And I was naked."

Carter snorts. "Gross, dude! Think of the shrinkage."

Renzo looks right into the camera and raises an eyebrow. "Mine never shrinks. Ever."

"Then you take after your father," Maria says from a chair next to the couch.

"Mom!" Alex complains.

Renzo snickers in a way that's not at all self-conscious. I glance over at him, then back at the television, and it's kind of surreal. I know they're the same person, and yet there's a distinct difference. I've never considered the various attributes that combine to form our identity. The way we carry ourselves and speak are just two traits out of many, but they change how others perceive us. I wonder if Renzo feels like he's a different person now, or if he feels the same except in a body that won't cooperate.

We watch more videos. Not all focus on climbing, but most of them do. The gym is left behind, and I watch as Carter and Renzo scale outdoor cliffs and rappel down again or stand atop high places and hold the camera out to capture the gorgeous views behind them. I'm not as interested in these achievements as I am the segments where the two friends interact. They were close. Incredibly so. I thought Carter and I were too, but I'm no longer sure if we've reached the same intensity.

When the videos end, Alex complains that we haven't watched any of his, so I'm treated to a clarinet recital. It's mercifully short. When he suggests we watch another, Maria steps in.

"That's enough family time. I'm sure the boys would like their privacy."

"Let's go to my room," Renzo says.

I'm up for that. Carter helps him up by gripping his left hand, which seems to work better than his right. After he pulls Renzo to his feet, he clasps his shoulder. They smile at each other, but only Carter has tears in his eyes. Renzo carefully picks up the LEGO set on the way, which again, seems a little odd to me.

Even more so when I see his room. Renzo doesn't have a hospital bed or any sort of special equipment. He has all the usual furniture. What stands out is how almost every flat surface is cluttered with LEGO builds.

"Wow," I say. "You uh… You sure like LEGO."

"It's part of my recovery," Renzo says, setting his newest prize on the bed. "Hand-eye coordination. The more I practice, the better I get."

"That's what he claims," Carter says, addressing me at last. I feel like we haven't spoken since we got out of the car. "He had LEGO even before the accident. Just not this much."

"Now I have an excuse," Renzo says with a cackle. "Want to help build the diner?"

"Yeah," Carter says, looking at me for feedback.

"Sounds fun to me," I say. I never need much prompting to embrace childish things. They never stopped being fun. I guess I just reached an age where I felt like I was supposed to move on, but screw it. Fun is fun.

We put on music before we get started. It quickly becomes apparent that Renzo has a lot of pride and determination. He refuses help so often that I learn to stop offering. He insists on opening the box and the individual plastic bags inside. This takes more time than most people need, but he gets it done. Once we're faced with a giant pile of multi-colored bricks, we sift through them to find the pieces he needs.

This is surprisingly satisfying. We share a common goal and a point of focus, which makes it easy to chill. I can see why Renzo uses this activity for rehabilitation. His hands are shaky, so he really has to concentrate when putting two pieces together. I notice he prefers using his right hand, even though his left seems to work better. He's pushing himself to improve. Sometimes the bricks don't go together like he wants, which makes him cuss and try again. Only rarely does he pass the more frustrating connections to Carter or me to complete.

The hours fly by. At ten o'clock Renzo starts yawning over and over again. This is contagious, and we start doing it too.

"You still get tired early?" Carter asks.

"Yeah," Renzo says. "I hate it. I can never stay up for *Saturday Night Live*. I record it, but watching it during the day feels wrong."

"You've gotta start pounding energy drinks." Carter yawns. "It's been a long day for us too."

There's a knock on the door and Diego sticks his head in the room. "Need help getting settled in?"

"In a minute," Renzo says.

"Okay." Diego looks at us. "We have the living room set up for you boys."

"Thanks," I say. "We'll be there soon."

It seems like he should go, but Diego wavers. "Son?"

"In a minute!" Renzo snaps.

Diego finally disappears. I'm willing to ignore the outburst. I get annoyed with my parents too, but Renzo feels the need to explain.

"I do okay on my own," he says. "But it's not easy getting undressed."

I grin at him. "I can help you with that." Yeah, I'm flirting with him, but so what? Just because he took a hit on the noggin and isn't as buff as before doesn't mean he's no longer handsome.

Renzo laughs. "And I have to use the restroom."

"That could be interesting too."

"Jesus, Andrew!" Carter hisses.

Renzo doesn't mind. He just grins at me. That makes me wonder again about the nature of their relationship. I know Carter said that the girls were always more interested in Renzo, but that doesn't mean he was interested back. Although he did have a girlfriend at one time. I wonder what happened to her?

We say goodnight and go to the living room, where the couch has been pulled out into a sofa bed. The house is dark and quiet now. I'm eager for some alone time with Carter. As usual. I just hope that he's feeling talkative.

"Don't get Renzo started," Carter says as he yanks down the sheets. "He's always been a shameless flirt."

"Do you think he's interested?" I ask.

Carter makes a face. "Are you?"

The question trips me up. On a superficial level, I'd be open to the idea, but my heart already belongs to the person standing in front of me. "I just think he's cute. That's all."

"You and everyone else," Carter grumbles. "I guess we should get our things from the car."

I'm confused by how angry he seems. It might not be directed at me, but it feels that way. I try to give him his space as we unload the car, and once we're inside again, we take turns using the restroom. I go last. When I return, Carter is shirtless and sitting up in bed. He doesn't seem to notice me, even when I strip down to my underwear and climb in too. I'm wondering if I should leave him alone and go to sleep when Carter surprises me by speaking.

"He makes it sound like a joke."

"Renzo?"

Carter nods. "The accident wasn't funny. At all."

I lick my lips, almost afraid to ask, but I can't resist. "What happened?"

"I fucked up," Carter says, his voice cracking. "In more ways than one. When we first started out… Renzo was a gymnast. You saw the way he moved in those videos. That came later. He didn't have any climbing experience. I met him on his first day at the gym. He watched me climb and was impressed enough to ask me to teach him. Renzo's always been that way. He treats everyone he meets like a friend. I think it was the second or third day of us hanging out when he asked if he should buy a helmet. I said no." Carter turns intense eyes on me. "Do you know why?"

I shake my head.

"Because they look dumb, and they're uncomfortable. You'd be surprised how many climbers feel the same way. Most of them, actually. I saw some recent polls on the subject, and it's *still* that way. Renzo asked me again when we started climbing outdoors, and I gave him the same stupid answer. Can you believe that?"

I open my mouth to tell him that he couldn't have known, but I shut it because I think he needs me to listen instead of react.

"Pretty soon he was teaching me tricks," Carter says. "Renzo was an amazing climber. People at the gym called him Spider-

Man. He was just as good once we took it outdoors. I wasn't bad, either. We had this sort of competition going, and for a while it was like..." He shakes his head. "Like we were made for each other."

I swallow, and it hurts my throat because now I don't want Carter to be gay or straight. I just want him to be mine.

Carter looks over at me self-consciously and says the only thing that could make me feel better. "It was like you and me. All we wanted to do was hang out together. We started camping so we'd have more time out on the rocks. We never got tired of it. Everything was good, until I fucked it up. I was belaying, and like he said, we were facing a five point ten at least."

"I don't know what that means."

"Oh. Which part?"

"All of it," I admit.

"It was a tough climb," Carter translates, "but we had a lot of experience. We both thought we could handle it, and it probably would have been all right, but I got distracted. I was belaying, which means I was on the ground and slowly feeding him rope. You saw in those videos how if someone falls, the person on the ground braces to slow and stop their descent?"

I nod. In one of the home movies, Carter had slipped and plunged toward the ground. Renzo, as the counterweight, was lifted up and swung forward to brace his feet against the cliff wall, stopping Carter in mid-air.

"I should have been paying attention. I wasn't looking at my phone or anything. I was just daydreaming." Carter's hand clenches the sheets, his fist trembling with rage or frustration. "That's all it took for me to ruin his life. On a climb like that, I should have been alert, not staring into space. Renzo fell, and I tried to stop him once I noticed, but it was too late. He flipped upside down and hit his head. It smacked against the rocks and was the most horrible sound I've ever heard. I can still hear it. Even though it all went by in a blur, that moment when his head hit the cliff is crystal clear. I knew he wasn't going to be okay. He just dangled there without moving. I thought he was dead. That's how bad it was. Even when I lowered him, I couldn't tell if he was breathing."

Carter whimpers, and I try to imagine myself in that scenario, seeing the person I love so broken and knowing that I could have prevented it.

"I could barely get a signal on my phone," Carter squeaks out. "We weren't that far from town. Just enough that it took freaking forever before—"

Carter hunches over and buries his face in his hands as he begins to sob. I reach over and rub his back as he cries, but I take no pleasure in it, because it hurts me to see him in such agony. My heart is aching for him. I want to bear this pain so he doesn't have to.

"Everyone makes mistakes," I say. "You didn't do it on purpose."

"No," Carter croaks, "but I wish it had been me instead. You don't know what I put him through. Renzo was in a coma for two weeks. When he woke up, he couldn't talk. He didn't react to anything. He wouldn't even look at you when you spoke to him. I thought he was brain dead. It went on long enough that—" Carter's lips tremble. "—that I started to wish I *had* killed him, because this was worse."

"It must have been horrible."

"It was." Carter wraps his arms around his stomach and rocks back and forth like it hurts. "I ruined his entire life."

I'm afraid to give my honest response to this, but I need to. "He seems happy to me. He wouldn't be if you'd ruined his life."

"That's just Renzo," Carter says dismissively. "He was always like that. Nothing ever upset him."

"Then he's still the same person," I say. "That's a good thing, right? Sure he's facing new challenges physically, but you were both into that before. Just in a different way."

"Challenges? Like not being able to take a piss by himself or get ready for bed?" Carter looks over at me, tears running down his cheeks. "He should hate me. So should his family. You should too."

"Too bad," I say, my throat tight, "because I love you. I mean it. Honest Andrew, remember? I love you, Carter."

"Thanks," he says, wiping his eyes on the inside of his forearm. "But that doesn't mean I don't hate myself. Because I do."

He doesn't get it. It felt good to finally tell him, but he doesn't realize how deeply I love him. Now isn't the time. This is about him, not me.

"If I march into Renzo's room," I say, "and tell him that you hate yourself, do you think that will make him feel better?"

Carter shakes his head. "No."

"Then stop. There's no point. You can't undo what's already been done. There's no sense in beating yourself up. It's a waste of energy. Even worse, it might seem like you pity the life he has. If Renzo is happy, even after everything he went through, then you should be happy for him too."

Carter keeps shaking his head. "You don't know what he was like before."

"I don't care! You were different too. So was I. The past is the past. Get over it. Renzo is a cool guy. Yeah, he has a lot to deal with, but who doesn't? Life stops being simple when we grow up."

Carter glares at me. Then his expression softens. "You're right. He's so freaking amazing. Renzo had to relearn everything. Talking, walking… all of it. If that had happened to me instead, I don't think I would have been that strong."

"I don't agree, but I do think he deserves our respect. Renzo is cool."

"You really think so?"

"Pffft. Yeah!"

Carter manages a smile. "Thanks."

"No problem. I just wish you had told me all of this sooner."

"I thought you would hate me. Or stop trusting me. I'm going to keep my promise, Andrew. I'll never let you get hurt. I swear. I won't make that mistake again."

"I've got your back too," I say. "If it makes you feel better, the chances of me getting any kind of sports-related injury are extremely low. I don't even like Quidditch. I usually skip those parts."

"That's so wrong," Carter says, spluttering laughter. "Hey. Can I show you something? Alex made a video about Renzo's recovery. It's online, but I have to warn you, it's hard to watch. He looked pretty bad the first couple of months in the hospital."

"Show me," I say.

It's easy to be brave for him. I feel like I can face anything or become anyone I need to be, if it's for Carter. I only hope, now that he's finally opened up to me, that I can inspire the same kind of courage and help him get past this.

Chapter Thirteen

The parking lot is nearly empty, the morning still young, when we pull up to a blockish building with few windows. We're not in the Fiat. Diego drove us here in a minivan. I'm in the backseat with Carter, who is leaning forward between seats to look out the windshield. He asks the same question running through my mind.

"What are we doing here?"

"Memory lane," Renzo says from the front seat.

I look around and notice a sign for the business. It has "rope" in the title, so I'm guessing it's a climbing gym. "Is this where you guys met?"

"Yeah," Carter says.

He somehow manages to make even this single syllable sound grim, so I thwack him in the chest with the back of my hand and make a face. I'm not going to let him turn this into another platform to wallow in guilt. Especially since Renzo was so excited as we piled into the van. I feel vindicated when he turns to us wearing a smile.

"Ready?" he asks.

"They aren't open yet," Carter replies.

Renzo laughs. "For me they are."

We get out and slowly walk to the entrance. Renzo knocks on the door, which unlocks and opens. The woman who answers is short and slender, but her muscles are toned. "Oh hey," she says. "You brought an audience."

"My friends," Renzo says.

That's flattering. When I notice Carter's solemn face, I thwack him again and smile. He loosens up and thwacks me back, his grin a welcome sight.

"Do I finally get to see you climb?" I ask him as we enter the building.

"What?" Renzo says to Carter, sounding surprised. "You still aren't climbing?"

"No," Carter admits. "It doesn't feel right."

"It does to me," he replies.

Carter stops in his tracks. "What?"

My attention is pulled away from this exchange by the bizarre interior. The ceiling is at least two or three stories above our heads. All around us are artificial cliff walls, but it's as if Mother Nature lost all sense of style and made everything as tacky as possible. Most of the cliffs are covered in oddly shaped multi-colored bumps for climbers to grab or stand on. Elevated metal walkways run down the center of each corridor. I'm not sure if that's just for spectators or something more. I guess I'll find out. Right now I return my attention to the conversation.

"You're climbing again?" Carter asks.

"Yup! Three times a week. Soon it will be five. This is my trainer, Sharon."

We shake hands with her, then watch as Renzo gets geared up. He wears a helmet this time. I notice that he doesn't look at Carter while putting it on. I don't think he's bitter. Most likely he's aware that it's a sensitive subject. Sharon helps him with the waist harness, and that's when Renzo addresses Carter directly.

"It's okay if you don't want to climb. You never were as good as me."

Carter scoffs. "Then you're forgetting the speed record. Which of us was faster, huh?"

"I don't remember," Renzo says mischievously while tapping on his helmet. "Must have forgot when I bumped my head. Was it me?"

"I'll show you who it was!"

Before long, Carter is geared up too—helmet and all—and to my abhorrence, I'm also expected to participate. I insist on watching first, since that seems like the most basic place to start. A staff member comes over to help us and to belay or whatever it was called. Renzo climbs first. He's slow and cautious going up, but from what I can tell, he does just fine. I look over at Carter and see him biting his lower lip. His shoulders are shaking too. If he wasn't such a guy, he'd be crying outright, and I'm certain they would be happy tears. When he claps, it's loud and firm as Renzo makes his way back down.

"Fucking badass, dude!" he shouts. "You've still got it!"

"But do you?" Renzo asks once he's down. "Don't hold back. Show me how fast you are."

"I've gotta warm up first," Carter says. "It's been a long time!"

I am predictably impressed as I watch Carter scale the wall. He makes it look effortless. I've admired his body since the first day I laid eyes on him and seeing it in motion now is truly beautiful. To my surprise, he's critical once on the ground again.

"I'm stiff," he complains. "And my hands have gotten weak."

"You used to be quicker for sure," Renzo says. "Want to go up together?"

"Yeah!"

I'm moved as I watch them climb as a pair. They're still competitive and unabashedly critical of each other, stopping to point down at grips the other should have taken or other technical things I don't understand. They seem to be in their natural element. This is where their friendship was forged, and I'm content to stand back and watch the blacksmith of experience hammer it back into shape again.

If only I could remain so idle. Before long, Carter and Renzo are insisting that I try too. We move to the beginners' wall, which looks like something an eight-year-old would have no trouble mastering, so of course I'm ridiculously awkward as I try to scale it. Past my initial embarrassment, I have to admit this is fun. After enough encouragement, I move on to a tougher wall. Then I make an excuse to stop because I really want Carter and Renzo to have their time together. I didn't realize how important that would be when planning this trip. Now it has become a priority, because learning all I can about Carter isn't enough. I also want him to be happy.

We're in Reid Park, which is trying hard to be green. The ground is covered in actual grass, although it's short, patchy, and struggling to survive. The ponds help ward off the dry desert climate, and the trees that ring the water's edge are a welcome sight. Dogs walk with their owners, children chase each other, and the sun shines in a cloudless sky. I try not to take any of this for granted, especially after my brother texts me a photo of the blizzard that is pummeling the city back home.

Despite the tranquil surroundings, I'm feeling jittery. I knew we would meet *her* sometime during this trip. I expected it to happen sooner. We drive home in a few days, but she's been busy with family obligations and—Ugh! I need to get my nerves under control. Melanie isn't a celebrity. She's only Carter's ex-girlfriend, the one romantic relationship he's ever had, that I know of. I envy her.

She's really pretty too. I keep sizing her up from across the picnic table where we sit, but it's hard to find flaws. She's not wearing much makeup, if any at all, and her long blonde hair is natural. No styling product or highlights. She has it pulled back in a pony tail so it won't blow around too much in the light breeze. Simple as that. I'm starting to have some *Silence of the Lambs* fantasies about wearing her skin so I can seduce Carter. Not really, but I am eager to learn more about their time together.

"They were always like this," Melanie says, nodding away from us. Beneath the shade of a nearby tree, Carter is gripping Renzo's ankles as he attempts to walk on his hands. Renzo is wearing a helmet, or I'd be more worried, but it still seems…

"Isn't that a little risky?" I say to her.

Melanie laughs. "I can't count how many times I've said the same thing. I *hated* their daredevil antics. All I did was worry about one of them getting hurt. The guy I'm dating now doesn't even ride a bike. He's that boring, and I love it."

"I bet. How long did you and Carter date?"

"About a year. Or two. Things got a little confusing toward the end."

"How so?"

Melanie exhales. "After the accident, Carter withdrew into himself. Has he told you about that?"

He hasn't, but I know enough to wager a guess. "When he stopped talking?"

"It was bad. Really bad. Renzo was still in his coma, and Carter was becoming more upset by the day. All he did was cry, which was hard to witness. When Renzo finally woke up and couldn't speak or do anything else, I think Carter convinced himself that he had forfeited his own right to those things. Nobody was angry with him. Both families knew the sort of risks their sons were taking and lectured them about safety, but try making a teenager listen to anything, right?"

That's something else I've learned. Melanie is older than Carter and me. Just by a year or two, but she does seem very mature. I want to come across as that way too, so I say. "Yeah, no kidding."

"I suppose Carter decided to punish himself, if no one else would. He stopped talking, stopped climbing, stopped doing anything fun. Even television. He woke up, went to school, and ate, but that's it. I tried to be there for him. He wouldn't allow that either. Renzo couldn't be with Tracy, so he couldn't be with me."

"Tracy was Renzo's girlfriend?"

"Correct. She wasn't able to handle his recovery. I try not to judge her for that, since we all have our own methods of coping. She still could have been his friend. I stopped being hers. I'm not sure if that was nice of me, but I felt like Renzo needed me more."

"Oh. Like…"

"Just as friends," Melanie says. "As far as I was concerned, Carter and I were still together. The problem was, he wouldn't talk to me about our relationship or anything else. That's why I can't say how long we dated. I didn't hear from him again until his parents moved with him to Chicago. I thought that was a terrible idea at the time, like they were separating Renzo and Carter so at least one of them could get better. Now I think they were right, because seeing Carter now…" She shakes her head. "I'm glad he's his old self again."

She's dropping so much information that I feel like taking notes. "That must have been really hard on you, losing a special guy like Carter."

She smiles at me in a funny kind of way.

"What?" I ask.

"Nothing. I'm just not used to hearing a man talk about another man that way. It's sweet."

"Oh," I say with a chuckle. Then I lean forward and say in a conspiring whisper, "Don't tell Carter, but I have a *huge* crush on him."

"I thought you might," Melanie says. She's smiling like she's okay with the idea, which gives me the courage to press on.

"It's probably hopeless though. Right?"

She raises her eyebrows at this, which I can understand. "You're asking if he's…"

"Hope springs eternal. I know he likes women. I can tell by the way he talks about you. And from the way he obsesses over this girl at school. I'm probably deluding myself, but you know… Maybe he likes guys too."

Melanie looks to where Carter and Renzo are now lying on the grass and laughing together. "I did wonder a few times."

"Really? Any reason why?"

Melanie starts to shake her head before she reconsiders. "They're unusually close. I had a friend like that once, so maybe it's not so strange. Except…"

"Except?" I say, not hiding my anticipation. I already know that if she clams up, I'll kidnap her and hold her hostage until I get the answers I need.

"I always found it odd how they used to sleep together."

"*They what?*" I don't mean to shout this, but I do.

"Don't believe anything she says," Carter calls over to us.

"It's all true!" Renzo yells.

I make a face at them and turn to Melanie again, fearing that our time is now limited. "Do you mean—"

"Not like that," she says, her face a little red. "Not exactly. When they went camping and the temperature dropped at night, they would combine their sleeping bags and hold each other if it got too cold. Carter told me about this after it had already happened a few times. I suggested that they should get warmer sleeping bags so they wouldn't have to, but… I didn't really mind. I was being practical, not judgmental. Anyway, when I made that suggestion, it was like Carter hadn't even considered the idea."

I try to imagine Carter and Renzo spooning together beneath the stars. Any potential jealousy I might feel is preempted by my need for this to be true, because if it is, maybe hope isn't just a spring. Maybe it's a dam bursting at the seams.

One more night before we begin our drive back to Chicago, and even though I'm exhausted, I don't want to leave. I'm enjoying myself too much. We spent more time at the climbing gym than I ever wanted, but we also went for a hike, enjoyed a few swims, and took a road trip to Phoenix, which we toured on foot.

Renzo never misses an opportunity to rehabilitate himself. Everything we do, even when we stay inside and play video games, he treats as an opportunity to hone blunted skills. I've talked to him about this and learned a lot, like how he damaged his cerebellum, which is responsible for physical coordination. The doctors didn't think he would walk again, and once he did, they decided he would never be able to do so unaided. They were wrong. He's still young, and as Renzo explained to me, that means his chances of making a full recovery are stronger. It would be interesting to see how much he's improved in a year's time, but I know that I won't wait that long to interact with him again. We're friends now. We've exchanged numbers and plan to stay in touch.

"Boom!" I say, closing my suitcase and zipping it up. "I'm done packing. You?" All the competition I've witnessed over the past week is rubbing off on me.

"Almost," Carter says.

He's standing on the other side of the sofa bed, a pair of socks in one hand, his phone in the other. His lips always move when he reads, sometimes to sound out the words. I think it's adorable. He's even cuter when his face lights up.

"Holy shit," he whispers.

"What?"

"Just a sec." He seems to be rereading, his eyes darting back and forth. "Yeah… Yeah!"

"You want to be alone with that thing?" I joke.

Carter looks up at me and grins. "She broke up with him."

My stomach sinks. "Who?"

"Olivia. She broke up with Bobby! At least I think so. Listen, it says, 'We're done now. I can't put up with him anymore.' That means they broke up, right?"

"Let me check." I grab my phone and send a text to Jackson, asking him if it's true. I keep my attention on the screen while I wait for a response because I don't know how to react to this news, or to Carter's excitement.

Yeah, Jackson finally replies. *They split up yesterday. It was messy. He's over here now.*

Doing what? Treating Jackson like a whore he doesn't have to pay? Ugh! I don't want to go home. Ever. We'll transfer to a school down here instead.

"Well?" Carter says. "Did you text her or Bobby?"

"Jackson," I say. "It's true. They broke up yesterday."

Carter stares at me. "You know what this means?"

"That you better finish packing."

What it really means is that I'm almost out of time. We have a two-day drive ahead of us. If I have any hope of getting Carter to see us as more than friends, it's now or never.

— — —

Carter's body glides beneath the water of the hotel pool, tan and sleek. The week in Tucson has reawakened an athletic side that he had been denying himself. I might end up regretting this trip because I have a feeling our relationship is going to be a lot more physical from now on. Not like that... But maybe that too.

Water drips from my hair onto my shoulders as I sit on the edge of the pool and watch him. I will my heart to stop beating so fast, but the treacherous organ stopped listening to me around the time he and I first met. I've been buffeted by an emotional hurricane ever since, especially during our return trip to Oklahoma. Every mile felt like a countdown, my chances slipping away with each turn of the odometer. Carter and I aren't traveling alone this time. Fear sits in the backseat, whispering nightmares into my ear. Some are more detailed than others, such as a vision of Olivia meeting us as soon as we arrive home and taking Carter into her arms—enveloping him so completely that he's lost to me forever. This seems unnecessarily elaborate, because all it really takes are five words to make me shudder and want to give up hope.

Nothing will come of this.

If that's true, I don't know if I can deal with it.

Carter surfaces, sees that I've gotten out, and swims over to join me. I stare openly at his arms as he lifts himself from the water and his biceps flex. I want him to know how attractive I find him. I need him to know that he can have me, and that it will be like nothing he's ever experienced because I won't hold back. I'll give all of myself to him. Anything he wants. Emotionally, physically, spiritually... It's all his. He just has to want me back.

"I wish this trip would never end," Carter says, spinning around to sit next to me.

"Same here," I admit.

"Hey, do you think we can do it again soon? How about spring break?"

"Yes! Count on it!"

"Cool," Carter says, his grin dopey. "Maybe we can bring Olivia with us."

I look over at him incredulously. "Why?"

Carter seems just as puzzled. "It could be fun."

"Yeah, but I like it when it's just us."

"Huh? What about Renzo? And Melanie? There's no point in

making the drive if we don't get to see them."

I don't agree. Not entirely. "We can hang out with as many people as you want once we're in Arizona. It's the drive back and forth that I like. It's better when it's just us."

"So she's supposed to drive down on her own?" Carter says, sounding frustrated. "Or fly?"

"I don't really care either way," I mutter.

"That seems mean."

I roll my eyes. "Fine. She can come with us. I'll bring Jackson."

Carter makes a face. "Why him?"

"Never mind." This isn't going how I wanted it to. It's already night. We ate dinner hours ago. The pool is closing and soon we'll be going to sleep. I can't waste a single minute being petty. "Sorry," I say. "I just get frustrated sometimes because…"

He looks over at me. "What?"

"Our time together is special. Like some sort of treasure." I wince and shake my head. "That sounds hokey. I mean that I value it more than anything else. The things we talk about, all the dumb stuff we do, it's the best. I've never been happier than when I'm with you."

"Wow." Carter thinks briefly and nods. "I feel the same way. I guess I don't mind as much when other people are around though. That can be fun too."

"Can we just forget about everyone else for the rest of the night? Especially right now, because you say you feel the same way, but I'm not sure that's true. And I need to know."

Carter's face grows a little red. "Okay."

He doesn't say more. It's up to me. I search for the right words. I don't want to say it outright, but I've been hinting and hoping for months now, and that hasn't worked. It's time. "I love you, Carter."

"I love you too. You're my best friend."

He says this like it's an obvious fact and not a confession. Never has the term "best friend" seemed so inadequate, so I try again.

"I'm not sure you get it. I'm *in* love with you."

"Oh."

Together we listen to the water lapping against the side of the pool. I stare into its depths, at a submerged light illuminating his feet, which had been kicking just seconds ago. Now they are still.

"Do you ever think of me like that?" I manage to force out of an increasingly tight throat. "Is there any part of you, no matter how small, that loves me as more than just a friend?"

"I don't know."

That's already enough to make me despair, because there's no doubt in my mind. I love him. So badly that my chest never stops aching. "Can you at least try? For me. Just to see if we can have that together. I need you to, okay? I know it's asking a lot, but sometimes when I look at you, I feel like my heart is either going to burst or break, and I need to know which it's going to be. I can't take this anymore."

Carter's hands grip the concrete edge of the pool tighter. "What am I supposed to do?"

"I don't know," I admit.

I shouldn't have said anything. I should have carried this secret until it destroyed me because now I'm realizing how much I've gambled. This could ruin our friendship. I could end up with nothing. In fact, I'm pretty sure I will.

"Let's go up to our room," Carter says. He pulls his legs from the water. "Let's go up there, and I'll try."

I don't know how to respond as I rise on shaky legs and fetch my towel. I hand Carter's to him and notice his worried expression. I want to reassure him that he can't do anything wrong. Everything with him has always been right, even when it's flawed. We pad on bare feet down the hotel hallway, and when we pass through the lobby to reach the elevators, the person behind the desk notices our lack of shoes and frowns in disapproval. Carter and I laugh as soon as we're safely in the elevator, and it feels good. Everything is okay. We're still us, and best of all, this is going to happen.

"Did you already know?" I ask him. "Sometimes I felt like I was being obvious. Other times…"

"I suspected," Carter says. "Once or twice. Like after Halloween."

"I've been wondering about that. Was it only physical for you? Did you feel anything?"

Carter's eyes dart to mine and away again. "I love you, Andrew."

The elevator dings and the doors open, revealing a couple

old enough to be our parents. They also look us up and down. I guess it is unusual to see two guys wearing nothing but swim trunks in the middle of winter. As we walk to our room, I wish I'd had time to say it back. I love him too. I want him to know, but I don't want to cheapen it through repetition. My hand shakes as I unlock the door.

The room is dark when we enter. I'm reaching for the light switch when Carter grabs my wrist and moves my hand away. He doesn't let go. He steps closer, letting the door close behind us. Then he presses me against it, releasing my wrist so he can touch me elsewhere—a hand on my shoulder, the other on my cheek. His legs are intertwined with mine, his waist pushing against my own. I'm reacting. I can't tell yet if he is too, but I feel something down there.

I don't care about that as much as I do his face. The curtains are open, the light from the parking lot allowing me to see him as my eyes adjust to the darkness, and I want to cry because he's so damn handsome. Carter brings his face close to mine. He's breathing through his nose like a huffing bull, his gaze intense as he touches his forehead to mine. He holds it there, our mouths tantalizingly close, and yet still infuriatingly distant. I can't take it anymore. Figuring he needs me to lead, I tilt my face forward.

His moves back, just before our lips touch.

I don't let this dissuade me. I slide my hands up his body, reveling in the feel of muscles still warm from exertion. My palms come to rest on each side of his neck and I try again, needing to kiss him before we go further.

Carter flinches. Then he pulls away, the shadows enveloping his face.

"I don't want to lose you," he says, voice strained. "I only recently got Renzo back. That's how it feels. I don't want you to... Sorry. I'll shut up."

He steps forward again, but this time when my hand touches his chest, it's to hold him at bay. "You don't have to pretend," I say. "If it's not how you feel, it's not how you feel."

Carter's mouth moves before he gets the words out. "I wish I was gay. For you. I wish I could make myself feel that way. But I can't."

"Of course you can't," I say, turning my head so he won't see my lip tremble. "It's not a choice for either one of us."

"I'm sorry, Andrew. I really do love you. Not in the same way, but it's still love. I promise. I love you."

"I love you too," I say. "And don't worry. You're not going to lose me."

Carter plows into me, and before I know it, I'm wrapped in his arms. It feels good. Platonic, but good.

"Thanks for trying," I murmur against his skin. I let myself enjoy the sensation—my cheek against his shoulder, my lips brushing against his neck. Knowing it will be the last time we're ever this close, I reach up and tangle my fingers into his hair. I squeeze Carter close to me like it might make the impossible come true.

Then I let go.

I'll no longer put him through this or torture myself. I don't know what I'll do, but I care about him too much to push this further or to take advantage of him in moments of weakness.

"I'm going to get dressed," I say, slipping into the bathroom.

I close the door behind me and reach for the lock. My hand drops before reaching it, because there's no need. He's not interested. I flip on the light and squint against the brightness. Then I stare at myself in the mirror, baffled by how mere physical differences—having one part instead of the other—could amount to so much. Not just for him, but for me as well. I hate it, but I understand.

I avert my eyes, take off my swimsuit, and start getting dressed. I'm pulling on my jeans when I can't take it anymore. I fall to my knees, rest my head on the edge of the tub, and cry. I allow myself to feel bitter. I think petty thoughts, blaming this on *her*. I silently declare myself a victim and curse the world and all its injustices.

Then I give in to sorrow and close my eyes, wishing he had at least kissed me. I would have liked that. Just one kiss that I could cling to while mourning everything that could have been. Or maybe it's better not to know the touch of those lips. It would be too much like a drug that I would choose over eating, sleeping, living…

Enough.

I pick myself up and finish getting dressed. I wash my face

in the sink so all of it is wet, not just my cheeks and eyes. This doesn't help. It's still obvious I've been crying, but I can't stay in here all night. I won't be that pathetic.

Trying to hold my head up high, I leave the bathroom. The lights are on now. Carter is dressed too, his damp swimsuit hanging on the back of the desk chair. He's sitting on the edge of the bed, looking bewildered.

I try to sound like my usual self when I say, "Is it just me, or does it feel a little awkward in here? Maybe we should crack a window."

He sees right through this. "Are you okay?"

His kindness nearly sets off another round of tears before I manage to swallow them. "Yeah. I'm fine. Are you?"

"Yeah."

"We need to pretend this never happened," I blurt out. Then I shake my head and grimace. "Easier said than done."

"No kidding," Carter says, attempting a smile.

I stare, wishing I no longer found him so attractive. What's the point? All that's left is to salvage what we had. "I don't want this to mess with us. That's what I mean. I can't change how I feel, but this isn't anything new. I've felt this way for a long time, and we were still able to be friends. I want it to stay that way."

"I do too," Carter says. Then he seems to reconsider. "I want you to be happy."

"Like I said, when I'm with you, I'm happy." But not fulfilled. That's different. I feel emotion rising, so I grab the remote to give us something to focus on. After an hour of watching TV, everything almost feels natural again. We hit the vending machines, and Carter fills the ice bucket to overflowing. Frozen cubes tumble over the edge and scatter on the carpet, but he only stops when I start laughing. By the time we crawl into bed, I'm able to make myself believe that our friendship is okay. I hope he is too.

I'm not. I'm anything but okay. My back is to Carter. I'm trying to give him plenty of space so he knows I won't try anything again, although I'm imagining a different room where our swimsuits are balled up on the floor together next to the door. Where instead of pretending to sleep, I'm showing him all the ways I love him, one touch at a time.

The only thing I'm touching now is my own face as I wipe away more tears. Carter shifts in bed, moving closer. He wraps an arm around me, and I don't know how to react until he whispers, "I'm sorry."

I place my hand over his as he holds me. This is love. Maybe not the kind I had been hoping for, or what I wanted to give back, but the fact remains...

This is love.

Chapter Fourteen

Most of us live a dual existence, our lives taking place simultaneously in two different worlds—one unyielding and physical, the other an ever-changing landscape of emotion. Both can be confusing. We meet others in the external world, where we try to interpret through clues and experience what the other person is feeling. Here it is possible to deceive, to smile despite the pain, and to laugh when our insides are begging us to cry. We don't have as much control over the internal world. We are forever subject to its whims and inclinations. The most we can do is to wrap our arms over our stomachs or press a hand over our hearts in the hope that those feelings won't manifest—that the truth will remain inside where no one can see.

This is what I attempt on the rest of the ride to Chicago. Carter and I joke around. We talk about the books we like, we make fun of people who annoy us, and we stop to inhale burgers and fries when we get hungry. On the surface, everything is fine. It's only when there's a lull in conversation or while we're listening to music that I think about a future without him. I feel empty inside. Carter King will never be my boyfriend. There are depths of his soul that I will never know, parts of his body that I will never touch. Carter will never love me back in the same way that I love him.

I let myself think these words and try not to recoil from the pain. This is necessary, like learning that a flame is dangerous, no matter how enticing its dance. I may not be able to control my heart, but I hope it remembers this ache—this unbearable emptiness with just enough left behind to hurt—so that it never does this to me again.

As we continue driving north, the sky grows gray and we're forced to crank up the heater. I want more than anything to turn around and drive back to a place filled with sunshine. A place where he and I still felt possible.

"Remember my big writing project I keep mentioning?" Carter asks.

"The one you always bring up before reminding me that it's a secret?"

"Yeah. Sorry. I'm ready to tell you now. If you still want to know."

I nearly sigh. Of course I still care. I wouldn't be this upset if I didn't. "Please tell me it's not about Olivia," I groan as I ease the car into the slow lane. We'll need to exit soon to get gas, and I'm tired of driving. Time for him to take the wheel.

"It's not about her," Carter says. "It's about Renzo."

"Oh yeah? How so?"

"I want everyone to know his story," Carter says. "That's my main motivation for writing it."

"So it's biographical then?" I ask. "I'm surprised, because we're close, and you weren't comfortable telling me until we went down there. A book that anyone can read…"

"That's why I decided to make it a sci-fi story." Carter shifts in his seat, turning to face me. "It's about an astronaut who is supposed to travel to three planets and set up these satellite antennas so that humans can contact aliens. Scientists were able to detect their civilization, which is really far away. Out of our reach. The aliens are way more advanced than us, but we can't get their attention. To them, we're just ants in the grass."

"And Renzo is the astronaut?"

"Yeah. He does the first two installations just fine, but when he lands on the third planet, his spacecraft crashes and he takes a nasty blow to the head."

"Just like the accident."

"Right. The rest of the book is about him having to rehabilitate himself and set up the final satellite antenna, even though he's pretty messed up."

"How does he even survive? Renzo was in a coma, right? Is your character in better condition after the crash?"

"No, but he has a faithful robot who helps take care of him. It even carries him around, because it can transform into a cart."

"A cart?" I say, stifling a smile. "And does this robot happen to be you?"

"Yeah," Carter says sheepishly. "It's dumb, isn't it?"

"Not at all!" I think it's sweet, but I'm not about to tell him that. I've regurgitated my feelings for him enough lately. "So what happens? Does he get all three satellite antennas… Hey, how about communication beacons instead?"

"I like that! And yeah, the astronaut gets all three up and working. He makes contact with the aliens, and one of them comes to see him. Not only that, the alien fixes him. They have high-tech medicine, so by the end of the novel, the astronaut is all better."

"And he lives happily ever after with his faithful robot?"

"No." Carter clears his throat and faces forward again. "There's actually a really sad part where the robot sacrifices itself to save the astronaut from a meteor storm."

"Oh."

"It reads better than it sounds."

"I'm sure it does," I say diplomatically. "A sad ending then."

"Not really," Carter says. "The astronaut and the alien return to earth together and become national heroes. No, *interstellar* heroes!"

"Nice!"

"Yeah. So I was thinking, would you uh… Would you like to be the alien?"

I laugh. I can't help it. I'm flattered, but mostly I'm struck by how, even in the middle of my misery, Carter is still able to make me feel better. More than that, he makes me believe there can be a happy ending to our story too.

My first day back at work is nice and easy. A snow storm blew in an hour after my shift began, and even though it's a Saturday, everyone seems to have decided that no pizza is worth venturing out into this weather. Thank goodness we don't deliver. Jackson and I have given up standing behind the counter. We've moved to a booth, where we've been watching the snow pile up and cars slide across the road.

"By the time our shift is over," I say, "we'll be snowed in. We'll have to sleep here."

"There's plenty of food," Jackson says. "And we can keep the pizza oven going so we stay warm."

"Think we can make a bed out of pizza boxes?" I ask.

"Filled with napkins. Like a mattress."

We're content to watch the hypnotic flurries as they blow against the window. That's the funny thing about him. Carter and I never stop talking. Jackson and I do okay with silence. We can be around each other without needing to say everything that comes to mind. I like that. Especially when my thoughts are so troubled.

"I never would have left that warm weather behind," he says.

"I'm thinking of driving south and never looking back."

"Sign me up!" I entertain the fantasy until my heart grows heavy. "Then again, we'd both probably miss our friends too much. Two of them in particular."

"Or maybe not," Jackson says.

That piques my interest. "What do you mean?"

"Bobby and I aren't getting along so well."

"Did something happen?"

"Yeah. When you were out of town. He came over to my place looking for the usual."

"He wanted you to blow him," I say.

Jackson glances around, even though the place is empty and the only other employee bailed an hour ago. "Right. I refused."

"Really?" I lean forward and place my elbows on the table. "Has that ever happened before?"

"No. You know how I always pretend to be reluctant? He must have thought that's what I was doing, like it was normal, because he didn't let up." Jackson glares at the table's surface. "I kept saying no. Bobby got really forceful. I had to throw him out."

"Not cool." I refrain from saying more, but only because I want to respect that Jackson has feelings for him. "I guess he thought he could have you again after Olivia dumped him."

"Not exactly. They hadn't broken up yet."

"What?"

"They weren't getting along. He didn't even get her a present for Christmas."

"So he decided to cheat on her instead." I regret saying this as soon as it passes my lips. Carter is a much better person than Bobby, but even if someone found a legitimate reason to criticize him, I wouldn't want to hear it. I'm sure Jackson doesn't want to hear anything bad said about Bobby either. Or so I thought.

"It was super fucked up," he says. "For a lot of reasons."

"And now he's pissed at you?"

Jackson shakes his head. "He's sad. Bobby really loved Olivia. I haven't been hanging out with him as much lately. So he can't try anything with me again, I keep telling myself, but the truth is, it's rough being around him when he's so down. I want him to be happy, and that makes it tempting to give him what he wants."

"I wouldn't trust myself in that situation either," I say. "Speaking of which, I got my answer when it comes to Carter."

After we arrived home from the trip, I promised myself I wouldn't tell anyone what happened. I'm a little embarrassed. Hindsight might be flawless, but I still feel like I should have figured out the truth sooner than I did. I was deluding myself. Begging a straight guy to be with me, just to see if we could make it work, isn't my proudest moment. I still consider that night special, even if it didn't lead anywhere. I had planned to keep it close to my heart—a secret that only Carter and I shared. Not that we agreed to never talk about it. He'll probably tell some girl eventually, and she'll think he handled it in the sweetest way possible. Which he did.

That's why, when I reach the end of the story, I don't tell Jackson how Carter held me that night while I cried. I know it's the kind of tenderness that he always wanted from Bobby and never got. It feels good to tell him the rest though. Better than I expected.

"At least you know," Jackson says. "Now you can move on."

"Ha!" I say without humor. "You first."

Jackson clenches his jaw, his head shaking. "I mean it. I'm done."

"Then tell me your secret so I can be done too."

"You'll get there," Jackson says. "Everything being one-sided gets old. Like talking to yourself, it doesn't stay entertaining for long. Although with Bobby, it was more like talking to someone who never answered back."

"I still envy you," I say. "Seriously," I add when Jackson makes a face. "At least you got to sleep with him. I'd take that over nothing."

A smile tugs at Jackson's cheek. "I did like it. For a while."

"For a while? From what you've told me, you liked it for years." I roll my eyes in exasperation. "Does he at least have a big one?"

Jackson starts shaking his head again, but he's smiling now. "My lips are sealed."

"They sure weren't before! And you don't have to say a single word. Grab some dough and show me instead."

"What?"

"Why not? Make me a Bobby-sized pizza. Come on!"

I rise and pull on Jackson's arm until he stands up. Then we return to our work stations and make a pizza that's definitely not on the menu. Soon I'm presented with a tube of dough, and I have to admit it's bigger than I was expecting. We even add two balls, and once it's rolled out, we decorate it with toppings to add color and texture.

"I am *not* eating that once it's done," Jackson says.

"It's not like you haven't before."

"You suck."

"Not as often as you do."

Jackson grabs the back of my neck and starts to push, like he intends to shove me in the oven. I resist, and we don't exactly wrestle, but we do a lot of playful pushing and shoving. He's chasing me around when the door finally opens and we have a customer. Sort of. The guy is clearly homeless.

"Mind if I warm up?" he asks.

"No problem," I say.

He smiles a mostly toothless grin. "Sure smells good in here!"

"Then it's your lucky day," Jackson says, a demonic glint in his eye. "How would you like a very special pizza?"

The man accepts, of course. I cut the pizza into stripes before serving it, and the homeless man is none the wiser as he happily fills his stomach with Bobby's pizza penis. We don't mean any disrespect. It's simply better than the food going to waste, even though I honestly wouldn't have had trouble eating it myself. We let the man stay until closing time. As we're locking the doors, I turn to Jackson and grin.

"You might want to text Bobby and let him know that he's officially on the rebound. He just made it to third base with a homeless dude!"

Jackson doesn't seem to hear me. He's looking toward the corner the homeless man had disappeared around. "Where's he going to sleep tonight?"

"Oh. I don't know. A shelter?"

"Around here? This isn't the inner city."

Jackson pulls out his phone and types something. I catch a glimpse of a map before he pockets it again. "Text me when you make it home," he says. Then he hurries to his car.

I can guess where he's going, and what he'll do. I hope Jackson does become a police officer, because it's obvious that he'll be a good one.

— — —

It's the middle of January before the inevitable happens. I'm alone at our usual lunch table in the school cafeteria when Olivia sits down across from me. Her dark eyes search mine. I don't need to be psychic to know what's coming.

"I haven't answered him yet. If you're wondering."

Okay, that's not what I was expecting. I thought she would ask if Carter is still interested in her, but I suppose she doesn't need reassurance. I look to where he's standing in line to get them both lunch. Carter is grinning like he's at an amusement park instead of a cafeteria.

"Carter asked you on a date?"

Olivia looks surprised for a moment. Then uncomfortable. "Last night. I figured he already told you."

There it is. The first crack in our friendship. We're supposed to tell each other everything. "Maybe he mentioned it and I wasn't paying attention." I'm not sure if I say this is for her benefit or mine.

Perhaps both. She's not purposefully intruding. Olivia used to pair up with another girl in class until that student transferred out of the program. Once that happened, she was on her own, and joining us simply made sense. Why wouldn't she? Olivia is part of our circle of friends. She was still with Bobby at the time, so she was more of a distraction than a threat. But now…

"What's there to think about?" I say. "It's Carter. If we were in normal classes, he'd have all sorts of girls after him." I swallow. "And maybe a few guys."

"That's what I'm worried about," Olivia says.

She means me. Her expression is sympathetic, and I wonder if she knows about my clumsy attempts to win Carter over. I'm not ashamed of my feelings, but I would be embarrassed if other people knew how desperate I had become. "The only thing that matters is who he wants to be with," I say, my throat tight.

"I disagree," Olivia says. "Maybe I'm wrong. I'm running on instinct here. And the way you look at him."

I shake my head as if to deny it, but there's no point. "I've already accepted that it's not going to happen."

She reaches across the table and places her fingers over mine. "I don't want you to get hurt."

God damn it! I wish she would be a bitch. Instead I'm forced to accept that she's a decent human being. "Just because I can't have him, doesn't mean I want him to spend the rest of his life alone. This is going to happen eventually. At least with you—"

She looks up sharply and I follow her gaze. Carter is back with two trays, his smile like a beam of sunshine. He looks a little puzzled as Olivia pulls her hand away from mine, but we smile back at him, and he decides that everything is okay. I suppose it is. For them.

Carter sets a tray in front of her, and after sitting, passes me a chocolate milk. I didn't ask him to get me one. It's a nice gesture, but it feels like a consolation prize, especially when Olivia gets an entire meal. I make the most of my sack lunch, staying quiet so they can talk.

I can't help but envy her in the same way I do Melanie. I'm not transsexual. I've never felt like I was born in the wrong body, but ever since I met Carter, I've often wished I could wave a magic wand and become something I'm not. Maybe it still wouldn't be enough. Judging from what transsexual people go through, gender is more than just the physical, so I'd probably still be missing something that Carter needs. If I was able to change that too, I wouldn't be myself anymore, and as much as I love him, that sounds like a step too far. With this in mind, after Carter leaps up to whisk away our trash, I say, "I know what my answer would be if I were you."

Olivia's eyes widen. "Are you sure?"

I swallow again and manage a nod, putting into motion one of my worst fears.

"The outline doesn't need many changes," I say.

We're in the downstairs family room at my house. Or my apartment, as I've started calling it since Reed moved out. When my parents get on my nerves, that's what I tell them: that I'm leaving and going to my apartment. I think it's funny. They don't.

Thanks to Jackson's gift, the temperature is no longer freezing down here. The space heater requires a couple of hours to really warm up, but once it gets going, everything stays nice and toasty. My make-believe apartment has become something of a sanctuary. Olivia is with us during the school day, and we often hang out with her and the others afterwards, so only here or the rare trips to Carter's house do we have time alone.

Working on his stories is my favorite excuse, since it's not a group activity. I like sitting on the couch with him and letting our creative impulses mingle. Carter enjoys it too. Usually. Tonight he keeps checking his phone.

"It's the end I have an issue with," I say, hoping to reclaim his attention. "The alien shows up and fixes the astronaut, but that feels wrong to me. Doesn't the astronaut prove he isn't broken? That despite his difficulties, he's still a complete human being who can achieve his goals?"

"Right, right," Carter says. "That makes sense."

"I don't want it to seem like there's something wrong with Renzo. He might be fighting a disability, but he himself isn't a problem that needs to be corrected."

"Hm."

I wait until Carter finally looks up from his phone again. Then I continue. "What if, when the alien finally shows up, it doesn't have legs? I know Renzo does, but I'm thinking the alien's natural physiology might be a little more limited than ours. Like its species had to learn to overcome the same issues. That would make the astronaut the perfect ambassador, turning his disability into a strength."

These are premium ideas, which makes it all the more frustrating when Carter grabs his phone after it vibrates and starts mouthing along to the text he's reading. Then he looks up, his expression pure joy.

"She said yes!"

"Who?" I say.

"Olivia!"

"Did you ask her out? Because that seems like the sort of thing best friends tell each other." I'm being petty. I don't like how the venom tastes on my tongue, or how it feels as it slides down to my stomach. This is his moment of victory, and I'm turning it into another battle.

"Oh," Carter says. "I wasn't sure what she'd say. If she shot me down, I would have been embarrassed so… Sorry."

"It's fine," I say, my anger draining away. "Just promise you won't forget about me when you two fall madly in love."

"I won't!" he says with a guffaw. "Can you believe it? Oh man, I'm freaking out."

"You better text her back," I say.

I study him as he does, taking in details that I have

memorized so thoroughly that I can conjure them up when my eyes are closed. Especially late at night when I'm lying in bed. That's all I have of him now. A fantasy.

After he sends the text and sets aside the phone, Carter finally pays attention to the story again.

"What were you saying about the alien? No legs, right? So what are you thinking? Like a slug? Are they slimy and gross?"

I don't remind him that the alien is supposed to be me. Nor do I let my irritation show each time he looks to where the phone rests on the table. Instead I focus on improving his stories, which used to make me feel like I had an advantage that made us closer. Now it doesn't feel like enough. I can no longer compete. Not with her.

What do you think?

It's the weekend, and I'm in my room, relaxing before I start my shift at work. And by relaxing, I mean that I'm doing everything in my power to distract myself, because Carter and Olivia go on their date tonight. I imagine them kissing, or doing more, and it eats me up inside. I want to throw a tantrum. I want to stop the date from happening. What I really *really* want, is to quit obsessing over it because there's no point.

A text message should have been a welcome distraction. Instead, as I stand there with the phone cradled in my palm, I'm staring at a photo Carter has just sent. In it, his hair is slicked back and he's wearing a zip-up hoodie with a dress shirt beneath it. He looks like a complete doofus. It takes me a minute to realize that he's getting dressed for his date. This is good. I won't say a thing about his appearance, he'll meet Olivia, and she'll reject him, because right now, he's the polar opposite of a bad boy. And then…

Then it will all be the same. I'll still want him, he'll still want her, and we'll both be unhappy.

I'm coming over, I text back. Just to be safe, I add, *Do not send her that photo!*

A few minutes later, I'm standing at his front door and shivering as I wait for it to open. When it does, Vicky is standing there instead of Carter. She looks worried, even after she ushers me in.

"Are you okay?" she asks.

"Yeah. I didn't think I'd need a coat because you guys live so close. I was wrong."

She shakes her head like I'm not making sense. "No. The date. Are you upset?"

We're standing at the bottom of the stairs. I look up them to make sure we're alone. "Carter told you."

"Told me what?"

I sigh. "Then it's obvious."

"Since day one," Vicky says. "I don't know how to feel. I like Olivia but—"

"I like her too," I say quickly. "And so does Carter. So let's just be happy for them, okay?"

Vicky nods, but she's still frowning. "You would have made an awesome brother-in-law."

I allow myself to imagine the wedding. Carter and I are standing in front of the altar and he's about to kiss me, but he's still wearing that stupid outfit. "You'll have to settle for us being awesome friends," I say to her. "Now if you'll excuse me, I have an emergency to tend to."

"Have you seen his hair?" she asks, following me up the stairs.

"Exactly. Wish me luck."

She doesn't come into his bedroom with me, but she does stick her head in long enough to snort. Carter seems oblivious. He puts his hands on his hips and smiles like he's the sexiest guy alive.

"No," I say. "Sorry, but no."

Carter's hands drop to his side. "You don't like it?"

"Why do you think I said not to send her the photo?"

"So she'd be surprised!"

"She will be if you show up like that." I walk a critical circle around him. "What's with the dress shirt?"

"I want to look nice," Carter says, glowering at me.

"And the hoodie?"

"It's cold outside!"

"Take it off." When he complies, I say, "All of it."

Carter stares at me. "Why?"

"Worth a shot," I say with a smirk. "You have a maroon sweater with a V-neck. Is it clean?"

"I think so." He goes to his dresser, pulls out the sweater, and turns to me. "What sort of T-shirt should I wear under it?"

"None, unless you want to wear three layers. The sweater goes over your dress shirt."

Carter makes a face. "You're dressing me up like Gerald."

"Who has better taste than you. Besides, everything he wears is a lot busier. I don't think he owns anything that's a solid color. Try the sweater."

"It'll mess up my hair."

"Good! You look like a wet dog."

"I was going for James Bond."

"I'm sure she'll be plenty impressed with your guns, double-oh-seven. Here." Half the dress shirt collar is trapped under his sweater and the sleeves are all wrong, so I step forward to help him. I undo the top button of his shirt and tug the fabric so it's even before I look into brown eyes. He's adorably insecure, and of course I have the urge to kiss him, but I no longer get my hopes up or struggle to find some way of making that happen. I'm learning. Instead I work on his shirt sleeves, yanking on them until they poke out slightly. Then I brush his sweater down with my palm, and to my credit, I don't allow my hand to linger there or go where it's not needed. My work complete, I step back. The jeans are fine. He looks…

"Very handsome," I say, the words almost catching in my throat. "She won't know what hit her. Boom. Instant crush."

Carter smiles at me. Or at the thought of her. Either way.

"Then there's the hair," I say, unable to resist taking him down a peg. "It's better how you usually do it."

"Be right back," he says.

After he leaves, I sit on the edge of his bed. I'm tempted to bury my face in his pillow or raid his underwear drawer. I'm pretty sure neither of those things will make me feel better, so instead I stand and leave the room. Carter is putting the final touches on his hair when I enter the bathroom.

"What do you think?" he asks, watching me in the mirror. "Am I good to go?"

"Yeah. Much better."

"Cool." He licks his lips nervously. "Hey."

"Yeah?"

"Can I borrow your car?"

"What? I have to work! I thought you were borrowing your mom's?"

"She's going to a movie with a friend, and Dad is out of town. Olivia said we could use hers, but you know what a junker it is. Besides, I want to pick her up."

"That's very old-fashioned."

"I just want everything to be perfect. I can drive you to work so you don't have to walk."

I sigh. "Fine."

Carter turns around and hugs me. It's a nice reward. Except…

"Is that a new cologne?"

"It's my dad's," he says, pulling away. "Why?"

"Do you really want to smell like someone's dad?"

"Oh."

Carter looks like a scolded puppy, which makes me sigh again, but not out of irritation.

"Wash it off," I say. "Reed left behind a really nice bottle when he moved. I never use it because it would be weird to smell like my brother, but Olivia will love it. You can put it on when we go to my place for the car."

"You're the best!" Carter says.

I refrain from pointing out that isn't true or he would be taking me out instead, but I know it wouldn't be fair. Nor do I point out that he once promised to never let anyone hurt me. Does that not include himself? Because I'm beginning to fear the constant ache inside of me is permanent. If so, at least Carter will have forever left his mark on me.

I keep these thoughts to myself, and when we return to my house, I make sure he doesn't put on too much cologne. Then I hand him my car keys, wish him luck instead of saying that I love him, and let go. As much as I can or ever will, I open my heart and release him for another to find.

I don't enjoy my shift at work. Every heterosexual couple I see is, in my mind, another version of Carter and Olivia. Their age doesn't matter. If it's a couple in their sixties, I wonder what Carter will look like then, and if he'll tell his grandchildren how he married his high school sweetheart. A pair in their twenties make me picture how Olivia might be the one to help Carter with his dyslexia in college. Maybe she'll be editing his stories by then. When people our age come in for pizza, I'm reminded how it's normal to actually go on dates, rather than imagining other people on theirs. I really need to get it together.

Jackson is in the mood to joke around, and I try to match his spirit, but it's tough. I just want the night to be over. Tomorrow too, when I'll no doubt have to listen to every happy detail. Once I get past that chore, maybe I'll finally be over him. I'm reaching the point where I'd rather rewind to the previous summer, when I felt lonely because my heart was ready to be filled rather than it being scraped empty, like it is now.

At last my shift is over. I'm standing by the doors while waiting for Jackson to finish shutting off the lights. He's always the one to lock up. I could just go, but we always leave together.

"Where's your little clown car?" he says while walking toward me. He's wearing a big grin.

My expression is the opposite. "You did not just make fun of my Fiat."

"Doesn't Mr. Bean drive one of those?"

I cross my arms over my chest. "If he does, that only makes it cooler."

Jackson nods toward the parking lot as we step outside and pulls the door shut behind him. "Seriously," he says while locking it. "I don't see your car anywhere."

"Carter wanted to borrow it."

"What for?"

I don't answer. I'm too worried about how Bobby will react when he finds out Carter is dating his ex-girlfriend. I know he and Jackson still talk. Their relationship might be strained, but they have more history together than he and I do.

"Come on," Jackson says, pocketing the keys and pulling out another set. "I'll give you a ride."

My toes are already starting to go numb from the cold. I don't know why anyone chooses to live in Chicago. Cost of living is high, gun violence is out of control, the highways are always backed up, and the weather sucks. The people are nice, as I'm reminded when Jackson opens the car door for me. Once he's in the driver's seat, he revs the engine a few times before we pull out of the parking lot.

"Gets the heater working faster," he explains. "It's a waste of gas, but it's better than freezing to death."

"Too late," I say, sticking out my tongue and letting my head go limp.

He laughs and guns it down one of the neighborhood streets. "You didn't say why Carter needed your ride."

"He's on a date," I admit.

"Oh." Jackson says. "*Oh!*"

I shouldn't have said anything. "You can't let Bobby find out! He'll kill them both. Please."

"He won't kill them," Jackson says. Then he reconsiders. "Okay, he might kill one of them."

He means Carter. "Promise me you won't tell him."

"I won't. But if they become an item, he'll find out anyway."

"I know. Any advice?"

Jackson grimaces as he slows at a stop sign. "Hope that Bobby finds someone else before then."

"Know any girls who are interested?"

Jackson is quiet, and I mentally kick myself because he probably hates the idea of Bobby dating someone else. I can relate.

"I'll tell them to be careful," I say.

"How are you doing?" Jackson asks.

It's a loaded question, and I give him a loaded answer. "I feel like a junkie who's trying to kick a bad habit, when really, I'd do just about anything for another fix. The only problem is that my dealer is giving his best stuff to some pretty young thing who caught his eye."

Jackson laughs. "Sorry," he says, "but that's textbook melodramatic."

I smile. "Yeah. I guess it is. I know I'll get over this. I just wish I could skip to the part where I already have."

"But you want to."

It's hard for me to say it, but it feels true when I do. "Yeah."

"Then you've made it past the biggest hurdle. My mom always says that we fight our most difficult battles inside ourselves. Everything else is easy."

"Do you think she's right?"

Jackson stops the car in front of my house. He puts it into park and looks over at me. "I hope so."

"Me too." I should go inside and try to get some sleep, but the car is getting warm and I don't want to be alone. I'm about to invite him inside when I remember that he never accepts. "Why are you so scared of my house?"

"Huh? Oh." Jackson rolls his neck, working out the kinks before he answers. "I'm still not ready to come out."

"That's fine, but I'm only asking you to come in."

"Yeah, but..." He looks to the house. "Your parents are home, right?"

"Yes."

"And they'll see us together."

"Probably. I wouldn't mind introducing you. Why?"

Jackson looks over at me with an apologetic expression. "Won't it be obvious?"

"What?"

"A gay guy brings another guy home. They'll just assume."

I laugh. I can't help it. "Carter and I sleep in the same bed *every weekend*. They've never once asked me if he's... Okay, my mom did at the beginning. And my brother. But I'd be willing to lie for you. I don't usually. Being in the closet is different though. This is about protecting you until you feel safe."

"You'd do that for me?"

"Sure! If it means you'll come play video games with me. Or we could watch Netflix. You pick the show. I don't care if I've never seen it and you're in the middle of the fifth season. I just want to hang out. When my parents ask me later who the handsome guy was, I'll tell them that you dated Becca and that I'm not your type."

"You don't have to lie."

"Technically, I wouldn't be. So..."

Jackson shakes his head, like I'm being foolish. Then he undoes his seatbelt. "Okay."

"Really?"

"Yeah."

"Finally!" I try to open the car door in my excitement. As always, it doesn't cooperate. "What's with this thing? Is it rigged?"

"It's all in the way you handle it," Jackson says, leaning over to open it for me.

Except he doesn't reach for the door. His hand lands on the seatback next to my shoulder, and his lips... I barely have time to react before they touch mine. At first I don't do anything. Then I think of the guy who always makes sure I never walk home in the rain or snow. The same guy who has patiently listened to my every problem, who bought me a heater so I wouldn't be cold, and who chased after a homeless man just to make sure he'd be all right. That kindhearted person is kissing me now, which makes it easy to kiss him back. And it feels good.

"I know," Jackson says when he pulls away. "You still love Carter. I guess I still love Bobby." He settles back into his seat. "But I thought maybe you and I could move on. Together. We can take it slow. See what happens. I like you, and if you like me too, at least we're capable of loving each other. We can give that back if we ever start to feel it. You know?"

"Yeah," I say.

With anyone else, it would seem unfair. He's right. The kiss was nice, but I still love Carter. I didn't realize how much that has blinded me. The guy sitting next to me is handsome and noble. He has issues, but so does Carter. So do I. At least Jackson and I are messed up in the same way. We both want guys we can't have. The closeted thing doesn't bother me. I can help him with that. If he wants. We could be together. We could try!

"I was hoping you'd say a little more," Jackson says, his eyes darting over to me nervously.

"Sorry!" I say. "I've been lost in my own thoughts lately. I feel like you just woke me up."

"Does that make you Snow White?"

"I mean, I *am* pretty white, but you're thinking of Sleeping Beauty. She gets awakened with a kiss, remember?"

Jackson shakes his head. "Nope. It's Snow White. She's in a glass coffin and the prince wakes her up with a kiss."

"Can't be. If she's in a coffin, she's dead, not sleeping."

He scrunches up his face. "Weird. Maybe you're right."

"Then that's what we'll watch. Snow White."

Jackson looks me over. "What if I'm right?"

"Then you get to kiss me again," I say.

"And if you're right?"

I give him my best evil grin. "Then you get to be Snow White next shift and do all the dishes for the pizza-loving dwarves."

"Agreed. Let's get this over with."

Turns out that Jackson was right. In the Disney version, at least. I still feel like I won. Especially after I say goodbye to him and crawl into bed, because I haven't been thinking about Carter and his date. The entire time I was with Jackson, it was the furthest thing from my mind.

Chapter Fifteen

I'm not surprised when I see less and less of Carter. His date with Olivia went well. Naturally. He's a good conversationalist, good looking, a good guy… Ugh. All that good stuff. I get to see this first-hand during school. They never stop talking. They often remember I'm there and try to include me, which is kind, but there's only room for two on a honeymoon.

I try not to take it personally. I did the same thing when I first started dating Scott. I didn't like my friends any less. I simply couldn't think of anyone but him. A new relationship isn't a great experience for those left standing on the sidelines, but for the couple falling in love, it's one of the most euphoric highs out there. So I'm happy for Carter, and I tell myself that this might be good in the long run. I need to get over him. Time spent apart will help.

In theory. As the weeks go by, I miss Carter more and more. He'll never be my husband, but he *is* my closest friend, and that leaves a gaping hole in my life. Jackson does his best to fill it. Not like that. We kiss sometimes, but we've been taking it slow. We haven't gone further. He often hangs out at my place now, and even invited me over to his. I got to meet his family. I tried to be charming and personable. After I left, he told them the truth. My truth, anyway. They know I'm gay. Jackson says they don't care. At all. He's still concerned that they'll have a different reaction if he comes out, but I'm not worried. They seem like kind, intelligent, loving people. With that sort of combination, it's hard to go wrong.

By the time February rolls around, I'm focusing less on what I can't have and appreciating more what I do have. Carter and I still have fun, on the rare instances that we hang out alone. He tends to give any private time to Olivia, so it's more common I see him when we're all hanging with Bobby's band of misfits. Olivia only makes token appearances, and when she does, she doesn't interact with Carter or Bobby much, since the situation is too complicated. Instead she sticks close to me. The more I socialize with her, the happier I am that Carter has such an awesome girlfriend. It's official now. They're together, even though it has to remain a secret. We're all too worried about how Bobby will react.

I hang out with Vicky on occasion. That began because I was missing Carter and wanted to be around someone like him. As it turns out, she doesn't have much in common with her brother, but she and I have fun regardless. She's been spending time with the entire group more often, which is nice. She and Olivia really hit if off. I'm hoping they start doing more together so Carter isn't as busy.

Working at Blaze Pizza continues to be tolerable, thanks to Jackson. He's always joking around, especially when I lose myself in morose thoughts. He seems to sense my downward spirals and catches me before I can plummet too far. We've lined up our shifts so we're always working together, which is practical. Carter often needs to borrow the Fiat. Each time I hand him the keys, I fight down a smile because I know Jackson will give me a ride home. These days, whenever Jackson reaches over to open the door for me, he kisses me first. He's sweet, and more and more, I find myself fantasizing about him.

Overall, I'm content. My life is good, but not without its issues. When I get home from school one afternoon, my mom is already there, which is unusual. She tells me that my grandpa is in the hospital with pneumonia. I was never very close to him, but I'm crazy about my grandma, and I don't want her to lose her husband. Or for my mom to lose her father. His condition is serious enough that my parents are flying to Albuquerque for the weekend. Reed is coming to stay with me. He's the first person I call once I'm alone in my room.

"I need a favor," I say.

"Let me guess," Reed replies. "You don't want me there this weekend."

"I figured you'd be too busy to babysit. You really don't need to. I can take care of—"

"Save it," Reed says. "I'm not Mom and Dad. I know you want to throw a party, and you're right, I've got better things to do than chaperone."

"Thank you!"

"You owe me."

While I'm on the way to work, my mind fills with possibilities. I could invite all of my friends over. Pedro always knows where to score weed. We could get fried and chill. Or it could just be Jackson and me. Maybe now is the right opportunity to explore what we have together. Or maybe I should go really big and invite everyone who's in the OCP.

I still haven't decided when my shift begins. I keep weighing my options without mentioning the idea to anyone. That changes when Carter and Olivia show up. Once they're seated in a booth and sharing a pizza, I make up my mind.

"Hey," I say to Jackson. "It's dead right now. Let's go sit with them."

"Mood killer?" he says pointedly.

Oh. Right. I guess they are on a date, but… "I've got exciting news for them. You too. Come on."

I sit next to Olivia so I can see Carter better. I might be trying to get over him, but I can still enjoy a little eye candy. This works out even better when Jackson sits next to Carter. Two handsome guys instead of one! Before my libido can lead me down that rabbit hole, I tell them my plan.

"My parents are out of town this weekend," I say. "What if we keep that a secret between us?"

"A party?" Olivia asks.

"A very small one," I reply. "Just the four of us."

I look at Jackson to gauge his reaction. He seems a little uncomfortable, probably because nobody knows about us yet. If we're even a thing. So far there haven't been any titles or expectations.

"What do you think?" Carter says to Olivia.

She raises her eyebrows. "That depends on what you're expecting to happen."

"Nothing!" he says hurriedly, his face turning red.

I start laughing before she does. Then I look at Jackson. "You in?"

"Yeah," he says, smiling at me and no one else. That's refreshing. I'm tired of competing.

We discuss potential plans. Should we try to get alcohol? Make a fancy dinner? Each time a customer comes in, Jackson and I serve them, then return to the booth to talk more. Carter and Olivia are getting ready to leave when the door opens again. I'm rising so she can slide out of the booth when I glance at the entrance and see Bobby there.

I freeze. Not a good move because I look like someone who has just been caught. I'm poised somewhere between sitting and standing, my eyes wide. Then I smile and say his name, so that the others will know he's here.

"Bobby! Hey! How's it going?"

"What's going on?" Bobby says as he walks toward us.

The door opens again, and this time Mick comes in. I don't know where Pedro and Felipe are. I'm not worried about anyone but Bobby, who is eyeing the table as he nears, sizing up the situation. I do the same. It doesn't look too bad. Carter and Olivia aren't sitting on the same side. Wait, would that be better, or worse? I don't know. I'm freaking out. Jackson looks nervous too. This isn't good.

"You should have told us that we're all hanging out tonight," Bobby says. He's most interested in Olivia, although he spares a few glances for Carter.

"Jackson and I are working," I point out. In a conspiring whisper, I add, "Or we're supposed to be." I thought this would help explain why so many of us had gotten together without him. But if I'd had more time to think, I might have reached the same conclusion that Bobby does.

"That means you two are enjoying a night out on the town," he says, looking between Carter and Olivia. "Together."

"No," I say quickly. "Olivia was already here. I promised her a pizza for helping me with my Calculus test. I texted Carter and told him to get over here, because I have exciting news. I was about to text you too."

"You never text me," Bobby says without humor.

"Now I won't have to start because you're here. My parents will be gone Saturday night. We're having a party."

It's the only thing I can think of. I don't dabble in deception. I'm not good at playing mind games. My punishment is instantaneous because my dream of a cozy night with my favorite people is now gone. I had to sacrifice it to stop Bobby from having one of his psychotic incidents. I'm getting tired of us dancing around him and hiding our feelings just because we don't want to deal with how nuts he is.

"A party," Bobby says, pulling up a chair so he can sit. "Now we're talking!"

And talk he does. Filipe has an uncle who will buy us booze if we all chip in. Weed is a sure thing too. I don't mind. It's my senior year. I'm okay with getting wild. I just don't like the idea of inviting Bobby into my home. When I risk a look at Jackson, he nods at me, and I know I did the right thing. Strange how it still feels so wrong.

I'm just about to get undressed and crawl into bed when I get a text from Carter.

You still up?

Yeah. I answer. *What's going on?*

He's not the fastest at replying. I'm used to that, but when minutes pass and I don't see the indicator that he's typing, I go to the side entrance of my house. Sure enough, when I open the door and stick my head out, I see Carter hurrying down the sidewalk, his every breath a cloud in the air.

"Fuck this weather," he hisses.

"Fuck it to death," I agree.

He rubs his hands together once he's inside. Then we silently go back down to my room where my parents won't hear us.

"Is everything okay?" I ask. It must be important if texting isn't an option.

"Yeah!" Carter says. He looks around my room like he hasn't seen it in ages. "It just kind of clicked tonight how long it's been."

"Oh?"

He turns to face me with a sheepish grin. "I wanted to say that I'm sorry. I miss you, man!"

"I miss you too," I say with a chuckle. "It's okay, though. I totally get it."

"Yeah?"

"Yeah. How are things going with her?"

"Fine," Carter says. "We can talk about other stuff though."

"Okay."

I wait, knowing that his entire life has been consumed by Olivia, Olivia, Olivia. I watch him squirm as he tries to think of anything to say that doesn't begin with her name.

"How have you been?" he tries.

"Fine. Now stop being polite and tell me everything. Have you guys… you know."

Carter groans and flops down on my bed. I join him.

"Girls are so hard to figure out," he complains. "We've done some stuff. Playing around. But we haven't done that yet."

"Is she not willing or…"

"I don't know," Carter admits. "I don't want to push my luck. There's never an opportunity. At my place, my sisters are around. My parents too. At her house, she has three older brothers, and they're all *huge!*"

I laugh. "Sounds dangerous. Maybe you'll have more luck this weekend. You guys can take my parent's room. If she wants to stay the night, that is."

Carter looks over at me. "How will I know if she's ready?"

"Ask her," I suggest. "I know it's revolutionary, but there's this wacky thing called communication. You should try it."

"Won't that... I don't know, kill the spontaneity and romance?"

"Or it'll let her prepare so she's ready and comfortable. The act itself is romantic enough. If she's not ready yet, ask her to let you know."

Carter blinks a few times. "Now that you say it, it's kind of obvious."

"Yup."

He grins. "So this weekend we might—" The smile slides off his face. "Are you okay with this? I don't want to... um."

"Hurt my feelings?"

"Yeah."

"I'm okay," I reassure him. "In fact, there's something I've been meaning to tell you. It's a secret, because he's still in the closet, but I've been seeing someone. Sort of."

Carter sits upright. "That's awesome! Who?"

"Jackson."

"Ha ha. Seriously. Who?"

"Jackson," I repeat.

Carter studies my face, probably expecting me to laugh. When I don't, he says, "You're messing with me!"

"Nope! What do you think?"

The question has him too overwhelmed to respond, so I tell him everything. With the exception of Jackson's history with Bobby. That's private and not mine to give. After I get him up to speed, the first question he asks surprises me.

"Do you love him?"

"I have feelings for him," I say carefully. "Why? Do you love Olivia?"

He hesitates, so I reassure him again that I'm okay. Only then does he nod.

"I'm crazy about her."

"Cool."

"Yeah?"

I search my heart, and while it's not in complete agreement, there is at least a general consensus. It's good that my best friend can finally be with the girl he loves.

"Yeah. I'm happy for you. Just be sure to watch out for that pillow."

"Huh? What pillow?"

"This one."

I grab my favorite pillow and swing before he can react, knocking him on the side of the head. Then I scurry out of bed, feigning and dodging to avoid his lunges. He'll make me pay when I finally get caught, but hey, at least he's the one chasing me. That's a nice change of pace!

I like to dance. Even if I'm the only one feeling the groove, but hey, it's my party and I'm in the mood. Bass shakes the family room as my phone streams all of my favorite songs. Everyone is watching me, and when I get tired of being the sole source of their amusement, I grab Carter's hand and pull him off the couch, thinking he will resist. Instead he hops to his feet and starts shaking his hips and pumping his arms. He's not bad! After I get past my surprise and stop laughing, we dance together and I freaking love it. I never expected him to be the type, although I suppose he is athletic, and we are getting some serious exercise.

The party has been great so far. I'm a little drunk. And high. Everyone seems to be having a good time. I was most worried about Olivia, due to the tricky situation. Being around an ex and a secret boyfriend at the same time? Awkward. That's why I invited Vicky, so Olivia would have someone to talk to without Bobby freaking out.

Speaking of Mr. Psychopath, he's brooding in one corner of the room. He seems intent on getting wasted. That's fine with me. Hopefully he'll pass out soon. Mick and Pedro are keeping him company. Felipe is too, until he walks over and asks Vicky to dance. She's not as easily coaxed into the center of the room as her brother, and she seems even more intimidated when Felipe shows us his moves. The boy can dance! I should get to know him better. I notice Jackson plopping down on the couch to keep

Olivia company, so I stop worrying and get lost in the music.

When I open my eyes again, it's just me and Felipe. The others have given up. When the next song ends, I bow to him like he's king of the dance floor and leave to find myself a drink. I hang out with Mick and Pedro while I guzzle a beer to parch my thirst. Halfway through it, I notice that Bobby isn't with them or anywhere else in the room. I try not to worry about that. Maybe he needed to pee. And is doing so on my parents' bed or something crazy.

I go upstairs to check. The house is silent, so I return to the basement. I stick my head in my room, which was dark when I left it earlier in the night. Now the light is on, and Bobby is standing there, sucking on a beer.

"What the fuck is this?" he asks, gesturing at my wall.

"Photos," I say, walking over to join him.

"I mean *this*," Bobby says, pointing with the lip of his bottle. I ignore the beer that slops out onto the carpet and look instead at the photo.

It's of Jackson. We were at work when he carved a microphone out of a zucchini and started singing to me. An entire song! He wouldn't stop, no matter how much I begged him to, or tried to embarrass him by snapping photos. He was shameless, and it cracked me up.

"What about it?" I ask.

"I'm not surprised that you sit in here jerking off over Carter," Bobby says, motioning to all the photos of him. "I didn't realize you have a thing for Jackson too."

"We work together," I say. "We're friends."

"Is that why you put him right in the middle?"

I'm never surprised when Bobby is an asshole. When he's observant, that's when I'm caught off guard. The photo of Jackson is a new addition, and yeah, I did put him right in the middle because more and more, I'm thinking that's where he belongs—in the center of my world.

"I wanted to put your photo there instead," I say, not hiding my sarcasm, "but you didn't give me one of your yearbook pics."

"Yeah, where am I, Andrew?" Bobby says, looking over at me. "Aren't we friends?"

"Right here," I say, pointing at a group shot at the park. I put it there for this very reason, so nobody would feel like they weren't included. "But if that's not good enough…" I take out my phone and snap a photo of him glaring at me. "I'll print this out and add it to the wall. Soon I'll be jerking off over you too. Happy?"

He doesn't look happy. "Jackson never seems to have time for me lately. Why is that? Huh?"

I shrug, like I don't know or care. "Ask him. Are we done in here?"

"Yeah," Bobby says. "We're done."

I don't realize how tense I am until he leaves my room and I shut the door behind us. Bobby scares me. Always has. When he goes to get another beer and hang out with the guys, I pretend to ignore him and go over to Carter, when what I really need is to talk to Jackson. I want to know what he thinks about Bobby's comments. Are they suspicious or is he just being a dick? I have another question for Jackson too, one that's been burning inside of me all week.

"Hey," I say to Carter after I feel enough time has passed. "I'm going out back for some fresh air. Could you tell Jackson to meet me there? Not right away. Ten minutes?" I remember the cold. "Better make it five."

Carter grins slowly. He's not entirely sober either. "You guys are going to mess around. Aren't you?"

"Maybe," I say, elbowing him playfully. "You might want to ease up if you expect anything to happen later tonight."

"Oh shit!" he says.

He and Olivia had their big talk, and she confirmed that she's ready. They're going to sleep together. Tonight. I'm trying not to obsess over that.

Carter sets aside his beer. Then he nods. "I'll tell him. Hey, will you walk my sister home? Her curfew is almost up. I figure that's a better excuse, anyway."

"Good idea," I say. "Thanks."

I make sure to look bored on my way out of the room. I don't think anyone notices me go. Bobby is lost in a cloud of smoke with Pedro and Mick. Felipe already left, having to work a nightshift. I hope everyone else will clear out soon.

I collect Vicky, who resists. She can't stay the night. Her parents think she's out with friends. Carter doesn't have to worry about a curfew since he has permission to stay over with me, although his parents don't know that mine are gone. I'm worried they'll figure it out anyway, because Vicky is a giggling mess. During the walk, I try to get her to remember that, officially, she was out bowling instead of smoking bowls. She pulls herself together when we reach her house. Once she's safely inside, I hurry back to my place. Jackson is waiting by the back door when I get there.

"Hey," he says, eyes a little glassy.

I hate to kill a good buzz, but this is important. "I think Bobby is on to us."

Jackson goes still. "What?"

"He saw that photo of you on my wall."

"That's it?"

"Yeah."

Jackson relaxes. Then he pretends he's holding a microphone and starts singing. "*Very superstitious…*"

"You are not singing that song again!"

"*Writing's on the wall.*"

I shake my head and laugh. "Stevie Wonder, could you please give me Jackson Pearson back? I need to talk to him."

"*Very superstitious…*"

I grab the imaginary mic from him, throw it to the ground, and stomp on it. "Seriously. The way he was acting freaked me out."

Jackson's arms fall to his side. "It's fine."

"How do you know?"

Jackson turns his face away, the distant light from an orange streetlight deepening the shadows on his face. "Because he doesn't care about me."

"His loss," I say, touching his chin and turning it toward me. "I mean it." I kiss him, and my heart skips a beat, reminding me of what I really wanted to talk to him about. "Do you want to stay the night with me?"

"That was the plan," Jackson says. "My mom already gave me the all clear."

"Yeah, but…" I grin. "I'm asking if you want to be with me. Tonight. Because I like you."

Jackson's expression remains cool. His smile is subtle as he jerks his head upward. "All right."

I push him playfully. "I thought you'd be more excited than that!"

He moves close to me again. "You'll see how excited I am. Later."

I bite my bottom lip, loving the way he looks at me. "Okay. Let's go back inside. I'm cold."

"Or we can stay out here and I'll warm you up."

Jackson is wrapping his arms around me when we hear the door squeak open. The outdoor light is off and we have enough time to leap away from each other, but my pulse still kicks into overdrive when Bobby steps outside.

He looks at us in silence. We stare back.

"I fucking knew it," Bobby growls.

"Knew what?" I ask, playing dumb.

Bobby ignores me. He focuses on Jackson. In the darkness, I don't see the knife until I hear a metallic click. Then I look down as Bobby marches over to Jackson, the blade held low.

"What the hell is going on here?" Bobby says, shoving him against the house. "Huh? You want to tell me about it?"

"Fuck off!" Jackson says, pushing him away.

Bobby comes right back, this time with the knife raised, and I stop breathing when the point touches Jackson's throat. I don't dare make a sound or move an inch, because the knife is pressing against the skin of his neck, but so far it hasn't punctured the surface.

"What are you going to do?" Jackson says. His words sound brave, but he's back up against the house as far as he can go. "You gonna cut me? For real this time?"

"You're a faggot," Bobby snarls. "Aren't you?"

I've never felt so helpless. I want to pull on Bobby's arm to get the knife away from Jackson. I even brace myself to tackle him, but I'm too terrified to take action. One wrong move and blood will splatter across the concrete walkway. Still, I have to do something!

"Calm down," I say, inching closer.

"I'm not talking to you," Bobby says.

Then he notices that I'm near and shoves me away with his free hand like I weigh no more than a dried leaf. Jackson's brow furrows and his lips pull back. I think of Gerald, and his warning that lives can be lost if anger spirals out of control. I try to remember my lessons. If all of this had already happened, what would I do if given a second chance?

Reason with him.

"He's not a faggot," I say, pleading with Bobby. "He's your best friend. Look at him! You've known each other since grade school, right? Since you were little boys! You used to play together, and now you have a knife to his throat. Why?"

"Because he's a traitor," Bobby says, his hand starting to tremble.

I see a drop of dark liquid trickling down Jackson throat. He's bleeding, and I want to scream for help or maybe cry because I can't stand the idea of him getting hurt. I've got to keep my cool. I'll be useless if I give into despair.

"Talk to him," I tell Jackson. "Tell him how you feel."

"I'm your friend," Jackson rasps. "Always."

Bobby's teeth are bared and grinding together. I'm positive he's going to kill Jackson. Then he moves, and I tense, but no more blood is drawn. Bobby steps away from Jackson, puts the knife away, and sounds disturbingly calm when he says, "That's all I wanted to know." He pats Jackson on the shoulder, like they're old pals. On his way to the door, he looks me right in the eye. "Nice party, Andrew."

I can't find words as he goes back inside. I'm still rigid with fear. "We have to call the cops," I say, pulling out my phone.

"No," Jackson says, placing a hand over mine. "It's fine. Forget about it."

"How can you say that?" I shout. "He nearly killed you!"

"It's fine." Jackson rubs at his neck, looks at the blood on his palm, and grimaces. "He's done this before."

"What? When?"

"I told you that I always pretend to be reluctant."

"That's so fucked up," I say, shaking my head. "Seriously. You want to be a police officer? Don't you think this is the sort of thing that should be reported? How many times has he done this to you?"

"Once," Jackson says. "This is the second time. Like I said, for him it's about power. He saw that he has it over me. He's happy now. I don't think he really cares if I'm gay. He doesn't care about me at all."

"At least we agree on something," I say. "Let's go inside. I'm worried about the others."

"Don't tell them," Jackson says.

I halt on the way to the door, my mouth falling open. "Are you kidding me? No way. I'm telling them."

A hand on my shoulder stops me when I try to walk away.

"Please," Jackson says. "I don't want them to know the truth. You're the only one I trust."

I turn to face him and sigh. I'm not sure if he doesn't want the others to know that he's gay or that Bobby abuses him. It doesn't really matter, because I've already decided to respect his wishes. But this has to stop. We can't keep making excuses for Bobby. If we do, he'll end up killing one of us. I'm sure of it.

When we go back inside, the only person still there is Carter. He squints at us and laughs. "Is that a hickey?"

Jackson covers his neck where Bobby cut him. "No. Who would give me a hickey?"

"He knows about us," I whisper.

Jackson looks surprised.

"It's cool," Carter says. "Actually, I think it's great. Oh. Everyone else is gone. You don't have to whisper. Olivia should be back a little later."

The plan was for Bobby to see her leaving so he wouldn't suspect anything. I'm especially glad we're being so cautious now.

"Come on," I say to Jackson. "Let's go take care of that hickey."

"Go easy on him," Carter calls after us.

I don't say anything until Jackson and I are standing in the bathroom. I move his hand away from his neck. "It's just a prick," I say, wadding up toilet paper to press against it. "Barely worse than a shaving cut."

"You told Carter," Jackson says.

"Yeah." I meet his gaze. He seems more hurt than angry. "Just about us. Carter is a good guy. You can trust him. Oh. He doesn't know about the stuff with Bobby."

"He wasn't always like this," Jackson says, expression pleading with me.

I don't respond. I know he won't listen because love has blinded him too. I'm only now starting to understand how he's been mistreated over the years. I want to help him. I can be there if he needs me to listen, and if he ever seems open to it, I'll try to talk sense into him.

Jackson's throat moves beneath my hand as he swallows. "I still want to stay the night. If you want me to."

"Of course," I say. "Come here."

I take him into my arms, but they feel small and weak. I wish I could protect him. I just don't know how.

The house is quiet. The door to my bedroom is closed. Jackson is reclining on my bed, and I know he's expecting something to happen between us, but we haven't so much as kissed. I'm still too jittery with adrenaline. He watches me pace back and forth as I try to purge Bobby from my mind.

"Can you at least admit that he's crazy?" I say, unable to let the subject drop.

Jackson sighs. "I think he could use therapy."

"Is that a yes?"

"Fine. Yes. Over the past few years, Bobby has gotten more… unstable."

Unstable doesn't begin to describe it. "Then maybe we should help make therapy happen."

"How?"

"I don't know, but ignoring his outbursts won't help."

"Andrew…"

I stop and face him. "What?"

"Can we talk about this tomorrow?"

My shoulders slump. I know he's right. Bobby already ruined part of the evening. I won't let him destroy the entire night. "Sorry. I'll check the house and make sure everything is locked. When I come back, I won't mention him. It'll just be me and you."

Jackson smiles. I like his teeth. Is that weird? Maybe I'm falling for him. I'm tempted to forget about the rest of the house and lock the door to my bedroom instead, but I need to feel safe. "Be right back."

I check the side entrance at the rear of the house first. The bolt is in place, and the outside light is on. I'm tempted to check the windows on my way through the house, but Reed made sure those were locked tight at the beginning of winter. They haven't been opened since. That just leaves the front door. After yanking on it to make sure it's locked, I peer through one of the windows to confirm that the porch light is still on. The house is as secure as can reasonably be expected, although maybe I can talk my parents into getting an alarm system. I turn around and look up the stairs to their room. They aren't home, of course, but their bed isn't empty.

A longing stirs inside me, and before I know it, my foot is on the first step. I creep up the rest of them, stopping whenever a board squeaks. I know what I'm doing. I try not to think about it, but I can't deny what I want.

I make it up the stairs, then get on my hands and knees and crawl along the carpet in slow motion, terrified of being detected but unable to resist my sick desire. If I can't be with him, I can at least hear how it would have sounded. The taste of his skin and the sight of him naked—these things will never belong to me, but sound… Give me at least that, because from it I can create a soundtrack for an impossible world where he and I are together.

The top floor is a converted attic, so space is limited. There are only three doors. One leads to a closet, another a bathroom, and the final… I hear the rhythmic sound of sex behind it. Murmured words spur me forward. I need to know each so I can pretend he's speaking them to me. As I slowly get to my feet, I wonder what Carter is like in bed. Gentle during their first time together, I bet. Tender. Or maybe he's playful, making jokes while nipping at my neck. *Her* neck. I carefully press my ear against the door. I hear gasps and moans, and finally…

"You're so beautiful."

One of the steps behind me creaks. I turn around and my heart shoots into my throat. Then it plunges down to my stomach, because Jackson is standing there. I want to tell him I'm sorry, but I can't speak without giving myself away. Tonight is supposed to be about us, and now he's caught me obsessing over Carter. Again.

All I can do is make an apologetic face and tiptoe over to where Jackson stands. I reach for him, wanting to whisper an explanation in his ear, but he catches my wrists. Not to push me away. Instead he leans close to my ear.

"It's okay," he says quietly. Then he pulls back, and gestures with his head for me to follow him.

We slowly work our way down the stairs, and once at the bottom, he moves faster, walking through the house toward the basement stairs.

"Hey," I hiss after him. "Wait."

Jackson turns around in the kitchen. "I get it," he says. "You don't need to explain. I've done the same thing."

Not what I was expecting to hear! "You have?"

"Bobby was with this girl and yeah, I totally get it."

"This doesn't mean I'm not…" *Into you. Over Carter.* I hesitate, no longer sure what's true. "I don't want to feel this way," I admit, my lip trembling.

Jackson takes me in his arms, and this time, no one interrupts us. "We both need to move on," he says. "I'm coming out."

I pull back so I can see his face. "What?"

Jackson clenches his jaw and nods. "Tomorrow. To everyone. And if Bobby has a problem with it, then he and I are done."

"Wow."

"Yeah. I'm sick of feeling this way too. No more fear."

"That's awesome!"

"Thanks." He lets go of me and steps back. "We don't have to do anything tonight. I understand if you're not ready."

I stare at him, focusing on the feelings he stirs up inside of me until the rest fades away. Carter, Olivia, Bobby… All of them are gone from my thoughts until Jackson becomes my everything. Then I take his hand and lead him downstairs to my room. There's no need to tell Jackson I'm ready. I'll show him instead.

Chapter Sixteen

I have a boyfriend now. Not only that, but he's a man of his word. Jackson came out the next day, just like he said he would. First by telling Carter and Olivia during breakfast. He woke up early and went to get us donuts that were only half as sweet as the gesture itself. When Jackson went home that day, he told his family. I wish I could have been there, but such moments are private. I squeezed every detail out of him anyway. His family had a lot of questions, and there were a few tears, but they've chosen to support him.

Jackson needed another week to work up the courage to tell Bobby. This also happened behind closed doors—of his Camaro, this time—but Jackson wasn't as forthcoming about that conversation. When I saw him next, I could tell he was hurt, but he wouldn't say why. Although he did have something he wanted me to know.

"I asked him if he was gay," Jackson says while sprawled out on my bed. He's resting his head on my bare chest and we're both basking in the afterglow. "Or maybe bisexual. Bobby just laughed."

"As in, 'Ha ha, this question makes me nervous, can we please change the subject?' That kind of laugh?"

"No. More like, 'Ha ha, you still don't get it, do you?' But I do. It's just like I said. I was convenient for him and he got off on the sense of power."

"At least you have your answer," I say.

"Yeah. I waited years to ask him that."

"And he accepts you? You'll still be friends?"

"Uh huh."

Jackson clings to me, and I try to be happy for him. If I'm honest, I was hoping that his friendship with Bobby would end.

"I'm proud of you," I say. "You've come out to everyone important in a single week. That's amazing!"

I'm not the only one who is impressed. Carter and Olivia are downright inspired because, as they tell me in the school library the next day, they want to come out too.

"We only have one person to worry about," Carter says. "You and Jackson had to tell everyone. We keep reminding ourselves of how much easier we've got it."

As much as I appreciate his understanding, I have my concerns. "You need to think about the best way to break the news to Bobby. There's no telling how he might react."

They still don't know about the incident with the knife. Whenever I bring up that subject with Jackson, he rolls his eyes and points out that Bobby was drunk that night.

"Maybe I should tell him alone," Olivia says. "Bobby might pick a fight with Carter, but he won't try that with me."

I don't share her confidence. "Carter needs to tell him," I say. "Otherwise it'll seem like he's hiding behind you. Bobby will interpret that as weakness."

"I bet he's right," Carter says.

"But," I stress, "you shouldn't do it alone. Meet him in a public place. How about at my work? That way I'm there. Jackson too. We can call the police or intervene if Bobby freaks out."

"I don't think he will," Olivia says. "It's been nearly two months."

"It doesn't hurt to take precautions," I say. "You know what? Jackson is his best friend. We'll see what he says. If he thinks it's a good idea, then we'll do it. Agreed?"

They nod at me. I look to Gerald, who is across the room tutoring a student. I want to run the idea by him as well. When it's my turn for some one-on-one tutoring, I ask him a question.

"Do you mind if Carter joins us? It's important."

"Not at all!" Gerald says.

Soon the three of us are sitting at a table, two pairs of eyes trained on me.

"Carter and I have a tricky situation coming up," I say. "We want to make peace with someone, but this person is emotionally volatile."

"Great way to phrase it," Gerald praises.

I smile. "Thanks. I've learned a lot from being his editor." I gesture at Carter. "Anyway, we have some news for this person that he won't be happy about. He needs to hear it, but I'm worried about how he'll react."

Gerald purses his lips. "Does this have anything to do with our anger management discussions?"

"Yeah. We need to stay calm. This other guy, we're pretty sure he's going to freak out. But like you keep telling me, if there are two people and only one of them gets angry…"

"Then the other person should be able to defuse the situation or move themselves out of harm's way. Are you able to share more details of the scenario?"

"He's the ex-boyfriend," Carter says. "I'm the new one. Except he doesn't know about me yet."

"Ah." Gerald takes off his glasses to polish them. I swear he only does this when he needs to buy time. "Yes. That can indeed be difficult. I would suggest, first and foremost, that you let him know he's being informed out of respect. Assuming he still has feelings for his ex, you might choose to remind him that you have that much in common. You both love this other person—"

"It's a girl," Carter says helpfully.

"I see. Remind him that you both love this girl and want the best for her. Is this other boy a friend of yours?"

"Yes," Carter says instantly.

Not the answer I would have given, but okay.

"I would suggest explaining that you were happy for him when he was dating this girl, and that you hope he can feel the same way so you can continue being friends."

"What if he doesn't take it well?" I ask. "This guy is the kind of person who always knows how to make you mad. He'll say something terrible, guaranteed."

"Then you have an advantage," Gerald says. "You can predict his behavior and prepare for that moment. When the time comes, instead of reacting to *what* he says, ask yourself *why* he's saying it. For instance, let's say you just broke the news to me, Carter, and that I'm very unhappy. I might tell you that your mother is a disgusting fleabag and that you're nothing more than a slimy egg she laid."

"Hey!" Carter complains. Then he laughs. "That's pretty good, actually."

"Thank you, although I bet this person will have something much more personal to say. Go ahead and imagine what that might be."

Carter shakes his head. "Like you said, it's not important. I need to ask myself why he wants to hurt me or make me angry."

Gerald smiles. "Exactly. And?"

"He'll be jealous. Or maybe he'll feel insecure, like he's comparing himself to me. Or maybe he just misses her."

Gerald nods. "Are any of those good reasons to be angry in return?"

"No."

"There you have it. If this young man screams that he hates you, ask yourself why. You've already narrowed it down to the likely truth. His anger has very little to do with you and more to do with whatever unpleasantness he's feeling inside. Try not to take his reaction personally."

"I won't," Carter says. "This is cool! How do you know all this stuff? I bet you're a spy or something, aren't you? This teacher gig is just a front."

Gerald laughs. "If only I was so interesting. My wife piqued my interest in anger management. She's an attorney, and as you can imagine, emotions are often high in the courtroom."

"Is that legal?" Carter jokes.

"You're such a dork," I say, rolling my eyes. "So your wife learned how to keep her temper in check because of her work?"

"And our relationship, I'm sure," Gerald says wryly. "Staying calm is an infuriating advantage in an argument, so I finally read the book she kept mentioning and found it was useful in many aspects of my life. Especially when it comes to dealing with teenagers."

"I'm already into it," Carter enthuses. "I want in on all of your tutoring sessions, Andrew. You've been holding out on me."

I wouldn't mind, but Gerald reminds us that we have tests to study for. Math still doesn't seem as important to me as learning how to navigate through life, but I'm eager to make him proud, since Gerald is quickly becoming my favorite teacher of all time.

We settle on a school night in the middle of the week for the big reveal, figuring that Bobby is less likely to be high or drunk. We want him as rational as possible. There isn't a single detail we haven't deliberated over, which is ridiculous and not the kind of thing anyone would need to do for a normal human being. I make sure to point this out. I'm met with silence, although nobody outright disagrees with me.

When the night in question arrives, I'm working the register and Jackson is running the oven. Between the two of us, we have a view of the entire restaurant. Carter plans on sitting near the counter, and we'll have more than just visuals, thanks to a clever idea of Jackson's: Carter is going to secretly call me on speakerphone beforehand so I can monitor the conversation. As for safety precautions, I've asked Jackson to have his phone ready to dial 911, and if necessary, I'll run over to their table with a wooden pizza paddle and smack Bobby over the head with it. That last bit is my own private plan. I haven't discussed it with anyone. I almost hope it happens.

Not really. I keep thinking of the knife and what it could do to Carter. My stomach is gurgling with nerves by the time Carter and Bobby finally show up together.

"Hey!" I say, trying to sound surprised. I don't do so well. Maybe I should ask Gerald to give me acting lessons. "What are you guys up to?"

"You're dating my best friend," Bobby says as he approaches the counter, "so I thought I would date yours. I just hope he puts out as easily as Jackson does."

I can think of a number of responses to that, but I want him in a good mood, so I only say, "Then consider me officially jealous. What can I get you?"

Bobby is only an asshole most of the time. We manage to complete the order without any more slights. I'm eager for them to take a seat, and Carter suggests they do, but Bobby is more interested in loitering around the ovens and talking to Jackson. That wasn't part of the plan. Carter was supposed to get up from the table when the pizza was ready and call my phone on his way to pick it up, but we adjust quickly enough. After getting a drink, Carter returns to my counter. While pretending to text, he calls me. I answer and mute my side of the conversation. That way they won't hear me talking to customers. My headphones are already plugged in, only one earbud inserted, like I'm with the Secret Service.

Once the pizza is ready, they finally sit. I listen to them eat while I'm helping other customers. Carter casually checks on me during this and sees we're busy working, so the reveal doesn't happen yet. We work as fast as we can, and finally, when there's a lull, Jackson walks over to join me.

"Give me the other earbud," he says.

"Okay. We should probably pretend we're listening to a song together."

"No problem."

He starts bobbing his head to an imaginary beat. I do the same.

"Jesus," we hear Bobby say through the earbuds. "Look at those two. Like they needed to tell anyone that they're queer."

My head stops moving until Jackson widens his eyes at me. Then I remember to keep pretending.

"It's cool they found each other," Carter says. "Were you surprised when Jackson came out?"

Oh god. This could be bad. Especially if Bobby says something mean like—

"If I'd known he was gay, I wouldn't have slept over at his house so much."

I wince in sympathy. Jackson tries not to react, but I can tell it hurts.

"What difference does that make?" Carter asks, starting to sound huffy.

Uh oh. If they get in an argument over this, the rest of the conversation will only be worse.

I take out my earbud and quickly grab a couple of cookies. Then I run them over to where Carter and Bobby are sitting.

"On the house," I say. "All part of our loyal customer appreciation program."

They both grin, because who doesn't like cookies?

By the time I get back to the counter, another customer is waiting. Jackson and I help them as quickly as we can. I keep looking at the dining area but can't tell what they're talking about. Even with the earbud in, I have to tune them out to pay attention to the customer. I only hear keywords, and Olivia is one of them.

"—really like her," Carter is saying once I'm free again. "I was always envious when you guys were dating."

"She's not that special," Bobby says.

"I think she is. You're not surprised, right? I figure it's obvious that I like her."

"Painfully."

"Oh. Well, I have good intentions. I'm not looking to take advantage or anything. To be honest, I'm in love with her."

It's not news, but it still stings to hear this. I wish Jackson was listening with me, but he's waiting on the most recent order to finish baking.

"What's your point, Carter?"

"That you guys didn't work out, and I'm really sorry about that, but—"

"I'm not sorry."

"Good. Then you won't mind that we're dating."

I risk looking at the table. Bobby is either staring or glaring. It's hard to tell from this distance.

"Huh," he says. "I thought you were about to ask my permission."

"That's not yours to give," Carter says, "but I respect you, and I want you to be okay with this, so what I'm asking for is your blessing."

Bobby doesn't sound happy. "Maybe you should have asked for that before you went behind my back! You're already screwing her?"

"We're dating. The only reason we kept it a secret is out of respect for you."

Bobby laughs but doesn't sound amused. "Respect. That's how you're selling it? When did this start? Before we broke up?"

"No! Absolutely not! I didn't think she was interested in me. That's why I didn't ask for your blessing sooner. I didn't even tell Andrew before I asked her out, and I tell him everything. I was too embarrassed because I was sure she would shoot me down."

"Why? She gets around, if you haven't figured that out already. I don't think she's ever told anybody no. Olivia is a free ride for anyone who's desperate enough. You might want to double up on condoms and get tested."

Here we go. Bobby is trying to make him angry. I hope Carter hasn't forgotten Gerald's advice.

"That's not how I see her," Carter says calmly. "At all."

"You're not interested in the truth?"

"All I'm interested in is making sure you're cool with this. I really care about her. And I like you. You're my friend. I'm hoping we can make this work somehow."

Go Carter! Sure we rehearsed these lines and many others, but he's performing them well. I would have already cracked under pressure.

"I don't give a shit who she dates," Bobby says. "If you're into sloppy seconds, that's your problem. Just remember who got there first."

"Okay."

Even from here, I can see that Carter's face is red. With anger, most likely.

"And if you have trouble making her come," Bobby says, "I can give you some pointers. I managed every single time."

"I'll keep that in mind," Carter growls. He's about to lose it.

Jackson finally walks over to join me, but there's no point in giving him an ear bud. I'm thinking we should pull the fire alarm. Or cause some other distraction.

"Let's go hang out with them," I say.

I don't wait for a response. I hurry over to their table, and as I'm taking a seat, I "accidentally" elbow Carter's drink and knock it over.

"Oh crap! Sorry! Hold on." I grab napkins and make a big scene. And it works. By the time the mess is cleaned up, Bobby is stewing but no longer lashing out.

"Come smoke with me," he says to Jackson.

"I can handle the oven if a customer comes in," I say, eager to get Bobby away from the table.

Once they're outside, I exhale and look at Carter. "You did good."

"I hate him," Carter mumbles. "You were right. From the very beginning, you were right about him. Did you hear what he said about her?"

"It's not what he said that's important," I remind him. "It's why. Bobby loves her. She broke up with him. And now she's with you. Think how that would make you feel."

Carter scowls. "You're defending him?"

"No. I'm trying to keep you calm. He isn't worth it. You've got Olivia. You've got me. All Bobby has is bitterness and rage."

"And his loyal dog Jackson," Carter spits. "That doesn't worry you?" Then he sighs. "Sorry. I needed to vent. That wasn't fair."

"It's okay," I say, looking toward the door they disappeared through. "And yeah, it definitely worries me."

We hold our collective breaths for the next few days, waiting for something bad to happen. It doesn't. The weekend comes and goes, and everything seems normal. The next time we hang out as a group, everyone is perfectly civil. Or at least as civil as a group of teenagers can be. Olivia doesn't join us. She's keeping her distance, which is wise. After another week comes to an end, we finally relax.

Then the unexpected happens. I finally go on a date with Carter. He's taking me to a rock-climbing gym, which isn't my first choice—or even second or third—but I'm sure we can make it romantic if we try. Oh yeah, Jackson and Olivia will be there too, so technically it's a double date, but whatever.

"You wanna sit up front with me?" I ask Carter as I stand next to the passenger-side of the Fiat.

"Uh…" he says, looking to the backseat and no doubt dreaming of being snuggled up with Olivia. "Don't you want your boyfriend sitting in front with you?"

"I don't mind," Jackson says, shooting me a wink. "If you want, I can drive so you and Andrew can sit back there together."

"Yes!" I say.

Carter looks between us. Then he groans. "You're messing with me, aren't you?"

"A little." I open the door for him and pull the handle to tilt the seat forward, so he can climb in. Once he's back there, I return the seat to its upright position and kiss my boyfriend while he's still outside the car and easily accessible. I adore that Jackson isn't the jealous type. At all. He understands my need to make little jokes like this—to slowly disarm the disappointment and pain until it's a harmless puff, rather than a heart-breaking explosion. He's wonderful that way.

"Maybe we should let Carter drive," I murmur against his lips, "so we can get in the backseat together."

"Or we can take my Camaro instead of your little clown car—"

"You love the Fiat," I remind him.

"I love you," he says. His eyes go wide, like he didn't intend to say it. "I mean—"

"It's okay." I shut the passenger-side door to give us privacy. "If that's how you really feel."

"It is." Jackson's chin juts out. "I don't need you to say it back, Andrew. You shouldn't until you really mean it."

"I'm crazy about you," I say, my mind racing because maybe it's true. Maybe I love him too. I haven't reassessed lately. Is love the sort of thing that needs to be thought about? Should I just open my mouth and say whatever comes to mind?

Carter knocks on the window. He looks confused. And impatient. I feel annoyed, which surprises me. Usually I'm happy for any scrap of attention Carter gives me, but all of a sudden I wish Jackson and I were going on this date alone.

"We can talk about it later," Jackson says. "If you want. I think he's worried about being late to—"

I interrupt him with a kiss. "We'll definitely talk about this," I say while grinning. "Later."

I open the car door for him. Then I go around to the other side, and drive to Olivia's place. She lives in an apartment complex not far from our school. Carter is texting her as we ride over, occasionally asking us how a word is spelled, so I'm not surprised when we get there and she's waiting outside. Once she's squeezed into the back, it's off to the climbing gym.

We drive out to the suburbs to reach our destination. There are closer gyms, but Carter did research to find one that he approves of. I'm not really concerned about the quality. I'm more looking forward to dinner afterwards.

"Are you into this sort of thing?" I ask Jackson as we're walking across the parking lot.

"I don't know," he says. "Never done it before, but I can't wait to try."

Great. I was hoping he would be as apathetic as I am. Olivia is my last hope. Ideally she'll stay on the ground with me and gossip. But no. As soon as we're inside, she's excited, even when it comes to renting the necessary equipment.

"Pink helmet," she asks, lifting it in one hand, "because it's so adorable, or blue helmet," she holds up another, "because it matches my hair?"

"Blue helmet," I advise.

She nods and sets down the pink one.

I grab it and laugh. "Sucker! I only wanted it for myself."

Jackson and Carter both choose boring gray helmets. Once we're dressed in harnesses and take a few selfies, we head to the beginner's wall. Thank goodness. I need a refresher. The next hour is fun. Olivia isn't very athletic. Carter stays with her on the beginner's wall to give her plenty of personal attention. He couldn't look happier.

Jackson quickly takes to climbing and wants us to move on to the next level, so I go with him, alternating between flirting and trying to impress him with my meager skills.

"My harness is all tangled up," I complain at one point.

"Turn around and I'll check it out," Jackson offers.

"That's too easy. I want you to do it by touch alone."

"Why? Oh." His eyes are half-lidded as he moves close and puts his arms around me. "Is this better?"

"It's getting there," I say.

"Mind if I livestream this?" a familiar voice says.

I look over and laugh. "Vicky! What are you doing here?"

"I'm on a date," she says.

That explains why she looks so pretty. Vicky is normally a tomboy. She's not caked in makeup now, but she's clearly making an effort. I've never seen her in a blouse before, and the jeans are so pristine that they must be new. "So are we! Your brother is here too."

"I noticed," she says, looking to where Carter and Olivia are still practicing.

"Who's the lucky guy?" I ask.

Vicky looks nervous, and I don't understand why until I notice someone approaching. He's the reason Jackson's arm slides off my shoulders. He's also the reason I turn my head to check on Carter, because this won't go over well.

Vicky's date is Bobby Tucker.

"Hey, homos," he says. "How are things?"

"What are you doing here?" I ask.

"Same thing as you." Bobby puts an arm around Vicky and pulls her close. "I'm on a date."

I look to Vicky for an explanation. "How long has this been going on?"

"It's recent," she says, making a face. "Lighten up."

"Sorry," I say carefully. "I'm just surprised you're here. Like... *Here*. Did Carter tell you where we'd be?"

Vicky shakes her head. "Bobby said he had a surprise for me."

"And you guys surprised us by being here," he says.

Right.

I check on Carter again, but he's not where I last saw him. He's much closer and marching toward us.

"Vicky," he says, jaw clenching when he sees Bobby's hand on her hip. His fists ball up as his pace increases.

"It's a triple date now," I say quickly, stepping into his path. I don't want this to escalate.

Olivia shares my concern, hurrying to catch up with Carter. She grabs his arm to stop him.

"What the fuck are you doing here?" Carter huffs, glowering at Vicky and then at her date. If looks could kill, Bobby would be a splatter of blood and guts on the far wall.

"They're on a date," I say before Bobby can make a rude comment. "It's not a big deal."

Carter's face turns a deeper shade of maroon. "Not a big—"

"I only have good intentions," Bobby chimes in, his tone sickly sweet.

"Not *too* good, I hope," Vicky says with a grin. "It was a joke," she adds when Carter bares his teeth. "Calm down."

"For real," I whisper, my hands on Carter's shoulders. "Don't play into this."

"What's that, Andrew?" Bobby says.

"Mind your own business," I respond as I turn to face him. "Are you guys here to talk or to climb?"

Bobby nods at us. "Yeah, where can we rent some gear?"

"Over there," Carter says, pointing a shaking finger toward the entrance.

"Do we have to wear helmets?" Bobby asks. "Because you guys look like a bunch of retards. That guy over there isn't wearing one."

I check on Carter, worried he's about to explode, but his attention is on Vicky now. "Wear a helmet," he says. "You know why."

"I will," she says, sounding pensive. "Come on, Bobby."

"No problem," he says, leading her away.

He keeps his arm around her.

"I'm calling our parents," Carter says.

"To tell them what?"

"He's too old for her!"

"She's a junior. He's a senior."

"It's *Bobby*," he snarls. "Are you okay with this?"

"No, but… Listen, if you flip out and forbid her to see him, what's going to happen? Olivia, what do you think?"

She grimaces. "Vicky won't stop seeing him. She'll probably do the opposite, just to prove that you aren't in charge of her. That's how I feel with my older brothers. Even when they're right, I get sick of them bossing me around and treating me like I'm helpless."

"There you go," I say. "So you can let Bobby make you mad and guarantee that Vicky will stay with him, or you can let it go so we can keep having fun."

I can tell that Carter still wants to murder him. He's glaring in the direction they went, but the anger softens when I step into his field of vision and disappears entirely when Olivia takes his hand.

"Come on," she says. "Let's keep going. I was just getting the hang of it."

When she walks away with Carter, I turn to Jackson.

"Did you tell him that we'd be here?"

"He knew we were going on a double date. I didn't say where."

"Do you guys share your GPS location with each other?"

"Oh." His guilty expression is all the answer I need.

"It's fine," I say. "I do the same thing. So it's not an accident that he's here. He wants to upset Carter."

"Probably. Or he might actually like Vicky."

I resist an eyeroll. Jackson always gives Bobby the benefit of the doubt. I understand why. Even if love wasn't involved, they've been best friends for most of their lives. It doesn't matter to me either way. Even if Bobby is genuinely in love with Vicky and wants to marry her, he's still a psychopath. It's only a matter of time before he hurts her. The thought alone makes me clench my jaw, but I'm not sure what to do.

The situation continues to trouble me as we resume climbing. Vicky has experience and isn't interested in the beginner's wall. Bobby has none, but his fragile ego makes him refuse to start there, so we're all on the intermediate level. Bobby doesn't do so well. No thanks to Carter, who coaches the rest of us and doesn't tell Bobby what he's doing wrong until it's too late. Vicky starts giving him advice instead. I notice Bobby's irritation at this, but he quickly swallows it and becomes increasingly flirtatious with her, casting the occasional glare in Carter's direction to make sure he's watching. What a jerk!

"I want to move to the advanced wall," Carter says to Vicky during a break. "Can you belay for me?"

"You just want to show off."

Carter grins at her. "Exactly."

We pick up our things and begin moving toward the advanced wall.

"I'm going out for a smoke," Bobby says.

"I'll join you," I say instantly, because I've reached a few conclusions.

Those lessons Gerald has been giving me boil down to two things; trying to figure out why I'm angry, or why other people are, which distracts me long enough that I don't get angry.

That's the first part. The rest is attempting to defuse someone else's anger. This involves a combination of understanding their perspective and reasoning with them.

I believe that's worth trying now. Maybe I'm crazy. All I know is that if I had continued to dismiss Jackson as being one of Bobby's lackeys, then I would have missed out on meeting a wonderful man. As I later learned, Jackson has his own reasons for supporting Bobby. I might not agree with them, but that doesn't make him a bad person. Now that he and I have a relationship—now that we're talking instead of staring each other down—I hope to bring Jackson around to my way of thinking. Even if that never happens, I still like him. A lot, which makes it all the more ironic that I once feared him instead.

Will I ever reach a similar place with Bobby? I don't know. I think about that as I take off my helmet and grab my coat on the way out the door. I have to try. We'll never change people's minds by grouping them all together and labeling them with an unpleasant name. That dehumanizes them, and I'm not okay with that. Everyone deserves a chance. Even if they do seem like a monster.

Bobby doesn't wait for me. He's already leaning against the wall and smoking when I step outside. I join him, and together we look out across a half-empty parking lot with miniature mountains of snow in each corner, accumulated from repeated shoveling.

"Vicky, huh?" I ask, deciding to skip over any pleasantries. He always sees through them anyway.

"That's right," Bobby says. "I don't think her brother approves but fuck him."

"He'll get over it," I say, not taking the bait.

"Doesn't it bother you?" Bobby asks.

"Vicky is a big girl. She can make her own decisions."

Bobby snorts. "Not that. I'm talking about the date you're on. You have to stand there all night and watch Carter drool over someone else. You're in love with him, aren't you?"

"Who told you that? Was it Jackson?"

Bobby scoffs. "He didn't tell me. It's obvious. And messed up. You shouldn't be dating Jackson if you're hung up on someone else."

"I could say the same to you," I shoot back.

Bobby laughs. "You know what I'm doing. You aren't stupid."

"Neither are you, which is why I don't understand this. Any of it. You seem to get people. You're really observant, and when you want to be, charming. Everyone I talk to makes excuses for all the crazy stuff you do because you inspire a weird sort of loyalty. Sometimes I think about the kind of person you could be if you'd stop being…"

"An asshole?"

"Yes."

Bobby doesn't seem offended. If anything, he seems bored as he stubs out one cigarette and lights another. "I used to be like you. Back before my dad ran off. I used to think that adults knew what they're doing, and that if I was good, everything would work out fine. Then my mom showed up at school one day with a black eye and a missing tooth. She had them pull me out of class. I still remember the way the principal looked at her like she was scum, when all she was trying to do was to make sure my dad didn't run off with me. He threatened to. I don't think my dad cared about me. He just wanted to hurt her. The police weren't much better when we went to file a report. My mom had dried blood on her chin, and they treated her like she was overreacting. Or like she had it coming. If my uncle hadn't stepped up and tried to kill him, my dad would have beat her to death eventually."

"Jesus," I breathe. "I'm sorry. I had no idea."

"You still don't," Bobby says. "Adults are just as messed up as we are. Maybe more so because they no longer believe the lie. The smart ones, anyway. The rest are just gullible idiots who do as they're told. The people in power… Look at the White House. Do you think any of those politicians got to where they are because they paid attention to bullshit like rules and morality? No. They do whatever they want. They get richer and stronger by taking advantage of the poor and weak. How? By telling them the same crap. That if we keep our heads down, work hard, and obey, all of our dreams will come true. That's not how it's works. That's not real life."

"So what are you saying?" I ask. "That you're dreaming of a career in politics?"

Bobby snorts. "No. Not me. I'm going out in a blaze of glory. I just don't know when."

He still scares me. I have to try anyway. I can call him names or just walk off, but that won't make anything better. It won't keep my friends safe. I can't fix Bobby's life. I can't undo his past, but I can focus on the present and attempt to make it better for all of us.

"You're right about me," I say. "I do love Carter. I've been obsessed with him since the day we met, and for the longest time my worst fear was seeing him with anyone else. I was glad when you started dating Olivia because it was obvious he liked her. I tried to deny that, but it didn't do any good. That's just how it is. People can't control who they want. It's out of our hands, so when she asked me if I was okay with them dating—"

"Wait. Olivia asked your permission?"

"No. She was worried about hurting me because like you said, my feelings for Carter are obvious. I wanted to tell her that she couldn't have him, but that wouldn't have changed anything. They still would have been into each other, and I still would have been single. So I let him go. Hell, I even helped him choose an outfit for their first date. Try to imagine that. Think about helping Olivia look her best so she can go on a date with someone else. That wasn't easy, but I did it because it was the only thing that makes sense. At least they can be happy with each other. I'm a lot happier now too, thanks to Jackson. I wouldn't have gotten there if I was still clinging to what I can't have. So if you really like Vicky, that's awesome. I hope you learn from the past, from your own father, and treat her right. But if you're only dating her to take revenge on Carter, you won't end up happier. None of us will. Why put yourself through that? The way I see it, no one is at fault. We can't help the way we feel."

Bobby takes a long pull on his cigarette. I'm not sure if he's heard a word I've spoken until he says, "You're right. People can't help the way they feel. They don't get to choose who they love or make it stop when they don't want to anymore."

"Sad but true. I wish it wasn't that way, but it is. There's no one to blame."

Bobby flicks his cigarette, sending an orange glowing arc through the air. "That's where you're wrong." He pushes away from the wall and looks me right in the eye. "There is someone to blame. I just had the wrong guy."

Some primal instinct deep inside tells me to run, but I manage to resist the urge. Even when Bobby cracks his knuckles and looks like he's about to start pummeling me. Instead he smirks.

"Thanks for the pep talk, Andrew. It was very enlightening."

And with that he walks away and goes back inside.

I stand there and shiver, and not just from the cold. I think back to my first day of school and how two emotions were born that day. That's when I started loving Carter, and also when my hatred for Bobby began. I've tried and failed to fight off both emotions, but when it comes to me and Bobby, the feeling is mutual. And now we're back to square one. I can make my peace with that. I might have returned to being a target, but at least this way, he'll leave my friends alone.

The Fiat is idling outside Jackson's house. I'm about to make a joke about dropping *him* off rather than the reverse when he reaches over and takes my hand. More than that. He grips it like he's worried that I'll try to escape.

"I'm sorry if Bobby ruined the night," he says, "but I don't want to talk about him anymore."

I'm surprised, but I understand. "He didn't ruin the evening," I say. It's true. Bobby and Vicky didn't follow us to dinner once we were finished climbing. Maybe what I said had a delayed reaction and I got through to him. More likely, he's decided that he wants to make me suffer and isn't interested in torturing Carter anymore. "We don't have to talk about him. But something good came out of it all."

Jackson looks over at me. "It did?"

"Yeah. You've been through a lot. Enough that you have good reason to be angry at the world, but instead you want to start a career that will enable you to help people. You're sympathetic. To a fault. I like that too." I bite my bottom lip and smile. "You might even say I love that about you."

Jackson catches on. He leans closer to me. "There's got to be a better way of phrasing that. Shorter. Not so many words."

"There probably is." I nod at the dashboard clock. "Too bad your time's almost up."

He follows my gaze. Then he swears. "Damn. I've gotta be the only senior who still has a curfew. Can we pick this up tomorrow?"

"Sure."

He pecks me on the lips. Then he reaches for the door, but I'm ready for him. The Fiat's doors might not stick, but I push down on the automatic locks just as he tries to open his. The door doesn't budge. It's obvious why. He looks at me and laughs.

"Let me get that for you," I say, unbuckling my seatbelt and leaning over. I'm not really reaching for the door. Neither of us expects me to. He meets me halfway, the smell of his skin filling my nose, the light hairs on his neck soft beneath my fingers, but I don't kiss him yet. I rest my forehead against his, gaze into big browns eyes, and say, "I love you too."

Jackson stares. Then he kisses me… and won't quit. I'm loving it, even when he tries to climb over to my seat. I laugh and remind him of the hour, and when he kisses me one final time and reaches for the door, I don't try to stop him. Although I almost do, because I love him. I love him, and I want more.

Chapter Seventeen

I'm standing in front of Carter's house on a Sunday afternoon. When the door opens, it's the person I was hoping to see.

"Hey!" Vicky says. "He's not here."

"Carter is old news," I say dismissively. "I'm here to hang out with you."

Vicky starts to smile. Then her eyes narrow in suspicion. "You're here to talk."

"That too," I say, rubbing my arms to remind her that it's still winter. I'm pretty sure it should be spring instead, but that's Chicago.

"Come on," she says. "You can help me clean my room."

For a tomboy, Vicky's bedroom is surprisingly feminine. She doesn't have an abundance of pink accents or bottles of perfume lined up on her dresser, but the space is nicely decorated. Instead of just taping photos to the wall, she has tasteful frames for each. A number of decorative pillows occupy her bed, and she even has a little corner set up with two chairs, which is where we sit. She was only joking about needing to clean, thankfully.

"I will pay you to make my room this nice," I say, nodding to the shelf beneath her window. "Are those cactuses from Arizona?"

"Yeah. I wanted to bring a piece of home with me. Oh, and I was planning on going into landscaping, but I don't think so anymore."

"No?"

"No. I'd rather be a park ranger."

"Very cool," I say.

Vicky watches me patiently, her eyebrows slightly raised. She's clearly waiting for me to broach the most obvious subject.

"Bobby isn't good for you." And we're off!

Her response is an exasperated sigh. "I expect that kind of bull from my brother. Or my *dad*. I thought you of all people would get it."

"Get what?"

"That neither one of us is feeble and helpless just because we're not heterosexual men."

"That's not what this is about," I say quickly. "I'm not trying to mansplain anything or protect your virtue. When it comes to boys, I'm with you. They're trouble, but who cares. I love 'em."

"Me too. So what's the problem?"

"Bobby isn't like other guys. He's crazy. A psychopath. He's not a sexy bad boy who's going to break down in tears during a tender moment with you."

"You mean like he did the other night?"

I don't hide my surprise. "What?"

"Bobby cried in front of me. While telling me why his parents split up."

He told me the same story and had seemed irritated at most. Maybe he's good at hiding how he feels. "Okay. I don't know that side of him, but I've seen another, and it's bad."

Vicky shrugs. "I'm all ears."

I want to tell her about Bobby holding a knife to Jackson's throat, but I promised to keep it a secret. That doesn't leave me with a lot. I describe what he did to me on the first day of school, and I do mention that he flashed the knife, but she's nowhere near as shaken as I felt.

"He can be a prick," she says. "I'm not letting him get away with such things anymore. Like when he called you and Jackson homos the other night. I told him later that if he wants to be with me, that sort of thing needs to stop."

"It's more than the way he talks," I say. "He's a user, like…" How he used Jackson. Another secret. Most of it. "Like how he expects Jackson to give him a free pizza whenever he swings by Blaze. Guess who ends up paying for those?"

"Dick move," Vicky says. "I agree. I'll talk to him about it."

"I'd rather you didn't," I say, knowing it would get back to Jackson. "Listen, I need you to trust me. There are things I can't talk about, but they're bad. *Really* bad. Oh! I know! Bobby pushed someone down the stairs at school, just because the guy was badmouthing Olivia. You can't tell me that's normal."

"I've seen guys beat the crap out of each other over girls before. I agree that it's stupid. I don't like it either, but it's not a deal-breaker. If it makes you feel better, I'll remind him that I can fight my own battles. Let me ask you something."

"Okay."

"Who's tougher, me or Olivia? Don't overthink it. Just answer."

"I don't know. You're about the same."

Vicky makes a face. "Really?"

"Fine. You seem tougher."

"So what makes you think I can't handle dating Bobby when she did all of last semester?"

"Have you asked her what it was like dating him?"

"Yeah. He's a jerk. I knew that going in, but I still like him."

I shake my head in frustration. "What is it with this guy? Am I the only one who can't see it?"

"Carter hates him too," Vicky says. "He flips out every time I mention his name."

"What about that?" I say. "Don't you trust your brother's judgement?"

"I do," she admits, "but straight guys don't treat their girlfriends the way they do each other. It's a completely different relationship."

"Are you his girlfriend? Is it that official?"

Vicky nods. Then she looks away and sighs. "You don't understand. It's not easy for girls like me. Most guys want a princess, not a warrior goddess. They find out that I like sports and digging around in the dirt, and they assume I'm a lesbian or tell me I need to wear more makeup."

"I know what it's like to not have many options," I say.

"Good. Then you can imagine how you'd still give Jackson a shot even if he had a bad reputation because it's better than being single. Right? It's better than nobody asking you to the dance."

I nod grudgingly and let the subject drop, the battle lost. I just hope for her sake that she knows what she's doing.

"I'm happy," Carter says to me. "You?"

I snort. "Are you kidding? I would have had to do this on my own!"

We're standing in front of my house, surveying the freshly completed work, and leaning against our snow shovels like two old wizards with their staffs. Carter worked most of the magic, clearing the sidewalks and brushing off the walkways. He was clever enough to turn his lawnmowing business into a snow removal service, and he's earning a lot more because of it.

"What do I owe you?"

"Oh please," he says, like the idea is absurd. Then he hesitates. "Although, if you wouldn't mind loaning me the car…"

"Done," I say. "Whenever you want it." Reed used to shovel the snow. We were both supposed to, but he always told me I was useless and would send me back inside. I was always eager to comply.

"Awesome," Carter says. "But I meant are you happy in general. Like with your life."

"Oh." I don't need to think long. I have a boyfriend, a best friend, and a lot to be thankful for. I could imagine being happier if not for one person, but I don't want to be greedy. A single irritation isn't much of a burden. "Yeah," I say. "I'm super happy."

"So am I," Carter says. "I don't want this to end."

He means high school. I don't think he's that fond of it, but it's the only thing standing between us and college. Most of the other seniors talk about the next stage with endless enthusiasm, but for us, it's a complicated subject.

"If we both get accepted into one of the Arizona schools," he continues, "do you think Jackson would want to move down there?"

"I honestly don't know. Jackson applied to a lot of schools, but I don't think any of them were in Arizona."

"Oh," Carter says. "Olivia is open to the idea. She only sent an application to Phoenix though."

"Hey, that's where you're from!" I tease. "It's so much cooler than Tucson."

"Shut up," Carter says with a grin. Then his expression becomes serious. "I want us to stay friends. I know we will no matter what, but if we go to the same school, we'll actually see each other. The same with Olivia. Vicky too. I want Jackson there for you. If we're in Arizona, I'll be close to Renzo. That just leaves our families."

"I'd miss Reed," I say. "And my parents. Maybe. But we could take trips to Chicago to visit them."

"Yeah!" Carter wipes at his nose, which looks just as frozen as mine feels. "What am I worried about? I probably won't be accepted into *any* college."

"You will. Wait and see."

"They won't be the same ones that want you. Hell, they'll *all* want you. You'd be slumming it if you go to any school that's interested in me."

"Don't sell yourself short," I say, nudging him playfully. "We nailed your applications. I put more effort into yours than I did my own, so you might be slumming it with me somewhere instead."

"*If* we get accepted into the same school. What if we don't?"

I don't know, and it worries me. I've found a group of people I genuinely love, and I don't want to lose any of them. "We'll make it work. Somehow. If worse comes to worst, we'll stay in touch. We'll take vacations together, visit each other often, and be the best man at each other's weddings."

"Yeah," Carter says, putting on a brave face. "And when we settle down, we'll be neighbors again. We'll make sure to buy houses right next to each other."

We stand in silence, a winter wind blowing around us. My torso is still warm from shoveling snow and my extremities are too numb to feel the chill anymore, so I don't have the usual urge to run inside to escape the weather. Maybe I'm just getting used to it.

"Hey," I say. "Ever built a snowman?"

"Nope," Carter says. "You?"

"Uh-uh."

We look at each other and smile at the same time. Then we fall to our knees and start rolling snow into balls. We might not have many more days like this. I don't know what our adult lives will bring or where any of us will end up. Right now, there's only one thing that I'm certain of.

"I'm really glad we're friends," I say.

Carter stops and looks over at me. It's probably just the biting chill causing them, but I see tears in his eyes.

"Yeah," he says. "I am too."

I've become obsessed with the weather app on my phone. I once dismissed such things as an old person's hobby, but not anymore. I'm constantly checking it for any sign of spring. March is over. April has just begun, but I can't see any hint of the traditional showers or the flowers they are supposed to bring. I don't leave the house unless I absolutely have to, and it's giving me cabin fever. Even a simple walk around the block would be welcome. Give me rain! I can deal with being wet. Just no more snow. Please.

I'm staring out the living room window on a Saturday, letting the sun warm my skin while I dream of green leaves, when my phone rings. It's Carter.

"Hey!" I say. "What's—"

"Can you come over?" His tone is urgent.

"Is everything okay?"

"It's Vicky," he says. "She won't talk to me."

I don't understand, but I'm not going to play twenty questions when my best friend needs me. "I'm on my way. Meet me at the door."

I throw on a coat and leave the rest of my winter gear behind. Then I hustle over to his house. When Carter opens the door, he looks upset. And confused.

"What going on?" I say.

He turns and leads me deeper into the house. "It's Vicky. She came home crying. She won't tell me why. I thought maybe she would talk to you."

"Where was she?"

"Out with Bobby. I think."

My stomach sinks. He doesn't need to say more. Carter and I finally share the same opinion of him. On the way up the stairs, I hope it's something simple. Maybe Bobby broke up with Vicky because he no longer wants to make Carter angry. That's the most obvious explanation. Please let it be that. Vicky probably doesn't want to hear Carter say he was right, or that she should have listened. I promise myself not to say those things either. I only want to make sure she's okay. I reach her bedroom door and knock on it.

"Go away!"

"It's me," I say. "Andrew. I'm worried about you."

"I'm fine."

"Then let me in."

We hear someone moving. I whisper to Carter to go away before she sees him and slams the door on both of us. He ducks into his bedroom. As soon as Vicky opens the door, I can see why he was so concerned. Her hair is a mess, and her face is swollen from crying.

"What happened?" I say.

She sends a withering glare toward her brother's room. Thank goodness Carter had the foresight to close his door. "Did *he* send you?"

"I'm your friend and I'm worried," I reply.

Vicky sniffs. Then she stands aside so I can enter, closing the door after me. I search for clues of what happened, but all I see are wadded up tissues on the bed. Vicky goes to the chairs in one corner. I follow her, not saying a word as we sit. I figure she needs someone to listen, more than anything.

"I'm fine," she repeats.

"Obviously," I say. "What happened? Please talk to me. Don't do the annoying thing your brother does where he goes all quiet. I can't stand that."

"Neither can I," Vicky says, spluttering laughter. She rises to fetch a box of tissues, brings it back with her, and blows her nose before sitting again. "You should have been there when he didn't talk for months."

"I can't imagine. Are you all right? What happened? You were with Bobby, right?"

She raises her guard again, but at least she nods.

"Did you two break up?"

She considers the question. "Not yet. But I'm done with him."

I wait. I can tell that she's struggling internally. She wants to tell me, but something is holding her back. "You can't repeat any of this to Carter," she says at last. "He'll make it into something it's not."

"Like what?"

Vicky pulls her legs up close to her body. "Rape."

"Is that what happened?" I say, my voice rising.

"No. But it wasn't good."

She doesn't say more.

"Olivia told me he was pushy," I say. "It's one of the reasons I worried about you dating him."

"She said that?"

"Yes." And now, more than ever, I believe her. "What happened? Don't worry about your brother. I'll handle him. I promise."

Vicky nods. She's unable to meet my eye. Her feet hit the floor again. She grabs the box of tissues and plays with it absentmindedly, tearing at the thin cardboard. "I wanted to have sex with him. I was planning on it. Just not yet."

"But you did have sex with him?" I ask.

"Yes."

"Did he force you?"

Vicky's chin trembles before she regains control. "It's complicated."

"Then tell me everything from the beginning," I say.

She nods, gathers herself, and begins. "We were hanging out in Bobby's room. At first everything was fine. We were just talking. Then we kissed. Or I guess we made out. When he wanted to take off my shirt and bra, I didn't mind. I wanted to see him shirtless too. That's as far as I wanted it to go. When he undid his jeans, and I told him to stop. I wasn't angry. Everything was still chill. I told him there was no sense in taking his thing out because I wasn't going to touch it. Bobby seemed okay with that too. He got on top of me and we kept kissing. That's when he got aggressive."

"Aggressive how?"

Vicky rolls her eyes and sighs, like I'm foolish for even needing to ask. Maybe I am. For all I know, this could be a common experience among women.

"He whipped it out anyway," she explains. "And he kept trying to get into my pants. I figured I had gotten him all riled up, so I could at least give him a handjob or let him play with me."

"You were still willing at this point?"

"Yeah. But it wasn't enough. He kept trying to go further, and I told him no."

"Then that's it. You said no, and he didn't listen. I'm sorry, Vicky, but that's rape."

"It's not!" she shoots back. "He wasn't holding me down. I wasn't kicking and screaming."

I take a deep breath. "I hate to even ask this, but why not?"

"Because I didn't want to be a victim," Vicky says, tears spilling from her eyes. "He wouldn't get off of me, and I tried pushing him away, but he's stronger. Bobby got this look in his eyes, like he didn't care about me or anything else. I was scared and decided I'd rather have sex with him than find out what would happen if I kept resisting. So that's what happened. I'm a stupid little girl after all, okay? I got nervous and had sex with him even though I didn't want to."

"You told him no," I reiterate. "That's all it's supposed to take. If someone doesn't listen, then it's on them. Did you say it more than once?"

She nods, unable to speak as she pulls more tissues from the box.

"Loud enough that he heard you?"

"He kept saying that it would be okay, that he loves me. He wouldn't stop though."

"Then we need to call the police."

"It wasn't against my will," Vicky reiterates.

"Because you went along with him physically? That has nothing to do with what you wanted. You already made that clear."

"Would you stop?" she says wearily. "I'm fine. I just need a bath. Or a shower. Could you do me a favor?"

I nod. "Of course."

"Get rid of my brother. I'm worried he'll read into it if I lock myself in the bathroom."

She's worried that he'll figure out the truth: that she feels the need to wash herself after being violated by a slimy creep.

"I will," I say, "but only if you promise to think about pressing charges. This is a serious crime, and I know you don't like how it sounds, but you're a victim." Her mouth becomes a thin line. Enough lecturing. "I'm so sorry, Vicky. What a horrible thing to live through. You deserve better."

"Thanks," she says. "Lesson learned, I guess."

"One more thing before I go. Were you safe?"

She looks pained as she shakes her head. "I'm on the pill, so at least I don't have to worry about that."

"I'll go with you when you're ready to be tested," I say. "That needs to happen."

"Okay."

"I'm not going to lie to Carter about this."

"You know what he's going to do!"

"I'll stop him. But I have to tell him something. He's worried about his sister. You should have heard him on the phone. I thought someone had died."

"Oh."

"I'll get him out of the house. You think about filing a report with the police. Promise me."

"Fine. I'll think about it."

"Good. Do you feel like a hug right now? I understand if you don't."

She looks small and vulnerable when she nods. When she's wrapped in my arms, she feels even tinier. I don't understand how anyone could do this to her. It's a testament to what Gerald has been teaching me that I've managed to contain my anger for this long. When I step out into the hall, I nearly give into it. I want to search the house, find any weapon I can—a shotgun, preferably—and do the only thing guaranteed to stop Bobby from hurting anyone ever again.

I can't afford to feel that way. Not now, when I have to face Carter and somehow tell him the truth. I knock on his door and suggest we go for a drive. When he realizes that I won't answer his questions until we do, he agrees. I make sure we travel outside the neighborhood far enough that if he tries walking back, I'll have plenty of time to stop him. If I feel like murdering Bobby, I can't imagine how Carter will react. I pull over in a grocery store parking lot to find out.

"Are you finally going to fucking tell me?" he grumbles.

We're off to a great start. "Bobby got forceful with her."

"You mean sexually? Did he rape her?"

"She didn't want to have sex with him, but she didn't fight him, either."

"What's that supposed to mean?" Carter says. He shakes his head. "Doesn't matter. Start the car. I'll ask Bobby about it right before I rip his goddamn throat out."

"We're going to take him down," I say. "We won't let him get away with this, but we'll do it the right way."

"We'll do it now," Carter snarls. "Start the fucking car!"

"Because that'll make Vicky feel better," I spit. "It's bad enough she's been through this, but now you're going to make her feel guilty for being the reason her brother ends up behind bars, possibly for life."

"Worth it."

"Don't be stupid."

"I need to do something!" Carter yells, his voice cracking. "I can't stand the thought of her being hurt. It's my fault! I should have told our parents. I should have killed Bobby before he could ever lay his disgusting hands on her."

"I want to kill him too," I say. "I promise you, I do. But that'll only make things worse. It'll feel good in the moment, but think what it would do to our families. Okay? Seriously. Think about it. We'll take him down. But we've got to be smart."

Carter's expression is pleading with me to understand, to not argue and to do what we both want. If I saw Bobby walking across the parking lot right now, I'd run him over. I know I would. Instead I make us sit there until Carter calms down. It takes hours. We even leave the car and go for a walk to blow off steam, and by the time we return he finally agrees. We'll take care of this. The right way.

I don't have much time. If Carter runs into Bobby again, he won't keep his cool. A fight, or worse, seems inevitable if I don't act quickly. Besides, I promised him I would find a solution the next day. It's the only thing I could say to keep him in check. Now it's Sunday afternoon, and four people are squashed onto the couch in my family room, watching me. Jackson, Vicky, Carter, and Olivia. I honestly have no idea if any of them will cooperate. I thought about talking to them individually, but they always have their reasons for wanting the bad things to stay secret. It's time for that to stop. I hope seeing the complete picture will change their minds.

I start with myself. "On my first day of school, after I addressed the class, Bobby pulled the chair out from under me when I tried to sit again. I landed on the floor and it hurt. What's worse, when I stood up to him, he made sure I saw his knife. He wanted to scare me. It worked. A day or two later, he threatened to beat me up on my lawn where my mother could see."

I look to Carter next because I know he's on my side. "You're the only person I told about the knife, and you weren't surprised. You said you had seen it before."

Carter nods. "We were at the park, just me and him, and he was using the knife to carve his initials into a picnic table. Then he told me to spread my fingers wide, and stupid me, I did. Bobby grabbed my wrist so I couldn't get away and started playing that game where you stab the knife in between each finger, trying not to hit yourself. That's how it usually works. He was doing it to me instead. Keep in mind, it was getting dark out. I could barely see, and man, was I freaking out!"

"That's all he wants," Jackson says. "It's Bobby's way of letting you know that you shouldn't mess with him, but you need to understand where that comes from. His dad used to beat him and his mom. Bobby was too small to stand up to him, so he would do crazy things instead. One time he knocked everything off the dinner table—plates, glasses, food, everything—because his dad had his mom cornered. Bobby made a scene and ran outside so his dad would chase after him instead of hitting her again."

I know what Jackson is doing. He's defending Bobby. Maybe not consciously, but I think he's been doing it for so long that it's become a habit. "Too bad he didn't have his knife then," I say. "Have you had any experiences with it, Jackson?"

I didn't give him any forewarning that we'd be discussing this. Jackson looks shocked. And hurt. He thinks I've betrayed him. Maybe I have, but I'm tired of secrets, and this is bigger than the both of us.

"You have a long history with Bobby," I say. "You don't need to tell us everything. Or anything. That's fine. I was a witness to one occasion, though, and I have every right to say what happened. I know you'd rather I didn't, but believe me, I'm only doing this because it's important."

I look at Vicky. She refuses to meet my eye. That's not a good sign. I need her story most of all.

"Fine," Jackson says while glaring at me. "Bobby held the knife to my throat. More than once."

"The most recent time is enough," I say, hoping he sees that I still respect his privacy. Some of it, at least. "What happened?"

"He caught us outside your house together, the night of the party. I think he wanted to scare you. And to remind me where my loyalties lie. Or are supposed to. So he backed me up against the wall. He wouldn't have cut me. It was just an act."

I nod my appreciation. "Thank you."

Jackson glowers at me, shakes his head, and looks away.

Yeah. This isn't going well. I turn next to Olivia. "You once told me that Bobby is pushy. What did you mean by that?"

Her eyes dart over to Carter, no doubt worried about his reaction. To what exactly? Nothing substantial, potentially. Many guys don't like to hear about their girlfriends being with anyone else. It could be as simple as that.

"It's important," Carter tells her. "Trust me. I won't be mad."

Olivia sighs. "Bobby doesn't like being told no."

"In regards to what?" I press.

"A lot of things," she snaps.

"Including sex?"

Olivia starts to shake her head. Then she rolls her eyes and nods.

I hate having to ask my next question. "Did you ever tell him that you didn't want to have sex?"

"Yes."

"Did it happen anyway?"

Olivia crosses her arms over her chest. "Is there a point to this?"

"Yeah," Carter interjects. "It matters to me. I need to know the truth. Please."

"Fine." She sighs again. "With Bobby, it was easier to give in than put up a fight."

Vicky finally speaks. Sort of. She makes a whimpering sound, probably from holding back tears.

Olivia uncrosses her arms and puts a hand over Vicky's. "Oh no… What did he do to you?"

Vicky swallows, reluctant tears trailing down her cheeks. "He wouldn't take no for an answer."

The mood in the room changes instantly. Jackson makes eye contact again, finally understanding. Olivia is hugging Vicky as she cries, and Carter… He's a mess. He looks at his sister and then to me with pleading eyes. I can't fix this. Not on my own. The truth is, we need each other. All five of us.

"It's just a matter of time before someone else gets hurt," I say. "That might mean another rape. Bobby might get careless with his knife again when he's drunk or high. He's already drawn blood."

"I don't think he meant to," Jackson says. Then his shoulders slump. "But you're right. The next time it happens, I'm to blame."

"We all are," I say, "unless we do something to stop him."

"Like what?" Olivia asks.

"I think we should start by writing down everything we've just talked about. Then we can take it to the police."

"Will it be enough to put him away?" Carter asks. "I want him behind bars."

I look to my boyfriend. "Jackson?"

He exhales. "Tough to say. The police won't ignore it. They'll talk to him at the very least, but without evidence…"

I can't believe it. "The word of five people isn't enough?"

"It might be," Jackson says. "Something will happen. It's hard to say what. That would depend on the judge, if it goes to court. The police will take it more seriously if our parents are involved."

"No way!" Vicky says.

"I'm not crazy about the idea either," Olivia says. Then she looks over at Vicky. "But if it helps…"

"What if it doesn't?" Carter says. "If the police talk to Bobby and nothing else happens, we need to be prepared because he'll want revenge."

Jackson nods. "He'll go ballistic."

"We can't keep being afraid of him," I say. "That's why we've all stayed quiet until now. If we keep doing that, Bobby keeps hurting people. Or worse. I know he's your best friend, Jackson. He needs help, and this might give it to him. We might stop him from becoming a murderer."

"Fine," Jackson replies. "But we need to be cautious."

"You want to be a cop," Carter says to him. "Do you have any contacts that could, I don't know, assess the case or whatever? That way we'd know if it's worth reporting or not."

Jackson shakes his head. "I wish."

"I know someone," I say. "Gerald's wife is an attorney."

"Who?" Vicky asks.

"Our teacher at school. His wife would know, right? She must see cases like this all the time."

"Depending on what kind of attorney she is," Jackson points out.

"It's worth a shot," I say. "I know we can trust Gerald. He's cool. Isn't he, Carter?"

"Yeah."

I nibble on my nails for a second, trying to get it all organized in my head. "We'll write down what we've each been through. I'll explain to Gerald that we're nervous about taking action, and he'll show it to his wife. Once she gets back to us, then we'll decide. Agreed?"

The murmurs of consent are a huge relief.

"Until then," I say, "none of us confront Bobby. We don't let him see that we're angry, no matter how pissed off we feel." I look directly at Carter. "Promise me. All of you."

"I promise," Vicky says. Then she reaches across and thwaps her brother's stomach. "Say it."

Carter clenches his jaw a few times, but he nods. "I promise."

Olivia and Jackson do too, and some of the tension leaves me. I don't know if our plan will work, but at least I know that nothing will fall apart for the next few days.

— — —

"I'm sorry," I say, hoping these words won't be among the last that I ever speak to my boyfriend. That's up to him.

Jackson is leaning against his Camaro, his attention on the pavement beneath his shoes. Everyone else has gone home. Before they did, we wrote it all down, but it wasn't easy. Not for any of us. Jackson especially. I wish he would look at me. I'm standing right in front of him and worrying that I've gone too far.

"Sorry for what?" he asks, still not raising his head.

"For betraying your trust. I told Carter that you're gay before you were ready for him to know. And I just told everyone what Bobby did the night of the party, even though you didn't want me to."

"It's fine," Jackson murmurs.

That's not the same as saying I'm forgiven. "I didn't know what else to do. I tried reasoning with Bobby. I really did. And it's not like we're making things up to get him in trouble. All we're doing is telling the truth. Other people will decide what to make of that, but it needs to be known."

"You're all about the truth," Jackson says, turning his head to look down the street. "Aren't you?"

"I try to be," I say meekly. "I'm not perfect. I mess up all the time."

Jackson finally makes eye contact, although I have a hard time understanding what I see there. "Coming out made me happy," he says. "*You've* made me happy. Do you think this will too?"

"I think it's going to hurt," I tell him. "Doesn't it already? I can't stand seeing you suffer. I love you, Jackson. If I thought there was any other way…"

He sighs. Then he reaches for me, almost reluctantly, and pulls me close. When he hugs me tight against him and whispers that he loves me too, I know it's another truth. The kind that heals.

— — —

I'm sitting alone with Gerald, five hand-written and signed statements on the table between us. I explain to him that we need his wife's help and let him read the statements. He remains calm until he gets to Olivia's and Vicky's stories. That's when he starts taking breaks from reading to look up at me. Then he finishes and glances over at Olivia and Carter, who are studying at a table on the other side of the room. Or pretending to. I know they can't concentrate right now.

"I'm obligated to report all of this," Gerald says.

"That's what we want," I say. "But before you do, we want to be sure that Bobby will be put away. If not, then there's no point."

"I disagree," Gerald says.

"I know what you're going to say. We also want to stop him from hurting other people, but if he's not going to get in trouble, none of this will do any good."

"I can promise you there will be disciplinary action," Gerald says, looking at the statements again and shaking his head. "I wish you had told me about the knife sooner."

"I know, but it was a similar situation. Sometimes all tattling does is make you a target."

"Not if the school does its job right. I'll need to inform your parents."

"What? No! That's not the deal."

Gerald takes off his glasses. He doesn't polish them. This time he sets them down and leaves them off. "There is no deal, Andrew. These are serious allegations."

"I thought I could trust you!"

"You can trust me to do what's right."

Before he can stop me, I reach across the table and take back our written statements. "Then we'll deny it. We'll say it was a prank, or that we were trying to mess with him."

This doesn't provoke Gerald. Of course it doesn't. Instead he sighs and puts on his glasses again. "If I show these statements to my wife tonight, and she feels there is enough there to press charges, will that satisfy you?"

"Yes," I say. Then I reconsider. "Will he be put away?"

"That's for a judge to decide, not an attorney, but I'll ask her what is most likely to happen."

"Then yes."

Gerald studies me. "And at that point, you would be willing to get your parents involved?"

I don't want to, but it seems inevitable. "Yeah."

"Very well." Gerald holds out his hand.

I return the statements to him.

"I'm very sorry," he says. "I wish none of you had to go through such horrible experiences."

"That's life," I say wearily.

"It shouldn't be. I'll let you know first thing in the morning."

"Thank you."

Now we wait. None of us are hanging out tonight. Jackson and I have to work. Carter is escorting Vicky home and staying there with her. Olivia is going straight home too. One more day, and hopefully this will all be over.

Chapter Eighteen

I'm the first one in the library the next morning, Carter right behind me. We hoped Gerald would already be there. He isn't. Our heads turn every time someone approaches, but no one comes in except other students. The bell rings and Gerald still isn't there. He's not the only one missing. Olivia hasn't shown up yet either.

"I'm going to go look for her," Carter says, standing up.

Another teacher arrives before he can go. I don't know who she is.

"Have a seat please," she says, noticing Carter. "Mr. Thorp will be here shortly. Go about your usual business."

Carter and I exchange a look after he sits.

"What do you think?" he says.

I shrug. "No idea. It's probably fine."

I'm sure it's not, but there's no sense in us both being nervous. I'm unable to focus on our work. The minutes crawl by without Gerald showing up. Olivia isn't responding to texts. I'm beginning to worry that Jackson had a change of heart. If he told Bobby about this and something happened to Olivia… This could be bad. Very bad.

Someone else finally shows up. Jill, the school counselor. She speaks first to the substitute teacher. Then she walks over to us.

"Carter," she says, smiling pleasantly. "Could you come with me please?"

"What's going on?" he asks.

"I'll explain everything on the way."

"Can I go too?"

"Not just yet," Jill says to me. Then she adds, "Everything is fine."

Carter hangs back, like he doesn't want to leave me.

"I'll be okay," I tell him. "Good luck."

Once he's gone, I'm left alone with my worries. I check my phone so often that I'm told by the teacher to put it away. When I feel it rumble in my pocket, I take it out again regardless. The text is from Carter.

polise parents

His parents are here. The police too. But why exactly? Our statements? Or did something happen to one of us?

Any sign of the others? I text back. *Vicky? Olivia?*

Oh god, what if it's Jackson?

I'm about to add his name when the phone is plucked from my hands.

"I told you to put this away," the substitute says. "You can get it back from Mr. Thorp at the end of the day."

I nearly tell her where she can keep it until then. I get myself under control but regret it. Getting sent to the office might be the best course of action, so I can see what's going on there. If that's where Carter was taken. I decide not to add to my troubles, but the next two hours are grueling. I feel like I'm about to lose it when Gerald finally shows up.

The second he looks at me, I stand. He nods, but holds up a finger, telling me to wait. Gerald has a quick word with the substitute. Then he gestures for me to follow him.

"What's going on?" I ask before we've left the library. "Is everyone okay?"

"Everyone is fine," Gerald says. "The police have been informed. So have your parents. Before you get angry with me, I need you to understand the situation I was placed in. If another student was raped or stabbed by Bobby and I was sitting on information that could have prevented it… Well, what would you have done in my shoes?"

"I get it," I say. "I don't suppose you showed the statements to your wife?"

"Who do you think reminded me of how foolish I was being by waiting even a day? I have good news in that regard. With all of the attention issues like these are getting right now, she feels confident that it will be handled with the utmost seriousness."

"But will Bobby be put away?"

"That's out of my hands," Gerald says. "Be honest with the police and tell them everything you know. This isn't the time to be concerned about getting in trouble with your parents or protecting your friends. The more the authorities know, the more they can help."

I nod, even though I won't tell them everything. Jackson's feelings for Bobby—what he used to do for him—that's none of their business.

As Gerald leads me down the hall, I'm glad I didn't flip out in class because we don't go to the principal's office. Instead he takes me to the school counselor, and when Jill opens the door, my parents are sitting at the table with a police officer. My friends are nowhere to be seen, but that's fine. I'm not as worried now. We're going to be okay.

My parents aren't mad at me, exactly. They weren't thrilled I threw a party, but they weren't surprised either. More than anything, I think they're grateful that nothing terrible happened to me. Not compared to what Olivia and Vicky went through, or even Jackson. I tell the police anything relevant I can think of, details that didn't make it into my first statement, like how Bobby more or less admitted he was dating Vicky to get back at Carter. Intent is important. I feel even more confident that he'll do time for this.

I wish I knew for sure. In all the commotion, I forgot to ask Gerald to get my phone for me. Now I'm at home again. The principal thought we needed the remainder of the day to discuss things with our parents or whatever. Normally I would be thrilled, but not when I feel so cut off. My parents want me to stay home. When I ask if I can go over to Carter's house, they say his family needs privacy to deal with things too. This wouldn't be such a big deal if I could text him. Without my phone, I'm clueless as to how everyone is doing.

My parents can't keep me walled up forever. I'm scheduled to work in the late afternoon, and after a small argument, they finally allow me to go. Sort of. My parents are coming along. For pizza, they claim, when in reality they don't trust me anymore. They even drive me to work. So lame!

When I walk into Blaze and see Jackson behind the counter, I decide I don't care what they or anyone else thinks. I go right up to Jackson and grab hold of him. He hugs me back.

"Are you okay?" he asks. "You aren't answering my texts. Or calls."

"My phone got confiscated," I say. "Have you heard any news?"

"Yeah." He nods at the line of customers, my parents among them. "Later, okay?"

Today has been one long waiting game. A little longer won't

kill me. Besides, I'd rather talk to him when my parents aren't standing nearby. Half an hour later, the line of customers has been served and we're finally alone behind the counter.

"Bobby got expelled," Jackson says. "He won't be back at school this year."

"That's it?" I say.

Jackson looks pained, and I have to remind myself that he has a much different picture of Bobby than I do.

"Sorry," I say. "But you know what we were hoping for."

"That happened too. I talked to his mom. Bobby is in a JDC."

"What's that?"

"A juvenile detention center."

"Juvie," I say. "That means he's been arrested, right? He's being formally charged?"

Jackson nods. "Yeah."

"That's—" I almost say good. Then I think of Carter, since that's the easiest way for me to understand where Jackson is coming from. If I had put Carter behind bars, even for his own good, I'd be feeling dreadful right now. "Are you okay?"

"No," Jackson admits. "But I know this is right. I keep thinking about what happened to Vicky. Olivia too. It's my fault."

I shake my head. "I don't see how it could be."

"No? Remember how I always pretended to be reluctant when Bobby wanted—" He glances at the dining room. "You know. I'd always fight him before giving in. It's like I was training him to do this to other people."

"No," I say firmly, "it's like he was already that kind of person. It doesn't matter if you actually wanted to. When you told him no, that should have been the end of it."

"Yeah?" Jackson says, looking vulnerable.

"Yes. You aren't to blame. At all." I wish we were somewhere private so I could hold him or even hug him again without it being awkward, but more customers have walked in, and we have to get back to work.

When I get another free moment, I go over to my parents and update them on the news. As soon as they hear that Bobby is locked up, they're willing to leave. This makes me feel a burst of love for them. They didn't follow me here because they don't trust me. They wanted to make sure I would be safe.

On my break, I borrow Jackson's phone so I can call Carter.

"How's it going?" I ask, after explaining to him why I've been unreachable.

"Fine," Carter says, sounding grumpy. "Vicky is emotional but doing better. I'm in trouble, I guess."

"What do you mean?"

"I'm the one who took her to the parties, introduced her to Bobby, and everything else. They haven't said I'm grounded, but I'm not allowed to go anywhere."

"That sucks."

"Yeah. Any news?"

When I tell him that Bobby is in juvie, his tone changes.

"I don't care if I'm grounded for life," Carter says. "Totally worth it! I'm glad you made us do this."

"I hope it helps," I say.

"It does. And it will. I'm going to tell Vicky now."

"All right. I won't have my phone until tomorrow. I'll see you then."

"Yeah. And hey… Thanks."

I smile, even though he can't see me. "Don't mention it."

After I hang up, I feel good until I look over at Jackson and remember his pain. This will pass. I can't wait for it to. I try to imagine waking up and having so many positive things to look forward to without any of the negative. It almost sounds too good to be true.

I'm sitting in the school cafeteria at the end of the week when I see Bobby again. It doesn't even register at first. After all, he isn't out of place. He goes to this school. He never shared our lunch period, but I would sometimes see him in the halls before or after class. Just not here. My brain needs a moment to register how wrong this is. Bobby is walking between crowded tables, leering at me as he nears. I check his hands, expecting to see the knife or even a gun. Maybe he'll just beat me to death instead, I'm not sure.

I must appear panicked as I look to where Olivia and Carter are still standing in line for lunch. Bobby follows my gaze, his grin even bigger when he turns to face me again. I don't know how to react. Last I heard, he was still in juvie. His court date isn't until next week.

"Relax," Bobby says, taking a seat across from me. "I just wanna talk."

"What are you doing here?" I ask.

"Cleaning out my locker. Or at least that's what I'll tell the police when they call. Should be any second now. That's house arrest for you."

"House arrest?"

"Take a look at my ankle."

I don't budge.

Bobby laughs. "Under the table, stupid. Go on. You can check out my package while you're down there. You know you want to."

I look, but not because I'm interested in his body. I want to know if he's telling the truth. I lean over until I can see beneath the table, my eyes darting back to his face repeatedly because I don't trust him. Sure enough, when he lifts one leg of his jeans, I see a bracelet on his ankle. It's hard to hear over the noise of the cafeteria, but it's beeping and saying something about an exclusion zone.

"I thought house arrest meant staying at home," I say.

"I know, right?" Bobby sighs as if exasperated. "I told you how fucked up this world is. This shows you how seriously the authorities take people like me. Now if I was Jackson, I'd still be locked up."

"Because he's black?"

"Way to go, detective. Can you also figure out why I'm here?"

Whatever his reasons are, they can't be good. His hands are on the table. I can see that they're empty, but this is Bobby. He could do anything, like grab the fork from the guy sitting nearest to us and stab me in the eye with it. I start scanning the crowd, searching for a teacher or a security guard.

Bobby notices. He briefly looks over his shoulder at the lunch line. I do too. Carter and Olivia are being served. In just a few minutes, they'll walk over here, but I can't decide if that's good or bad. Carter will flip.

"I came to let you know that we're not finished," Bobby says. "You and me, we're going to settle things soon."

"You'll only make it worse for yourself," I say, my voice shaking. "Kill me if you want. It'll just mean you get a life sentence."

Bobby laughs. "Who said anything about killing you? That's too quick. Too kind." He leans across the table and speaks in a whisper. "Why do you think I did that to Vicky? It's so much more satisfying to make you watch your friends suffer. That's what really gets to you, isn't it? When they get upset and you have to see them cry."

I grab him by the shirt. With both hands, unfortunately, when I should have left one free to punch him.

Bobby isn't fazed. He merely smiles, and when a ringtone fills the air, he pulls himself free from my grip. "Saved by the bell," he says, whipping out his phone. "What were you going to do, Andrew? Kiss me?" He places the phone to his ear, sounding much more civil when he answers it. "Yes, officer. You're right. No, I was just cleaning out my locker. I'm on the way out of the school now. Of course. I'm sorry, sir."

Bobby stands, and while continuing his conversation, walks away. A minute later, Carter and Olivia sit across from me in the same space he had just occupied.

Carter passes me a chocolate milk, and when I reach for it, my hand is trembling. He notices and asks, "You all right?"

"Yeah," I say, my throat dry when I swallow. "Never been better."

School is over for the day. The Fiat is idling outside Carter's house. I turn off the engine and get out so that Vicky can slip free from the backseat. She rides home with us every day now. Jackson lives closer to Olivia, so they've paired up too. This makes me feel better, but I don't like how we're mostly on our own after we get home. We might have families, but the only thing keeping Bobby from us is his determination, which I'm starting to realize has no bounds.

"See you tomorrow," Vicky says. "I'm so sick of being grounded. This isn't fair."

"We're not grounded," Carter says, climbing out the passenger side.

"What are we then?"

"We're being cautious."

We watch Vicky walk to the house, and once she's safely inside, Carter turns to me. "We're totally grounded, and it's super unfair."

"I saw Bobby today."

I need to tell someone. I've kept it to myself so far, trying to decide on the best course of action, but I can't think straight when I'm so damn scared.

"When?" Carter asks. "Where?"

I explain what happened, and I can tell that I sound like I'm freaking out. Because I am. The entire situation has spiraled out of control.

"I won't let him lay a finger on you," Carter says.

"You heard what he said. He'd rather go after you guys."

Carter looks back at his house in concern. "Do you think he's planning something? Or he is just trying to shake you up?"

I'm cold but don't care. I lean against the car and gulp in fresh air, trying to calm down. "I have no idea what Bobby is capable of anymore. He's on house arrest, and he still shows up at school? That's not normal."

"He's crazy for sure," Carter says.

His arms are crossed, and he's standing directly in front of me, looking up and down the street like my own personal bodyguard. I want to hug him. I want any kind of comfort I can get, especially if it's physical because that doesn't involve thinking. I won't let myself touch him though. Not so soon after I've moved on.

"Do you think we should call the police?" he asks.

I shrug. "They know he was at school. I can tell them he threatened me while he was there, but it's my word against his. He'll sweet talk them or make it sound like we told each other off when passing in the hall. They're not going to arrest him for something like that. Fuck! I can't believe they sent him home before the court date."

"That's seriously messed up," Carter says with a scowl. "They wouldn't do that if one of *their* sisters had gotten raped."

"No kidding."

"So what do we do?"

I take another deep breath. "We tell the others that he's out on house arrest. Maybe we can set up a code. If one of us sees him, we'll text everyone else in the group with... I don't know. Nine one one?"

Carter nods. "We should make sure we're sharing our GPS location with each other too. All of us."

"Yeah. Good idea. You tell Vicky and Olivia. I'll tell Jackson."

"Okay. I better get inside."

"Same here." I'm starting to shiver.

"Is anyone home at your place?"

"No. But I'll be fine."

Carter doesn't move. "My mom is off work, but I'll ask her if you can come in. At least until your parents are back. I'm sure she'll understand."

I start to refuse, not wanting to give in to fear. Carter doesn't listen. He grabs my hands, pulls me away from the car, and puts an arm around my shoulders as he guides me toward the house.

I'm wrapped in a blanket on the couch, the space heater steadily adding to the electric bill. Netflix is streaming on the television, but I'm barely watching it. My primary focus is on my phone because it keeps me from feeling alone. I don't even feel afraid. Not with so many creature comforts surrounding me. I'll be nervous at school tomorrow and at work where I'll be even more exposed, but for now, safe at home, I'm fine.

Got some big news today, Reed texts.

You're pregnant? I send back.

No. And neither is Dakota. I found a new job.

I sit up straight, excited for my brother. *Really? Is it a good one?*

Yeah. Wicker Park. Lots of nightlife, which should mean lots of tips.

I grin at my phone. *Awesome. My birthday is coming up. I expect a really expensive present.*

After a minute, he sends me a photo of a golden turd.

I'll take it! I send back. Hey, gold is gold. *For real though, congrats.*

Thanks.

I watch one of those cooking competition shows until my phone vibrates again. Another photo, this time from Jackson. It's a selfie. I think. The photo is fuzzy from being taken at night. There's not much light, but I can see his confused expression. And flakes of snow in the air.

LOL I text. *What are you doing outside? Where are you?*

He sends another photo, this time of a map, a little blue dot showing his GPS location. He's not on a street. He's surrounded by a solid chunk of green with the name of a park off to the left. Millers Meadow. I've never heard of it. Rather than googling the name, I open the app we use to track each other. Sure enough, he's still there. The park isn't too far away.

Seriously, I reply. *It's way too cold to be out.*

Jackson sends another photo in response, and my stomach

sinks. He isn't alone. Bobby is standing next to him, flipping off the camera. Jackson is smiling. Sort of. He still seems baffled.

My fingers are stiff as I send another text. *What's going on? Are you okay?*

He's fine, you stupid faggot.

The text isn't from Jackson. It can't be. Neither is the next one.

If you don't do what I say, he won't be fine for long. Don't tell anyone where we are or what's going on or…

A photo finishes the sentence for him. Bobby is looming over the camera, a finger pressed to his lips, instructing me to be quiet. Gripped in his other hand is an open knife.

I leap off the couch, ready to rush there to help Jackson. Then again, police can probably get there quicker. My thumb moves to the phone to place a call when another text pops up.

If I hear sirens, I'll gut him like a fish.

My hands are shaking when I text back. *What do you want?*

For you to join us. Alone. If I see anyone with you, Jackson is dead.

I don't know how to respond, so I back out of the conversation and tap Carter's name instead.

911. Come over. Now.

Then I pace back and forth, knowing I have to say something to Bobby before he gets suspicious, so I text him with, *I'm on my way.*

You better be. I'm watching you.

The next photo he sends is another GPS map. This time it shows my house. The little blue dot is me. Sharing our location had seemed like a good idea at the time. Now it's become a liability. A thought occurs to me: If Bobby can track my location, then he can track Carter's too. I better warn him.

Leave your phone at home. He's tracking you.

I grab my shoes since they are closest, when what I really need is my boots. I might be walking through half-melted snow, but there's no time to be picky. I only pause to text Carter that he should bring a coat.

What's taking so long? Another text from Bobby. *You've got two minutes to leave.*

Damn it! As soon my shoes are on my feet, I run for the back door. I'm outside and shrugging on my jacket when Carter comes tearing around the corner, an aluminum bat in hand.

"Is he here?"

"Worse," I say. "Come on. We've gotta drive!"

As soon as we're in my Fiat, I pass him my phone. "The text messages from Jackson… Read them!"

Then I gun it down the street, wanting to make sure my GPS location changes.

"Oh shit," Carter says. "You don't think he'll really hurt Jackson?"

"I hope not. It's me he's after. Send him a text that I'm on my way." Technology isn't always reliable, and I'm worried that any blip could cost Jackson his life. "No, wait," I say, swerving to the side of the road. "Let me."

I grab the phone. I feel bad, but if Carter makes one of his trademark typos, Bobby will know I'm not alone.

After sending the text, I map the park's location and keep driving.

"What are we going to do?" Carter asks. "Should we call the police?"

"Are you kidding? You read what he wrote!"

"Won't they know where he is anyway? The tracking thing on his ankle. Remember?"

This gives me hope until I imagine police cars swooping in on Bobby's location, sirens blaring. I swear and push down on the accelerator. "We have to get there first. Oh fuck, oh fuck, oh fuck! If something happens to Jackson…"

"Do you think they're in this together?"

"Of course not!" I'm panicking. Bad. I don't realize I've run a red light until Carter asks me if I'm going to run them all. I can't afford to get pulled over now, so I slow down and try to drive safely even though it goes against my instinct.

"Bobby can't see you when we get there," I say. "You need to stay out of sight."

"You distract him," Carter says. "I'll come up from behind and take him out with my bat."

"Only if Jackson is in the clear, okay? If Bobby is holding the knife to Jackson's throat, stay back."

"We can take him," Carter says. "All three of us. *If* we can still trust Jackson."

"Stop saying that! Just keep your distance unless you're sure that Jackson will be safe."

"What about you?"

I don't know the answer to that. Bobby said he would rather make me watch my friends suffer. Maybe I'm only racing across town to witness Jackson's murder. I grip the steering wheel tighter and swear again.

"Turn here," Carter says.

"But the phone—"

"Turn!" Carter says, grabbing the wheel.

I push his hand away and slow, making the turn.

"This isn't where the phone says we should go," I complain.

"Yeah, but it looks like they're on the trail. This will get us closer. I've been here before."

The road Carter has me turn down runs along the edge of the park, concrete bumpers and white lines off to each side to create parking spaces. We don't see any sign of life until the pavement ends. A rope dangles between two posts, a sign hanging in the middle denying us entry to a deteriorated road beyond. A single vehicle is parked in front of this.

"That car," Carter says. "It belongs to Bobby's mom."

"Lean your seat all the way back," I hiss. "He could be inside and watching us."

Carter complies. As I park, I make sure the headlights sweep across Bobby's car. The interior is empty. My phone vibrates. Carter hands it to me so I can read the newest text message.

You sure took your time. Hurry up. He's bleeding all over the place.

"Change of plan," I tell Carter. "Stay here."

"But—"

"Stay here!"

I have to do what Bobby says. I can't risk Jackson's life with any heroics. I unbuckle my seatbelt, open the car door, and start running. The road past the dividing rope isn't nearly as wide, and although it was once paved, nature has broken it down to pieces over the years. Skeletal trees rise to either side of me, the night sky glowing orange from too many city lights. I feel like I'm running through an alien landscape.

I slow to check my phone. Just a little farther. All I can think about is Jackson. I see his brown eyes in my mind, except now they are squinting against the blood pouring down his face. I should have taken the bat from Carter. I glance behind me, worried that he's too close before I remember that I asked him to wait. I wish I hadn't. I don't want to be alone.

The road ends as the trees open up suddenly, a wide expanse ahead of me. The meadow this park is named after. Bobby and Jackson are somewhere to my left, according to my phone. I follow a paved path that runs between the woods and the meadow. It's quiet here. Even the typical sounds of the city are distant. I check my phone again and stop. I'm lined up with the dot now. It's to the left of me, through the trees. I start picking my way along a narrow trail, my heart thudding as I leave the last vestiges of civilization behind, because it could be any second now that—

"So glad you could make it."

The voice is behind me. It's Bobby. I turn around slowly, expecting to feel the blade of a knife stab into me. The trail is dark. Bobby is just a shadow. This only makes him more terrifying.

"Where's Jackson?" I ask.

"You want to see him?"

Bobby rushes forward, and I cringe. He grabs one of my arms, pulling on it as he passes me.

"Come on!" he says, sounding gleeful. "Let's go see Jackson!"

I'm yanked along behind him until we reach water. A river. I can see more trees on the other side and beyond them…

"It's a graveyard," Bobby says, releasing me. "Appropriate, don't you think?"

"Where's Jackson?" I repeat, my voice shaking.

"Huh." Bobby spins around, as if confused. "I swear he was here just a second ago. Check your phone."

My hands are shaking as I do. The blue dot is overlapping my own.

"Strange," Bobby says. "Maybe try texting him."

I know he's fucking with me, but I don't know what else to do.

Are you okay? I send.

Something on the trail lights up a few seconds later. Jackson's phone.

"Oh, that's right," Bobby says, scooping it up. "He won't be needing this anymore."

I don't know what that means. I can imagine, but I don't want it to be true. I feel like pissing myself. I want Carter to show up. I want help. What about the police? I don't hear any sirens. Maybe I can call them. Dialing won't be hard, but the second I put the phone to my ear, Bobby will attack me. I'm not sure if calling and not saying anything would get the police's attention. Not in a city with plenty of other problems. So I pretend to be stupid.

"I don't get it," I say, my fingers moving like I'm sending Jackson another text. "Where is he?" I even hit a few random keys so that Bobby will see on Jackson's phone that I'm typing. Then I back out of that screen and see a list of names, all of them impossibly distant. Carter doesn't have his phone with him, my parents are sleeping, and I'm screwed. Reed's name leaps out at me. I know he's working tonight. He'll still be awake.

"You don't understand?" Bobby is saying mockingly. "I fucking killed him, you idiot! Do you really want to see where Jackson is?"

911 GPS help

My trembling hands make it hard to send the text, but on the third try, I finally hit the right button. When I look up, I see that Bobby is suspicious.

"Give me your phone," he says, already reaching for it.

"No!"

"Give it to me!"

I throw my phone into the trees. "Fuck you!" I shout, backing away from him. I want Carter to hear us. Is he still sitting in the car? A glint of metal draws my eye downward. Bobby has his knife out. Oh shit! I scurry back until my feet plunge into freezing cold water. I think about turning and diving into the river, but Bobby grabs me by the jacket before I can. The point of a blade touches my throat.

"Sorry it's not the same knife," he says. "The police took my favorite away from me." He holds it up so I can see. It's huge with jagged teeth. Before I can do anything to escape, he presses the point against my neck again. "This one will hurt worse. Of course, that's your fault, isn't it? I fucking hate you, Andrew. I never knew it was possible to hate anyone this much. First you force your way into my group of friends with all of your bleeding heart bullshit. Then you goad Carter into going after my girl, and if that's not enough, you steal my best friend and make him a faggot like you."

The knife twists against my neck until I feel a sting. Warm liquid drips down my chilled skin. I'm bleeding, but it's hard to care because I'm pretty sure I'll be dead soon. I accept that, the fear easing up, and decide to say what I'm thinking. "Did you love him?"

"What?"

"Jackson. Were you in love with him? Is that the real reason you hate me? You loved Jackson and you wanted Carter."

Bobby is quiet. Then he starts laughing. "Jackson told you, didn't he?"

"How you used him? Yeah."

Bobby laughs again. He sounds manic. "He was a hole! That's all. A warm convenient hole. You think I'm some twisted closet case? I guess in your mind, we're all gay, aren't we? You fucking wish. I'll tell you who I love. You helped steal her away from me."

"Olivia broke up with you," I manage to croak. "I didn't do anything to—"

"Shut up!" Bobby shouts. "I'm so sick of listening to your whiney voice. I was willing to look past it all. You know that? Even after the crap you pulled, I was willing to let it go. You got everything you wanted, but apparently that wasn't enough. You just had to tell the police. I'm not going to graduate from high school, Andrew. Not this year. Not ever, because I'm sure as hell not going back. Are you fucking happy yet? When I do time, will that finally be enough for you?"

I want to answer him, to explain that I was only trying to protect my friends, but the sting of the knife has become a searing burn, causing my panic to rise again. I don't want to die!

"You want to see where Jackson is?" Bobby snarls. "Turn around." He finally moves the knife away. "Turn around!"

He grabs my shoulder and spins me around, my feet sloshing through the water. I nearly fall, but he has too tight a grip on the back of my jacket.

"*That's* where he is," Bobby whispers into my ear. "He's somewhere down there."

I stare at the broken mirror of the river, huge sheets of floating ice obscuring its dark depths, and I know what's coming next. That's where I'll end up too.

Bobby's breath is hot against my ear. "Are you ready to join him?"

This is it. If I'm going to survive, this is my last chance. I know I'll be cut to hell if I try, but it's better than certain death. I gather all my strength and strike behind me with my elbow.

I hear a thud, my arm connecting with nothing but open air as I spin around and lose my balance. I fall into the river and scramble to get up again so I can assess what's going on and protect myself.

I see two figures on the ground. I can't tell who is who in the dark, but as I climb up the slick riverbank, I find a baseball bat on the ground. Carter is here! I reach for the bat before I'm knocked aside by a heavy weight. My shoulder hits the hard frozen soil first, then my head. I hear a ringing in my ears, the lights in my eyes blinding me temporarily. I force myself up again, dizzy and confused. Two bodies are tangled together on the ground and struggling. I guess that's what hit me. I can't tell them apart in the commotion, but I hear Carter cry out. By the time I find my feet, one person has the other pinned by sitting on him. Please let it be Carter who's winning! When an arm raises up high, knife in hand, I know he lost.

I lunge and grab Bobby's wrist to stop him, but he's strong. I can only hold him at bay by using both hands. This leaves me vulnerable when Bobby elbows me in the side. I don't dare let go. Even though it hurts as he keeps hitting me. I won't let him kill Carter.

Finally tiring of my interference, Bobby twists around and launches himself at me. I'm still holding on to his wrist, but I'm forced to let go when his body plows into mine and knocks me over. I'm on the ground now, a knife sweeping down in an arc. I move to the side just as it whizzes past my cheek and strikes the ground. He won't miss a second time. Bobby is on top of me, pinning me down, and the knife is in the air. I think of Jackson and how I'll soon see him again. There are worse fates, I suppose.

A hollow cracking sound rings out. One with a metallic timbre. The knife comes down, but only to hang loosely at Bobby's side before he topples over. I look up and see Carter, huffing as he grips the bat in both hands.

"Get off of him!" he shouts, using his foot to shove Bobby away.

I'm finally free of Bobby's weight, another surge of adrenaline shooting through me and making me feel like a maddened bull as I roll over onto my hands and knees. My world shrinks to Bobby and nothing more, instinct telling me to eliminate the threat, even though he's not moving. Maybe he's unconscious. He should be dead. That's the only way any of us will ever be safe. I see the knife next to him, my hand snatching it up. I feel all the rage of the past year building inside of me. From that first encounter at school all the way until the day I sat in Vicky's room and watched her cry. I hate Bobby, and now… Now I'm going to kill him.

Why?

I hear Gerald's voice. It's only in my mind, but it's enough to make me hesitate. It won't stop me. The biggest reason why is standing not far away, hands on his knees as he tries to catch his breath, but he still wastes air to say, "Oh Jesus! Man. Are you okay? That was messed up!"

Bobby is going to die because of what he did to the people I care about. Carter especially. He wanted to hurt Carter, so I have to… No, Carter *is* hurt! He's clutching his chest like he's having a heart attack. I drop the knife, my anger forgotten as I get to my feet. Carter hugs me when I get close, clutching at me and whimpering, but I don't know if it's emotion or physical pain that makes him do this. I force him away from me, wanting to see if he's okay. The dark makes this difficult, so my hands move over his body. I feel something wet and warm. When I pull away, my palm is covered in it.

"You're bleeding!"

"I think he stabbed me," Carter says. "It all went so quick."

"We need light. Where's my phone?" I remember throwing it into the trees, but I don't know exactly where. "Or Jackson's phone," I say, looking around for it, but with no luck. Forget light. We need to call for help. I think of the tracking device on Bobby's ankle. Maybe I can trigger it somehow and get the police to come here.

I try explaining this as I bend over Bobby and start clawing at his shoes and jeans. I try one ankle. Then the other. The device is gone. He must have cut it off. We're on our own.

I turn around to ask Carter what we're going to do, but he's not standing anymore. He's fallen to his knees.

"Dizzy," he manages to say.

I rush over to him, my hands useless as I try to find exactly where he's been injured. "Show me where he stabbed you," I say.

"I don't know. Chest?"

How could he not know? I feel along his chest, but it's soaked. There's no way of locating the source. I start trying to undress him, but he's fighting me.

"I'm cold," Carter complains. "Stop!"

"Then we have to get up and go somewhere," I say, looking around. All I see are trees, the river, and a graveyard. "Come on. Can you stand?" I try to lift him, but he's heavier than me. In fact, he's mostly dead weight. "Stay awake," I say. "Come on."

Together we hobble along the path. Progress is slow, and Carter is getting less responsive. We still have far to go. Even if we make it to the car, I don't know where the nearest hospital is. I wish I had paid more attention to things like that, but at least I can drive him somewhere. A gas station maybe, where the attendant can call for help.

When we finally reach the meadow, a new wave of fear washes over me. A car is barreling down the path, engine roaring. The headlights blind me, and I try moving us to safety, but Carter isn't cooperating.

The car screeches to a halt, the driver-side door opens, and I hear my name.

"Andrew?"

It's Reed. I want to cry I'm so relieved. A squeak comes out of my throat as he reaches us. Then I try again. "We have to get Carter to the emergency room."

Reed scoops up Carter in his arms like he doesn't weigh a thing. I run to the car and open the back door. Then I climb inside so I can help get him in. We rest his head on my lap. With the overhead light on, I can finally see where he was stabbed. Most of Carter's clothes are wet with blood, the fleece lining of his jacket stained pink, but there's a much darker spot on his chest toward his right shoulder. I put my hand over this and tell Reed to drive. Then I start praying, because Carter's eyes are now closed, and I honestly don't know if he's going to make it.

"Are you okay?" I ask him. No response. I'm pretty sure it's important to keep people awake in situations like these. Or is that only for a concussion? I don't know, but Carter's breathing is shallow, and I don't want to lose him, so I risk a gentle shake. "Hey! Talk to me!"

His eyelids flutter and open. Carter's voice is weak when he speaks. "Renzo?"

"No. It's me, Andrew, but you've got to keep it together. Renzo will be pissed if he doesn't get to see you again. You don't want to let him down, right?"

Carter's eyes are still open, but they're not focused on me. He doesn't seem to be looking at anything.

"Or what about Olivia?" I say, trying again. "Huh? Do you really want her crying over your grave? She's too young to be a widow. If you survive this, she's going to be all over you. Think about that. She's crazy about you, Carter."

This makes him smile, but it doesn't last. Carter coughs and retches. I'm worried he's choking on blood or something, so I shift and get my arm beneath his back, using all of my strength to lift him slightly. My arm is already shaking from the effort, but I won't stop, no matter how bad it hurts. My throat aches too, from the effort of holding back tears.

"I need you to stay with me," I say. "Please, Carter. Do it for me. I love you! You know that. I love you so much that if you die, it'll kill me too, so don't. Don't do this to me. Stay here. I need you."

I'm crying now, and as I try to wipe some of the tears on my shoulder, I catch Reed watching me in the rearview mirror. I can tell that he's hurting for me. Does he know that it's hopeless? He returns his attention to the road, a bright rectangle shining outside as the car slows. A hospital sign! We made it already.

I look down to tell Carter the good news, but his eyes are shut. He's not moving. At all. I stare in disbelief, but his chest never rises.

"He's not breathing!" I say. "Reed! He's not breathing!"

The car goes faster, breezing past parked cars. "Almost there. Hold on!"

"There's no time! Reed! Pull over!"

I hear the breaks squeal and the horn honk. I glance up to see an emergency room entrance, but nobody is coming out to assist us.

"Help me get him inside!" I shout at my brother.

He gets out of the car and opens the back door, staring in shock until I yell at him to grab Carter's feet. He does, and I take his shoulders, but it's a huge effort to get him out, every passing second feeling like an eternity. It's too late, too late, too late. By the time we get him inside the hospital…

"Put him down!" I cry once I'm free from the car.

"Shouldn't we—"

"Now!"

We lower him to the pavement, Reed covering his mouth and shaking his head. "Andrew, I think he's—"

"Go get help!"

I look away from him, not liking what I see in his eyes. The pain and shock are bad enough. The acceptance is even worse. Seconds later, I hear him running away, and I'm left trying to figure out what to do. Carter needs air. He needs to stop bleeding. I can't do both. Can I? I put my hands over the wound to stop the flow of blood and do compressions like I've seen on TV, but it doesn't help. Carter is unresponsive, no matter how much I jostle him. It's unsettling to see him so still. He was always so vital before, even in the dark of winter, as if he carried the sun inside his heart. He's too strong to let this kill him. Oh god, please don't let this kill him!

I lean over Carter, tears striking his pale skin like drops of rain, and I kiss him at last. My lips touch his, and I give all the air from my lungs, along with every ounce of love I feel for him, to try and reignite his spark. The miracle I need never comes. I try again and again, alternating between chest compressions and breaths of air. I can hear people rushing toward us. Toward me, I suppose, because I'm pretty sure I'm alone now. Carter is dead.

I won't quit though. I keep breathing for him, and just as a hand on my shoulder pulls me away, I swear I finally feel a breath returned.

"He's not dead!" I shout, fighting against whoever is restraining me. Someone takes my place, slipping a mask over Carter's mouth, and I see him wince against this intrusion. Carter is moving. He's alive! My body shakes with tears. I watch as Carter is stabilized and placed on a stretcher, my brother's arms tightening around me as everyday heroes do their best to prevent another life from being lost.

I want to be with Carter. I would stay out of the way. I'd let the doctors do their work, but I want to be there at his side. Whether he lives or if he dies, I want to be there.

This isn't allowed, so instead we sit in the waiting room, and I shake. From cold or shock. I don't know. Reed tries his best to comfort me. I keep telling him to call the police. I need something to focus on, because there's another fact I haven't faced, and it hurts so bad it might kill me too. I don't want to think about that. Not until I know if Carter is going to be okay. Maybe then I'll have the strength to bear it. Or not. When the police arrive and I explain to them what happened, I can't stop denying it any longer. Jackson is dead. Carter might be dying. All the good things in my life have been taken away. I guess that's how Bobby felt, but I don't feel any sympathy for him. Between bouts of sobbing, I experience blinding fury when I think about who is to blame for all of this. Bobby. I hope he froze to death out there in the park.

My parents arrive while I'm talking to the police. My mother and father sit to each side of me, trying to provide whatever comfort they can. Their presence gives me the strength to get through my story, especially when I'm asked to go over the same details again and again. Not only to various police officers, or the doctor who inspects me, but Carter's parents as well. That's the hardest. All I can tell them is the truth: that I wish I could trade places with him. I'd give my life to save Carter, if that were possible. Without hesitation. I make sure to tell his parents that their son saved me. He's a hero. So is my brother. I don't feel so heroic. All I feel is guilt, but focusing on that right now would be too self-indulgent.

When the questions cease, I'm free to lose myself to misery. Jackson is gone. I begged the police to contact his family to be sure, but none of the officers returned to say he's okay. If there was good news, I would have heard it by now instead of this silence—heavy and impermeable like a blanket that is slowly suffocating me. That's fine. Even if Carter pulls through this, I'm not too motivated to go on living. I succumb to numbness as my dad forces me to wash up in the restroom and to put on the clothes my mom retrieved for me. I won't go home to shower or use the one at the hospital. I need to be ready to see Carter if he's okay or to hear the news if he's not. I'm cleaner now, and I'm dry, but inside I'm all gushing wounds.

It's nearly three in the morning when the automatic doors to the emergency room slide open and Jackson walks in. Part of me wonders if grief is making me hallucinate, but it's too real. Right? It's really him? Jackson is looking left and right, searching for me. I'm certain he isn't a delusion now. I open my mouth to call to him. Nothing comes out. Instead I start crying. Again. But this time because I'm relieved.

He finally sees me, and it's like I can breathe again. We run to each other, and after I slam into Jackson, he holds me. I keep crying as he does. I don't know how long we stand there. A small forever. Even then it's not enough.

"He told me you were dead," I croak.

"What?" Jackson takes a step back, but his hands remain on my shoulders. "Who?"

My chin trembles, and his expression shifts to one of guilt. He knows exactly who I mean. "Tell me what happened," he says.

I try hard to calm down enough to speak. It's starting to feel like a rehearsed play, I've repeated it so much, but it never stops being so emotional. I cry through most of it, pulling myself together at the end, because I need answers too.

"What really happened? Were you ever at the park with him?"

"No," Jackson explains. "Bobby stopped by my house earlier in the night. I was surprised to see him, but he acted like things were cool between us. He'd cut off his house arrest bracelet and was going to drive to Canada or Mexico. He wouldn't say which, just that he was never coming back. He wanted to borrow my phone to get to where he was going. Promised to mail it back. I had no idea what he was really planning, I swear."

"I believe you," I say, gripping his hand.

"Those photos you saw, Bobby said he wanted them to remember me by. He didn't even ask. He just started taking them. He was acting weird. I knew something was wrong. I figured he was eager to get away before his mom noticed the car missing." Jackson scowls, the hands on my shoulders balling up into fists. "I should have called the police. I should have texted you guys the second he showed up, like we agreed to."

"Yeah, same here. We were both doing what we thought was best."

"Sure," Jackson says, "but at least you were trying to rescue me. I was trying to protect him. Like always. When will I freaking learn?"

"You have a good heart. It's one of the things I like about you."

Jackson looks insecure. "I'm surprised you can still like me at all."

If anything, having thought I lost him has only intensified my feelings, but I can't let myself focus on anything so happy. Not until I know. A nurse walks into the waiting area, drawing my attention away. She addresses Carter's parents. She doesn't share any news. Just that the doctor wants to speak with them. Half an hour passes before his mother returns. She's pale and shaken, but she manages a smile as she approaches me.

"He wants to see you."

I'm on my feet and following her deeper into the hospital when I look back. Jackson is still sitting there. He nods, like it's okay, and I'm almost unable to leave. How can I when I just got him back?

"Andrew?" Carter's mother says, puzzled that I've stopped.

"One second," I say. I rush back to where Jackson is sitting and press my lips against his. "I love you."

He touches his forehead to mine, his hands on my cheeks. Then he kisses me back. "I love you too. Don't keep him waiting."

I feel bad, because the other guy Jackson loves, we're not sure what happened to him. Bobby might be dead. I don't know, but I do manage to care, if only for my boyfriend's sake. Jackson has been through enough. We all have. I'd rather Bobby be locked up somewhere. There's no doubt of that happening, if he survived getting hit by that baseball bat. As for the person who did the swinging…

I walk into a hospital room and see a guy sitting up in bed who looks like he's been through hell. I suppose he has. Him and me both.

"You gotta get me out of this Muggle hospital," Carter stage-whispers. "They sewed me up with a needle and thread instead of using a healing spell."

"Barbarians!" I say.

"Are you okay?" he asks. "Your neck."

"I'm fine." A doctor already looked at it. She sealed the cut with liquid stiches and put an adhesive bandage over it. "What about you?"

"I lost a lot of blood, apparently. I'm sure we can find it once the sun comes up."

"Along with my phone," I say.

"Ouch," Carter says with a grimace. "I'd rather lose another couple of pints than that." He leans over to see past me. "Hey, Mom! Can you go home and get my phone? It's on the couch."

"I'm not going anywhere!" she says.

"How about a candy bar or something? I'm starving."

She purses her lips and wags a finger, but she leaves the room.

"I'm milking this for whatever I can get," Carter says.

I'm done joking around. I can't pretend to be brave. "Are you okay?"

"Yeah," Carter says with a swallow. "I guess it was pretty close. I almost died. They think I might have actually."

"You seemed dead," I say, my voice cracking.

Carter's smile is gentle. "Good thing you were there to save my life."

"You saved mine first," I say.

Carter stares at me, his jaw clenching as tears trickle down his cheeks.

"Stop," I tell him. "I can't cry anymore. It literally hurts."

"Then get over here." He scoots over and pats the mattress next to him.

Our arms brush together as I stretch out next to him. The physical contact is reassuring. I put my hand over his. He flips it over and intertwines his fingers in my own. Everything we want to express is contained there. We grip each other like a promise to never let go again. I do though. I'm the first to move my hand away. I don't want either of us getting hurt again. Not by feelings that can't be returned in full. I search instead for a change of subject. "This is nice," I say. "You should ask your parents for a bed like this at home. Talk about deluxe!"

"Check this out," Carter says, pushing buttons to make the backrest raise and recline. He doesn't stop, making it jitter and jerk until we're both laughing. "I definitely need one of these," he says. "Think there's a way of making it react to music? It'll be like dancing, except for the super lazy."

I don't respond. The situation is too surreal. Mere hours ago, we were fighting for our lives. Now everything feels good again. Just like it always does when we're together.

"You okay?" Carter asks when he notices me staring.

"Yup," I say, scooting down and leaning my head on his shoulder. "I'm just glad you're okay."

"Aw," he says with a chuckle. Then he shifts, puts an arm around me, and pulls me closer. "I'm glad you're okay too. Now how do we put this thing in drive? I'm ready to get out of here."

By the time his mother returns, I'm making motor noises while Carter pretends to steer. We still have to face all the consequences of this harrowing night, but for now, I'm content to lose myself in love again. Love for my family and my friends. Love for my boyfriend, who I plan on kissing until he begs me to stop. And love, of course, for my straight boy. I'm okay with that now. I no longer want him to be something he's not. Nearly losing Carter made me realize that he's already one of the most special things imaginable.

He's my best friend.

Epilogue

The years go by too quickly. I've gotten used to this. When my life slows down enough for me to realize that entire *decades* have passed, that's when I look back and realize how much has changed. It never takes long for my mind to drift back to high school. I only spent a year of it in Chicago, but that time was so intense that it dominates all other memories. I often compare this to how war veterans go through a terrible ordeal and spend the rest of their lives reminiscing about it. I can relate. Those experiences were so emotionally intense that they've burned themselves into my psyche and settled deep into my heart.

I lived through some dark times, twenty years ago. Not just being lured out to the woods at night and attacked, but what happened afterwards. We learned the next morning that Bobby wasn't found by the police when they checked the park. His mother's car was gone too. Another day went by before we heard about an accident in northern Wisconsin. Bobby had driven the car off an overpass, either by accident or design. Nobody knows for sure and never will. He can no longer tell us, because his life ended when the car flipped and landed upside-down. I'm told it was most likely a quick and painless death.

Part of me was relieved to know that Bobby would never hurt me or my friends again. The rest ached for Jackson, who took the news hard. I never spoke a critical word about Bobby after that. Not to him anyway. I often wonder what Bobby intended that night. I'm pretty sure he wanted to kill me before he left town. That he had also needed to hurt me by pretending Jackson had died was especially cruel.

Age has made me look back on those events with more compassion. I've seen far too many school shooters on the news, damaged children who felt they had no option but to unleash their pain and confusion upon others. I wish Bobby could have had a better upbringing or gotten the help he needed. I wish I could have found a way of making him see me as a friend instead of an enemy. Most of all, I wish he could have been happy. He wasn't though, and never did I question if we were better off without him. I tried to undo the wreckage he left behind. I gave

Jackson all the comfort I could, and I embraced those stragglers Bobby had taken in. Filipe, Mick, and Pedro. We hung out with them often, all the way through graduation, and in Filipe's case, years beyond.

College changed everything. That's the hardest part of looking back now. The ragtag bunch of people I would have died for and nearly did, how could I lose touch with them all? That's what happened though. Some more slowly than others.

Jackson and I went to the same college for two years. Our relationship didn't last quite as long. At a certain point, he needed to focus on his career. An associate degree was enough for his purposes, and once he was accepted into the Illinois State Police Academy, that became his primary focus. I was still floundering, more interested in partying than trying to figure out what sort of career I would have. So we went our separate ways. Not just because of our different priorities. I believe Jackson always associated me with losing Bobby. He never blamed me, even during our worst arguments, but it's not hard to imagine how us meeting and Bobby dying were forever linked in his mind. He's still one of the greatest loves of my life. Whenever I'm in Chicago, we often meet to share a meal. Sometimes more, in the rare instances we both happen to be single. Those days are over now that Jackson is married. I'm proud of him for making detective, and when I'm feeling ornery, I tell him I'm proud of having *made it* with a detective.

Olivia and I still talk on occasion. She took an office job shortly after graduating from high school, climbing corporate ladders until she reached the top of a pharmaceutical company. We rarely meet in person, and when we do, we mostly reminisce or ask for updates on the others. I don't know what happened to Pedro or Mick. Felipe went to the same college as me, and was just as interested in partying until he met the right woman and started a family. Supporting them soon became his sole focus. Vicky had plenty of kids of her own and became a park ranger. She's always good about sending me photos, first of grubby kids playing in the dirt with her, and later of awkward teenagers clustering around their mother. Occasionally I'll get one of her brother too, looking overwhelmed by the gaggle of nieces and nephews.

I regret losing touch with him most of all. Carter was accepted into a university in Arizona. I never took it personally that he wanted to move there to be close to Renzo again. I stayed in the north. My parents were insistent that I go to what they deemed to be a better school. They were paying, making it hard to refuse. Carter and I promised to keep talking, and to visit each other, and for that first year we did. Then life got in the way, and the gap between calls and texts became longer until entire months went by. By the time I was about to begin my junior year of college, we weren't talking at all.

That's about the time I decided I'd had enough of winters that last six months.

"Can I have an ice cream?"

I turn away from the Arizona sun. A boy with dusty skin, brown eyes, and a mop of black hair is standing next to my deck chair. "I'll give you money," I say, "but you have to ask your father."

I look elsewhere in the park to find Carter, who is helping his daughter climb a tree. She's sitting on his shoulders and reaching up for a branch. Once she grips it, he ducks to free himself and squats to talk to his son, who has run over to him. Soon they're both looking at me. Carter nods, hands his son something, and then walks over.

"I was willing to pay for it," I say.

"You can buy me one later," Carter says, shielding his eyes as he looks after his son, "from the freaking ice cream robot."

I snort. "You know, if we had put something like that in one of our early sci-fi novels, people would have left scathing reviews telling us how cheesy and unrealistic we are."

"They wouldn't be entirely wrong," Carter says. "Speaking of which, maybe it's time we try something different. I have an idea for a historical novel. It's about a power-mad tyrant who—"

"No talking about work on the weekend," a voice interrupts. "How many times do I have to tell you that?"

I look over at my husband, who I thought had fallen asleep in his deckchair. One of Renzo's eyebrows appears above his sunglasses. "I mean it!"

"Fine," I say. "But now I've decided I want an ice cream too."

"Oh yeah, I also need one," Carter says, making a puppy dog face. "Pleeeease?"

"I know exactly what you're doing," Renzo says as he stands.

He still walks with a limp, but he hasn't needed to lurch or struggle since his early twenties. Most people who meet him never realize that he was in an accident at all. Occasionally, when Renzo is tired or especially drunk, he'll sound a little thick-tongued, and his short-term memory can still give him trouble. Otherwise, through a tremendous amount of determination and few advances in science, he's made a full recovery. Not that it matters to me. If we woke up tomorrow and Renzo had reverted back to the way he was when we first met, it wouldn't change the way I feel.

"By the time I return," he says, "you better be done talking about it."

We watch him walk away. Then I nod in his direction. "Is it still weird for you sometimes?"

"That you turned him gay?" Carter asks, flopping down into the chair that Renzo had abandoned.

"He's not—"

"I know, I know. He's bi. And it's not your fault. I'm pretty sure it happened when he hit his head on that cliff. Hey, maybe that's where all gay people come from! You ever hit your head?"

"Easy now," I say with a smile. "You're starting to sound like Bobby Tucker."

We both laugh and share an awkward moment of silence. "It's been twenty years," I tell him. "Do you realize that?"

Carter sucks in air. Then he swears. "Can't be!"

"I know." He still looks great. Authors aren't supposed to be so hot. They're supposed to be pale and feeble from sitting inside and typing so much. Most of that work falls to me, these days. We're a good team. Partners in a way I never expected. Maybe that's why I still regret the time apart in college. I've had years with Carter since, decades, but it's still not enough. I always want more.

"You know I love you, right?" I tell him.

Carter looks surprised. Then he smiles. "I think you told me that once. In a hotel room, if I remember correctly."

"Shut up," I say, rolling my eyes, even though he can't see them behind my shades. "And it was by the hotel pool, if you'll recall."

"Ha! You're right!"

"I usually am."

"Not about me, you weren't," Carter says.

"Rub it in. Go ahead," I say with a sigh. "I take it back. I don't love you."

"We both know that's not true," Carter says. He looks me over. "Do you remember what I told you that night? How I feel?"

"No."

He studies me. Then he snorts. "It's a good thing you don't lie much, because you're terrible at it. Fine. I'll say it again." He clears his throat, like he intends to announce it to the entire park. Instead he leans close and whispers, the words meant for me alone to hear. "I love you, Andrew. Always will."

I swallow. "Thanks."

"Hey." He reaches a hand toward me. "Let me see those sunglasses."

I take them off and hand them to him. He notices the tears in my eyes. I can't help it. I've only gotten more emotional with age, but I smile to show him that I'm happy.

He smiles in return. Then he puts on my sunglasses and flops back in the chair. "Way better. That sun is bright!"

"I'm just going to make Renzo give me his," I say. "Think how squinty and red his little eyes will be by the time we leave here. That'll be your fault."

"Totally worth it," Carter says. "You should thank me. Now you have an excuse to put sunblock on his eyelids again."

"I've never done that! You're thinking of his ears. Although it might be worth trying. Just once."

"You're welcome! It's going to be adorable."

We settle down in our chairs to enjoy the sun. I suppose "settled" sums us up nicely. Our lives are established, and while we might not be the old married couple I once envisioned, I have no doubt that our future will be spent in the best way possible—how I've wanted it to be since the very beginning.

Together.

Who the hell is Jay Bell?

Jay Bell is a proud gay man and the award-winning author behind dozens of emotional and yet hopelessly optimistic stories. His best-selling book, *Something Like Summer*, spawned a series of heart-wrenching novels, a musically driven movie, and a lovingly drawn comic. When not crafting imaginary worlds, he occupies his free time with animals, art, action figures, and—most ardently—his husband Andreas. Jay is always dreaming up new stories about boys in love. If that sounds like your cup of tea, you can get the kettle boiling by visiting www.jaybellbooks.com.